Acclaim for Ruth Reid

"Reid has written a fine novel that provides, as its series title claims, a bit of 'heaven on earth.'"

—*Publishers Weekly* review
of *The Promise of an Angel*

"If *The Promise of an Angel* is anything to judge by, it looks like she's going to become a favourite amongst Amish fans."

—*Christian Manifesto*

"Ruth Reid captivates with a powerful new voice and vision."

—Kelly Long, best-selling author of
Sarah's Garden and *Lilly's Wedding Quilt*

"Ruth Reid's *The Promise of an Angel* is a beautiful story of faith, hope, and second chances. It will captivate fans of Amish fiction and readers who love an endearing romance."

—Amy Clipston, best-selling author
of the Kauffman Amish Bakery series

"*The Promise of an Angel* is a fantastic read! This page-turner kept me up late at night as this unique and refreshing story unfolded. Fast-paced and with an ending that brought a happy tear to my eye, fans of Amish fiction are going to love this first novel in the Heaven on Earth series by debut author Ruth Reid."

—Beth Wiseman, best-selling author of *Seek Me with All Your Heart* and *Plain Proposal*

An Angel
by Her Side

Also by Ruth Reid

The Promise of an Angel
Brush of Angel's Wings

An Angel by Her Side

A Heaven on Earth Novel

Ruth Reid

THOMAS NELSON
Since 1798

NASHVILLE   DALLAS   MEXICO CITY   RIO DE JANEIRO

Published in Nashville, Tennessee, by Thomas Nelson. Thomas Nelson is a registered trademark of Thomas Nelson, Inc.

Thomas Nelson, Inc., titles may be purchased in bulk for educational, business, fund-raising, or sales promotional use. For information, please e-mail SpecialMarkets@ThomasNelson.com.

Scripture quotations are taken from THE KING JAMES VERSION and from THE NEW KING JAMES VERSION. © 1982 by Thomas Nelson, Inc. Used by permission. All rights reserved.

Publisher's Note: This novel is a work of fiction. Names, characters, places, and incidents are either products of the author's imagination or used fictitiously. All characters are fictional, and any similarity to people living or dead is purely coincidental.

Library of Congress Cataloging-in-Publication Data

Reid, Ruth, 1963-
    An Angel by Her Side / Ruth Reid.
       pages cm. -- (A Heaven On Earth Novel ; 3)
    ISBN 978-1-59554-790-3 (trade paper)
    1. Amish--Fiction. 2. Tornadoes--Fiction. 3. Disaster relief--Fiction. 4. Christian fiction. 5. Love stories. I. Title.
    PS3618.E5475A83 2013b
    813'.6--dc23
                            2012040487

Printed in the United States of America

12 13 14 15 16 QG 5 4 3 2 1

An Angel by Her Side is dedicated to those teachers who identify and work with students with dyslexia. I especially applaud the Centennial Elementary and Centennial Middle School teachers in Dade City, Florida, who have influenced the growth and educational development of my son, Danny. Through your skillful training, he has reached milestones despite his struggle with dyslexia. Thank you!

Through the LORD's mercies we are not consumed,
because His compassions fail not. They are new
every morning; great is Your faithfulness.

Lamentations 3:22–23

Pennsylvania Dutch Glossary

ach: oh

aemen: amen

aenti: aunt

alend: trouble

Ausbund: Amish hymnal

bloh: blue

boppli: baby

bruder: brother

bu: boy

daed: dad

denki: thank you

dokta: doctor

Englisch or *Englisher*: a non-Amish person

fraa: wife

geduld: patience

geh: go

grossdaadi haus: a small house on the same property where the grandparents live

guder mariye: good morning

guder nacht: good night

gut: good

haus: house

hungahrich: hungry

jah: yes

kaffi: coffee

kalt: cold

kapp: a prayer covering

kumm: come, came

leddich: unmarried

Loblied: an Amish praise song

mamm: mom

maydel: girl

mei: my

meiya: tomorrow

nacht: night

nau: now

nay: no

nett: not

onkel: uncle

outhaus: outhouse

Pennsylvania Deitsch: the language most commonly used by the Amish

redd-up: clean up

rumschpringe: running-around period that begins when the person turns seventeen years old and ends when the young person is baptized into the Amish faith

schee: pretty

schul, schulhaus, schulwork: school, schoolhouse, schoolwork

sohn: son

teetshah: teacher

wedder: weather

wilkom: welcome

wundebaar: wonderful

yummasetti: a sweetened meat and noodle dish

Chapter One

Agust of wind swept through the open windows of the one-room schoolhouse and sent the children's papers skittering across their desks.

"Keep working on your math problems, children," Katie Bender said without looking up from her desk. Another burst of air lifted the paper she was trying to grade. Katie tossed her pen on her desk and stood. The initial breeze was welcoming, especially after the past week of unseasonably sultry weather, but she couldn't have the classroom disrupted by children chasing their papers across the room.

Katie crossed the room to the window. She pushed down on the window casement, but the wood was still swollen from the prolonged rain last month, and the casement wouldn't budge.

In the distance, dark clouds rolled rapidly over the Masts' nearby field of winter wheat. The little town of Hope Falls didn't need more rain, not after the ten straight days of it in late April nearly ruined Katie's garden. Amos Mast's winter wheat field looked as though it still needed drying out yet too.

The shifting direction of the wind pushed another fitful gust through the window. Katie shivered from the noticeable temperature drop. Her prayer *kapp* ties flapped over her shoulder as she worked to jiggle the casing loose. She pressed harder, and finally, after using all the brute force she could muster, she freed the jammed window. It slammed closed, vibrating the plate glass.

Katie brushed the peeled-paint chips from her hands and moved to the next window. She was all for recycling, but installing old, refurbished windows hadn't made sense five years ago when the schoolhouse was built, and it certainly produced frustration when the casings swelled on humid days like today.

The sunlight disappeared behind the clouds, and the room darkened.

"The sky is green," one child said.

Several other children murmured while they shifted in their seats to look out the windows.

"Children, please continue your studies."

She scooted in front of the next window. It slid down with ease and she paused to inspect the sky. The children were right. The sky had turned an eerie pea-soup shade. A shudder crawled down her spine. In her five years of teaching, it had never been so dark at noon that she had to light the oil lamps.

She craned her head toward the pasture. During one storm last growing season, her frightened mare snapped her harness and trampled the Masts' wheat field. Amos Mast voiced his complaint to the bishop, which prompted the men to fence an area for Peaches to graze while school was in session. Her buggy mare wasn't grazing now. The pending storm had the horse on edge. With her ears perked and nostrils flared, Peaches paced the barbed wire fence.

Katie squared her shoulders, not wanting the children to notice the razor of panic cutting through her, and returned to her desk. Raindrops pinged against the tin roof. She disregarded the noisy distraction and continued correcting the stack of papers before her, until the thrumming annoyance changed into a heavy barrage of what sounded like mothballs beating down on the roof. That wasn't easily ignored. She clenched her pen.

Noah Zook, seated in the back of the room, raised his hand. *"Teetshah?"*

"Jah, Noah." She cleared her throat to settle the quiver and hoped his question wouldn't require a lengthy reply.

He pointed to the window. "That's hail *kumming* down."

She pushed off her chair just as a cast-iron bell clanged in the distance. The faint sound didn't register until she reached the window and looked outside. Hailstones littered the lawn.

Katie whirled around to face the children. "Everyone"—she took a calming breath before continuing—"please hold hands and form a line at the door." She motioned to two of the oldest boys, Noah and Eli. They hurried to her, and she pulled them aside. "Once we're outside, I'll need your help to open the cellar doors."

The boys nodded as the two youngest students sidled up to Katie.

"I'm scared." Ella Sue's lips trembled.

Mary Lapp whimpered, "Me too," and clutched Katie's dress.

When a low rumble of thunder vibrated the glass in the windows, even some of the older students echoed their fear.

Katie squatted to the five-year-olds' level and put her arms around them. "God is watching over us. Do you know that?"

When they nodded solemnly, she stood to address the others. "Everyone hold hands." She made a quick scan of the group, then headed for the door. "We're going straight to the cellar. Do not let go of each other." She touched Eli's shoulder, and he and Noah opened the schoolhouse door.

Short bursts of whirling wind kicked up gravel from the driveway and pushed them a few steps backward. She wasn't sure which stung worse, being pelted by gravel or hailstones. Katie tucked her chin against her chest and pressed forward, leading the way. The boys lost their straw hats in the wind as they ran ahead to the side of the building.

Noah and Eli worked in unison, yanking on the cellar's wooden door. Once it flapped open on its hinges, the children filed into the underground storage area. Katie entered last and tugged on the door.

"It's stuck," she yelled over the boisterous wind. "Give me a hand, boys."

Her muscles quivered, fighting against the wind's forceful pull. Finally, with the boys' help, she managed to get the door closed. The storage area went black except for a few pinholes of light surrounding the door frame. They were safe for the moment, but with only a flimsy inside latch, she wasn't sure how long the hinges would hold under the wind's force.

Katie hunched over to avoid hitting her head on a beam and inched away from the door. "Is everyone sitting?" Her voice cracked, and she silently chided herself to control it. For the sake of the children she must remain strong.

"*Jah*," they replied in unison.

"I'm *kalt*," said one girl.

"We all are, Sarah," one of the boys replied sharply.

"This isn't the time to get lippy *nau*." Katie blindly followed the foundation's stone wall and, finding an empty space, lowered herself to the cold, dirt floor. She inhaled deeply, trying to calm herself, but instead gagged on the musty odor.

The cramped space wasn't meant to house a classroom of children. Rather, the old dug-out root cellar offered a dry storage area for the wood under the school. At least the diminished winter's supply meant more space. A blessing for sure.

"As I say your name, I want you to answer." Katie called out the first names that came to mind, pausing between each one to listen for their reply. "Rebecca Fischer? Sarah Plank? Emily Trombly? Peter Wyse? Esther Miller? James Yoder?" She stopped. "James?"

"He stayed home sick today, remember?"

"*Jah, denki*, Eli, for reminding me." Between the thrashing wind and whimpering youngsters, her concentration waffled. "Sarah Plank?"

"*Jah*, but you already called me," Sarah replied.

"Sorry." She needed to calm herself before everyone panicked. *Think*. Who hadn't been called? "Have I called Daniel Hershberger?"

"I'm here," he said.

Inside the classroom, she knew immediately who was absent by what desk was unoccupied. Now in the dark and under stress, she didn't want to rely on her memory. She rattled off several more names. "Did I miss anyone?"

"You didn't call me, Mary Lapp."

Katie squeezed the child's hand. "That's because I'm sitting next to you."

Five-year-old Ella Sue squirmed on her other side. Katie tapped the girl's knobby knee. "And I know this is Ella Sue King on *mei* right, ain't so?"

"*Jah*," she said faintly, then poked Katie's rib and whispered, "I have to use the *outhaus*."

"*Nett nau,* we must stay—" Katie's breath caught. "Samuel Fischer, are you in here?"

Silence.

"Samuel?" But even as she repeated his name, she remembered giving him permission to use the outhouse. He hadn't returned to the classroom. Her stomach knotted.

"He's *nett* answering, *teetshah,*" Ella Sue cried.

Ach, nay. Bile burned the back of Katie's throat. "Everyone stay put," she said, pushing off the floor. Then, tangled in a web of sticky threads, she flailed her arms, batting the spider's clinging web away from her face, and stifled a scream. *Don't panic.* But she was panicking and she'd run into plenty of spiderwebs in the barn before.

"Don't leave us." Mary pulled Katie's dress hem.

"I have to find Samuel. I'll be back." Katie eased her way to the entrance and nudged the door with her shoulder. At the same time, the wind caught the door and slammed it against the building, jetting her outside. The boys scrambled to pull it closed while Katie leaned into the wind and tromped toward the school. A nearby tree cracked under the wind's force, then shed one of its limbs. It hit the ground with a thud.

"Samuel?" She swiftly panned the area and stopped on the overturned outhouse.

Oh, Lord, please don't let him be harmed.

Pressing forward, she ran to the site. As she searched the area, the flailing branches of a weeping willow whipped against her, stinging her face and entangling her with their ever-bending rod-like shoots.

"Samuel!"

No answer. No sign of him at all. She broke loose from the willow and ran toward the schoolhouse. She barged inside the abandoned building. The windowpanes rattled against their casings as though someone were knocking.

"Samuel!" She rushed toward the front of the room and called again.

A movement under a desk caught her eye. Crouched beneath the wooden desk with his arms hugging his chest and his head buried between his knees, the eighth grader rocked on his haunches. Samuel lifted his head, his reddened eyes vacant and wide.

"*Kumm* on, we have to get to safety."

The pale-faced boy continued to stare at nothing in particular.

"Samuel," she said strongly, "we must hurry. *Nau*, you *kumm* out from under that desk." When her words didn't seem to register, she grasped his hand firmly. "You must listen to me, Samuel," she said, tugging his arm.

Samuel stood. He looked about the room, still dazed. "Where did he go?"

"Who are you talking about? All of the students are waiting in the cellar."

"The man with white hair." Again, Samuel canvassed the classroom with his eyes. "He led me in here and said I'd be safe until you came for me."

The building groaned, and Katie steered Samuel toward the door. "We have to get out of here *nau*." She looked over her shoulder but didn't see anyone else in the room.

They sprang outside into an eerie calm. Although the wind had died down and the hail had stopped, in the distance, a dense wall of ash gray with a low-hanging funnel cloud moved toward them. Thankfully, she needed only to point at the approaching tornado for Samuel to regain his senses. Even with his childhood limp from falling off a barn roof, he kept stride with her as they raced for cover.

She gripped the cellar's handle and, with a jolt of adrenaline that burned her veins, yanked the door open. The two of them tumbled into the makeshift shelter, wrestled the door closed, and collapsed against the wall, unable to catch their breath.

The floor joist above them vibrated and dirt sifted through the cracks. "Everyone, crouch down and cover your head." Katie braced for impact.

The door burst open again, flooding the area with light. Katie lifted her head as a man entered, then pulled the door closed behind him. The cellar darkened once more.

"I hope you don't mind if I seek shelter with you. I saw you and the boy take cover in here," the man said.

A rumbling noise similar to the sound of a train filled her ears and the ground rippled with tremors. Katie's eyes burned with tears. "God have mercy on us all."

Chapter Two

Seth's eyes hadn't adjusted to the darkness when something outside thumped against the cellar door. He'd made it to shelter just in time. As the whirling cry of the wind careened closer, he heard a tinny wail, a metallic scream that was quickly swallowed by the din of the storm. The woman next to him shrieked, jolting upright and knocking heads with him.

"You okay?" He rubbed his forehead.

"What was that?" she said through panting breaths.

He almost said his head, but he knew she meant the noise outside. "I'm pretty sure that was the roof." He'd worked in construction and easily recognized the flailing sound of distressed roofing tin. More flapping noise carried into the distance.

"Ach." Her gasps feathered his face with warm air.

Assuming the roof was gone, the walls would collapse next,

but he couldn't tell her that. At the rapid rate she breathed, he expected any moment for her to faint from hyperventilating. The full impact of the storm hadn't even hit yet. But as his thoughts rambled, the structure gave off a high-pitched screech as boards pulled away from their nails. Daylight seeped through the cracks where a moment ago it was dark.

"Get down!" he yelled.

It seemed as though time stood still before the howling wind passed. When it did, an unnatural silence loomed.

"Is it over?" A child's frail voice broke the silence.

"I . . ." The woman cleared her throat. "I think we're safe *nau*, children."

Children? He'd only seen one running with her for cover.

More whimpers came from the opposite direction. Seth shifted his eyes, but without more light than what penetrated through the cracks, he couldn't decipher anything but shadows in the dark.

"How many children do you have?" His thoughts escaped aloud.

"Twelve," she replied. Then added, "Is everyone all right?"

The children might have thought she sounded composed, but he heard the tremor in her voice. He sat quietly and listened as the children's faint responses rang out.

A small hand tapped his arm. "Where did you *kumm* from, mister?"

"Mary, don't be so bold," the woman corrected.

"I'm sorry," said the child in a weakened voice.

"I'm Seth Stutzman." His hands gritty, he wiped the dirt on his pant leg. "I'm from the Saint Joseph County settlement in Centreville." With his district 135 miles south of Hope Falls, he didn't expect the child to know where he was from, but he said his district for the woman's benefit.

"Seth from Centreville, would you mind opening the door for us?"

Good idea. He lunged off the dirt floor, banging his head on the overhead beam.

"What was that?" asked one child.

"Only me." He rubbed the sore spot.

"Are you okay?"

Hearing the woman's motherly concern, he smiled. "*Jah,* at least we know one beam is intact. My thick head didn't seem to shift the structure any."

"That's a blessing," she said.

"Having a thick head?"

Several children laughed, and the woman hushed them immediately.

"I meant the sound structure is a blessing," she clarified, her voice a mix of authority and jitters.

He chuckled as he moved cautiously to the door. Maybe his thick head would figure out a way out of here. He patted the wooden door, searching in the dark for the handle. Gripping it firmly, he nudged the door with his shoulder. It didn't open. He tried again, using more force. Still, the door wouldn't release. "It's jammed."

"That doesn't make sense. It must be latched," the woman said.

"*Nay.* I heard something slam against it just after I entered." The noise was loud enough that she should've heard the same racket outside the door. Then again, firsthand experience had taught him how fear paralyzed one's senses.

"Are we going to have to stay in here forever?" a small voice squeaked. Several of the children sniffled.

He wasn't thinking straight. He should've held his last comment and not riled the children.

"We'll be rescued soon." The woman's soothing voice settled most of the whimpering.

Seth rammed the door harder and vibrations rippled throughout his body. The hinges rattled, but the door wouldn't give. Whatever had struck the door during the storm was solid and somehow had lodged itself against the entry. He drew a deep breath. As a builder, he'd belly-crawled through several narrow crawl spaces and never felt claustrophobic, but now, trapped with a woman and her frightened children, he expected the walls to close in.

"I'm hungry," one child said.

"Me too," another one added.

The woman shushed the children as he barreled his shoulder against the door again. The force dislodged debris from overhead, causing an echo of shrill cries in the darkness behind him. He readied for another shove, but a hand grasped his arm and he stopped.

"Are you sure forcing the door open is safe?" the woman whispered.

"Do you have a better idea, Mrs. . . . ?"

"Katie." She dropped her hand from his arm. "And *nay*, I don't have a better idea."

He plowed his weight against the door once again. This time the structure groaned. Beside him Katie let out a similar noise under her breath. He peered up at the new pinholes of light. What was he thinking? He couldn't risk a cave-in.

"You're right. Let's sit down," he told her.

Her shadowy figure shuffled away from the door.

"Is there a lantern in here?" He moved gingerly so as not to stumble over one of the children. Before he lowered to the floor, he dug his hand into his pocket, hoping he had a pack of matches.

"*Nay*, we didn't think to bring one," Katie replied.

Just as well. He hadn't found any matches. His fingers

touched the brass casing on his pocket watch and his breath caught. He pulled it out but couldn't inspect it properly without enough light to see the face. At least in the shuffle of seeking shelter, the watch's chain remained intact and the glass face didn't feel broken.

It was noon when he checked the time last. His niece had announced that the meal was ready, and he had glanced out the kitchen window and noticed his nephews struggling against the strong wind to push the buggy into the barn. After going out to help his nephews, a strange noise caught Seth's attention and he sent the boys into the house while he checked out the source of the wailing. A sorrel mare tangled in the barbed wire had put up a fight. She'd bolted away once freed, and that's when he'd caught a glimpse of a funnel cloud as it spun closer.

Seth sat on the damp dirt floor. He hoped his nieces and nephews were safe. With their father in town, picking up supplies . . . Seth squeezed his eyes closed. He refused to think about anything happening to his late sister's children. *God, please send your angels to watch over them. Keep them safe.*

The volume of chatter rose until Katie cleared her throat. "Children, if you're unable to talk quietly, we will resume our earlier lesson." Immediately the noise level dropped and she redirected her attention to Seth. "I thought that would settle them," she said. Then added, "What brings you to our settlement on this dreary day?"

He leaned against the woodpile next to the woman. "I arrived yesterday to help *mei* brother-in-law, Amos Mast."

"*Ach.*"

He wished there was light. Her reluctant reply fed his curiosity, and he would've liked to have seen her expression.

"Your brother-in-law, you say?"

"*Jah,* I *kumm* to help him set up a honeybee farm." Certain he detected her muttering under her breath, he asked, "Is something wrong?"

A stretch of silence passed as though she were choosing her words carefully. "I thought perhaps he'd changed his mind about the beehives. I hadn't seen any boxes."

"I just finished building them. We plan to set them up this next week."

"Your sister was a fine woman. I miss Erma a lot."

Without knowing Katie, he couldn't be certain, but it sure sounded as though she intentionally shifted the conversation away from the beehives.

"*Denki,*" he said.

Talking about his sister was still difficult for him. His brother-in-law's household struggled too. Amos seemed steeped in anger while a cloud of depression hung over his children.

The prattle of young voices grew louder again, pulling Katie's attention away. Just as well. He didn't want to talk about his sister's family or about Erma's untimely death. Her cancer had consumed more than her own life; it had practically devoured her husband and children.

Seth tilted his head up to view the cracks in the subfloor. If he had his tools, he could cut an opening large enough to evacuate everyone. "Are there any tools in here? Perhaps an ax?"

"I'm *nett* sure. The wood is already split when it arrives at the *schul.*"

"*Ach,* this is a *schulhaus.*" Her shadowy figure certainly looked far too lean to have mothered twelve children. "*Jah,* that makes sense." Hearing the sound of relief in his own tone caused heat to creep up his neck.

"Excuse me?"

"Your voice sounds young for having . . . so many children."
Dig a little deeper, he inwardly scolded.

"I'm the *teetshah* and I'm twenty-nine—if that was your
next question."

He coughed into his hand, caught off guard by her bluntness.
Nay, surely he would've caught himself before saying something
that offhand. Most *leddich maydels* were secretive about their
age, especially since schoolteachers past twenty-six were considered old maids in his district.

"I don't feel an ax at this end," said a boy at the far side of the
room. "But I think I've seen one in here."

"*Denki,* Eli." Katie pulled up to her knees and reached to the
woodpile beside Seth.

"Stay put. I'll look for it." It wouldn't be safe having too
many people move about.

"I suppose you're right," she said and lowered back to the
dirt floor.

He raked his hands along the top of the woodpile, made
his way to the end, then felt the wall in search of an ax leaning
against it or hanging off a nail.

"Nothing."

Loose dirt sifted through the cracks and landed on his head.
He combed his fingers through his hair as more debris fell. That
couldn't be good. Without saying anything, he slid his hands
along the rocky wall, feeling for any indication of disturbed
mortar. Once he reached the corner, he prodded the support
beam for gaps between it and the wall.

Wobbly. Just as he suspected. It meant the brace for the
support timber was compromised too. Sweat trickled down
the middle of his back. Only in his dreams had he relived this
predicament. The outcome was always the same—disastrous.

God, I beg you not to let another tragedy happen. Send your angels to save these children.

More loose sand sifted between the cracks.

"God has heard your plea, child." Elias reached up and supported the entire load span of the structure.

Seth swiped his shirtsleeve across his sweaty brow and peered at the ceiling.

"Touch the support beam again. See that the wall no longer wobbles. See for yourself that God has indeed answered your prayer."

The man groaned under his breath. He glanced over his shoulder, but not for long. Meanwhile, his driving heartbeat and heavy respirations indicated his lack of peace. His lack of trust.

"Why did you pray and not expect God to answer? You will fail in your own strength." Elias chanted words only the Master understood. Given orders to instruct Seth one last time, Elias pleaded, "Child, you have prayed. Trust God that he has not abandoned you. You asked for help, yet you do not rest in his power."

With the limited light quickly fading, Katie couldn't figure out what Seth was doing. He already said he couldn't find an ax, yet he pawed the wall like he was searching for something.

Something poked her ribs and she rotated to Ella Sue on her other side. "Something wrong?"

"How will *mei daed* know where we are?"

"God will lead him to us." Katie hadn't turned, but she sensed Seth's towering presence beside her.

He dropped to one knee and leaned toward her. "Can you get everyone moved away from this back wall?" Even as he whispered, panic laced his tone. *"Nau?"*

"Why?"

"Don't ask." He pushed off his knee and stood.

She placed one firm hand on Mary's back and the other hand on Ella Sue to guide them. "Let's all move forward." Thankfully, the children didn't question the instructions. As they all scooted together, she glanced over her shoulder at Seth. He was busy moving wood from the pile to a new corner location. Only he was stacking the pieces high enough to reach the ceiling.

"I'm scared," Ella Sue said.

Katie tapped her legs. "*Kumm* sit on *mei* lap."

"I want *mei mamm*." Mary Lapp's voice grew shaky.

"Me too," yet another child whimpered.

She had to find something to distract them. "How about we think on *gut* things?" Katie suggested.

"That's a *gut* idea," Seth chimed in as he sat down beside them.

Katie leaned toward him. "Did you get things situated?"

"As best I could."

"What does that mean?" Her voice quivered, trying to whisper.

"Think of *gut* things," he said, then added, "like ice cream."

Food wasn't exactly what she wanted to discuss, not with a roomful of hungry children. Her stomach had started growling before the storm started. No doubt the children were also half-starved.

"I'm hungry," one child said. The others agreed.

Seth leaned closer to Katie. "I'm sorry. I shouldn't have brought up ice cream."

Ella Sue squirmed into a position on Katie's lap to face Seth's direction. "I like chocolate."

Little Mary sidled up beside Katie and interweaved her arm around hers. "Are we gonna have to stay here all *nacht*?"

Katie balanced Ella Sue on her lap while pulling Mary into a hug. "Lord willing, we'll get out soon." *Please, Lord, let that be your will. That you send us help and don't leave us closed up in here all* nacht.

She glanced up at the dim light spilling in through the cracks. Almost nightfall. She didn't want to dwell on what might be keeping the children's parents. "Let's focus on other things. Perhaps when this is over we'll have a frolic."

"With ice cream?"

Katie smiled. Maybe Seth bringing up food was a good distraction. "Of course, and I'll make a couple of pies."

"Are you *kumming* too, mister?" Mary asked.

"Sure. I'll bring the ice cream," Seth said. "What's your favorite flavor?"

"Vanilla."

Several other students shouted out their preference before Seth's question returned to Katie. "And what is the *teetshah's* favorite?"

"Straw—"

"Save that thought. I think I hear footsteps," he said.

Chapter Three

C an you hear me?" The door hinges rattled under the man's heavy rap.

"*Jah!*" they all shouted in unison.

Katie shifted her rigid body to push off the floor, but Seth tapped her shoulder.

"Stay put," he said. "I don't want anyone to get hurt."

"Okay." She eased back down. Seth was right. They didn't all need to crowd the door. Besides, her legs tingled from several hours locked in the same position, and she wasn't certain she could stand. "Stay seated until the door is open," Katie instructed some of the antsy children who had already scrambled to their feet.

After the man outside explained that a fallen tree had blocked the door, Seth suggested they synchronize their effort and try forcing the door to open in the opposite direction. This time instead of thrusting his shoulder against the door, Seth braced his foot against the stone wall and yanked on the door. Their effort failed. The building, however, released an eerie creak.

Katie clamped her hand over her mouth to muffle her gasp. Dirt sifted between the cracks overhead, and she blinked several times to clear her vision. Flanked at her sides, Ella Sue and Mary clung tightly to her arms.

"I think the wall moved," Samuel said.

"*Jah*, I felt something too," confirmed another child.

"Slide closer together, children." Consumed with huddling the children into a tighter bond, Katie missed most of the conversation between Seth and the rescuer.

"This isn't working. What's left of this structure is unstable," said the man outside.

Seth blew out a breath. "What about from above? Can you cut the planks of the subfloor to gain access?"

"I'm frightened," Ella Sue whimpered.

Mary squeezed Katie's arm tighter. "Me too."

Katie wanted to listen to the rescuer's reply, but the children pulled her attention away with their cries. Even Seth would find it difficult to communicate with the man if she didn't settle the children.

Seth eased away from the door, his urgency nearly palpable. He leaned over Katie's shoulder to whisper, "Can you have the children clear the center area?"

She froze. Had the boys been right about the wall moving? Prodded by Seth's nudge on her shoulder, she shifted into action.

"You heard him, children. Let's squeeze together. It won't be long *nau*." She hoped. The children had handled the fright and discomfort of the day's events without much complaint. But now, jammed together, dirty and uncomfortable, it wouldn't be long before tension and fear gave way to temper.

Sawdust sprinkled from above as the man worked above

them and sliced through the schoolhouse floor. Katie coughed from inhaling the fine particles. The floor would need repairing prior to the frolic . . . She gnawed on her bottom lip, remembering the sound of the peeling wind and how Seth assumed they'd lost the roof. Perhaps only a section was missing. Lord willing, she could hope that was the extent of the damages. In her mind, she'd already begun to plan the children's ice cream frolic. With this the middle of May, they didn't have many more weeks before school broke for the summer. Ending the year with a treat like ice cream was a fine idea. *Jah*, she'd see to it that something good came from all of this.

Katie's growling stomach mimicked the sawing noise the blade made cutting through the subfloor. With mounting anticipation of being able to stretch from their cramped positions, it seemed as though several hours had passed before lantern light spilled over the newly cut opening.

The children's elevated cheers of excitement drowned out the man's voice.

"Children, settle down." Katie couldn't lose control of her group now.

"Are you all okay?" A lantern swung from the man's hand.

"Jah!" the children all responded. The chatter rose as they sprang to their feet.

Seth glanced over his shoulder toward Katie, his face masked in shadows from the lantern light shining behind him. "Let's send the youngest ones up first."

Katie stood. "That would be Mary and Ella Sue." She guided Mary by the hand to Seth, who then hoisted her up to the man on the other side of the opening. He directed her to the cement porch steps. Katie sensed Ella Sue's reluctance and squeezed the child's small hand.

"It's your turn," Katie told her.

"But I want to wait with you," Ella Sue whispered.

Katie squatted next to the girl and wrapped her arms around the child. "I won't be far behind you."

Meanwhile, as she continued to console Ella Sue, Seth hoisted a nearby child through the opening with a sense of urgency.

"*Kumm* and do as I say." Katie stood and gathered Ella Sue into her arms. "Your *daed* will be looking for you."

The child sniffled. "Okay."

Once Seth finished helping another child out, he extended his arms to Ella Sue. But an eerie sound of creaking boards caused the child to bury her face in the crook of Katie's neck. She didn't like the rickety noise either. They couldn't get out of the dark cellar fast enough for Katie. Her heartbeat hadn't stopped racing since she'd seen the approaching funnel cloud.

"We need to speed it up," Seth said, reaching for another child. Once the boy was safely out, he hurried to hoist another, then another into the air and through the opening. Meanwhile, the older children lifted each other up to reach the escape hole.

With Seth's quickened pace and the stranglehold Ella Sue had around Katie's neck, she lost track of how many children were out of the cellar. She should've counted. Katie peeled Ella Sue's arms from around her neck and drew a deep breath. "Be a *gut maydel*." She passed Ella Sue to Seth despite the child's protest.

In one swift movement, he lifted Ella Sue out. The child cried, mumbling something about not seeing her *daed*. Not seeing anyone. Then one of the older children called Ella Sue over to them and Katie breathed easier.

She craned her head but couldn't see anything beyond the lamp glow. "Have you been counting?"

"*Jah*, you're next." Seth wrapped his hands around her waist without waiting for her approval.

"Just a moment."

She needed to confirm that the children were all safely out, but her feet left the ground and for the first time she noticed the missing roof. Mesmerized by the open view of the sky, she lost her focus for a second.

After a swift breeze extinguished the lantern light, the children cried out, bringing her back to her senses. But just as she reached for a crack in the floorboard, Seth's grip on her waist tightened.

Instead of lifting her higher, he pulled her back through the hole. His jerking momentum caused them both to lose their balance and they landed on the dirt floor.

"Well, I certainly wasn't expecting that." She swiped her dress sleeve over her mouth to remove the gritty taste of dirt from her tongue. She shouldn't have been gazing at the sky; she should've grabbed onto the floorboards earlier and crawled out. But she didn't consider herself so heavy that he couldn't have held on to her a little longer.

"I thought I heard the walls groan."

"I sure didn't hear anything." Except the children fussing. She started to push off the dirt floor, but Seth placed his arm around her shoulder and kept her from moving.

"Wait a minute," he said.

"I can't leave the children—"

This time the creaking timbers stopped her from moving. Something solid struck the floor with a thud, causing a rippling tremor to spread from the overhead truss supports down the cellar wall studs. Dirt and debris rained down as the opening closed off.

"That's what I thought would happen," Seth mumbled.

"Wha—what?"

"The wall collapsed."

Ach, *the children* . . . Katie scrambled to shove off his chest, but he pressed his hand over her shoulder blade and with a strong grip held her firmly against him.

"Don't move," he said.

"I must check on the children," she insisted. Katie lifted her head away from his chest. "I must go to them."

"*Nay.*" He tightened his hold on her. "I'll get you out, but stay still until I tell you." His warm breath skittered down her neck. "I'm sorry. I didn't mean to sound harsh." He relaxed his hold but kept her close enough that her ear rested against his chest.

She counted every one of his racing heartbeats. Perhaps the thumping came from her heart. She hadn't been this close to a man in seven years. Not since James died.

"Did you see how many walls were standing when I lifted you?"

"*Nay* . . . I guess I got sidetracked."

"I didn't want to alarm you earlier," he said. "The back wall isn't stable. I made a makeshift support restacking the woodpile, but any sudden movement and we'll be digging our way out . . . and that's *if* we survive."

Katie pulled in a sharp breath, taking in the mixed scent of dirt and sawdust. No wonder he was hoisting the children up so quickly.

"I thought I should explain why I don't want you to move around." He jostled her shoulders. "Are you okay?"

No, she wasn't okay. How could he ask her such a silly question? She was doing her best to concentrate on other things besides his strong arms around her. She couldn't. Her insides were too jittery to stay put any longer. She jolted her head up and unintentionally clipped his chin. Without thinking, she reached out to caress the injury like he was one of her students but jerked her hand back when her fingertips met with his bristly jaw. "I'm sorry."

"You feel better *nau*?"

"I'm sorry." She was doing her best to control her trembling and not fall apart, but his strong arms around her waist weren't helping matters. "I didn't mean to—"

"Find out if I had a beard."

She gasped.

"I'm *nett* married," he chortled.

She narrowed her eyes. Not that he could see her scorn in the dark and take a hint. "I'm beginning to wonder if you're Amish. You certainly don't behave like any of the Amish men in *mei* district."

"Have you been trapped with a man in a cellar about to cave in before?" He chuckled, but a hint of nervousness spilled into his quiet laughter. "*Nett* that it gives me a right to hold you this close."

"I should say *nett*."

He gave her a gentle squeeze. "Think of this time like having an abscessed tooth pulled. It feels uncomfortable, but it's for your own *gut*."

"I know what's for *mei* own *gut*." She pushed off him and slammed into the wall. What felt like a bucketload of dirt slid down her backside. "It's caving in!"

He pulled her close. "I was serious when I told you *nett* to move. You squirm more than an earthworm about to be hooked on a fishing line."

"Didn't you say it was the other wall?"

"*Jah* . . . just don't move around anymore."

She closed her eyes. *Think of other things* . . . "Are you sure all the children are out?"

"*Jah*, I counted twelve."

Her stomach rumbled.

"Was that yours or mine?"

"Mine," she replied.

He patted her back. "What you need is a big bowl of ice cream."

She appreciated his attempt to make light of their situation. "I was thinking more like a bowl of vegetable soup." After the hours she spent in this cold, damp cellar, she'd need something warmer than ice cream, and as much as her stomach flipped in this awkward wait for him to decide it was safe to release his hold, she would need a glass of bicarbonate to settle the upset.

Ach, why was she wasting time on useless thoughts? She should be praying. *God, I've tried to live* mei *life in accordance to your Word. If this is* mei *hour—*

"Why are you so quiet? Changing your mind about the ice cream, *jah?*"

"I'm praying. Maybe you should take a moment to make certain your heart is in right standing too."

The planks above them creaked under what sounded like footsteps. Then a heavy rattling of chains hit the floor and dispensed a dusting of fine sand particles, which sifted into the cellar cavity like flour. It didn't take the rescuer long to drag away the collapsed wall. Once he did, the faint sounds of the children's chatter sounded musical to her ears.

Once again, lantern light entered the narrow opening.

He gave her a gentle push. "Can you get up?"

"Jah." She pushed off him and wobbled as she stood. As she peered up, a shaft of blinding light flooded the area. Katie squinted and lost focus on the man standing at the opening.

Seth rose to his feet and, standing behind her, leaned close to her ear. "Once you're up there, disperse your weight by crawling off the floor." He gripped her waist and lifted her up. "Watch for nails." His voice strained as he raised her higher.

She clawed the floorboards, searching for a crevice to pull herself up.

"Take my hand, child."

Without looking into the searing light, she extended her arm, and an oversize, firm hand lifted her out of the hole. Once she was out completely, the man released her hand.

"You are safe now, Katie. Go in peace."

His faint voice drifted over what sounded like an incredible distance, yet she was very aware that he'd just let go of her hand. Having spent so many hours in the dark, her eyes still hadn't adjusted to the flood of lantern light and she couldn't look beyond the light's blaring intensity.

By the time she crawled across the width of the schoolhouse subfloor and reached the area where the children waited, her raw knees stung and she teetered a moment, standing to her feet. She glanced over her shoulder to look for Seth, but he wasn't following. There wasn't anyone near the escape hole. Not even the man who had rescued them.

The clumping of horse hooves on the gravel drive caught her attention and she reeled around. A string of lantern-lit buggies pulled into the school yard. She caught Mary and Ella Sue before they bolted with the other children to meet their parents. With their small size, a horse could easily trample them.

Katie clutched both girls by the hand and walked with them.

The bishop's son, Andrew Lapp, jumped out of his buggy and dropped to his knees in front of Mary, his daughter. "I was worried about you." He glanced up at Katie. "Is everyone okay?"

"*Jah*. A little shaken, but we're fine."

Mary wrapped her arms around his neck. "We were in the cellar."

"You have a smart *teetshah*, ain't so?" He took his daughter into his arms and stood. "*Denki*, Katie." He looked past her toward the school. "The building took a direct hit. Praise God you are all okay."

"*Jah.*" Katie glanced over her shoulder at the building lying in a heap. God's mercy had saved them. She scanned the area again for Seth and the man who had rescued them. Neither was seen. Once all the children located their parents, she would find Seth and thank him.

Ella Sue squeezed Katie's hand. "Can we find *mei daed nau?*"

Katie bent down and gathered Ella Sue into her arms. "*Gut* idea." The poor girl trembled and understandably so, since her father was always the first to pick up his only child. She glanced at Andrew. "Have you seen Timothy King?"

"*Nay*, but he would *kumm* from the opposite direction as I did."

Katie frowned. She hadn't wanted to frighten Ella Sue and say it aloud, but Timothy's house might have been in the tornado's path. A lump lodged in Katie's throat when she caught a glimpse of the child's quivering lips. Growing up without any siblings and having a deceased mother, Ella Sue was exceptionally close to her father.

"I'm sure he will be here shortly," Katie said.

Andrew nodded. "We had to stop and cut some fallen trees. His road might be blocked too." He craned his neck. "I'm looking for Samuel and Rebecca Fischer. Judith's parents' *haus* was hit, so they need to *kumm* home with me." Andrew motioned to another buggy pulling into the yard. "Maybe that's Timothy."

But it wasn't.

"I'll find out if anyone's heard anything about Timothy." Andrew spoke over his shoulder as he stepped away.

"*Jah*, please." Katie touched her throat, hoping to reduce the quiver as she spoke. She didn't want to frighten Ella Sue more. As an only parent, Timothy always picked up his daughter. Even though several of the other students walked, he didn't want Ella Sue walking the two miles home at such a young age.

Katie weaved through the crowd, clutching Ella Sue in her arms. Talk of the tornado's path saturated the conversations, and she didn't wish to engage in the dreary discussions, not with a frightened child clinging to her neck. From the bits of news she had overheard, it sounded as though their community was devastated. Houses, barns, businesses—all destroyed. Some had lost their livestock, others their grain shafts. But no loss compared to Ella Sue's if her only parent was— Katie couldn't bring herself to think about the possible tragedy. Timothy would arrive shortly. He had to.

A low rumble of thunder preceded the rain. The cooling sprinkle quickly changed into a downpour. Ella Sue curled in Katie's arms and buried her face in the crook of Katie's neck. With the schoolhouse gone, they had no place to flee the weather. She had a shawl stashed in her buggy. Lightning flashed, allowing a few seconds of brightness to search for her buggy. It was gone, her horse, Peaches, too. Another flash showed her the outhouse. Flipped on its side, it now lay several feet away from where it originally stood. She hoped no one walked blindly into the uncovered sewage hole.

Andrew lumbered toward her. "I have someone heading over to Timothy's place. We'll have news shortly." He pointed to his buggy. "*Geh* sit in *mei* buggy with Mary," he yelled over a clap of thunder.

Katie nodded and headed in that direction. With Ella Sue clutched in her arms, she climbed on the bench and sat beside Mary, who had huddled under a quilt.

The child poked her head out from under the cover. "Ella Sue, are you *kalt?* We can share."

Ella Sue's lips trembled as she crawled under the cover next to Mary.

Samuel and Rebecca Fischer, drenched from standing in the rain, piled into the back end.

"I heard part of our *haus* was hit," Samuel said.

"We're staying with Andrew and Judith," Rebecca added.

Lowering the blanket from her face, tears pooled in Ella Sue's eyes. "Is that what happened to *mei haus?*" She peeled off the cover and climbed onto Katie's lap. "I'm afraid."

"God tells us in his Word that he is with us and we shouldn't fear. It's hard, I know. But let's pray for strength." Katie forced an encouraging smile.

The child nodded while rubbing her eyes.

"God, *denki* for keeping us safe today. We pray for an outpouring of your generous mercy in this time of need." Katie's voice squeaked.

"And please," Ella Sue cut in, "let *mei daed* find me. *Aemen.*"

Forgive me, God, for lacking boldness to ask. But please hear the child's prayer. Protect Timothy King.

Katie kissed the top of the child's head, then softly hummed a traditional hymn from the *Ausbund.* A few moments later the child was lulled to sleep. "*Denki,* God," Katie whispered.

Lightning flashed and illuminated a shadowy figure darting into the Masts' wheat field. Katie continued to stare in the same spot long after the flicker of light vanished.

"Samuel," she whispered, so as not to wake Ella Sue, "do you remember telling me a man directed you to wait under the desk?" She wouldn't be surprised if he didn't remember; after all, she'd found the boy in a stupor.

"*Jah,*" he said reluctantly.

"You said he had white hair? Did you recognize him?"

"*Nay*, I'd never seen him before."

Her curiosity wouldn't rest. "Do you think he was Seth?"

"I doubt it. The man's voice was deeper than Seth's."

"What about the man who rescued us—did you recognize him?"

"*Nay*, why?"

"I wanted to thank him, is all," Katie said.

Ella Sue stirred on Katie's lap. She resumed humming, only a little louder, hoping the hymn would offset the sound of thunder. This spring weather wasn't like anything she'd seen before.

God, please allow this wedder *to pass over us.*

Andrew climbed inside the buggy; water dripped off the brim of his hat. "We're calling a meeting in the morning." He released the brake. "I'll take you home. There's no sense waiting in the bad *wedder*. You don't mind, do you?"

Katie shook her head. She didn't want to risk waking Ella Sue by answering aloud.

"I'm tired." Mary yawned and leaned against her *daed*.

Samuel lurched forward from the backbench. "Does this mean we don't have *schul meiya*?"

"*Jah*, Samuel," Katie whispered. She pointed to the children sleeping and pulled her finger up against her mouth.

He nodded and leaned back against the seat.

As the lulling rain tapped the roof of the buggy, Katie's thoughts flitted from Timothy to wondering if Peaches was injured or if her house still stood. Each time lightning flickered, more uprooted trees were visible. They skirted around the ones that earlier blocked the road. Andrew got out at one point and led his horse through the obstacle of fallen limbs.

She gazed at Ella Sue through blurred vision. *God, please have mercy on this child's father. Let Timothy King be okay.*

Andrew pointed ahead. "Looks like your farm is still standing. *Gut* news, ain't so?"

Katie dabbed the corners of her eyes with her dress sleeve. "*Jah*, a *gut* sight to see, that's for certain." *Denki, God. Denki.*

Ella Sue stirred, smacked her mouth a few times, but never opened her eyes.

Andrew veered the buggy into the driveway and stopped near the back door. He repositioned Mary, who had fallen asleep against his arm.

"Don't get out. I'll be fine." Katie eased out of the buggy with Ella Sue in her arms.

"I'll send word once I hear about Timothy."

"*Denki*, Andrew." Katie climbed the porch steps and entered the house. Once she had a fire started to dry Ella Sue's clothes, she would warm some soup. Hopefully Ella Sue would fall back to sleep without asking too many questions.

Seth fought to suppress his thoughts of Katie. Curiosity was all it was. Naturally, after they'd spent several hours trapped together, he would have some.

Once he'd climbed out of the cellar, he looked for her, but it seemed every woman there held a child either by the hand or in her arms. Unless he weaved through the crowd in the dark and listened for her voice, he wouldn't find her. Just as well. He didn't intend to stay in Hope Falls for long. Once he helped his brother-in-law get the honey business established, Seth planned to return to his district in Saint Joseph County.

Still, he didn't even know her last name. Seth shook his head. He couldn't allow another woman to capture his thoughts. He hadn't even worked out his feelings for Diana—or his lack of feelings—when he didn't respond to her ultimatum and she called off their engagement.

His nephew Thomas, at Seth's left, nudged his arm, bringing him back to the supper table at his brother-in-law's house. "*Onkel* Seth, you want green beans?"

"*Jah, denki.*" Seth spooned out some beans from the dish, then passed it to Paul, his nephew seated on his right.

"You missed the lightning. It brought the old oak tree down," Thomas said.

Amos nodded. "On the barn."

"How damaged is it?" Seth hadn't noticed the downed tree. By the time he crawled out of the cellar, it was dark. He trekked across the forty-acre wheat field, which separated the school from the back of Amos's barn, unable to see more than a foot ahead of him.

"The main road was closed because of downed trees and traffic was rerouted. I couldn't check out the barn. It was already dark." Amos sighed. "I'm sure it'll need some sort of repair."

Seth nodded. That was the uncertainty of a tornado. While it demolished one place, it left a neighboring farm unscathed. Located on the hillcrest, the schoolhouse hadn't fared well, but thankfully no one was injured.

Paul reached for another biscuit. "We heard a train noise and hurried into the basement."

"That was smart," Seth said.

"What was it like being *in* the tornado? Were you afraid?"

"I wouldn't want to go through one again." Seth speared some green beans with his fork.

"The building's completely gone?" Amos lifted his brows.

Seth nodded. "*Jah*, leveled to the ground." He gazed at his nephews seated beside him. Thomas, who was eleven, and Paul, who had turned ten, were of school age. The girls weren't. The oldest, Leah, was sixteen, and the baby, Annie, had only turned four last month. "Why don't you boys attend *schul?*"

"I don't like *schul*," Thomas blurted.

Paul shifted in his chair. "*Jah*, we don't need no learning. Ain't that right, *Daed?*"

Seth raised his brows. Admittedly, he knew very little about his brother-in-law, but when Amos shot a glare in Seth's direction, he understood the silent warning. Seth glanced at Leah. With her head tilted down, his niece poked at the food on her plate. She hadn't said much of anything since he arrived yesterday. At least not when her father was around.

Amos lowered his fork. "I suppose it don't matter *nau* with the *schulhaus* torn apart." He pushed his chair away from the table but paused before standing. "Why were you over there anyway?"

Seth looked up from loading his fork with roast beef. "I found a horse tangled in the barbed wire at the edge of the field. After freeing the mare, I noticed the funnel cloud." He shrugged. "I saw a woman and child running for cover and I followed them into a cellar."

Amos stood. "I can't imagine being trapped for any amount of time with that meddlesome *schul teetshah*, Katie Bender." He shook his head and muttered something about her stubborn disposition as he walked out of the kitchen.

Seth smiled. Bender was her last name. *Katie Bender.* His smile faded. What made Amos so adamant she was meddlesome?

Chapter Four

Despite a restless night, Katie woke as soon as the morning sunlight filtered into her bedroom window. She eased out from under the quilt, careful not to wake Ella Sue, who hadn't slept much during the night. Each time the child stirred, she cried out for her father. Seeing the little girl so distraught caused a hollow ache inside Katie.

Katie slipped into a dress and grabbed the brush from the top of her dresser. Wood shavings fluttered to the floor as she guided the stiff bristles through her long, dark hair. She'd brushed both hers and Ella Sue's hair prior to going to bed last night but obviously hadn't done a thorough job. She opened the top dresser drawer, fished out a fresh prayer *kapp*, and pinned it in place.

Ella Sue rolled over on the mattress, facing the door. The child sighed restlessly, but her eyes remained closed. Katie slipped out of the room. She wanted Ella Sue to sleep as long as she could, and preferably until Timothy came to fetch her so she wouldn't have to answer the child's questions regarding her father's whereabouts.

Katie padded to the kitchen in her stockings and peered out the window above the sink. Scattered tree limbs covered the lawn along with bits of newspaper and other debris. From her limited view, the barn appeared intact. She couldn't see Peaches standing near the barn entrance, so presumably the horse hadn't found her way home yet. Katie pulled away from the window. Until she knew the whereabouts of Timothy, she and Ella Sue needed to stay put. She would search for the horse later.

"Lord, I feel guilty praying for Peaches when all *mei* prayers should be for Timothy, but I don't want Peaches to suffer. Please look out for her and protect her as well as Timothy."

The cold front that spawned yesterday's tornado had cooled down the house such that the chilly kitchen floor made her wish she hadn't rushed out of the bedroom without grabbing a pair of wool socks to slip over her stockings. But once she stoked the woodstove in the sitting room and had a fire going in the cookstove, the drafty house would warm up.

She smiled at Seth's suggestion of ice cream. Unlike his brother-in-law, Amos, Seth certainly had a sense of humor. Amos had turned bitter since his wife passed. Other than complaining about Katie's mare trampling his winter wheat, he seldom uttered more than a grunt. That was, until she asked Bishop Lapp to have Amos reconsider the spot where he intended to place his beehives. The man had several acres. He could've easily chosen an area away from the school yard where the children played.

Her shoes were still wet from last night, but she shoved her feet into them anyway since the ash pan needed emptying before she could start a fire. Katie pulled the ash pan from the bottom of the stove, then carefully carried it outside to the garden to dispose of the ashes. She tipped over the metal pan and tapped it a few times. Fine cinder particles scattered with the breeze, then landed on the ground and soaked into the muddy soil. She peered at the storm clouds. She certainly didn't need more rain. Her garden seeds were already at risk of rotting.

None of that was important, though, with Timothy King still not making an appearance.

Where was he?

Patience wasn't one of her strongest virtues. She turned to go inside but paused when a buggy pulled into the driveway. She recognized the horse immediately as one of her brother's.

Isaac climbed out. "I thought I'd better *kumm* check on you." He reached inside the buggy and grabbed a jar of milk and a carton of eggs. "I just heard this morning about the *schul*. You must've been frightened."

"*Jah*, we all were." She climbed the porch steps, her brother following. "Any word yet on Timothy King?" Her brother's weighted sigh caused her hand to freeze from twisting the doorknob. "What is it?"

He grimaced. "They've gathered a search team. It doesn't look good."

Search team? Her stomach knotted. "I thought his road was blocked by fallen trees."

Isaac's forehead creased with wrinkles in the same way it had the day he broke the news of their parents' death.

"If you know something, you need to tell me *nau*. I've got Timothy's daughter staying with me, and when she wakes, she'll have questions."

"Both his *haus* and his shop are in shambles, but that's all

I've been told. I'm *nett* withholding anything." He lifted the milk container. "I stayed behind to finish the milking, but the boys took the plow team and went ahead with the others."

Her brother had one of the strongest pulling teams in the settlement. He clear-cut the trees on his property in the middle of winter with those horses.

"By the way, I didn't see your buggy or Peaches."

"I think the tornado took the buggy. I don't know what happened to Peaches." She didn't want to think of the possibilities either.

Isaac made a silent gesture toward her hand resting on the doorknob. She turned the knob and nudged the door open with her hip.

"I'm on *mei* way over to join the search *nau*. I'll spread the news about Peaches, and Abigail or I will bring you a horse and buggy to use." He carried the milk and eggs into the kitchen and set them down on the counter.

"*Denki.*" Katie replaced the ash pan under the woodstove, then rinsed her soiled hands at the sink. "You never said if your place had damages. Abigail must've been a bundle of nerves."

Isaac shook his head. "The storm missed us. There was a little hail, but *nett* enough to cause damage."

"That's *gut* news." Katie smiled. She loved Abigail dearly, but her brother's *fraa* probably would still be hiding in the basement if they had been in the storm's path.

"I'll send word when I have more news," he said.

"*Jah*, please. And I'll keep Timothy and all the workers in *mei* prayers."

Isaac's forehead wrinkled again.

She couldn't bring herself to say any more. Her parched throat made it difficult to swallow.

Isaac seemed to understand her speechlessness. He left without saying anything more.

Katie leaned against the cabinet and closed her eyes to pray, but the words wouldn't come.

Hovering in the ethereal realm, Elias approached Katie. "God has not given you a spirit of fear, but of power and of love and of a sound mind." Elias hoped his words resonated with his charge. "Be prepared to give account for the hope that is in you. You will be used to encourage the weak."

The bedroom door slammed and Katie jolted.

Ella Sue practically flew down the hall. She skidded to a stop on the rug at the entry, then yanked open the door, yelling, "*Daed*, wait!"

Katie rushed over to Ella Sue and knelt in front of her. "That was *mei bruder*, Isaac. He brought us some eggs and milk. I thought we would make pancakes. Would you like that?"

Ella Sue's eyes pooled with tears. "Where's *mei daed*?"

Seth ambled across the yard toward the barn. His nephews were right. The old oak had split in half. Unfortunately, it looked as though the larger portion of the tree had fallen against the lean-to attached to the calving barn.

Amos rounded the corner of the lean-to and met Seth next to the fallen tree. "At least the livestock have been moved out. What do you think of the barn's condition?"

Seth dug the toe of his boot into the soft ground, then glanced at the cloudy sky. "I'd wait. Taking that tree down will be tricky, and doing it in the rain would be too risky."

"I need *mei* barn functioning. I won't be able to hold those calves long in the other barn."

The tree's oversized limbs and branches blocked the most critical view. Seth stepped around the corner of the structure. Even from this perspective, he couldn't be certain the load-bearing wall wasn't damaged or if any of the shims or pegs had pulled away from the tenons.

"I don't think we'll know the extent of the damage until after the tree's removed," Seth said. Even then, he didn't want to be responsible for determining the safety of the building. Last night he woke with cold sweats after dreaming the cellar had caved in on Katie and the children. In the dream he couldn't reach them—just like he couldn't reach Abraham Raber after the building came down and crushed him.

Seth's chest tightened. He was no longer a builder. Everything he built now wasn't any larger than a box to house a swarm of bees. He wouldn't ever trust his mind to unscramble the numbers or rely on his calculations being correct again. His palms turned clammy and beads of sweat trickled from his brow into his eyes, causing him to blink hard to dilute the salty sting.

"You must have someone in your district who could inspect the supports."

Amos shook his head. "Don't need their help."

Seth pulled a rag from his pocket and wiped the sweat from his eyes. Surely his brother-in-law knew why he stopped doing construction—why he only built beehives. He would ask around. On Sunday he would talk with the men at church and find out who their lead carpenter was for the barn raisings. Until then he planned to stall.

Seth shoved the rag into his pocket and looked again at the sky. If the weather cooperated, it would rain and that would be reason enough to wait.

His niece Leah strolled across the yard, pulling at the sides of her dress. She stopped next to her father and eyed the length of the fallen tree. "It's gonna be tough to get that down."

Seth nodded.

"*Daed*, while Annie is sleeping, I want to take the buggy into town." She cast a pleading glance at her father.

Amos's eyes narrowed. "To do what?"

"We need a few grocery items. *Kaffi*, sugar, stuff like that. It wouldn't take me long."

Amos shook his head. "Make a list. I'll *geh* after the stuff."

"But I thought you and *Onkel* Seth—"

"*Geh* on *nau*." Amos pointed at the house. "I'll be in to get the list."

Leah trudged away with her head tipped downward, scuffing her feet along the walk.

From the glimpse Seth caught of her frown, he suspected the trip into town meant more than merely going after a few grocery items. He'd seen a canister filled with coffee earlier when he searched the cupboards for a coffee cup.

The interaction between Leah and Amos caused a knot in the pit of Seth's stomach.

"I suppose I'll harness the horse so I can get those grocery supplies," Amos said.

Seth nodded. "I think before it rains I'll scout out a *gut* location for the beehives."

"Check out the area near the creek," Amos said.

"*Jah*, I'll be sure to." Seth waited until Amos circled toward the barn before he wandered out to the pasture. Maybe he should've mentioned finding coffee in the canister earlier. He shook his head. It wasn't his business. He certainly wasn't a mediator. Yet something pricked at his conscience. Like a pickax takes hold of a block of ice.

Seth's boot sank ankle-deep into the wet ground. He pulled it loose and shook off the clumps of mud. Overhead, a vulture swooped over its prey. Amos's droopy wheat field resembled a flattened patch of grass after a deer had bedded down. Only it wasn't just a patch—his brother-in-law was in jeopardy of losing his entire field. He walked toward the circling scavenger bird.

Reaching the edge of the property, Seth stopped at the sight of the sorrel mare tangled in barbed wire. The horse raised its head off the ground, flared its nostrils in his direction, then lowered its head back to the ground.

"You crazy fool. I freed you yesterday." He crept closer to the horse. Dogs return to their vomit, but in this case, a lunatic horse had returned to barbed wire. Lying on the ground, she wasn't as spirited as he'd found her yesterday. Although judging by the depth the barbs pierced her coat, she hadn't surrendered without a fight. He needed wire clippers for this job. "I'll be back," he said, backing up slowly. Once he was several feet away, he jogged, slinging mud with each stride, back to the barn.

It didn't take long to locate the wire cutter, hanging on a peg in the barn, and he didn't dally in returning to the downed mare. Seth knelt beside the horse. "Easy, girl," he said, gliding the clippers between the horse's coat and the wire. The horse jolted when he made the first snip. He stroked the horse's neck a few times to calm the animal, then clipped the remaining wire.

"*Gut* girl," he said, coaxing the mare to stand.

Seth gazed in the direction he'd seen the funnel cloud. A wide row of spruce pines had snapped in half, and several oaks lay uprooted along the path. His gaze followed the trail of damage and stopped on the demolished schoolhouse. Boards lay in a skewed heap. Remnants of what was once a buggy littered the soggy lawn. He shook his head. Seeing the damage in daylight brought home the miracle that they'd all survived. "Your mercy is new every morning. *Denki*, God."

A fine mist of rain drew his attention away from the school. He made a slight tug on the horse's halter. Once in the barn, he lit the wick on the lantern and brought it closer to get a better view of the mare's wounds. The barbs hadn't penetrated as deeply as he originally thought. Still, they would need attention.

"You'll be as *gut* as new once I fix up those cuts." Seth patted the horse's neck, then grabbed the feed bucket off the floor and stepped out of the stall. The horse would respond better when he washed the wounds with iodine and applied a medicated balm if her belly was full. Seth tossed a scoop of oats into the bucket, then slipped it into the stall. He would feed her more prior to starting the procedure, but this would keep the mare occupied while he gathered the supplies.

He ambled across the yard and entered the house, met by the sweet scent of cinnamon rolls. It brought back memories of home. Before his sister married Amos and moved to this settlement to be near his aging parents, she used to bake cinnamon rolls to sell at the small bakery in town.

Seth headed into the kitchen where Leah stood bent over the oven and Annie sat at the table scribbling on a piece of paper.

"Smells *gut*," he said.

"*Denki.*" Leah pulled the pan out of the oven and placed it on the wire cooling rack.

"Your *mamm* liked to bake those."

"She told me how you would snitch one when she put them out to cool." Leah slid the spatula under a roll, lifted it out of the pan, and set it on the plate.

"She slapped *mei* hand with the spatula too." His mouth watered for a taste of the icing she drizzled over the hot rolls.

Leah nudged the plate closer to him. "I won't chase you away from mine."

Annie looked up from her paper. "I'm *hungahrich* too."

"You need to wait until they're cool," Leah told her.

The younger niece stuck out her bottom lip.

"*Geduld*, Annie, *geduld*," Leah said.

As wonderful as the rolls smelled, it was easy for Seth to understand Annie's lack of patience. Most Amish children learned self-control at a young age. Leah didn't bend to the child's pout, and Annie returned to marking on the paper.

Seth glanced at Leah. "I need to tend to a horse first. Do you have some iodine?"

"*Jah*, there's a bottle in the hall cabinet."

"What about coal tar? I want to make a salve."

She lowered the last roll onto a plate and rested the spatula on the counter. She stooped down in front of the cabinet. "Here it is." She rose and handed him the container.

"*Denki*."

"Who needs the salve?"

"I found a horse caught in the barbed wire."

"Another one?"

"Same one as yesterday. I think the storm has her disoriented." He glanced at the rolls. "Those would sure be *gut* with a cup of *kaffi*."

"I'll make a pot." Without hesitation, Leah opened the cupboard and grabbed the container of coffee.

Seth widened his eyes at the container, then at her as she scooped the coffee. Obviously she had misled her father.

"I didn't realize your *daed* was back from picking up supplies in town," he said, looking inside the half-filled coffee can.

She sucked in a breath, then glanced at her little sister. "Annie, *geh* put your papers away and wash your hands."

Annie shoved the papers into a pile and climbed off the chair. She dashed out of the room.

Leah opened her mouth, but Seth spoke first. "I've got a horse to tend." He was heading for the entrance when someone knocked. Seth opened the door and greeted the group of men.

"Hello. Is Amos home?" one of the men said.

"He went to town. I'm his brother-in-law, Seth Stutzman."

The man rubbed his grimy hands on the sides of his pants. "I'm one of the ministers, Andrew Lapp." He pointed at the man on his right, also covered in dirt. "This is *mei* brother-in-law and another minister, David Fischer, and these are his twin boys, Jacob and James."

The twins looked to be Leah's age. One nodded, and the other made a sheepish smile Seth assumed wasn't aimed at him. Seth casually glanced over his shoulder but already knew the young man had been eyeing Leah. Her face turned pink.

Andrew continued, "We've *kumm* to see how everyone is doing after the storm yesterday." He eyed his dirt-covered hands. "We *kumm* directly from Timothy King's *haus*."

Seth nodded, but not being a member of this district, he had no idea who Timothy was.

"He's still missing," Andrew explained.

"We hadn't heard news a man was missing." At least, Amos hadn't mentioned it to Seth, and surely his brother-in-law would've wanted to join the search.

"We couldn't do much more after the sun went down because it became too hazardous. So we're—" Andrew cut off his words, and the other man introduced as David stepped forward.

"We're checking on everyone in the district, trying to get an idea of what the needs are for the families," David said. He continued, "Of course, we won't address the issues until Timothy is found."

"We're grateful to God our family was spared." Seth looked at his niece, whose face had turned a rosier shade. He figured it had something to do with the young man still eyeing her. Seth averted his attention from Leah and focused on the men. "Other than a tree falling on the lean-to, we're in *gut* standing here."

"I'm sorry about your lean-to. I can put it on the list, if Amos wishes, but I'm afraid it will be awhile. We have to prioritize the losses," David said.

"I understand. What about the missing man—where and what time in the morning are you resuming the search?"

"We'll meet before daybreak at Timothy's *haus*."

Seth nodded. He wouldn't detain the men by asking directions. Amos would know the way to the man's house.

"Lord willing we'll find Timothy tomorrow," Andrew said. He glanced sideways at the older minister before continuing. "Once we do, we'll plan when to meet and organize the work teams."

David nodded. "Word was sent to the neighboring counties, but we're *nett* sure when and how many will *kumm*. So far, there are three barns and at least one *haus* destroyed."

"But we haven't talked with the folks on the north side yet. Our settlement is small and spread out amongst the *Englischers'* farms," Andrew explained, then added, "I'm sure once we've collected all the information on damages, the need will be much greater."

They hadn't mentioned the demolished schoolhouse. Seth supposed it was near enough to summer break that they would release the students early. It made sense. They'd need every hand, young and old, to rebuild the settlement.

"I'll be sure to tell Amos about Timothy and about the meeting too." Seth already felt the weight lifted off his shoulders in regard to Amos's calving barn. Now that the settlement had plans to create a workforce, Amos wouldn't have to rely on Seth to inspect the structure's stability.

"Are you visiting long? We can use all the help we can get."

Seth's chest tightened. The moment he heard about the missing man, he planned to offer assistance in the search, but staying to rebuild the settlement was entirely different. He wasn't a builder any longer.

"I only planned to stay long enough to set up some beehives for Amos." But even as the words rolled off his lips, guilt laded him.

Andrew and David glanced at each other and frowned.

Seth looked down at the floor. Selfish. God had spared his family. He needed to show his gratitude and help his fellow brethren, even if this wasn't his settlement. He lifted his gaze and forced a smile. "I can swing a hammer. Let me know when you decide to meet."

"We'll know more tomorrow if—when—we find Timothy," Andrew said, his words laced with fatigue.

Seth didn't want to detain them any longer. "Then I'll see you in the morning."

"*Denki*, and please tell Amos we hope to see him there too," David said as they turned to leave.

Hope to see Amos? Seth mulled the odd statement over in his mind. In his district, it would be assumed that everyone would pull together.

The men climbed into their buggies. The boy with the keen interest in Leah made another sheepish glance at her, then climbed into the back end.

Seth elbowed Leah's shoulder. "I'm surprised you didn't offer that *bu* one of your cinnamon rolls." Seth grinned when his niece's eyes widened.

Annie poked her head around the corner of the kitchen. "They're *gut*," she said, licking the icing from her sticky fingers.

"You didn't." Leah marched into the kitchen after Annie. "Who said you could get into those?"

Seth wagged his head and slipped outside to take care of the horse.

The sorrel mare's ears perked as he entered her stall. He hung the lantern on a nail, then doused a rag with iodine solution. Surprisingly, the horse remained calm through the entire application.

Amos entered the barn. He draped the harness on the hook, then plodded over to the stall. "What's her horse doing here?"

Squatted next to the horse, Seth looked up at Amos. "You know who the horse belongs to?"

"*Jah*. It's Katie Bender's, the *schul teetshah*. What's it doing here?"

Seth added more iodine to the rag. "The mare got cut up by the barbed wire," he said, dabbing the wound with the medicated cloth.

"Probably tore up *mei* wheat field too," Amos growled under his breath.

What had him so irritated? His wheat field was under water. Seth didn't want to aggravate him more by pointing out his failed crop. He recapped the amber medicine bottle and stood. "There's a meeting about the storm damages *meiya*."

"How did you hear that?"

"Andrew Lapp and David Fischer stopped by."

Amos pushed a blade of straw with the toe of his boot. "What else did they tell you?"

"They asked if you had any damages and said one man is missing. Timothy King."

Amos stared at the floor.

Obviously Seth knew very little about his brother-in-law. He expected Amos to show an interest in the man's welfare.

Seth cleared his throat. "They plan to resume the search in the morning. I thought after chores we could—"

"I don't know why they came here." Amos squared his shoulders. "I no longer belong." He aimed his glare at the horse. "That animal and its owner are nothing but trouble. I want it off *mei* property."

Chapter Five

"D oes Ella Sue know?" Abigail sipped her hot tea.

Katie shook her head.

"The poor child. Having *nay mamm* and *nau* her father—"

"We don't know that yet," Katie was swift to correct.

"*Jah*, but it's been over twenty-four hours. Isaac described the *haus* as a flimsy cardboard box all folded in on itself. How could anyone—"

Katie lifted her hand to stop her sister-in-law from continuing. She'd heard the news too. The porch steps were thrown as far as the ditch, and the mound of debris between his house and his shop amounted to more than the men could work through in one day.

Turning her eyes down, Abigail swirled the tea in her cup.

Sometimes Abigail's lack of faith surprised Katie. Her dear

sister-in-law was four years older, a devout believer, but still, Abigail worried excessively. Usually over things she had no control over—like Katie not marrying. Her sister-in-law had said more times than Katie cared to count how she wouldn't know what to do living alone.

Katie wouldn't say she enjoyed her lonely life. Had James not died seven years ago, she would be married and most likely tending to a household of children. But when her dreams of marriage and children died, she adapted. She had to in order to survive. Now, at age twenty-nine, she'd found contentment. Surrounded by her students and immersed in teaching, the thought of her *leddich* life wasn't so frightening.

"I heard word was sent to the other counties about the tornado," Katie said.

"*Jah*, Isaac said they expect workers to arrive soon." Abigail's eyes brightened and she wiggled her brows. "Some unmarried men too, no doubt."

Katie choked on her tea. She set the cup down hard on the table.

"This might be prime time."

"For what? Never mind." She instantly regretted her slip in asking. She knew Abigail well enough to know better than to ask her to expound on an idea about single men. She'd somehow invite them all over for dinner just to introduce them to Katie.

"The *schul* is gone. What will you do?"

"I'm still the *teetshah*. The *schul* will be rebuilt."

"You can work the vegetable stand with me . . ."

Before Katie started teaching, Abigail wanted her to run a fruit and vegetable stand. Katie wasn't interested in that five years ago and she wasn't interested in running one now, other than to fill in occasionally when Abigail needed a day off.

"Or you could get married," Abigail said as though that were a viable option. It wasn't, and her sister-in-law knew that.

Katie huffed. "It's *nett* that easy."

Abigail shrugged. "You never know who might *kumm* help build from the other counties."

Katie wasn't about to mention being trapped with Seth in the *schul* cellar. Her sister-in-law would already have her married off in her mind. She'd learned long ago when Abigail started in on finding her a husband to steer the conversation to another subject.

"I think I'll write something about the storm and submit it to the *Budget*," Katie said.

"That's a *gut* idea. Maybe more unmarried men will *kumm* to help." She slid the chair away from the table and stood. "This is *mei* laundry day. I should be on *mei* way home."

Katie walked her sister-in-law to the door, opened it, and caught a glimpse of the fenced gelding. "*Denki* for the use of the horse and buggy."

"Willow doesn't have much stamina, but he will get you around."

She leaned close and whispered, "I don't plan to go anywhere until Timothy is found."

"Hopefully that will be soon."

Katie nodded. She waited at the door until Abigail stepped into her buggy before returning to the kitchen.

Katie picked up the cups from the table and lowered them into the sink. She waved at Abigail through the window. Then her gaze fell on the scattered yard debris. Today would be a fine day to clean up the fallen tree branches, and it would keep both Ella Sue and her occupied. The child hadn't slept much, and sitting around the house only made matters worse.

Ella Sue shuffled into the kitchen. Her balled fist rubbed puffy eyes. "Did *mei daed kumm* yet?"

"*Nett* yet." Katie tapped the back of the chair. "*Kumm* and sit down. I'll make you some breakfast."

"I'm *nett* hungry."

"That might be so, but I want you to try to eat something." She tapped the seat again.

This time Ella Sue climbed up on the chair without saying anything.

Katie fried some scrambled eggs and buttered a slice of bread for each of them. Ella Sue picked at her meal; Katie had lost her appetite too.

The child's silence tore at Katie's heart. They had to do something besides sit in this house and mope. When they finished eating, Katie cleared the table.

"These dishes can wait. Let's put our shoes on and get some fresh air."

Ella Sue slipped off the wooden chair without a word and headed to the door.

God, she's frightened, and I'm not sure how to reach her.

Katie wiped her hands on a dish towel and tossed it on the counter. She met Ella Sue at the door. Working hard to tie her shoelaces, her little fingers fumbled awkwardly with the strings. Growing frustrated, Ella Sue huffed and dropped the laces. Her eyes filled with tears.

Katie knelt next to Ella Sue. "Here, let me help you." She looped the laces into a bow, tying it tight. "Does your *daed* do this for you?"

She nodded and dropped her head. The child's chin touched her chest and her shoulders sagged.

"Do not lose hope." Katie tugged firmly on the shoelaces

before tying them in a knot. "God loves you and hears your prayers. He is faithful," she said, standing to her feet.

Ella Sue rubbed her eyes. "Does that mean I'll see *mei daed* soon?"

Katie reached for Ella Sue's hand. "If that is God's will."

"Can we pray it be God's will?"

The crack in the child's voice caused Katie's throat to tighten. Ella Sue squeezed her eyes closed and bowed her head. Katie hesitated, unsure what to say. Above all, she wanted God's will, but she learned firsthand when her fiancé, James, died how difficult it was to truly accept his will in all things.

"God, please make it your will for me to see *mei daed* again," Ella Sue said. *"Aemen."*

Have mercy, heavenly Father. Have mercy. Katie pleaded her own prayer silently.

Ella Sue squeezed Katie's hand. "Are you going to say something?"

"God, *denki* for the love you lavish on your children. Your grace and mercy are bountiful. *Denki* that you have Timothy in your hand. *Aemen.*"

"He's going to be okay. I know he will *kumm* get me." She nodded. "He will, ain't so?"

Lord, this is hard. Katie needed more strength. Her throat burned as if she'd eaten a lump of coal. On top of that, it had swelled so tight she could barely swallow.

She smiled at Ella Sue patiently waiting at the door. "I better get . . ." She cleared her throat. "A trash bag." She retreated to the kitchen and grabbed some bags from the pantry. "The sticks we can burn, but the rest we'll need to throw out," she said, walking back to the door. "Ready?"

The little girl nodded.

Katie opened the door and stepped onto the porch. She

scanned the yard. Fallen limbs were everywhere. "*Ach*, where do we begin?"

"Look!" Ella Sue pointed above them at a large tree limb protruding through a hole in the porch roof.

Katie cringed. "That's *nett gut* to see." She grasped the child's hand and led her off the porch. "We'll leave that patch work to *mei bruder*." She bent down, collected a handful of wet newspaper that must have blown into her yard from one of her *Englisch* neighbors, and shoved it into the trash bag.

After several hours in the warm sun, they built up a sweat dragging fallen tree branches to one central pile. The larger limbs, Katie pulled over to the side of the shed. They needed to be cut stove-size, but that wasn't a pressing project. She had plenty of dried wood from last season to burn.

With the bulk of the debris picked up, the yard looked much better. But more importantly, it gave them something to keep their minds off of Timothy's unknown fate.

Katie glanced at Ella Sue tugging on a small branch.

"Would you like to stop for lunch?"

Ella Sue nodded but spun toward the driveway at the sound of a buggy approaching. Her small face lit with excitement. She dropped the branch and ran across the yard.

Katie hurried to catch her before she darted into the path of the horse.

When the man stopped the buggy and climbed out, Ella Sue's expression sobered.

Katie shared the same disappointment that appeared so blatantly on Ella Sue's face.

"Are you Katie Bender?"

"*Jah*," she said reluctantly. If he had news of Timothy, she hoped he wouldn't blurt it out in front of Ella Sue.

He smiled. "*Gut*, I wasn't sure if I got the directions straight after I turned off of Northland Drive." He flipped his thumb over his shoulder. "I think I have your horse."

Katie moved closer and craned her head toward the back of his buggy. Sure enough, Peaches was tethered behind the man's buggy. Her mouth dropped in disbelief as she moved closer to the mare.

"This is your horse, right?"

"*Jah.*" Katie reached out and hugged Peaches's neck, vaguely aware of Ella Sue, who clung to her hip. Looking over her shoulder at the man, she asked, "Where did you find her?"

"She was tangled in a barbed wire fence." He stepped closer, his gaze fixed on Katie. "I think the storm had her disoriented." The man shook his head as though dismissing other thoughts and then looked away.

"*Denki* . . . Mr. . . . ." Warmth dotted Katie's cheeks. Lack of sleep had messed with her mind. She should be able to recognize his voice; it sounded so familiar. "Forgive me, but I don't know your name." Her brother had mentioned that several men from other districts had arrived to help, but she wouldn't know any of them. Besides, if she'd ever looked into this man's deep blue eyes, she would've remembered the quiver his gaze produced.

"You don't remember me?" His brow quirked, probably his way of acknowledging her stare.

"I do." Ella Sue peeked around Katie's dress. "Did you bring the ice cream?"

"The man in the cellar," Katie muttered aloud unintentionally.

"Seth Stutzman." He grinned and squatted in front of Ella Sue. "I haven't forgotten about the ice cream, but I didn't want it to melt if I got lost finding your *haus.*"

"Seth from Saint Joseph County," Katie rambled.

"*Jah*, that's right." He peered up at her with those attention-grabbing *boppli-bloh* eyes.

"This isn't *mei haus*," Ella Sue said. She tugged Katie's dress, drawing her attention. "I'm only staying here until *mei daed kumms* to get me, ain't so?"

She cupped her hand over the child's shoulder. "Ella Sue and I are *redding-up* the yard."

"*Mei daed* is *kumming* for me soon."

Seth stood from his squatting position. "Is he helping with the search for the missing man?"

Katie's breath caught in her throat. She hoped that comment went unnoticed by Ella Sue.

The child peered up at her, eyes budding with tears. "Is he talking about *mei daed?*" She blinked and heavy teardrops spilled over her lashes and rolled down her cheeks.

Katie lowered to her knees and wiped the child's face with the palm of her hand. "We'll talk about this later. How about you run ahead to the barn and open the gate for Peaches." Ella Sue probably wouldn't have enough strength to open the iron gate, but trying to open it would distract her a few minutes.

Ella Sue sniffled, looked questionably at Seth, but turned and walked away.

Katie waited until she was out of earshot. "Her father is Timothy King. He's the man they're searching for."

Seth winced. "I didn't mean to upset her—or you."

Katie forced a smile. "I think she's handling it better than I would've at her age."

"Is she your niece?"

"*Nay*." She sighed. Had her fiancé, James, not died, Katie would've happily been the child's *aenti*.

Seth cleared his throat. "I hope they find him." He extended the horse's lead to her. "I should be going."

"You didn't say where you found Peaches. Please don't tell me in Amos's field."

His brows lifted.

Ach *dear, that didn't come out right.* She tried to restate it differently. "I suppose I shouldn't have said it so . . ."

"Strongly," he finished.

Her eyes followed his muscular arms as he folded them across his chest. Her thoughts flitted to the time in the cellar when he pulled her up against him. Something she would rather not recall so vividly.

"Sounds like the two of you had a falling out." His tone hinted that he already knew they had.

"I'm sure he's given you an earful about me." She wasn't proud of it. People don't leave the faith because someone asks you to find a different area to keep your bees. At least that's what Bishop Lapp's wife, Mary, said when she tried to console Katie. But Amos had.

"Amos's *fraa* died. He's under a lot of stress," Seth said, then added, "He's raising four children alone."

"And he thought nothing of breaking an ordinance and pulling them out of *schul*. *Nau* that is a shame." She nodded to reinforce her statement.

"I don't know, is it?"

If Amos had given Seth an earful of anything, it was his disapproval of her as a *teetshah*. He made that clear before Erma died. A steady, percolating boil shot up her neck. She bit her tongue, but the directive took more self-control than she could muster. "Are you implying that I'm *nett* a competent *teetshah*?"

He stared at her hard, like she did her quilt block when she searched for skipped stitches. His demeanor now wasn't anything like the man trapped in the cellar with her. Last night he'd disrupted her comfort zone with his forwardness, but today, instead of being witty and playful, he sounded provoking and judgmental.

Why did she care if he thought she was a *gut teetshah*?

Amos had used her as a scapegoat because he stopped trusting God, but there was no sense trying to hammer home that point. She faced Peaches and gave her attention to her mare.

"*Denki* for returning *mei* horse." She patted the mare's neck. "*Nau* all that's missing is *mei* buggy."

"What about the missing man?" he mumbled under his breath as he reached into his buggy. He pulled out an amber bottle and handed it to her. "I put iodine on her cuts. You should probably do it a couple of times a day to keep the area from getting infected."

She couldn't listen to horse care instructions after he made that unsettling remark about Timothy. Had he thought she'd placed more importance on a buggy than a man's life? The notion was ridiculous.

"By the way," Seth said, climbing onto the bench, "your buggy isn't lost. It's scattered all over the *schul* yard." He released the brake. "*Gut* day."

Chapter Six

Seth had satisfied his curiosity about Katie Bender. Amos had called her meddlesome, but better words would be *defensive*, *prideful*, or even *callous*. How could she be so unconcerned that Amos was grieving, raising four children alone? Perhaps now that Seth had met her face-to-face, he'd be able to stop thinking about her.

But . . . as much as he hated to admit it, he liked how wide her smile grew when she first saw her horse. To make matters worse, she was even prettier than he expected. She certainly didn't look like the spinster teacher he had growing up.

He clenched his jaw. *Ach.* Women like her were nothing but trouble.

And yet he couldn't erase the memory of how his hands felt around her small waist as he lifted her to safety.

Seth shook his head. He couldn't become hung up over the

time they'd spent together in the cellar. It was common knowledge that in times of extreme circumstances, people often acted out of character. He had. Her closeness had kicked up his heart rate—but he had to rid her from his mind. He groaned. He'd driven a hundred feet down the road but couldn't steer his thoughts away from her.

Several paces ahead a man ambled with a wooden cane along the shoulder of the road. Seth slowed the horse as he approached and stopped when he came up beside him.

"Need a ride?"

The white-bearded stranger tilted his head to peer over his wire-rimmed glasses. "That's kind of you." He loaded his cane, then climbed inside the buggy and plopped on the bench. "I'm headed to Timothy King's *haus*," he said, removing a hankie from his pocket. He dabbed away the beads of sweat from his forehead. "It's five miles up the road."

"That's quite a hike. I'm glad to help." In his district, someone would've made plans to pick up an elderly man, especially one using a cane.

"I usually prefer walking," he said as though he knew what Seth had been thinking. He wadded his hankie and shoved it into his pocket. "Gives me quiet time with God."

"*Jah*, I like spending time alone with God too. I'm Seth Stutzman."

He stroked his beard. "Yes, I know who you are." He shifted on the bench slightly to face Seth. "My name is Elias."

The horse's hooves clopped at a steady pace along the gravel road. At the corner where he should veer right to return to Amos's house, the elderly man pointed to the left. "His *haus* is a country block down this way."

Seth hoped Amos wouldn't be upset. He planned to deliver

the horse to Katie and then help his brother-in-law remove the tree. Last night when Amos stated he no longer belonged to the church, Seth wasn't sure what to do. In his district he would've helped locate a missing man regardless of whether he was Amish or *Englisch*. In the Bible, the good Samaritan didn't stop to check the injured man's religion before he offered his help.

"How long will you be staying with Amos Mast?"

"I had planned on leaving after I helped him set up his bee-hives, but a tree *kumm* down on one of his barns during the storm, so I'm *nett* sure what kind of damage it did or how much work it will require."

"A carpenter, are you?"

Seth shook his head. He was careful not to call himself anything.

Elias pointed to the right side of the road. "That's Timothy King's place."

What was left of the man's place now lay sprawled over the yard. Seth glanced to his right as he pulled into the drive. The wind had thrown the porch steps as far away as the ditch. They appeared intact as if the tornado had carefully set them down in that spot. A large fallen elm tree blocked the driveway near the house. The buggy wheel dipped deep into the soft ground as he followed the tracks across the lawn. Horses grazed on a mound of loose hay under the shade tree near the barn, still intact. Seth parked next to the other buggies.

"They haven't found him yet," Elias said, reaching for his cane.

A dry hollowness seized Seth's spirit. It wasn't right to turn away from helping these men.

A man who looked to be Seth's age lumbered toward the buggy. His face was beet-red and his shirt soaked with sweat. He stopped next to Seth's side of the buggy.

"*Wilkom.*" He blew out a breath and peered up at the sun. "Hot day, ain't so?"

Seth's stomach pitted with guilt as he nodded.

"I'm Andrew. I stopped by Amos's *haus* last *nacht.*" He extended his gloved hand. "I'm glad you *kumm.*"

When Seth gripped Andrew's hand, heat radiated off the worn leather. He glanced at Elias shuffling toward the pile of rubble, taking short steps and favoring his right leg. Seth jammed the brake in place. If a lame man twice his age could work in this heat, Seth could disregard his concern over Amos being upset. This *was* the right thing to do. Amos needed a new perspective. He needed a thankful heart.

"You can unhitch your horse and put him in the pasture with the others," Andrew said. "I better get back to work."

"*Denki.*" Seth climbed out of the buggy. He glanced at the laboring men removing by hand each torn section of the house. *Jah*, he couldn't leave without joining the search.

Seth removed the harness, led the horse through the gate, and set him loose with the others. Then he joined the men and dug into the pile. He hadn't worked too long before someone tapped his shoulder.

"Here." Andrew extended a pair of work gloves. "I had an extra pair in *mei* buggy."

"*Denki.*" Seth shoved his hands into the soft leather and returned to clearing debris. He grabbed the other end of a long piece of battered tin roofing as another man struggled to drag it off the pile.

The man holding the opposite end of the flimsy metal nodded with his head toward the scrap pile. "We'll dump it over there."

After tossing it on the pile, the man extended a gloved hand to Seth. "I'm Jordan Engles."

"Seth Stutzman," he said, grasping the man's hand.

"*Denki* for giving us a hand." He glanced at the sky. "It's been over forty-eight hours since the storm. We need to find him soon. He's got a young daughter."

Another man came alongside Jordan, pulling his gloves on. "Sorry I'm late. Naomi thought she might deliver, so I went after the midwife. False alarm."

Jordan's hands full with rubble, he motioned with a head jerk at the man. "This is William. He's a bit distracted; his *fraa* is due any day."

"Yours too." William looked at Seth. "Don't let Jordan fool you. He's as nervous as a hen on the chopping block. He's about to be a first-time father any day too."

"Is true." Jordan slung the Sheetrock off the pile and wiped his shirtsleeve over his brow. "I keep praying she doesn't have the *boppli* while I'm here."

William agreed.

Apparently the nervous men found it easier to talk instead of focus on what condition they'd find Timothy lying beneath the rubble.

Seth had to admit that sifting through the household goods had sent a few shudders down his spine. He pulled a wooden chair loose from the mound. A leg was missing. If he found the other leg, most likely the chair was repairable. Scanning the immediate area, his eyes caught a glimpse of blue cotton material.

A shirt?

"Found something." Seth didn't wait for the others but grabbed a large section of Sheetrock and flung it behind him. Underneath what looked like the wooden spindles of a banister, he saw more of the blue material. A man's shirt, but Timothy wasn't in it.

"False alarm." Seth blew out a pent-up breath. He stood upright. His muscles tightening into a knot, he pressed his knuckles against his back and kneaded his constricting muscles.

Jordan clapped Seth's shoulder. "That's been happening all day." He drew Seth's attention to a small pile of non–building materials. "We've been throwing any bedding and clothes we find into that stack. The stuff is wet and some of it torn, but hopefully it's reusable."

Jordan and the others returned to hauling debris away.

Seth stared at the pile. The child's tear-reddened eyes flashed before him.

This was hard.

He drew in a deep breath, taking in a foul scent that nearly gagged him. Spoiled food, he told himself, mindful of what the alternative might be.

As he bent to pick up more debris, a bright flash of light caught his attention. Only the reflective source wasn't some-thing in the pile, but something near the road. There it was again—something flickered. He couldn't be positive it wasn't just the heat getting to him, but he had to find out what the shiny object was.

Seth shielded his eyes with his hand and trekked across the soggy lawn until he came to Elias, standing next to the ditch culvert. "You don't have to walk. I'll give you a ride."

The elderly man held up his hand. "Do you hear that?" he said barely above a whisper.

Seth listened closely but only heard a bird chirping.

"There it is again." Elias tapped his cane on the porch steps. "We need to move this away from the culvert."

Seth glanced over his shoulder at the men working. "I'll get help."

"I'm not decrepit like you think." Elias tossed his cane on the ground and reached for an end of the steps.

The man had his end hoisted up before Seth grabbed the other side. Elias's strength certainly surprised Seth. They moved the steps aside effortlessly.

"You hear it now?" Elias asked.

Seth cocked his head sideways. *"Nay."*

Perhaps the man needed to sit in the shade for a while. With the intensity of the sun and the fact that he'd walked who knows how far before Seth picked him up, this might be an early sign of heatstroke.

"I could use a cold drink of water. How about you?" Seth motioned toward the barn. "There's a well pump—"

Elias shook his head and pointed to the culvert. "Crawl inside. You'll see."

Seth glanced at the stagnant water in the ditch. "In there?"

"You'll see."

Seth blew out a breath. He didn't want to be disrespectful, but he didn't want to get wet either. The water must be ankle-deep. He looked at Elias, but before he could ask if he was sure, Elias nodded.

"This is crazy," Seth murmured as he eased into the ditch. His boots sank into the ground and water rose past his ankles, but he dropped to his knees and bent low to see into the opening.

Nothing.

He glanced up at Elias. "It's empty." The intensity of the old man's eyes was just as prodding as if he'd jabbed Seth with his cane.

"Keep searching." Elias pointed his craggy index finger at the hole.

Seth crouched down and, against his own better judgment,

belly-crawled into the culvert. The farther he crawled away from the opening, the darker it was. His shoulders pressed against both sides, his elbows and knees fought for traction on the metal drain's slippery surface.

"What could the man hear in here?" Seth's magnified and tinny voice bounced against the ridges of the drain. The murky water smelled like tadpoles. He should've insisted Elias sit in the shade and drink some water.

Then his hand hit something stiff.

A boot.

He reached farther up, touched the hem of a pant leg, then a leg. He tapped the person.

"You all right?"

No response.

Chapter Seven

Seth grasped the person's ankles, but given the cramped space inside the culvert, he couldn't move his shoulders or get traction to pull the body out. Water sloshed around him as he wormed his way out backward to get a rope.

Seth reached the opening of the drain and spit out the mouthful of murky water he'd taken in. He gasped for air and struggled to pull his knees out of the muddy water. Thankfully Elias had called some of the other men over while Seth was inside the drainpipe. "Someone's in there." Seth pushed off the ground and stood. "I need . . . a rope."

"I'll fetch it," one of the twins said. The young man took off running, his brother beside him.

Andrew bent down and peered inside the culvert. An uneasy expression filled his face. "How far in is he?"

"Fourteen—fifteen feet."

"Alive?" Andrew noticeably struggled to ask the question. His brows straightened and his forehead wrinkled.

"Couldn't tell," Seth said.

Andrew frowned and redirected his attention to the drain.

The twins returned and handed Seth the rope.

"Denki." Seth placed it between his teeth and reentered the drain. This time he reached the body faster and quickly wrapped the rope around both legs. He crawled back out holding tight to the other end of the rope. Several others had stepped into the ditch. Seth handed one of them the rope as he moved away from the opening.

Within minutes, they dragged the limp form out of the culvert. A man. His eyes were closed and he was caked with mud from head to toe, but his chest had movement. Shallow breaths, but alive. Someone slapped his cheeks. "Timothy, can you hear me?"

Through cracked lips, he whispered, "Ella Sue . . ."

A lump formed in Seth's throat as several men picked up Timothy and carried him to drier ground. It felt good to be part of the rescue effort, but more importantly, the little girl with the piercing, tear-blotched eyes had her father back.

Seth slipped away from the crowd, filled with relief and songs of praise on his mind. He hadn't gone far before someone clapped him on the shoulder and he stopped.

"Denki," Andrew said, a broad smile filling his face.

David, the other man who had come to Amos's house, jogged up beside them. "What made you think to look in the drain?"

"Elias . . ." Seth looked over the area for the elderly man. "Elias said he heard something." Even as he spoke, the idea sounded odd. He hadn't heard anything but water whooshing and his own labored breaths as he crawled inside the culvert. He couldn't even determine if Timothy was alive or dead while he was inside the drain. What noise had Elias heard?

"We're glad you came to help today," Andrew said.

Several men lifted Timothy and carried him toward the buggies. Timothy's cough sounded congested and he muttered something about seeing his daughter as he passed.

The twins broke from the crowd and joined their *daed* standing beside Seth. "Jordan's taking Timothy to be checked out at the clinic."

Seth recognized the twin talking as the one who had sheepishly stared at Leah.

"*Denki*, Jacob." The boy's father glanced at Andrew. "I say we call this a day."

Andrew smiled. "A *gut* day."

Seth glanced at the falling position of the sun. No doubt Amos was already upset that he hadn't come straight back after returning Katie's mare. Seth couldn't understand how Amos could ignore his obligation to help search for the missing man. But Timothy was found and would soon be reunited with his teary-eyed child. A blessing for sure.

"We're expecting more workers from the other districts to arrive soon." Andrew's words broke the silence. "We've planned a meeting tomorrow to discuss the needs and organize work crews. Will you be able to join us?"

It'd mean having to hold off on setting up Amos's beehives. But it would give him a chance to find someone from this district to help Amos with his barn. Not that the repair needed to be rushed; Amos had a temporary area for his calves. Rebuilding houses, even in Amos's eyes, should take priority over an extra barn.

"*Jah*, I'll be there."

The following evening after Timothy's rescue, the members met at Andrew Lapp's home to discuss the settlement's needs. Katie parked the buggy next to the others, and before she set the brake, Ella Sue squealed with delight and bolted off the buggy bench. Excited to reunite with her father, the little girl sprinted across the yard and flew into Timothy's waiting arms.

Katie grabbed the plate of cookies that she and Ella Sue had made for the meeting and headed toward the house. This night was certainly a celebration for Timothy and his daughter.

A pang of regret shot through Katie as Timothy twirled Ella Sue in the air. Obviously he was still weak; he didn't lift her far off the ground before pulling her into a tight hug. Their tight bond reminded Katie of what her life lacked—a family of her own. After James died, she'd pushed aside those dreams. Teaching filled the void and gave her a sense of purpose, a sense of worth. Yet at times like tonight, with the air ringing with a child's giggle, she longed to be more than an observer.

Katie dabbed a hankie over the creases of her eyes. She hadn't been able to control her tears of joy since hearing the news of Timothy's rescue yesterday afternoon. She hadn't stopped thanking God for the miracle either. Even Isaac seemed certain that the doctor would insist on admitting Timothy to the hospital, if for no other reason than to observe him a few days. Timothy refused. Once he was rehydrated, no one could convince him to spend another minute away from his daughter. Timothy's devotion certainly showed now in the way he twirled Ella Sue again despite his weakness.

She headed up the porch steps carrying the plate of peanut butter cookies. The yard was full of parked buggies; the meeting should be ready to start soon.

"Katie," Timothy called as she reached for the doorknob.

She turned. *"Jah?"*

He joined her on the porch, Ella Sue clinging to his neck. "A simple thank-you isn't enough for all you've done." He made a slight head-nodding gesture toward his daughter. "She's all I thought about while I was—" His voice cracked.

"You have each other *nau*. God's mercy is far reaching, *jah?*"

Timothy smiled. *"Jah*, it sure is."

Katie winked at Ella Sue. "We had a *gut* time, ain't so?"

"Jah. We made cookies."

Timothy leaned to see the plate Katie held. "I might have to sneak one before the meeting starts."

"Ach, how thoughtless of me. Have you eaten anything at all since they released you from the hospital?" Katie pulled the cloth covering off the cookies and extended the plate. "Take a few, please." He needed more than sweets. He needed a good home-cooked meal after everything he'd gone through.

Timothy took a cookie. "One is *gut*, *denki*." He took a bite and winked at his daughter.

"He likes our cookies," she told Katie.

Timothy's mouth was full, so he nodded.

"I'm glad." Katie twisted the doorknob. "The meeting is probably getting ready to start. I should see if the women need help." She followed them into the house.

Apprehensive about leaving her father, Ella Sue continued to cling to his neck instead of going to the back room to play with the other children. Katie would've taken Ella Sue with her into the kitchen had Timothy asked, but with a little coaxing and reassurance, he was able to unlatch her arms and send her to play. Under the circumstances, Ella Sue probably could've stayed with her father without provoking too many disapproving frowns. But with so many important matters to discuss and the room filled with volunteers from neighboring counties, the meeting room wasn't the place for children.

The kitchen buzzed with chatter, mostly about the miracle of Timothy being found alive. Katie placed her plate of cookies on the table with the other food.

Abigail set a stack of plates at the end of the table. "Ella Sue must've been overjoyed to see her father."

"*Jah*, she showered him with kisses." Katie smiled, genuinely happy—no, *elated*—for Ella Sue and Timothy, but she couldn't mask the void she felt now that she wasn't needed. Feeling her smile fade, she turned away.

"I'm sure Timothy's grateful that you watched over his daughter," Abigail whispered.

Katie recognized Abigail's words held a deeper meaning. Her sister-in-law had already tried to match her with Timothy *nett* long after his *fraa* died, then recently when Ella Sue became one of her students.

Katie focused on Judith Lapp. "What else can I do?"

"I think we're all set. The kettle is heated for *kaffi* and the food is ready."

Katie glanced around the kitchen at the somber women. "I feel like an unknotted thread. Isaac didn't want to say too much in front of Ella Sue, so I never heard the extent of the damages."

As the women shared, it seemed almost everyone had some form of loss. Some lost their houses while others lost their barns or the majority of their livestock. Katie's heart ached for each family.

"We should focus on our blessings," said Mary, the bishop's wife. "*Nau* that Timothy has been found, we haven't lost anyone."

Katie hung her head. She'd been so focused on Ella Sue that she hadn't thought about how many lives could have been lost. God had spared them all.

"We are blessed, that is for certain," Judith said. She wrapped her arm around Katie's waist. "*Denki* for getting the children to safety. I heard how quickly you responded when it started to hail."

The other women surrounded Katie, patting her shoulder or squeezing her hands. Tears pooled in their eyes.

Katie withdrew the hankie she'd tucked up her dress sleeve. "The children were all so brave." Katie dabbed the cloth over the corner of her eye. "I don't know that I would've gotten the cellar door open without the boys' help."

"The Lord was with you," Mary said. "Just as he was with Timothy."

Everyone agreed in unison.

Katie wanted to pull Judith aside and tell her about finding her brother, Samuel, under the desk before the tornado and how he'd said a white-haired man directed him to safety. Judith would understand since she'd been the one whom an angel visited years ago by the river after Samuel had fallen off the roof. But just as she opened her mouth to say something, Judith spoke.

"Rachel Engels was relieved to hear you were watching her niece, Ella Sue," Judith said. "She wanted to be here for the meeting, but Jordan insisted she follow the *dokta's* bed-rest orders."

"That's wise—she's past her due date," Katie said. Tactfully, she didn't point out that it was understandable since Rachel's older sister had also had pregnancy complications.

A young man poked his head into the kitchen. "Bishop Lapp wants to start the meeting."

"*Denki*, Jacob," Judith replied.

The women quieted their sniffles and straightened their dresses, then joined the men in the sitting room.

Katie inched into the room and found a space against the wall just as Bishop Lapp asked everyone to spend a moment in silence and thank God for his hand of protection. A few moments later the bishop cleared his throat.

Opening her eyes, Katie hadn't realized how many men from the other districts had come to help. Seth stood against the wall opposite her. He was holding his hat in his hand, his sandy-blond hair flipped up at the ends where it would meet his hat if he were wearing it. She stole a peek at his strong arms that had lifted her up out of the hole. Sparked by the memory, her face heated. She redirected her attention to the bishop.

Bishop Lapp addressed the visitors, thanking them for their support. Then he shared the news about Timothy, who hung his head humbly as the men jabbed him in his ribs.

Bishop Lapp cleared his throat, bringing the roomful of people back to attention. He adjusted his reading glasses, and when the room quieted, he lifted a sheet of paper. "I asked the ministers to compile a list of the members' needs." He glanced over the first sheet before slipping it behind the second. "We have a lot of work ahead of us. But together—" His voice cracked and he turned to cough into his hand.

His wife, Mary, slipped into the kitchen and returned with a glass of water.

The bishop's face turned a sickly whitewashed shade. His hands trembled as he lifted the glass to his mouth. Katie glanced at Mary, who stared pensively at her husband, acutely aware of his distress. He took a sip, then handed her the glass.

"I'll read what information we've gathered so far." He listed those who lost houses and barns, livestock, and silos and storage bins. The list continued long past what little information Katie had heard in the kitchen. The bishop's voice weakened and he stumbled forward.

"*Daed!*" Andrew reached out and steadied him from falling. "Please, sit down and rest." He helped his father into a wooden rocking chair, then looked at the others. "I think we need to continue this meeting another time."

"*Nay,*" the bishop said. He clutched his chest and leaned forward, whispering something only Andrew could hear.

Andrew took the papers from his father's hands. "He asked me to . . ." He glanced at his father, who nodded to proceed. Andrew held up one of the sheets. "There's a complete list of household items needed, such as clothes, bedding, and kitchenware. I'll leave this for the women to work on." He passed that list to his *fraa*, Judith, but kept his eyes on his father. Then he finished reading the reports of damages.

"Is there anything I've missed?" Andrew asked, his attention flipping between his father and the crowd. "Are you sure you don't need to lie down and rest?" he asked his father.

Bishop Lapp shook his head. "Continue."

Andrew readdressed the group. "Does anyone have anything to add?"

Disregarding an inner voice telling Katie to wait, she lifted her hand.

"Did you have damages?" Andrew glanced at her brother, Isaac, standing off to his left. Isaac shook his head and peered with raised brows at Katie.

"You didn't mention the *schul,*" Katie said.

Andrew nodded. "I know, but rebuilding the *schul* will have to wait. Our resources will be limited. Which brings up the next issue." He looked away from Katie to address the men's side of the room. "The other ministers and I will be taking up an offering. I'd like you to pray about what you can give toward the lumber and building supplies that are needed."

Katie had plenty of household wares to donate. Her savings certainly wasn't enough to buy much material, but she would offer that as well. Once they rebuilt the *schul* and she was teaching again, she could replenish her savings fund. But they needed to rebuild by fall or she wouldn't have an income at all. Katie raised her hand again and waited for Andrew to recognize her with a nod.

"Shouldn't the *schul* at least be put on the list? We need it built by fall."

"Katie," Isaac cut in. "Tonight's meeting is to address the immediate needs." Her brother motioned subtly at the bishop still racked with labored breaths, then looked at her with a silent warning to hold her response. Shamed over her selfishness, she did.

Seth eyed Katie across the room, shoulders slumped and leaning against the wall. This was May. Even if school were still in session, it would end for the summer in a few weeks. It made perfect sense not to worry about the school until closer to fall. Several families had lost everything, yet she wilted against the wall as if her best friend had died when she heard the immediate plans didn't include rebuilding the *schul*.

The bishop wheezed. Maybe Seth's ears were keener to distressed breathing—God knew he'd been haunted by that sound—but none of the others in the room seemed to pick up that the bishop's labored breathing had worsened. Seth had even seen him wince when Andrew hadn't been watching. Perhaps the bishop didn't want to admit he needed a doctor.

Seth wished Andrew would get to the details about the work crews so he knew where and when to show up to help, but Andrew continued to answer miscellaneous questions. Then he briefly informed them about the township officials' offer of assistance.

"We've never accepted government assistance," Andrew said as though he needed to explain why the bishop had declined help from the *Englischers*.

The room of men muttered in agreement.

"Getting back to the work arrangements," Andrew said, pulling the men back to the purpose of the meeting. "Of those from the other counties, is anyone a master builder?"

Seth rejected the inner calling to step forward. He wasn't a master builder any longer. He built beehives—that was all. The room's overcrowding and lack of air circulation made Seth sweat. He tugged at his collarless shirt.

"If so," Andrew continued, "we can split up and do multiple projects at once."

Seth shifted his feet restlessly. He needed a drink of water. Stomach acid had climbed to the back of his throat, waiting. Someone needed to answer the call.

Andrew scanned the group, but his eyes fell on his *daed* and suddenly Andrew started talking faster. "We can figure this out in the morning." He looked over at the bishop still holding his hand over his chest. "Let's meet at— *Daed*, are you okay?"

The bishop had hunched forward. One hand gripped his knee, the other stayed planted on his chest. His rapid breaths and the rise and fall of his shoulders were evident even from Seth's point of view.

Andrew bent to one knee in front of the bishop and another man concluded the meeting. "Let's meet at Timothy's place at seven. We can divvy up the workload then."

Someone else mentioned there were coffee and snacks in the

kitchen as Seth turned to leave. He needed fresh air. Too much time in a crowded house. Too much need. Too many reminders of things that could never be repaired, even by a master builder.

He pulled his clinging shirt away from his back. Besides, he didn't need any caffeine or sweets keeping him awake. As it was, he planned to get up early and find out what Amos wanted to do about the tree. He hoped he could talk his brother-in-law into waiting a few days before they tried to move it, at least until the ground dried. Amos hadn't spoken more than a few words to him after Seth told him he planned to attend tonight's meeting. When Leah had asked if she could ride along, Amos shot the idea down. He'd made it clear his daughter wasn't allowed to attend any gatherings. His brother-in-law's icy stare didn't change Seth's mind. God directed his children to help one another in times of need. Amos was fully aware of God's Word; he knew to do good and yet he hadn't even blinked when Seth quoted James 4:17.

He weaved around several people and slipped out the door.

"Seth?" a woman said.

He wheeled around.

Katie pulled a shawl around her shoulders and stepped off the porch. "*Denki* again for taking care of Peaches."

"She wasn't a problem." He assumed they were talking about her mare.

"I put the iodine on her cuts like you said."

"*Gut.*" He allowed his gaze to linger and found it entertaining the way she fidgeted with the hem of her shawl.

She gestured toward the house. "There's *kaffi* and desserts inside."

He grinned. "I heard."

Her nose twitched. He wasn't sure if she was nervous or about to sneeze. When she twitched her little button nose again, he decided she was nervous and the gesture was cute. For an instant, he reconsidered staying for coffee.

"I should see if they need help in the kitchen." She turned but spun back around. "I didn't get a look at the man who helped us out of the cellar. Did you recognize anyone here that looked like him?"

"I never saw him. After you got out, I asked him to hand me a lantern so I could be certain we hadn't forgotten anyone. He was gone by the time I crawled out."

Her eyes narrowed. "To be certain? You said you counted the children. I trusted that you did."

"I did count them." He nodded stiffly. "Twelve, right?"

She twisted the edges of her shawl into her fisted hands. "You don't remember how many you counted?"

He cocked his head sideways. "You didn't count any of them, *teetshah*."

She gasped.

The door opened and a few men stepped outside and into the porch light. One man craned his head toward them and squinted, then shuffled away from the others and met Seth and Katie on the drive. "I'm Isaac Bender. I see you've met *mei* sister, Katie."

Seth nodded. He remembered the man from earlier but couldn't recall his name, and at the moment Seth was more concerned about having to explain Katie's hardened expression.

The man nudged Katie's shoulder. "This is Seth Stutzman. He's the one who found Timothy."

Her eyes softened, melting Seth's tension. He almost didn't want to admit it was Elias who led him to the culvert.

The screen door slammed and the bishop, with support from Andrew, stepped outside. Their wives followed, and without lingering to talk, they headed for the buggies.

"He doesn't look well," Seth said.

"*Jah*, this has been stressful on him," Isaac said. "He built up quite a sweat working in the heat the day we were searching for Timothy."

Katie's watery eyes shimmered from reflecting the flickering lantern light. She stared silently as the bishop ambled away.

Seth bowed his head, closed his eyes, and silently asked God to heal the bishop. When he opened his eyes, Katie's and Isaac's heads were bowed and their eyes still closed.

Timothy broke the silence as he approached. "*Denki* for pulling me out of the culvert. How did you figure out I was in there?"

Seth shifted from eyeing Katie to Timothy. "Elias told me to check inside. He said he heard something." Seth glanced at Katie, but her expression hadn't changed.

Timothy extended his hand and Seth shook it. "I'm glad you rescued me. Doc said I was severely dehydrated. I wouldn't have lasted much longer. As it was, he needed to replace the fluids I lost." He held up three fingers. "It took three IV bags before I started feeling like myself."

"Who is Elias?" Isaac asked.

Seth shrugged. He looked at Katie. "I picked him up walking *nett* far from your *haus*."

Timothy and Isaac exchanged startled glances.

Katie's eyes darted between Timothy and Isaac, then over to Seth. "I don't know any Elias," she said.

The screen door slammed and Ella Sue came bounding down the porch steps. "Don't leave me, *Daed*!" Timothy squatted and the little girl ran into his open arms.

"I have to work with the men," Timothy said. "*Aenti* Rachel said you could stay with her."

"I want to stay with Katie," Ella Sue whined.

Katie smiled. "It's okay with me if she stays, Timothy."

"Fine then." He released the girl and pointed to the house. "Go back inside until Katie's ready to go home."

Ella Sue peered up at Katie. "Don't leave me, okay?"

"I wouldn't do that." Her soft and reassuring voice brought a smile to the child's face. Katie reached for Ella Sue's hand. "Let's go inside and ask to borrow some of Mary's dresses so you have something clean to wear."

Seth couldn't explain the warmth that spread through his body as the two of them walked away.

Isaac cleared his throat. "How do you know where *mei* sister lives?"

Both her brother and Timothy had crossed their arms. It hadn't dawned on him until this particular moment that Katie and Timothy might be pledged.

Chapter Eight

K atie, arise and pray," Elias whispered in her ear. The woman flipped on the bed to her other side. "Katie, arise and pray," Elias repeated. This time his words reached her. She sat up in bed. "God has called you to pray."

Katie's eyes took a few moments to adjust to the dim room. For a moment she wasn't sure if she was dreaming. She glanced at Ella Sue sleeping beside her. Strange, she thought she heard someone whisper her name. She laid her head back on the pillow.

"Katie, arise."

This time there was no mistaking the voice. Her name. She jolted upright and looked around the room. A quiver spread like rapid fire, sprouting goose bumps along her arms.

"Arise and pray," Elias said.

Katie sprang out of bed. She'd never been woken like this before, but the prompting was too strong not to pray. But for whom?

Her hands trembling, she adjusted her prayer *kapp* as she lowered to her knees beside the bed. Hands folded on her lap, she bowed her head and closed her eyes.

She waited.

Nothing.

"God?" She shifted, straightened her back, and waited.

Silence.

Katie slumped to the floor. "Am I imagining voices?"

"Pray," Elias prompted.

Katie's heart hammered. "I'm *nett* sure who I'm to pray for." She drew in a deep breath and released it slowly. Without a name coming to mind, she began to pray for everyone: her brother and his family, the bishop's health, Ella Sue and Timothy—the sun had lightened the horizon before she exhausted all the names, and still she felt called to continue.

"Who have I missed? There must be someone I've forgotten."

Elias waited until the child's mind stopped reeling with names before he delivered God's instructions. "Love your enemies, bless those who curse you, do good to those who hate you, and pray for those who persecute you. Pray, child," Elias repeated. *"Pray without ceasing."*

Immediately, Amos Mast came to mind. He certainly disliked her, though she never considered him an enemy. She prayed for him anyway, and Seth too.

"Lord, I'm *nett* sure why I feel this urgency, but please send your angels to watch over Amos and his household. Let him see the power of your love so that he can find his way back to you. I ask that you watch over Seth and protect him . . ."

"Yes, Katie, God hears your prayers. Continue, child. Pray without ceasing," Elias said.

The morning sun peeked over the horizon as Seth headed toward the barn. In the ethereal realm, Elias marched alongside.

Elias's sword drawn and ready for battle, he towered as a mighty kingdom warrior in power. Through him, the brilliance of God's light illuminated the enemy's tactics and blinded his adversary's forces.

Tightening his grip on the sword handle, Elias canvassed the area for the archfiend, Razzen. He was near. His sulfuric stench lingered like the putrid scent of a beast's singed flesh. It hadn't taken the archfiend long to gain ground. Ever since Amos's bitterness gave the accuser a foothold, Razzen had rooted his talons into Amos's subconscious and made his presence known.

Elias had learned long ago of Razzen's stealthy entrances. The fallen angel's pride ruled his wrath, and habitually, when he struck, he created a ripple of collateral damage.

Usually Razzen draped himself next to Amos's ear and probed him with lies to stir up more strife. Today he perched his haunches on the barn roof, aimed his beady eyes of fire at Seth, the approaching mark, and waited for the perfect moment to launch his fiery darts.

Acutely aware of the enemy's devices, Elias unfurled his wings to shield Seth from Razzen's trickery.

Before Seth's arrival, Razzen could plant anything in Amos's head, deviate as far from the truth as he wished, and Amos believed him. Now Seth's faith posed a threat, and unknowingly he'd become Razzen's new target.

Elias moved closer to his charge. "Be watchful," he whispered into Seth's ear. "The enemy prowls, searching for those he can devour. He is deceptive; a liar and thief. His only motive is to steal, kill, and destroy."

Razzen swooped down, skimmed the top of Seth's hat, then entered the barn as they did. He propped himself against the milking post.

Amos sat on the stool, unaware of the wicked imp's presence.

Elias planted his feet shoulder width apart and stood guard between Seth and Razzen.

Seth drew a deep breath as he walked over to the milking area. Last night, after he returned from the meeting, he attempted to bring Amos up-to-date on the settlement's needs and relay how the bishop wasn't able to continue the meeting. Amos refused to listen. As far as he was concerned, he was no longer a member of the settlement and wasn't interested in their news or needs. Seth had gone to sleep praying for Amos, who, blinded from the truth, was wandering in darkness. His brother-in-law's heart had turned to stone. The further Amos strayed from the path of righteousness, the more Seth feared what would become of his nieces and nephews.

Amos looked up from his milking stool, glared at Seth, then returned to milking. Normally the rhythmic splatter of milk hitting the side of the metal can soothed Seth. Not today. Amos's silent treatment struck a raw nerve.

Seth cast an eye on his nephews hard at work mucking out the horse stall. "Need a hand?"

Thomas stopped shoveling, glanced up, and smiled. "Sure."

Paul eagerly extended the handle of his pitchfork toward Seth. "*Nay*, they don't need help," Amos interjected.

Seth circled around to Amos. "You want me to throw some hay bales down from the loft?"

His brother-in-law continued milking, ignoring the offer.

Seth tried to justify Amos's rejection of help. After all, Amos only owned one milk cow. Besides a few horses, a herd of pigs, a dozen or so chickens, and an old mutt who shared Amos's cantankerous personality, he didn't have many animals that needed tending. Still, Seth didn't want to stand around without something useful to do.

Seth sighed. "If you don't need help with the chores, I think I'll join the settlement work crew. I told you last night, they planned to start rebuilding today."

"He's more interested in helping those people in your old settlement," Razzen needled. Amos's jaw tightened and Razzen continued, "Face it; you have no one to rely on. Seth wants to run off and work with all those people who wanted to see you change your mind about raising honeybees—see you lose your farm."

"I thought you were going to help me take the tree down," Amos said without looking up from the bucket.

Seth halted midstride. He and Amos discussed this last night. Until the ground dried enough that the horses could get traction, it would be too dangerous to risk dropping that tree.

"I'll do it myself," Amos said.

Seth stiffened. "*Nay*, we both know that isn't wise." What was Amos thinking? That tree could shift at the last minute and drop the wrong way—crush one of the boys. "Must it *kumm* down today?" It wasn't necessary; they both knew it. The calves were safe in the other barn, so besides a few tools in the lean-to section, the barn was empty.

"*Jah,*" Amos mumbled under his breath.

Seth shook his head disapprovingly but agreed against his better judgment. "Okay, I'll get the ladder and chains."

Amos craned his head toward the horse stall. "Thomas?" He paused until he had his son's attention. "You and Paul harness the team."

"Okay," Thomas replied.

The man was more stubborn than Seth had thought. He headed outside. The ladder and chains were both inside the lean-to. Seth stopped at the split oak tree and studied the bend of the major limbs. Most of the leaves had wilted and already showed tinges of brown, fried by the lightning strike. Perhaps Amos was right. The tree needed to come down sooner rather than later.

Amos stepped out of the barn and motioned with his head toward the milk bucket in his hands. "I need to drop this off and grab us some gloves from the *haus.*"

"Okay." Seth needed a few more minutes to study the tree anyway. He wasn't keen on pawing through an unstable building in search of the saw and chains. If Amos would have waited as Seth suggested, he could've borrowed tools from someone in the settlement rather than risk going inside the dilapidated structure.

"God help us." He shook his head again.

"*Onkel* Seth?"

He glanced over his shoulder. "*Jah,* Thomas."

"Where should we tie the horses?" Thomas led one while Paul brought the other one out of the barn. Until seeing the draft horse's head towering over his young nephew, Seth hadn't realized how small Paul was to be leading such a massive creature.

With the main hitching rail blocked by fallen branches, Seth motioned to the post on the opposite side of the big barn. Until they were ready to attach the chains, the horses would be in the way.

The wooden door's hinges squeaked as Seth eased the door open wide enough to squeeze through. His eye caught the abnormal amount of light showing between the wall and the roof truss. He needed a lantern to do a proper inspection, but with a more-than-a-thousand-pound tree leaning against the structure, this wasn't the right time. The bowed wall, however, allowed enough light to enter that Seth found a handsaw and the chain hanging on the wall. He slung the chain over his shoulder and grabbed the ladder leaning against the wall on his way out.

"How does it look?" Amos grasped the end of the ladder, easing Seth's load.

"Definitely damaged, but there wasn't enough light to determine the extent."

They carried the ladder over to the tree trunk, and Seth set his end down long enough to shake the chain off his shoulder. The two men maneuvered the ladder between the limbs. Seth gave it a shake, then gingerly climbed the first rung. Sturdy enough. He took another step higher.

Katie poured a glassful of milk and handed it to Ella Sue.

"*Denki.*" Ella Sue sipped the drink, then darted her tongue over her lips, licking up the remaining residue. "Can we make cookies again today? I like peanut butter or chocolate chip." Her tongue made another sweep over her lips.

Katie chuckled. What a difference a day made. The child's giddiness was a refreshing change. "I think we'll have time to make a batch of cookies." She set the breakfast plate on the table, then sat across from Ella Sue.

The girl's eyes widened. "What else are we going to do today? Work in the garden? I helped *Aenti* Rachel with hers last year." She smiled, exposing her missing front tooth. "I can pull weeds."

Katie couldn't get over how the child jabbered nonstop like a pressure cooker expelling its built-up steam. She waited for Ella Sue to lift her glass and take another drink before she spoke.

"I need to gather some household supplies to share with the others. I also thought we would take sandwiches over to the men—"

"And cookies?"

Katie refrained from correcting the child's abruptness. Considering what she'd gone through, Katie could overlook the girl's poor manners this time.

"*Jah*, cookies too." Katie buttered a piece of bread and passed it to Ella Sue. "I don't think I have any chocolate chips."

"Peanut butter is *gut*," she said before chomping into her bread.

Yesterday morning Ella Sue had pushed her meal around on her plate. Katie liked seeing the girl's healthy appetite return.

Ella Sue jabbed her fork into the potatoes. "Do you think there will be ice cream there?"

"*Nay*, silly."

Ella Sue shrugged as she crammed the overfilled fork into her mouth.

Katie punctured her fried egg with her fork, and the yolk oozed over to the side of the plate with her potatoes. Her thoughts drifted to Seth and his offer to bring the children ice cream. Last night at the meeting, he probably thought she was too forward. She practically ran out of the house to remind him about the coffee and desserts. What prompted her to chase after a stranger?

Pray . . . pray without ceasing . . . The same words that woke her during the night echoed in her mind.

"Something wrong?"

Katie looked up at Ella Sue. "Stay here and finish your breakfast." She stood. "I need to take care of something." Katie walked to her bedroom, knelt beside her bed, and without waiting for direction, began to pray.

Razzen edged closer when Elias became preoccupied with steadying the ladder that Seth climbed. Razzen took position between Amos and his boys. He could easily take them all out if he so desired, especially if Elias's attention was split between Seth and the boys' safety. A simple diversion would have Elias scrambling . . .

A limb dropped to the ground. Razzen's eyes scaled the tree. Maybe he wouldn't have to use his own sword after all. On the ladder, the man's face contorted. The sticky tree sap caused resistance from his blade and required more force to saw through the wood. A sudden snap of the branch or shift of the ladder would disrupt his position—cripple them all.

Razzen nudged Amos. "Don't spoil your boys by letting them just watch. For it is good for a man that he bear the yoke in his youth." Razzen snickered at his own cleverness of using Scripture to his advantage.

Amos fell for it. He pointed at the branches. "Drag those out of the way," he told his sons.

The boys, quick to respond, grabbed hold of the limbs.

Razzen stepped on the limb, weighting it down and preventing the boys from moving it until . . . Razzen lifted the weight, and both the boys slipped at the same time the tree limb above them snapped.

As expected, Elias sprang into action and protected the boys from the falling limb. Elias's attention diverted, Razzen had full access to Seth.

Razzen scaled the tree, grabbed the saw blade, and tightened his grip to increase the resistance.

Seth stopped sawing. "Is everyone out of the way?"

"*Jah, geh* on," Amos replied.

"Yes, keep going," Razzen prodded.

Seth took a deep breath, then resumed sawing. The jagged-toothed blade snagged on something. His muscles tensed as he used more force to pull. Freeing the blade threw him off balance. He teetered a moment, but his footing slipped and the ladder went out from under him. He was free-falling.

Light flashed. In a split second, something broke his fall. Skewered with pain, he could only take short gasps of air.

"Are you okay?"

Seth couldn't decipher which nephew had asked. His ears rang and blinding white spots obstructed his vision. "*Denki*, God." He held tight to the limb until able to regain his bearings.

"Seth!" Amos grabbed the ladder and held it steady.

Seth sucked in a breath and swung his legs. His body slammed into the ladder and he let out a peeling groan.

A thunderous flapping din settled overhead with the arrival of more heavenly hosts. Razzen glowered at Elias.

"Did you think I wasn't prepared?" Elias asked him.

Razzen scanned the perimeter and hissed, suspending a tawny vapor of toxic fumes into the atmosphere. But the fumes didn't affect the hovering warriors. Razzen inhaled deeply and drove the burning sulfur back into his lungs where it dissolved. In defeat, he scampered off.

Seth finished clearing the branches, then climbed down the ladder. The tree wasn't as massive stripped of its branches. As Thomas and Paul dragged the limbs away from the work area, Amos crossed his arms and peered up the oak.

Seth stared at the lean-to, now damaged beyond repair. The skewed roofline of the calving barn didn't look too promising either.

"What do you think?" Amos asked.

Seth guarded his ribs with one hand and bent to pick up the chain off the ground. His brother-in-law had yet to consider Seth's advice. But he pointed to the limb midway up the tree. "That's probably the safest place to attach the chain." Before Amos asked about the structure, Seth draped the chain over his shoulder and started up the ladder. By the time he'd secured the chain and had climbed down, Amos had positioned the team. Seth handed the opposite end of the chain to Amos, who fastened it to the harness.

"Stand back," Amos said.

Seth and the boys backed up several yards.

Amos clicked his tongue and guided the team forward. The chain was long, and Amos and his team were far enough away before it became taut. With a smooth and steady pull, the draft team brought the tree to the ground, dragging it clear of the building.

"That's a *gut* supply of firewood," Seth said, then added, "I'll help you cut it up another day." He dug his hand into his pocket for his watch. The tree hadn't taken as much time as he thought. It was barely past ten. His ribs weren't hurting nearly as much as before, so he could still put in a complete day helping the men.

Amos's eyes narrowed. "Still plan to help the others?"

"It's the right thing to do," Seth replied, his tone forceful. His brother-in-law had a knack for making him feel guilty over doing what was right. "There's plenty of time to cut that wood. You don't need more kindling for the cookstove and you won't be burning wood for heat over the summer."

Amos grunted and led the team away.

Chapter Nine

Katie and Ella Sue caravanned with the other women to deliver the noon meal to the work crews. Along the way, Ella Sue gazed at the roadside in silence. Katie understood. Many of the larger trees that once canopied the road had snapped in half during the storm. The tornado had blazed a trail, leaving its mark. Many of the trees lay uprooted. Some, stripped of bark, stood among a scattering of maples, whose untouched branches full of bright green leaves basked in the sun.

Pulling into Timothy's yard, Ella Sue lifted higher on the seat, her eyes roaming the destruction. "Where's *mei haus*?"

Katie's chest tightened. "It's gone."

Ella Sue blinked several times. "Where is it?"

"Remember the storm at *schul*?"

"*Jah.*" Her voice cracked.

Katie wished she hadn't promised to help feed the men. This

was too much for Ella Sue to comprehend. She maneuvered the horse and parked the buggy next to the others, then shifted on the bench to face the child. "You're going to have a new *haus*."

Ella Sue continued to stare at the empty lot that was once where the house stood.

"You and I can sew new curtains. Would you like that?"

She nodded, her bottom lip trembling.

"Okay then." Katie's voice strengthened. "We need to feed these men so they can keep working."

Ella Sue nodded. Her eyes lit and she pointed toward the workers. "There's *mei daed*." Climbing out of the buggy, she waved at Timothy, then skipped toward the other children.

Katie went to the rear of the buggy, opened the hatch, and grabbed the plateful of peanut butter sandwiches.

A few of the younger men made a makeshift table from sawhorses and plywood. Once the food was all unloaded and arranged on the table, the men lined up to eat. Seth remained at the woodpile. Perhaps he felt out of place.

Curious as to the reason she was called to pray for Amos and Seth, Katie poured a cup of water, straightened her dress folds, then meandered over to him.

"I thought you might like a cold drink," she said.

He stopped hammering and looked up. Sweat beaded on his sun-reddened face.

She extended the cup. "Thirsty?"

"Denki." He drank the water in one continuous gulp, then handed the cup back.

"Do you want more?" She pointed to the table. "I can refill it."

He smiled and motioned to the pump a few feet away. "I've been drinking water all day."

"Ach." She looked into the empty cup. She wasn't sure what

she'd hoped for, but strangely, she felt deflated. Katie lifted her gaze. "Are you hungry? You can't get a sandwich out of a well."

"I suppose that would be a difficult task." His line of vision shot over her head in the direction of the other men. "I haven't been here long."

"That isn't answering the question if you're hungry or *nett*." Without thinking, her teacher voice came out.

He smiled. "The others have worked harder and are probably hungrier."

"So you are hungry?"

"What man is *nett* always hungry?" He quirked one brow, then pointed his hammer at the men sitting in the shade eating sandwiches. "I prove *mei* point."

"*Nett* very well." She waited until his blue eyes roamed back to hers. "If you're hungry, you should be over there eating with the men."

"I told you. I just got here."

Seth positioned a board with the pointed end of the nail aimed up. He struck the nail with the hammer and drove it through the board, then flipped it over and used the claw end to yank the nail out of the wood. He placed that board on the appropriate pile for its size and grabbed another one with nails.

"Haven't you heard the Bible story of the laborers who all received the same wages?"

"*Jah*," he said without taking his eyes off the board he was about to hit.

"It doesn't matter how long you've worked. You should eat."

He broke from his swing and lowered the hammer. "I guess you're right. I should eat." He scowled. "After all, you're keeping me from getting any work done."

She pushed aside his gruff behavior and redirected her

attention to the piles of weathered boards. "What are you doing with those?"

"Right *nau*, nothing." He tossed the hammer on the ground and folded his arms across his chest. "I was pulling out the nails so the boards can be reused."

She could tell he was orderly by the way he stacked the different pieces. "So many piles," she said.

He glanced at his work. "Do you cut the same size fabric for a dress sleeve as you do for a waistband?"

Did he think her waist required that much material? He had lifted her out of the cellar and his hands were on her waist. Her expression must've mirrored the dismay that ran through her mind, because he laughed. Some of the others looked their way. Her face heated and she looked down at her shoes. Was she that difficult to carry on a conversation with? She wasn't a pincushion for him to poke fun at.

He stifled his laughter and grew serious. "It's easier to pull the size of the lumber you need when it's not all piled in the same stack," he volunteered.

She couldn't lift her head until the wave of heat stopped spreading over her cheeks.

"What kind of sandwiches did you bring?"

"Peanut butter. But there's ham too." She smiled. "And cheese."

"I'll take a ham and cheese, *denki*." He picked his hammer off the ground.

She meant to say ham *or* cheese. She opened her mouth, but he struck the nail before she could clarify the selections. This wasn't like her to become so easily confused, at least not by a man.

⚭

Seth cocked his head sideways at the stacked plate of food Katie handed him. *"Denki."* Two sandwiches wasn't necessary. He didn't need someone else going hungry because of what she gave him.

She motioned to the plate. "The top sandwich is ham; the bottom one is cheese." She looked off to the right at the wood he'd stacked. "You plan to rebuild using old lumber?"

He took a bite of the ham sandwich and nodded.

"That's interesting." She held her stare on the wood a moment longer before aiming her eyes at him. "So this is enough to rebuild both the house and workshop?"

He shrugged. "That depends on the size of the buildings." She was certainly different than any other woman he'd known; at least, she was the first woman who appeared interested in construction. Then it struck him. This was Timothy King's place. His little girl was the child who clung to Katie as if she were her mother.

"Does it take longer to build with used lumber?"

"Jah, the nails have to *kumm* out."

Her brows bent, no doubt perturbed by his simplistic explanation. Even annoyed, her crinkled nose twitching was cute. He couldn't help teasing her a little.

"I meant to say, how much longer will it take to rebuild?"

He looked over her shoulder at the men eating. Preoccupied in conversation, Timothy didn't seem concerned about Katie talking with him so long. It would trouble a less secure man. It'd trouble him if Katie were his pledge.

"Maybe you should ask Timothy these questions."

The corners of her mouth turned down briefly, then she perked up and smiled. "How are the sandwiches?"

"Both are *gut. Denki* again." He glanced up as another buggy pulled into the yard. *"Ach gut*, more help."

Katie pivoted around. "Maybe *nett*. That's Andrew Lapp, probably with an update on his father." She took a few steps away. "I want to find out how the bishop is feeling," she said over her shoulder.

A crowd formed around Andrew. Seth set his empty plate on the ground out of the way and resumed removing the nails from the boards. He worked out one nail and glanced over at the group. Their faces turned long and sorrowful. The news must be bad.

Chapter Ten

Katie joined the others to hear what news Andrew brought about his father.

"He still needs our prayers." Andrew choked on his words and bowed his head as though gathering strength to continue.

A knot formed in Katie's throat. Perhaps this morning she hadn't prayed enough. Bishop Lapp was the one who helped her decide to become a schoolteacher. When her fiancé died, both the bishop and his *fraa*, Mary, counseled her and encouraged her to accept God's will. Shortly after, she lost both her parents, and Mary and the bishop were once again instrumental in helping Katie pick her life back up. She should've prayed more. *Please forgive me, Lord, for becoming sidetracked and praying for Seth instead.*

Isaac stepped forward. "We'll pray, but is there anything else we can do?"

Andrew shook his head.

"Please let him know everything is fine here. He doesn't need to concern himself with the rebuilding," Isaac said.

The others agreed.

Katie's thoughts jumped from the bishop's health to his wife. Mary wasn't exactly strong in constitution. She would need help. Katie's mind reeled with ways she could help. She'd make a casserole dish. Offer to run errands in town if they had any. Do their laundry . . . Outside of taking care of Ella Sue, she didn't have nearly the amount of household chores as the others.

"Does your *mamm* need help with anything?" Katie blurted.

When the other women voiced their interest in helping too, Andrew nodded. "Please, when Judith arrives, ask her. She would know better how to advise you." He redirected his talk to the men, changing the conversation to the building project.

The women drifted back to the food area to clean up.

"I can make something for tomorrow's meals," her sister-in-law, Abigail, said.

Others listed the meals they planned to prepare as they began to busily *redd-up*.

Katie picked up a crock of beans, then glanced over her shoulder at Seth. He pulled a nail out of a board, then tossed it aside. Busy spying on his activity, Katie jumped when someone nudged her shoulder. Abigail was at her side.

"The one you keep looking at, Isaac said, is Amos Mast's *bruder*-in-law."

"*Jah*," Katie mumbled. "Seth Stutzman."

Abigail's brows arched.

Katie couldn't believe she just admitted to watching Seth. She motioned to the bean crock in her hand. "You brought this, right?"

Abigail smiled. "I noticed you made him a plate of food."

Katie grew warm under Abigail's inquisitive stare. Although Abigail wasn't much older, she had a keen motherly sense and could pull information out of anyone.

"I'll put this in the back of your buggy," Katie said.

Her sister-in-law peered over her shoulder at Seth, then faced Katie. "I'll walk with you."

Once out of earshot of the other women, Abigail leaned in. "I was going to wait to say something, but weren't you trapped in the cellar with him?"

Abigail might be both her dearest friend and sister-in-law, but some things shouldn't be shared. Any information would only fuel Abigail's desire to pair them up. Katie stopped at the back of the buggy and waited until Abigail opened the hatch.

"You're *nett* going to tell what happened in the cellar?" Abigail frowned.

"You know the answer," Katie said. "Nothing happened." Katie set the dish on the floorboard. "And don't forget, there were twelve witnesses who were also trapped inside the cellar."

"*Jah*, and they all gave assorted accounts." She wagged her brows. "Sounds as though you had quite a frolic."

"*Nay*." Katie squared her shoulders. "We are *going* to have a frolic," she said, adding, "once the *schul* is rebuilt."

"You mean *if*."

Katie shook her head. "*When* it's rebuilt," she said sternly. The school must be rebuilt. The children needed a place to learn—and she needed a useful purpose.

"Don't hold your breath. Isaac said he and the other ministers went around for offerings and the people just don't have much money." Abigail looked upward. "We had more than our share of rain last month. If the crops fail, who could possibly spare what they don't have?"

Katie nodded. Still, she couldn't believe the members would shortchange the children's education. She'd given all she could to the offering fund.

"This side of the district needs their own *schul*. It's too far for the children to walk, and who can cart them all over to the other side every day?"

"Something will be figured out before next fall." Abigail patted Katie's arm. "If need be, you have a job at the vegetable stand."

A new schoolhouse was what the district needed. After all, the boys needed their math skills in order to be the settlement's future builders. Even the girls needed mathematics for measuring material and understanding how much ingredients were necessary for cooking. She could argue more reasons, like the time it would take to drop them off and pick them up on the other side of the district. Time unspent on chores or in the field. Certainly the bishop would be in favor of rebuilding the school. Mary, too, once Katie had a chance to make her point.

A buggy pulled up next to them and Judith Lapp stepped out. "Rachel's *boppli kumm* last *nacht*. A girl, isn't that *wundebaar*!"

Katie smiled. "How is she doing?"

"Both are fine."

"The women are organizing supper meals to take to the bishop's *haus*," Abigail said.

"I plan to bring a casserole over later today," Katie added.

"*Denki*. That will be helpful. I've been with Rachel most of the day. Apparently she promised her niece, Ella Sue, she could stay with her after the *boppli* was born." Judith scanned the construction area. "Have you seen Timothy? I thought I'd let the girls play a little longer, then take Ella Sue with me when I leave if he says it's okay."

Katie's heart grew heavy. Caring for Ella Sue had given her

something to keep her mind occupied while she was unable to teach. Suddenly she felt as useless as an empty spool of thread. She gazed at the construction site, but instead of looking for Timothy, her eyes stopped on the piled lumber they had salvaged. Perhaps rebuilding the school wouldn't require much money if the lumber could be reused.

Her focus shifted to the elderly man who pulled a board off the debris pile. Until now, Seth had worked alone pulling nails out of the lumber.

Seth stopped hammering when he caught sight of Elias in his peripheral vision. He hadn't seen the man since the day Timothy was found.

Elias approached Seth, carrying a board in one hand and a hammer in the other. "Need help?"

Normally Seth liked to work alone. But he hadn't seemed to make much of a dent in the debris pile, and the men were using the boards practically as fast as he could prepare them, so he didn't mind the company.

"Sure." Seth resumed hammering, then stopped. "I didn't see you earlier. Have you been here all day?"

"*Nay*, I was detained."

"I looked for you after I got out of the culvert . . ." Seth cocked his head to the side. "I still don't understand how you could've heard Timothy in the drain. You must have sharp ears."

Elias smiled.

"If Timothy responded inside the culvert when I tapped his leg, I didn't hear him." He held back from adding how his own voice sounded magnified inside the drainpipe.

The man bowed his head humbly. "God has given us ears to hear. Hearing is a gift."

"Then your gift is extraordinary," Seth said, lifting the hammer. He drove the nail through the wood with one strike, tossed the board on the appropriate pile, then dropped the nail into his tool belt. Later he would straighten what nails he could for reusing.

After a few minutes of pounding, Elias handed Seth a board that he'd removed the nails from. "What do you think?"

Seth eyed the length. It was splintered, but it didn't appear bowed. He pulled a pencil he'd tucked over his ear, drew a line a few inches across the section beyond the cracked part, and tossed it into the designated trim pile.

"You have a trained eye to see that it was splintered," Elias said.

The man probably expected Seth to say that God gave him eyes to see. God had. He wouldn't contest that fact. But a trained eye? *Nett* in construction. If that had been the case, a man wouldn't have died from a miscalculation Seth made. He would never be so foolish again to think he could conquer his learning disability.

Seth hoped Elias would view his silence as humble and not ill-mannered.

Elias cleared his throat, interrupting Seth's thoughts. When Seth looked up, Elias was pointing to Seth's nail pouch.

"If you want to hand me the nails in your pocket, I'll straighten them," Elias said.

"Sure." He dug his hand into the leather tool pouch and pulled out a mixture of 60-penny common nails along with some shorter 8-penny nails, and a few roofing nails. Of the roofing nails, stubby and next to impossible to straighten, he only saved the ones deemed reusable and pitched the others aside.

Elias took a level slab of wood and, using the flat surface, laid the nail out to tap it with the hammer.

Seth motioned with his hammer to the oak tree. "You might want to sit in the shade to do that." He caught sight of Katie loading her arms with dishes of leftover food.

It wasn't uncommon for a group of women to cluster around the food tables chatting after the men had eaten and returned to work, but he hadn't struggled to keep his attention on his job like he did today. Katie not only distracted him, she intrigued him. During the meeting, she was the only woman who spoke up. Even in his settlement, women rarely said anything in a mixed gathering, and especially not during a meeting.

Seth followed Katie with his eyes over to the parked buggies. She leaned inside, situated the covered dish next to the others, then returned to the tables. Lost in the moment, he continued watching her as she reloaded her arms and made another trip to the buggies.

"Hard to concentrate?"

"*Jah,*" Seth replied before the question registered. He spun to face Timothy behind him and swallowed hard.

Timothy chuckled. "The *schul* children love her."

Seth clamped his mouth closed. His words would come out garbled. Besides, nothing he said would explain why he was staring at Timothy's woman. He glanced at the depleted stockpile. "I guess I'm falling behind. But at least I have Elias to—" He scanned the area, but Elias was gone.

"Something wrong?"

Seth shook his head. "I think *mei* helper walked off the job."

Timothy laughed. "Those young boys are forever running off."

"Elias is elderly." He craned his neck to scan the area as he described his helper. "White hair, wire-rimmed glasses, walks with a cane." Seth faced Timothy. "Do you know who I'm talking about?"

"*Nay*, but there must be fifty people here today from other districts helping. I'll fix you up with a *gut* helper." He waved at one of David Fischer's twin boys.

The young man jogged over to them. "Did you need something?"

"*Jah*, how about giving Seth a hand for the rest of the day?" Timothy said.

"Okay." He looked at Seth. "What do you need me to do?"

"Do you have a hammer?"

"I'll get one," he said and sprinted off.

"That was Jacob. Sometimes it's hard to tell them apart," Timothy volunteered.

Seth nodded, although he recognized the young man as the one who eyed his niece. He'd made a mental note that his brother had a chipped front tooth and Jacob grinned a lot.

Jacob was quick to return and seemed eager to get started.

"I better get back to work myself." Timothy ambled across the driveway toward the house construction.

Seth positioned a board and demonstrated the easiest technique for removing the nail without excessively bending it. "I stash the nails in my tool belt pocket," he said. Seth stepped aside. "Go ahead and finish taking out the other nails."

Jacob missed the nail and hit the board.

"Choke up on the handle. You'll have more control," Seth explained. Jacob hit the nail on the second attempt. "How old are you?"

"Seventeen."

"That's close to *mei* niece Leah's age."

Jacob smiled. "*Jah*, she's sixteen."

"I think Leah has a birthday *kumming* up."

"Five weeks and two days." Jacob's eyes widened and he dropped his head.

The young man's face turned four shades of red. Seth held his observation but wondered if Amos was aware of the young man's attraction to his daughter. Seth grabbed a board. He didn't want to make the kid any more nervous. As it was, he hadn't hit the nail again since Leah's name was brought up.

Seth glanced over at the group of women and his gaze connected with Katie's. He held his stare without realizing that she was walking toward the construction area. Toward him.

Katie diverted her eyes away from his and walked past him. She stopped next to Timothy, who lowered his hammer and faced her. After a moment, a smile filled Timothy's face and he nodded.

Seth's heart sank unexpectedly.

You fool. Why are you so interested in her? Seth shook his head. "Stay focused on the work at hand."

Jacob stopped hammering. "Did you say something?"

"Nothing important," Seth mumbled. He snatched his empty cup from where he'd left it on the stump and headed for the pump. He wasn't thinking straight, allowing a woman to preoccupy his thoughts. Maybe a cup of cold water would clear his head. Once at the pump, he cranked the handle, filled the cup, and gulped the cold water.

Hopefully now he could get back to concentrating on work. He plodded over to the work area. He went to pick up his hammer from the makeshift table, and shiny nails captured his attention. Seth picked them up and turned them over in his hand. Perfectly straight, they looked brand-new.

Seth looked up and spotted Elias at the end of the driveway

near the culvert. So Elias hadn't left earlier like Seth had originally thought. Elias glanced over his shoulder, waved at Seth,
then continued walking.

Seth inspected the nails again. He'd never seen anything
quite like it.

Chapter Eleven

K atie stood on Bishop Lapp's stoop, a tuna casserole dish in hand, and waited for someone to answer the door. In the void of activity, a shiver slipped down her spine. She hoped the bishop's condition hadn't changed for the worse. She knocked on the door again, this time harder.

The door creaked open and Mary smiled wearily. "It's *gut* to see you, Katie." Mary's welcoming words didn't match the lackluster expression in her eyes. She opened the door wider despite looking as if she were not really up for company.

Katie extended the warm casserole dish. "I thought I would bring you something for supper and ask if you need any help." She scanned the sitting room for Bishop Lapp but didn't see him. "How is Bishop Lapp feeling?"

Mary sighed. "He's weak. I just helped him into bed." She motioned for Katie to follow her into the kitchen. "I'm concerned about him," she said. "He asked for *mei* assistance. It's *nett* like him."

Katie set the dish on the table. "Is there anything I can do?"

"Pray for his strength to return." She glanced over her shoulder toward the kitchen entrance, then lowered her voice. "He can hardly hold a glass of water in his right hand because it shakes so much. He's too weak to walk down the hallway without using someone for support." Mary's eyes glazed with tears.

Katie reached for Mary's hand and gave it a gentle squeeze before releasing it. "I'll be sure to keep you both in *mei* prayers." Tears formed in Katie's eyes. "You both mean so much. I wouldn't know what to do if—"

"Don't speak it," Mary said sharply.

Katie clamped her mouth closed. She needed more control over allowing such careless words to spill from her mouth.

"We must leave it in God's hands." Mary's voice softened. "Everything. Zechariah's health, the rebuilding of our settlement . . . God knows what we've been through."

Katie brushed the tears from her cheeks. "You're right." She forced a cheerful tone for Mary's sake. "I believe the *schul* will be rebuilt as well."

"I'm sure one day it will."

One day? A flicker of panic sped through Katie's veins. "Five years ago the bishop thought we needed another *schul* in the district."

Mary nodded. "*Jah* . . . I remember."

Mary's hesitance prompted Katie to ask, "Don't you think we need it rebuilt?" Katie continued without giving Mary a chance to reply. "When he's feeling better, will you convince him? Remember, you talked him into building it originally."

Mary had supported Katie during the teacher selection process. Surely Mary would support her now as well.

"We had more *schul*-age children then. And don't forget, every family in the settlement agreed and donated money to the building fund."

Katie pulled out the hankie she had tucked up her sleeve and dotted the wet creases of her eyes. True, she only had thirteen students when they were all present. Three of them were finishing their eighth and final year. That would leave her with only ten students starting in the fall, and that was if the Yoders rebuilt. Isaac had mentioned the possibility of them selling their land and relocating to Joseph's home district. If so, that would leave her with six students.

Mary cupped her hand over Katie's shoulder. "I'll see what Zechariah says, but *nett* until he's feeling better."

"Ach, denki." Katie exhaled a long sigh. With Mary's help, the bishop would see the need to rebuild the school and he would convince the other members. Katie's soul filled with renewed hope. She hadn't realized how important teaching was until there was a threat of the school not being rebuilt.

"I should be going." Katie motioned to the door. "Try to rest. And if there's anything I can do, anything at all to help, please let me know."

"Denki."

Katie climbed inside the buggy and veered Peaches toward the road. She hadn't traveled more than a mile when a bright flash of light startled Peaches. The leather reins slipped through Katie's grip as Peaches trotted faster.

"Whoa," Katie yelled. She scrambled to regain control of the reins. "Whoa, girl." Jerking back on the reins, it took all of her strength to slow Peaches. When she finally got the horse to stop, an elderly man, walking with a cane in the center of the road, came into view.

The moment Seth pulled into Amos's yard, the stump of the fallen tree came into view. The rest of the tree was stacked as firewood against the woodshed. Amos had to have sore muscles after chopping that much firewood in one day. But that was what came of pride.

Seth unharnessed his horse and opened the gate for Sage to join the other horses in the meadow. Not that there was much grass; the pasture was still under water from all the rain they'd had.

Seth rested his boot on the bottom rung of the railing and gazed at the grazing horses. It would be costly if Amos had to supplement the horses with hay during the summer because the farmland couldn't feed them.

He glanced at the sky. Hopefully the weather tomorrow would be pleasant like today. If the warm and dry weather continued, the other houses and barns shouldn't take long to put up. The men finished framing the shell of Timothy's house today. Because the rebuilt house was a single story, it was half the size. Timothy didn't seem to mind. Seth had overheard him say he and his daughter didn't require much space, and should a need present itself, he would build an addition at that time.

Seth couldn't help but wonder if the need Timothy referred to had anything to do with marrying Katie and starting a family.

He pushed off the railing to head inside and stopped. A giggle caught his attention. He spun around but didn't see anyone. Then Leah rounded the barn. Her eyes connected with his and her smile dropped. She glanced off to her right, then hurried to meet Seth on the other side of the gate.

"I didn't know you were back." She pointed to the house, her hand shaky. "I kept supper warm for you."

"*Denki.*" Something was up with her. He stopped and looked over his shoulder. Nothing.

"Are you *kumming* inside?"

"After I put the harness up." And checked out what was behind the barn. "You *geh* on. I'll be inside in a minute."

Her eyes darted over to the corner of the barn, then back to him. "I hope you like beef stew."

"*Mei* favorite meal," he said, walking away.

"*Onkel* Seth?"

Her tone was panicky, and he pivoted on the heel of his boot.

Leah's brows crinkled and her eyes seemed to focus on something beyond him.

"Do you like corn bread?" she asked.

"*Jah.*"

"Do you want milk or *kaffi* with your meal?"

He spun to face her. "Maybe you'd better tell me what's behind the barn."

"Wh-what do you mean?" She bit her bottom lip.

"Where is your *daed*?"

Leah lowered her head. "In the *haus.*"

"You best run along then." He pointed to the house. He wasn't sure he wanted to know what she was hiding, but he wouldn't be much of an *onkel* if he let things slip under her father's nose.

Seth trekked behind the barn, not sure what to expect. Sometimes when the youth reached *rumschpringe*, his niece's age, they decided to try smoking or drinking alcohol, but he couldn't picture Leah being interested in either. He scanned the area, his eyes stopping on a buggy parked alongside the dirt road running the length of Amos's field. From the distance where Seth stood, he could only make out a chestnut-colored horse he didn't recognize and the shadowed form of the driver.

Katie studied the elderly man ambling along the shoulder of the road. He kept up a good pace considering he used a cane and walked with a slight limp.

"Do you need a ride?" Katie called, bringing Peaches to a halt.

The man stopped and straightened his back, then turning to face her, he looked over the rim of his glasses, his eyes glimmering with the late afternoon sun's reflection.

"That's mighty kind of you." He climbed onto the bench. "Sure was hot today." He pulled a white hankie from his front pocket and dabbed it over his brow. "My name is Elias."

"I'm Katie." She clicked her tongue and Peaches lunged forward. "Where are you headed?"

"Just around the bend."

Katie crinkled her brows. Except for Amos Mast's place and the school, there weren't any homesteads this side of the river. At least not any Amish farms.

He tucked the hankie back into his pocket. "I'm staying, for the time being, at a place on the river." He gazed out the window opening. "The storm hit these parts hard, didn't it?"

"*Jah*," Katie mumbled.

Elias faced Katie. "Have you ever noticed that after a forest fire there's an abundance of new growth?"

As though he hadn't expected her to respond, he continued,

"Sometimes there are obstacles that need to be removed before something new can develop."

"I don't understand."

An easy smile spread over his face. "You will, child. In time you will." He motioned to the road. "You can let me off near that stump up ahead."

Katie pulled back on the reins and stopped the horse where the man indicated. She scanned the immediate area, her eyes stopping on the narrow footpath leading through the ferns and into the woods. She glanced at him. "Are you sure this is where you want to get out?"

"I'm sure." He collected his cane and climbed off the bench. "*Denki* for the ride."

Katie scooted on the bench and poked her head out the window opening. "I don't remember seeing that trail before." She passed this bend every day on her way to and from the school. She'd never seen the footpath cutting through the ferns.

"You don't spend time at the river anymore, do you, child?"

Anymore? How did he know about the time she used to spend at the river? Katie swallowed hard and shook her head. After James died in the river, she stayed away from that area of the settlement. She hadn't been back in seven years.

Chapter Twelve

Seth fastened the top button on his Sunday shirt, then pulled the suspender straps over his shoulders. By this time at home, he'd be hearing the bustling sounds of his family getting ready for church, but here in his brother-in-law's house, all was oddly quiet. He hadn't smelled coffee or breakfast either, and that was unusual. Seth snatched his nicer hat from the top of the dresser and headed for the kitchen where he saw Leah standing at the stove.

"*Guder mariye,*" he said.

Leah set the coffeepot on the stove, then faced him. She eyed his Sunday best and her brows rose. "Are you going to church?"

"*Jah,* it's Sunday." He glanced around the room. "Where is everyone?"

"*Daed* and the boys are out in the barn. Annie is still sleeping." She pulled a cast-iron skillet from the cabinet and set it on the stove. "I miss going," she said, dipping a spoon into a can of lard. She chucked the heaping spoonful of grease into the pan.

"Would you like to go with me?" He pulled a chair away from the table and sat.

Leah's eyes widened, but before she could reply, Amos entered the kitchen.

Amos eyed Seth. "I suppose you're going to services with those folks."

Seth nodded. *"Jah."*

Amos rolled his eyes. "It didn't take you long to fit in."

"I might *nett* be from this county, but they're *mei bruders* and sisters in Christ." Seth glanced at Leah, who had turned her concentration to cooking the eggs, then looked back at Amos. "Please *kumm*. God wants you and your children in fellowship also."

"Since when did you start speaking for God?"

His brother-in-law's mocking tone rubbed Seth like a chafing rope around his neck. He tugged the hem of his collarless shirt away from his neck. "I think if you ask Leah, she wants to attend."

"She has chores."

Seth shook his head slowly. "You know what way is right. And you know the importance of following God. Even if you choose *nett* to follow him, it's wrong if you hold your children back from serving the Lord. You'll bring judgment on your entire household."

Amos pulled the chair out from the table and slumped into it. "Still talking for God? Am I supposed to believe you're a prophet *nau* too?"

Seth stood. "I should go."

"You do not live in this settlement, so you're *nett* required to attend."

Seth paused at the kitchen entrance and looked over his

shoulder at Amos. "I'm going to service to honor God. That's what I know is right to do, and despite your disapproval, I serve God above man."

Seth caught himself looking at Katie on the women's side of the barn during service. He found her sitting ramrod straight on the bench, her focus on the minister reading the Scriptures. Sunlight peeked through the barn's planks and cast a warm glow over her face. Seth forced himself to look away. He hadn't come to service to be distracted by a woman, and yet he hadn't listened to much of what the last minister said because he'd been too preoccupied with Katie.

Please forgive me, God. I've allowed my distraction to take the focus off of you and your Holy Word.

Andrew called Isaac to close the service. Seth bowed his head as Katie's brother began to pray. The moment Seth heard *"aemen,"* he opened his eyes and stole another glance across the aisle at Katie.

She looked his way and smiled.

Seth stood, took a step toward her, but stopped when someone tapped his shoulder.

"I'm glad you could *kumm,*" Isaac said. "Our service was shorter than usual."

"I hope your bishop is feeling better soon."

"*Jah,* we all hope he has a quick recovery." He motioned to the barn door. "You're planning to stay for the meal, right?"

Seth smiled. His stomach had growled most of the morning because he had missed breakfast. Once the singing ended, he was sure the men around him heard his roaring hunger call. He followed Isaac out of the barn and migrated with him over to the area next to the fence where the men milled as they waited for the noon tables to be prepared.

"Where are we meeting tomorrow?" one of the men asked Isaac as he and Seth joined the group.

"After we finish Timothy's place, I thought we decided on Moses Plank's *haus*."

"Most of the *haus* is gone," Moses said. "We won't recover many reusable materials."

Isaac nodded. "We'll use the lumber from the *schulhaus*." He looked around the tight circle of men. "Anyone have an issue with that?"

Seth dipped his head down, then looked casually over toward the women setting the tables, and more specifically at Katie. Exchanging glances with her distracted him enough that when his name was called, Isaac sounded as though he'd said it more than once.

"I'm sorry." Seth turned back to the group.

"I thought since Amos's place is near the *schul*, you could start preparing the lumber in the morning. Do you mind?"

"Sure, I can do that."

Another man pointed toward the tables. "Looks like they're signaling us to *kumm* eat."

Seth took a few steps before Isaac flanked his side. "Abigail, *mei fraa*, thought after we finished working tomorrow you might want to have supper with us." He smirked. "She also mentioned something about inviting Katie too." Isaac made an apologetic shrug.

Seth had received plenty of supper invitations over the years only to find out he'd been set up with one of the *maydels* in the settlement. At least this time Isaac had given him warning.

"You can let me know tomorrow," Isaac said.

Seth caught a glimpse of Timothy stopping next to Katie. "Are those two—?"

"*Nay.*" He shook his head as though reinforcing his words. "Both his *fraa* and his *mamm* have passed on. Katie helped him with his daughter while his sister-in-law was pregnant and on bed rest. There isn't anything between them."

Seth smiled. "Supper sounds *gut*. Tell your *fraa denki.*" He couldn't help but wonder if Katie was privy to the guest list or if she would be surprised to see him.

On Monday morning the sun poked through the trees as Katie veered Peaches onto the dirt road leading to the school yard. She hadn't been to the school since the storm, and this was a fine day to inventory what items hadn't blown away that could be reused in the new building. Surely not all the desks and chairs needed replacing. But she hadn't been able to see the actual damage that night. They had climbed out from the cellar in the dark. Even the starlight had been washed away when it started raining again.

Katie clicked her tongue, encouraging Peaches into a faster trot. Over the years she'd made the trip to school so many times that Peaches automatically pulled into the driveway and stopped at the fence post.

Not prepared to see the school splintered into so many pieces and scattered so far, Katie climbed out of the buggy in a daze, then leaned against it for support as she tried to take in what her eyes were telling her.

Elias edged closer. He had expected her arrival and had waited at the site. He needed to give her a message from his Master but was instructed to wait until she was in the right mind-set to receive the word.

Katie squeezed her eyes closed, then opened them wide to blink back her tears. With such destruction, it was hard to believe no one had been hurt.

"*Denki*, God, for keeping us safe in the cellar. Buildings are replaceable, we know that, God, and we are taught *nett* to cling to anything of this world."

She moved forward, focused on the schoolhouse lying in a heap. She had to remember to breathe as she walked toward the pile of debris. She fixed her gaze on something shiny hurled by the wind and now lodged in an oak tree's branches. She moved closer. A tin lunch pail. Probably wouldn't be too difficult to recover it with a ladder. The detached stovepipe dangled from another broken tree limb.

On the ground, an assortment of ink-smeared papers littered the yard. She picked up one page of schoolwork from a puddle, a mathematics practice sheet. It fell apart in her hand. Her vision blurred with tears as she canvassed the destruction. She carefully collected as many papers as she could find, although she didn't know why she bothered—the papers were damaged, the ink smeared.

"Don't cling to anything in this world," Elias reminded.

With the children's papers clutched in her arms, she eased up the rickety steps leading . . . nowhere now. One cautious footstep at a time, she crept over the plank subfloor to the room's midpoint where they'd escaped the cellar through the cut hole. It seemed so long ago when they were trapped. She remembered them talking about a frolic. At the time she mistakenly thought they'd only need to repair the floor and maybe replace some of the tin roof. How foolish to believe it would only take a few weeks to do the necessary repairs.

"That isn't safe."

Startled, she dropped the school papers, which fluttered into the cellar.

"Let me help you down." Seth extended his hand.

"How long have you been standing there?"

He shrugged. "*Nett* long enough, or I would've kept you from climbing up there."

"It feels firm to me." She made a slight bouncing movement, then realized the floor had more give than it should.

"Stop playing and get down." He leaned forward, shot his hand toward her, and nodded. "Katie!" His jaw tightened, straining his demand.

She took a step, and the boards creaked under her weight. He was right. This wasn't a safe place to be standing. The moment she reached the edge, he grasped her waist, lifted her from the platform, and set her gently next to him. Standing this close, the bead of sweat on the side of his face looked enormous as it rolled down his neck and disappeared under his blue cotton shirt. She started to track another bead, this time on his jaw, but he tipped his face slightly and their eyes met. A tingle rippled through her as he peered down at her.

"What are you doing?"

"What do you mean?" She stepped away, placing more distance between them.

"Here. What are you doing here?"

"This *is* still the *schulhaus*." She tapped her chest. "I'm the *teetshah*, remember?"

His expression grew cold and disappointed somehow. He wheeled away, muttering something under his breath.

"You really should speak up," she said, stomping behind him. "I could only hear mumbling."

He pivoted back to her, almost knocking into her.

"Should I raise *mei* hand before I speak too, *teetshah?*" He lifted his hand mockingly. "I suppose you want me to stand in the corner *nau.*"

"*Ach, nau* you're being condescending." She looked away. Her eyes stopped on the stack of piled lumber. Single boards? Excitement laced her thoughts. She hadn't expected the school to be rebuilt so soon. "What's all this?"

"What's left of the *schul.*"

She crossed her arms and tipped her head. "What are you doing here?" Somewhat condescending herself, she knew he was preparing the boards to rebuild the school.

His eyes traveled up and down her as though sizing her up, then he winked. "Don't worry. I have no plans to enroll in *schul.*" He pointed over her shoulder at the building. "Stay off the flooring. It isn't safe."

He marched toward the flatbed wagon parked along the edge of Amos Mast's field.

She traipsed behind. "So where is everyone else?"

"They're finishing up at Timothy King's place." He stopped at the side of the wagon, then pulled off his hat and swiped his forehead with his shirtsleeve. He replaced his hat and motioned with a head nod toward the piled lumber. "I *kumm* out early to strip the boards of nails and organize what lumber can be reused." He motioned to the wagon. "Then I'll start loading it, but *nett* until I get these—"

"What are those?" She had a sneaking suspicion those wooden crates were bee boxes, but she had never seen one up close.

"Beehives," he said.

"Couldn't Amos put those in a different location?"

Seth shook his head. "That's *nett* likely." He climbed up on the wagon and loosened the strap holding the wooden boxes in place.

"But the bees are a threat to the children's safety." She placed her fisted hands on her hips. "Can you talk to him about moving them? He doesn't seem to listen to anything I say."

Seth chuckled. "You don't say."

"This isn't a laughing matter. I assure you, Mr. Stutzman, those bees are a real threat."

He sobered and jumped down from the wagon. "Miss Bender, I don't think anyone will change Amos's mind. Besides, with the river close by, this is the best location." He leaned over the wagon bed and pulled one of the boxes into his arms.

Seth was her only connection to Amos. He could convince his brother-in-law—if she could convince him. She trailed him to the fence post.

"So you won't try to persuade him?"

He set the wooden box on the ground and faced her. "I'd just as well *nett* get in the middle of your spat with *mei* brother-in-law."

"If you won't do it for me, do it for the children."

His expression seemed strained, or perhaps regret flitted over his face for the brief moment their gazes locked. He walked back to the wagon and grabbed the next box. Avoiding eye contact with her, he brought the wooden crate over to the fence and stacked it on top of the other one.

"You won't do it for the children?" She exaggerated her appalled tone to gain his attention. It didn't work. He ignored her and continued unloading the wagon. The man's resolve was impossible to penetrate.

"You're heartless." She paused a moment to see if he would respond. When he didn't, she marched, arms swinging at her sides, back to her buggy.

Elias shook his head. *The flesh is weak.* He rejoined her at the buggy. *Perhaps now that she was alone, he would reach her and be able to deliver his message. First, though, she must recognize the deteriorating condition of her heart and seek the Lord in repentance.*

"*Love your enemies. Bless those who curse you . . . Katie, pray. The Father has called you to pray.*"

Chapter Thirteen

eartless." Seth shook his head, listening to the fading clatter of Katie's buggy. Wait until she found out he was taking the building supplies away once he cleaned off this wagon. He eased the last beehive from the wagon bed and carried it to the designated spot. A good spot. Not far from the river and close enough to the blooming apple orchard, an ideal site for bee pollination.

He trekked back to the demolished schoolhouse.

If he thought the men planned to rebuild the school, he would talk with Amos about finding a new location for the beehives. But the children's safety was a moot point, since from what he gathered, the school wasn't to be rebuilt. Why else would they be using the lumber on another project?

Apparently someone had failed to inform the *teetshah*. She'd stalked around here as if evaluating how quickly the building would go up. She would have more ugly thoughts of him when she discovered he hadn't made her aware of the plans. But this wasn't his district. He certainly wasn't about to get in the middle of any battle.

Seth sat on a student chair and grabbed the hammer he'd left earlier. Why was he still dwelling on what Katie thought of him? She'd expressed her ideas.

So had Diana. And odd as it was, he hadn't cared this much about what Diana thought of him after she gave him the ultimatum. She'd wanted to marry a master builder, not someone who built beehives for a living.

He jerked a nail from the board and slipped it into his nail pouch. Preoccupied with Katie's ire, he grabbed another nail with the claw end of the hammer and yanked. Perhaps Katie was right; he was heartless. He should've explained everything to her.

Seth inspected the board for any nails he'd missed. Not finding any, he tossed it with the other salvaged lumber. He kept the same mindless pattern and readied the next board. This work wasn't demanding or difficult, just tedious. Preparing the lumber for reuse offered some satisfaction, but not anything like the thrill of doing actual construction. It used to be that at the end of a long hard day he would stand back and marvel at the finished barn or house. Now it seemed he measured a good day by how many pulled nails were recyclable.

Judging by the lack of jingle in his pouch, he'd better pick up his pace if he wanted to consider this a productive day.

He paused for a moment and tilted his face upward into the warming sun and closed his eyes. He couldn't suppress the memories. The August heat had clung to him like a wool blanket that day he built his last barn. His shirt dripped of sweat by the time he'd finished. But satisfaction coursed through him as he stood back with a jug of icy well water, gazing at the work of his hands. He boastfully predicted the barn would outlast them all—a prideful statement that haunted him now. *"When we've all gone on to be with the Lord, that barn will continue to be a safe haven for the swallows and a place of warmth during the winter for the livestock . . ."*

It wasn't.

The barn roof collapsed under the weight of the first heavy snow.

His heart heavy, Seth found it difficult to take a deep breath. He puffed a few shallow breaths, but the stabbing, sharp pains in his chest made him feel as though his lungs had collapsed.

"You're suffocating," Razzen said. "Now you know what Abraham went through, struggling to breathe after the barn you built collapsed on him." Razzen mimicked the crackling lung sounds Abraham made just before he took his last raspy breath. "You remember his last breath, don't you?"

Seth dropped to his knees. *"Ach,* God. Here I am again."

"Again?" Razzen hissed. "Do you think he wants to hear you beg to clear your conscience again?"

Seth sighed. "You must've grown tired by *nau* of *me* calling out to you." Warmth entered Seth's body, filling him with a strong desire to soak in God's presence and dwell in this moment. Overpowered with peace, his body went limp and Seth fell prostrate, unashamed.

Summoned by his heavenly Master when the young charge began to pray, Elias trampled over Razzen to reach Seth.

"God has waited for you to call upon him. He knows you are hurting,

child." As Seth continued his supplication, Elias's chants rang out as a fragrant offering of adoration and praise to the Holiest of Holies. "Your heavenly Father has heard your plea," Elias said. "Lay your burdens down at his feet and cast your cares upon him."

Razzen tried to weasel his way around Elias, but empowered by the Master the angel served, Elias easily blocked his attempt. Listening to his adversary's reassuring words sickened Razzen. He'd go elsewhere—visit a soul who invited his presence.

Elias continued, "God loves you, child. Be assured, he has prepared your way. Know that you've been called. You are here for a purpose and that is to bring glory to God. Don't let the enemy tell you differently. What you see with your own eyes will lead you astray. For what God sees is perfect. His way leads to the everlasting."

Elias delivered the message, then stepped from his glorified nature into the human form of the elderly man.

A shudder streamed through Seth. Although acutely aware of a presence, he dared not lift his head. He kept his face against the ground, breathing in the earthy scent.

Elias tapped Seth's shoulder. "Are you okay?"

Seth scrambled to his feet, his heart pumping with adrenaline. He took a few calming breaths before he could speak. Even then his stammering sounded more like rambling than coherent thoughts. "When . . . did . . . I didn't see—you."

"I frightened you. I'm sorry." A smile danced in Elias's eyes as he scanned the area. "You've been busy, I see."

Still breathing heavily, Seth couldn't muster an answer.

"I thought you might have more nails for me to straighten."

"*Ach, jah.* Sure." His hands trembled as he dug into his leather pouch and pulled out a fistful of bent nails. With shaky hands, he gave them to Elias.

As Elias gazed at the gnarly spent nails, his lips creased into a broad smile. "The men won't be here until tomorrow. I'll have these ready by then." He took a few steps, then glanced over his shoulder. "You don't mind if I bring them back tomorrow, do you?"

"*Nay*, I don't mind. That would be great. *Denki*."

The man nodded, then continued to leave. Seth called out, "Do you need a ride somewhere?" He didn't have his buggy, but the flatbed wagon would be better than walking.

"*Nay*. I like to walk. Besides, you've agreed to have supper with the Benders." He glanced up at the sun. "What time do you have?"

Seth dug his hand into his pocket and pulled out his watch. He stared at the numbers. Numbers confused him. He forever had to remind himself that a six wasn't a nine and the two wasn't a five.

"Something wrong, *sohn*?"

"It's half past—five." He hated having to say numbers aloud. Even in the form of time. Often enough, the numbers he saw weren't relayed correctly to his brain, because the numbers he spoke were seldom the same. Until he started building and he skewed his measurements regularly, he hadn't comprehended the magnitude of his condition. It still wasn't something he shared. The same way he never read aloud because his mind scrambled the words on the page.

"I suppose you'll want to get cleaned up soon," Elias said.

Seth looked at the watch once again. Where had the time gone? Elias was right. He didn't want to arrive at the Benders' looking like he'd worked in the field all day. The front of his shirt and pants were dirty from lying on the ground. He brushed his hands over his clothing. "Can I give you a ride home? It'll only take me a few minutes to gather *mei* tools." But when he looked up from cleaning the dirt off his pants, Elias was already walking away.

A little prodding in the area of self-reliance and Razzen had Amos climbing the ladder to work on the barn. Razzen clung to Amos's back. He wanted to stay close to the man's ear—feed his soul with thoughts of rage.

Amos climbed as high as the ridge vent and stopped. He craned his neck in the direction of faint voices.

"You're almost seventeen. Run away with me." Jacob Fischer leaned closer and kissed Leah.

Amos's face turned red.

A wirey-haired dog charged toward the ladder, growling and snapping his teeth. The animal's neck fur stood on end.

Razzen swooped down and, landing on the animal, spiked his talons through the animal's fur. The dog tucked his tail in submission. He slunk away, whimpering, the moment Razzen released his hold.

Amos leaned sideways trying to obtain a better view. "Leah!"

The uneven weight tipped the ladder. Amos grappled to hold on to the structure, but the ridge vent would not sustain his weight. The weather-rotten board split.

He fell, screaming.

The loose board slammed against Amos's head. Then another board, dangling by a nail, dropped and hit him.

"Daed!" Leah shouted.

Amos pulled up to his knees, then staggered to his feet. He wobbled for balance but managed to draw back and slap Leah's face.

Stunned, the girl held her hand against her cheek. Her lips trembled and tears filled her eyes.

He took a step toward the young man at his daughter's side and would've taken a swing at him if his vision hadn't blurred. Disoriented, Amos shifted his weight to his other foot.

"*Daed*, please, calm down." Leah came between her father and Jacob Fischer. "Jacob, *geh* on *nau*."

The young man looked at Leah with pleading eyes, then dug his heels into the ground and sprinted toward the field.

"You're *nay* daughter of mine."

Razzen wormed his way around Leah. "He means every word. You've disgraced his name," he hissed. "You've surely sealed his fate. Only a cursed man will act in violence, throw a rage-filled swing. He has turned completely from your religious ways. Because of you . . . because of you, his heart is cold."

Thomas rounded the corner of the barn and stopped abruptly. "What happened?"

Amos's words escaped his mouth in an inaudible slur. Ringing pierced his ears, knocking him off balance. A wave of nausea spread through him as he fought to regain his equilibrium.

Thomas brought his arm around Amos's waist. "Help me get him into the *haus*, Leah."

She hovered close to him. "I'm sorry," she cried.

Amos shut his eyes and slumped on his son's shoulder.

The girl's eyes widened. "*Daed?*"

"What do you mean he hit his head? How?" Seth scuffed his boots on the braided rug at the entry.

"Leah said he fell off the ladder." His nephew shrugged. "I suppose a board must've *kumm* loose and knocked him down. There was one on the ground and he held his head like it was sore," Thomas explained.

Paul entered the house carrying the milk bucket. He set it on the kitchen counter. "Did you hear about *Daed*?"

"I was just telling him what happened," Thomas said.

"He working on the calving barn, wasn't he?" Of course he was. Seth already knew the answer; he just didn't want to believe Amos was that stubborn. Seth had told his brother-in-law he would help him tomorrow. Why didn't Amos wait?

Seth crossed the room and peeked into the sitting room. Empty. "Where is he? Is he still out in the barn?"

"He went to lie down. He said something about resting his eyes and *nett* to let anyone bother him." Thomas glared at Leah, who sat at the kitchen table, her hands covering her face.

Seth placed his hand on his nephew's shoulder. "Something else troubling you, Thomas?"

"Ask Leah."

Leah lifted her head, exposing her tear-reddened eyes. She opened her mouth but only produced a squeak. Then she bolted out of the chair and rushed down the hall toward the bedrooms.

Seth furrowed his brows at Thomas. "There's no reason to use a harsh tone with your sister."

Thomas bowed his head.

Amos falling would've shaken Leah, and understandably so. His nephew was too young to understand Leah's struggles. She hadn't yet learned to control her emotions. She needed grace and gentle guidance. After all, her mother was dead. She lacked a woman's influence to model godly maturity.

Seth paced the kitchen. "I should check on your *daed*."

"I wouldn't if I were you. He's really angry at the moment. Besides, he said *nett* to let anyone bother him," Thomas said.

"I thought you weren't *kumming* home for supper," Paul said, changing the subject. He opened the cabinet and removed a plate, then lifted the lid on the pan and peered inside.

"*Jah.*" Seth looked down the hallway, but there was no activity. "I was supposed to eat at Isaac Bender's *haus*." He had to check on Amos. Seth headed toward the bedrooms, stopped in front of Amos's room, and knocked. "It's Seth."

"What do you want? I thought you had other supper plans."

"I heard you fell. I wanted to see if you were all right and if you needed anything."

"*Nay.* I'm fine."

Amos's gruff tone was normal, but Seth asked again, "Are you sure you don't need anything?"

"I said I didn't."

Seth wished he hadn't agreed to eat with the Benders. He'd lost his appetite. Still, they were expecting him. It would be rude if he didn't show up. Unless Amos needed him. That would be a *gut* reason to stay. He knocked on the door again. "Amos, are you sure you're all right? I can take you to the *dokta*. I don't have to go to the Benders' tonight."

"I don't need to see a *dokta*. I'm fine. *Nau* don't bother me again!"

Amos certainly sounded like his stubborn self. Seth looked down at his soiled clothes. If he hurried, he would have time to wash up and change into something clean. He entered the spare room, poured water into a washbowl, and peeled off his dirty shirt. After a quick shave, he changed into clothes he brought to wear on Sundays.

Muffled cries came from Leah's room as he passed through the hallway. Seth stopped and tapped on her door.

"*Jah,*" she said.

"It's *Onkel* Seth. Can I *kumm* in?"

"*Jah.*"

Seth wasn't sure what he would say to console his niece, but he couldn't leave without saying something. "I know you're shook up about your *daed*, but I think he'll be okay."

She wiped her eyes. "That's *gut*."

"Is there something else bothering you? Something you want to talk about?"

"*Nay.*" She sat on the edge of the bed, her head bowed.

He wasn't good at pulling information out of women. At least she'd stopped crying.

"Sure?"

She nodded without lifting her eyes to meet his.

He stepped out of the room. Not having a mother had to be tough on a girl. She worked hard, took care of Annie, and did the household duties alone. She deserved to have a meltdown every so often at her age.

He entered the kitchen, placed his hand on the doorknob, then paused. "Are you sure I should *geh*?"

Thomas and Paul exchanged puzzled expressions.

"We're wondering why you'd want to eat with the *teetshah* in the first place," explained Thomas.

"Doesn't sound like fun to me," Paul added.

Seth laughed. He felt the same way about his *teetshah* as a kid.

"I stopped by the *schul* today and found several desks and chairs." Katie used a butter knife to release the sealed lid on the canning jar of green beans. Once the lid popped, she emptied the contents into a pan and placed it on the stove.

Abigail's knife stopped halfway through the loaf of bread.

"Katie, don't get your hopes up. I told you. There wasn't enough money collected—"

"You never said what the occasion was." A steady fire roared in the wood cookstove. Katie stirred the beans to keep the juice from boiling over the pan.

"Just supper." But Abigail's jittery tone and the fact that she had peered out the window several times in the past few minutes said it was something more. Abigail placed the sliced bread on a plate and took it and the butter into the dining room. Returning to the kitchen, she went to the window and pulled back a corner of the curtain to gaze outside.

"That's at least the fifth time you've looked out the window." Katie couldn't remember the last time her sister-in-law had acted so nervous.

Someone knocked on the front door.

Abigail abruptly opened the cupboard. She glanced over her shoulder. "Will you get the door, please?"

"Sure." On her way to the front door, she glanced at the dining room table and stopped. Counting six place settings, she circled back to the kitchen. Isaac, Abigail, their two sons, and herself made five. "The table is set for six."

"I forgot. George was invited to the Troyers' for supper. There should only be five." Abigail nodded as though confirming her answer in her own mind.

Another knock and Katie narrowed her eyes. "What's going on? Who else is *kumming* to supper?"

Abigail shooed Katie with her hand. "Well, don't leave him standing on the porch. *Geh* answer the door."

"Him?" Katie widened her eyes, but Abigail turned her back to her. Katie headed back toward the door. "I should have known," she muttered. When she opened the door, Seth stood on the stoop. A mixture of surprise and dread sped through her. "I suppose you've *kumm* for supper."

He quirked his brow. "Hello to you too." He looked past her, into the house. "Is Isaac around?"

She'd just assumed with the extra plate on the table that he was the invited guest. "You didn't *kumm* for supper?"

"Would it break your heart?" He grinned.

She rolled her eyes.

He leaned closer. "Your hospitality is charming. Are you going to invite me in?"

She opened the door wider for him to enter. "Sorry. I thought— *Ach*, never mind."

He stepped inside but paused beside her. "You can't offend someone who's already heartless."

"*Gut* point." She looked beyond him to her *bruder*, Isaac, who had set aside his newspaper to come to the door.

"I hope you're hungry." Isaac smiled at Seth, then patted Katie's back. "You know *mei* sister, *jah*?"

She lowered her head, embarrassed by the obvious dinner setup. Had Seth known she was going to be here?

"Hello, Katie."

Seth drenched his greeting in syrup, but he didn't fool her. "I should go help Abigail in the kitchen." Katie brushed past Seth on her way to the kitchen.

Chapter Fourteen

"How did you two end up in the cellar together?" The boy's eyes darted from his *aenti* Katie over to Seth.

Isaac's *fraa*, seated next to the boy at the table, elbowed the youngster's ribs. "Reuben."

The boy crinkled his face at his mother. "Isn't that what you asked *Daed* the other day?"

Across the table from Seth, Katie choked on her coffee.

Seth lowered his fork. "I found your *aenti* Katie's horse tangled in a barbed wire fence, and after I freed it, I saw a huge black funnel cloud."

The boy's eyes widened.

Katie clutched her water glass and chugged its contents. Then leaped from her chair and took her empty glass to the kitchen.

If her watery eyes were any indication, Seth suspected the

coffee had scorched her throat. He leaned back in his chair and watched her refill the glass at the sink.

"Katie?" Abigail slid her chair away from the table.

"I'm fine," Katie said in a hoarse voice, returning to her place.

Seth forked his meat loaf and stole a glance at Katie, who avoided looking at him and had shifted several times on the chair.

"Were you afraid of the tornado, *Aenti* Katie?" Reuben restarted the conversation.

"Sure I was. It sounded like a freight train."

Seth still marveled at her bravery. "She saved the *schul* children by getting them into the cellar." He caught a glimpse of Katie's cracked smile as she dipped her head low and looked as though she were staring at something on her plate.

Isaac removed a biscuit from the bowl, split the biscuit in half, and added a pat of butter. "Were you able to get much done at the *schul* today?"

"*Jah*, but I found some carpenter ant damage on what would've been a complete wall. Those boards shouldn't be reused."

Isaac nodded.

"But just one wall, right? That shouldn't hinder the rebuild much." Katie's inquisitive eyes darted between him and Isaac. "One wall shouldn't cost much to replace, ain't so?" Her eyes stopped on Seth's.

Under the pressure of her stare, Seth directed his attention to his plate and rolled some green beans with his fork. How could he tell her about the plans to use the school's lumber on another project? He couldn't. Besides, Isaac should explain the district's decision, not an outsider like himself.

Abigail cleared her throat, breaking the silence. "What is it you do for work in your district?"

"He builds beehives." Katie's top lip curled slightly.

"That's right," he said, probably sounding more defensive than he should.

Reuben's eyes widened. "Do you wear the fancy hat and suit?"

Seth smiled. "*Jah*, if I'm extracting the honey or gathering honeycombs."

Katie plopped her fork down on her plate. "And why is it necessary to wear the *protective* gear?"

"Katie," Isaac said, drawing out her name, "don't interrogate him."

Seth shifted on his chair. He wasn't sure that it would help to explain, but he tried. "Honeybees are normally not threatening," Seth said.

"Normally," she interjected.

Seth glanced at Isaac. "Katie's upset about the hives I put up for Amos near the *schul*."

Katie squared her shoulders. "They pose a risk to the children." She set her glare on Seth. "*Someone* needs to talk with Amos about moving them."

"*Nett* anymore." Isaac speared a forkful of green beans. "The *schul* isn't being rebuilt."

Katie narrowed her eyes. "It has to be."

Seth picked up the quiver in her voice and wished more than anything he would have stayed home. He wasn't from their district. It shouldn't matter what they planned to do with the lumber, yet his insides wormed with guilt. Maybe if he'd said something earlier today, she wouldn't look betrayed like she did now.

Abigail slid her chair over the wooden floor and the screech drew everyone's attention. "I made a chocolate cake with peanut butter icing. Is anyone ready for dessert?"

"I am," Reuben said, pushing aside his empty plate.

"Katie, would you mind giving me a hand?" Abigail motioned with her eyes toward the kitchen.

Without saying a word, Katie rose from her chair, collected a few plates, and followed.

"I figured that would upset *mei* sister." Isaac sighed. "It is a shame about the *schul*. She's a *gut teetshah*." He took another bite.

Seth studied Isaac a moment. True, losing the school was a shame, but surely her brother noticed the determination in her eyes. During the tornado she proved her strength. No doubt, she'd weather this storm about losing the school with the same unmovable fieriness.

Katie skimmed the peanut butter icing across the rectangle cake with the back of a spoon, moving the icing from a heavy area to fill the scantly covered spots. "What will I do if the *schul* isn't rebuilt? Grow old with idle hands?"

"That wouldn't be God's will." Abigail motioned to the newspaper on the counter. "Did you send your article about the storm to the *Budget*?" She pulled the plates down from the cupboard.

"*Jah*, I did." After the heartache and turmoil her articles had caused in the past, she wasn't sure writing articles on a regular basis was the answer.

"I'm sorry." Abigail slipped her hand over Katie's forearm. "I wasn't thinking about James when I suggested the other day that you should write again."

Katie forced a smile. "It's been seven years . . . I shouldn't—" She shouldn't be stumbling over finding her purpose again. She was a schoolteacher. "I'm *nett* a writer. God's will for me is teaching. I already know. It's *nett* to be a *fraa* or a *mamm*, but a *teetshah*." She sliced the cake and placed a corner section on the first plate. "Mary Lapp thinks the *schul* should be rebuilt. She plans to talk with the bishop once he's feeling better."

Abigail smiled. "Then things are bound to work out for the best, ain't so?"

Katie glanced over her shoulder toward the dining area. "I still have to figure out some way to get Amos to move those beehives."

"Don't you think you were a little snappy toward Seth?"

Katie thought for a moment. "I suppose I should apologize." She glanced at her sister-in-law's steadfast nod. "I still think Seth could persuade Amos to relocate those hives if he wanted."

"Then you need to learn a new approach." Abigail picked up two plates and handed them to Katie. "And smile when you serve him."

Katie rolled her eyes.

"Make sure you ask him if he wants his *kaffi* warmed too."

"I think I can handle showing some common courtesy."

"Let's hope so." Abigail winked.

Katie forced a smile and followed her sister-in-law into the dining room. She handed Seth a plate.

"*Denki,*" he said.

"Can I refill your *kaffi*?" She purposely spoke in monotone, then winked at Abigail.

"Sure." He reached for his cup, tipped it and looked inside, then handed it to her. "*Denki.*"

"No problem." Katie caught a glimpse of Abigail's subtle nod on her way back to the kitchen. Apparently her sister-in-law approved of her changed attitude. Seth had a warm smile. It certainly shouldn't be difficult to return his kindness.

As Katie added coffee to his cup, she craned her head to listen to the conversation in the dining room.

"Are you going to move to Hope Falls?" Reuben asked.

"*Nay*, I'm only visiting," Seth replied. "I *kumm* to deliver some beehives I made for *mei* brother-in-law. I ended up staying longer because of the storm."

"Are beehives hard to make?"

"*Nay*, once you build one, all the others use the same pattern."

Seth's answer carried a ring of sadness. Katie couldn't imagine doing the exact same job day after day. As she entered the room, she caught a glimpse of dullness in Seth's eyes. She set the cup next to his plate. "You don't like building beehives, do you?"

"*Ach*, here we go," Abigail said under her breath.

Katie moved around the table and took her place, feeling his eyes following her.

"Why do you say that?" Seth asked.

She shrugged. "Just a guess." She sipped her coffee. "It's probably a family trade, *jah*?"

Seth shook his head. "*Nay*."

"Then you've been building them for so many years that you could build them blindfolded?"

Seth stared. His blue eyes changed from dull to vivid and intriguing.

Abigail cleared her throat softly, which Katie ignored until her sister-in-law kicked her under the table. Katie tore her attention away from Seth and faced Abigail's raised brows.

Isaac chuckled. "Do you feel like you're in the hot spot tonight with all these questions? We didn't invite you here to quiz you all *nacht*."

Seth smiled. "I don't mind."

Isaac drained his cup. "*Gut* to see you have a sense of humor."

Seth needed a good disposition if he intended to spend much time with Amos Mast. Katie's thoughts erupted into a chuckle.

Seth's brows rose. "You don't think I have a sense of humor?"

"*Nay* . . . I'm sure you have one . . . I mean . . . you'd have to have one spending any amount of time with—"

Seth grinned. "Amos said that about you too."

"Me?" Katie widened her eyes, playing as if the news appalled her. It didn't. Nothing shocked her about Amos. But she did find Seth's lopsided grin entertaining. For the time, it seemed, she and Seth had called an unspoken truce.

Isaac redirected Seth's attention by bringing up the topic of the weather and its effect on the winter wheat crop.

Abigail stood and collected an armful of dishes, and following her sister-in-law's cue to give the men time alone, Katie gathered the remaining dishes. She headed for the kitchen but stopped when someone knocked on the door.

Reuben jumped up to open it.

Jacob Fischer entered. He glanced at Seth, then spoke directly to Isaac. "*Mei daed* sent me to fetch you. He said it's important that the ministers *kumm* to Bishop Lapp's *haus nau*."

Katie hurried to set the dishes on the counter. "Something's wrong with the bishop," she told Abigail, who was stacking plates into the sink. Katie bit her bottom lip. This couldn't be *gut* news to call a meeting at supper time.

Abigail's expression sobered. She wiped her hands on her apron, then weaved her arm under Katie's as they walked together into the dining room.

Isaac pulled his hat off the hook. "Seth, I hope we can visit another time."

"*Jah*, for sure."

Isaac glanced at Abigail. "I don't know how long I'll be."

She nodded. "I'll say a prayer for Bishop Lapp."

"Me too," Katie managed to squeak past her burning throat.

Isaac disappeared behind the closed door.

Seth stood. "I should get going home." He looked at Abigail. "*Denki* for supper."

"We're glad you could *kumm*." She sniffled and wiped the corner of her eyes with her dress sleeve. "You drive by Katie's *haus*, don't you?"

Seth glanced at Katie. "Do you need a ride?"

Katie shook her head. "*Nay.*" She eyed Abigail. "*Nay*, I don't."

"I was hoping you would follow her and make sure she gets home safely."

"I don't need—"

"*Jah*, I'd be happy to see her home." He motioned to the door. "I'll get the buggies ready."

Katie pulled into her driveway, stopped the buggy next to the barn, and climbed out. Seth entered the driveway and parked beside her.

"I'll take care of your horse." He climbed off the buggy bench.

"*Denki*, but I can manage." Her fingers fumbled over the harness buckle. "I don't want to keep you. It's late." But it wasn't that late. Maybe half past eight. And it wasn't like she had a classroom of children to teach in the morning. Still, she needed time to process the evening. Toward the end, she had relaxed a little and even found sparring with Seth somewhat enjoyable.

He stood beside her. "Let me finish. Please."

Katie eyed him a moment. Something shifted inside her, sending a jolt of heat through her. She released the harness and stood back.

He slid the harness off the horse, draped it over his shoulder, and took hold of the mare's halter. "Should I release her into the pasture or do you want her in a stall?"

"The stall. I haven't fed her yet." Katie led the way and pushed opened the barn door.

He walked Peaches into the barn and stopped.

The darkness didn't disorient Katie, but it was awkward to be with a man alone and not have a lantern lit. She squeezed between him and the wall. "Over here to the left." She made her way to the stall and unlatched the gate. "Peaches can find the way. You can let her go."

"Keep talking, I'll find you."

"Um." It wasn't like her to be short on words. She scrambled to say something that didn't sound like babble. "*Mei* favorite hymn from the *Ausbund*? '*Loblied.*' *Mei* favorite color? *Bloh*. Um . . ."

He stopped short of the entrance. "Is that why you kept staring into *mei* eyes? Because they're *bloh*?"

For someone who wasn't sure which way to go in the dark, he certainly seemed to have little trouble finding her. He'd stopped close enough to her that his warm breath caressed her face.

"Yours are an . . . an unusual shade." The brightest blue she'd ever seen. She backed into the wall. "But I don't think I was staring."

"You don't think so? Hm. I suppose I could've been wrong." He continued into the stall.

Katie's jaw dropped. He seemed quite amused by his observation. At least with the barn dark, he couldn't see how his flirting affected her. Heat engulfed her cheeks like embers igniting bark.

"Do you have a lantern? I'd like to take a look at how Peaches's wounds are healing."

"*Jah*, there should be one on the post. I'll get it."

Katie rarely used a lantern. During the day, the paddock windows allowed enough light to enter. Besides, she kept the feed bucket and grain barrel in the exact spot her father had for close to thirty years, so on the rare occasion she was out here after sundown, she knew her way around the barn in the dark. At least she thought she did. That is until she stumbled over something on the floor and caught the rough-hewn post before falling.

"You okay?"

"*Jah.*" Embarrassed and probably bruised, but okay. She patted the beam, found the nail, but the lantern was missing. "Either one of *mei* nephews or Isaac moved the lamp when they were in here last." She headed for the door. "I'll get the one from *mei* buggy."

"That isn't necessary," he said.

But a moment of fresh air and time to regain her composure were necessary. She hurried out of the barn, drew a deep breath, and trekked to the back of her buggy. Once she lit the lamp's wick, she headed back into the barn.

A shadow shifted and Katie gasped. She aimed the lamp to the right side.

"What's wrong?"

"I thought I saw a shadow."

Seth chuckled. "You weren't afraid when it was dark, but *nau* that you have a light you're jumpy."

"*Jah.* Silly, isn't it?" She glanced off to the right again, then continued to the stall and handed Seth the lantern.

"*Denki.*"

While he inspected the healing wounds, she went to the grain barrel and filled an old coffee can with oats. Katie paused at the barrel, thinking she heard the rustling of hay above her in the mound.

"The cuts look healed," Seth said.

"That's *gut* news." She carried the tin filled with grain back to the stall and dumped the oats into Peaches's feed bucket.

"I suppose I should be going." He reached over the half wall and unlatched the door. Then he slipped through the gate and handed her the lantern.

Katie led the way out of the barn. "*Denki* for seeing me home," she said, pausing near his buggy.

"*Mei* pleasure." He motioned to the house. "I'll walk you to your door."

"That isn't—"

He placed his hand on her back and gave her a nudge. "I insist."

A tingle sped along her spine. Afraid any reply she made would come out garbled, she kept her mouth closed and headed to the house.

"The *haus* is dark. Do you live here alone?"

"*Jah.*" She climbed the porch and stopped at the door. "When *mei* parents passed away, they left me the *haus* and gave *mei bruder* the barn and land." She withheld mentioning that her mother feared Katie would never have a husband's support, and if she remained single, a *teetshah's* pay wasn't enough to afford a house.

Looking around the porch, he squinted at the roof, then reached for the lantern handle. "Can I use this?"

"*Jah.*"

He lifted it over his head and stared at the porch ceiling. "Is that a limb?"

"*Jah.* During the storm a limb broke off and punched a hole through the porch roof." She shrugged. "Isaac's been tied up with everyone's storm damage, so I didn't want to bother him with this. Besides, it's only the porch and that shouldn't be too hard to fix. I can do it myself."

He chuckled.

"You don't think I can?" She narrowed her eyes. "I fixed a leak under the sink. I ended up changing out the complete drain."

"You replaced the P-trap?"

"Did that too." She peered up at the roof and nodded. "I could do it."

"I'm sure you can do anything you set your mind on." He twisted the knob and opened the door. "You better go inside before you get the fool notion to do those repairs tonight."

She laughed.

Seth handed her the lantern. *"Guder nacht."*

"Guder nacht." She closed the door, then pulled the curtain back to look out the window. The moonlight fell on his shoulders as he walked to his buggy. She waited until he was down the drive before she pulled away from the window.

Katie moved the lantern to the counter and froze. Staring at the light dusting of crumbs on the counter, a shudder coursed its way to her core. There weren't any bread crumbs there when she left to have supper at Isaac's. Someone had been inside her house.

Katie grabbed the lantern and fled the house. Now she was certain she'd seen a moving shadow in the barn. She wondered what it was that she'd tripped over. That should've clued her then that things were wrong. She never left anything out to stumble over. Katie barged into the barn. She heard a soft gasp and she lifted the lantern higher.

Chapter Fifteen

K atie's stomach knotted. She was sure she'd heard something—someone—but now the only sound was the rhythmic drumming of her heart. She clutched the lantern handle tighter and extended her trembling hand above her head. Even with a wider perimeter of light, she fought to focus her sight beyond the hay mound.

"Is someone there?" Her voice shook. She waited a moment, then took a few steps toward the door and stopped. The alternative, going back inside a dark house, frightened her more.

"Do not fear," Elias whispered. "You are not alone. I am here at your side." Still, she continued toward the door. "Don't leave just yet." When she didn't heed the stirring of her conscience, Elias mimicked the sound of her horse's neigh to draw her attention.

Rational thoughts paralyzed, she was torn between what the safest plan of action was: locking the barn or running back and barricading herself in the house.

Peaches neighed again. This time the mare stomped her hoof on the straw floor.

Katie had her answer. She would hitch Peaches and drive back to Isaac's house. She marched to the stall, swung the gate open, and froze midstep.

Huddled in the corner, Leah Mast sat trembling.

Katie blew out a breath of relief. "Leah! You frightened me half to death. What are you doing here?"

The girl slowly turned to face Katie. "Is *Onkel* Seth still here?" Leah's voice cracked and she buried her face in her hands.

"*Nay*, he's gone. What's wrong?"

Leah stood. With her head bowed and her eyes avoiding Katie, Leah wiped the straw from her dress.

"What do you say we get out of this cold, dark barn and go inside where we can talk?"

Leah hesitated a moment, then shuffled out of the stall.

Katie placed her arm around Leah's shoulder. "Are you hungry? How about I make you something to eat and then I'll drive you home."

Leah moved back from Katie's embrace and shook her head. "*Nay. Nay*, I'm *nett* going back."

The warm evening breeze rushed against Seth's face on his ride home. His hands were still clammy as he gripped the reins. He hadn't felt this exhilarated since his youth. Sage's hooves clopped rhythmically against the pavement, and Seth couldn't stop thinking about Katie. She'd peered into his soul and understood his boredom with the beehive trade. They didn't even know each other, but she sensed a deeper reason. Unlike his fiancée, Diana. He spotted her disappointment long before she admitted she wanted to marry a master builder and not someone who just built beehives.

Seth cringed, recalling Diana's acceptance when he postponed their wedding. She agreed he needed more time, even said they would marry after he resumed the role as the district's master builder. In other words, when he came to his senses. It would never happen—his lack of good sense was what caused the tragedy to begin with.

As he turned into Amos's driveway, his thoughts drifted back to Katie. She was certainly unique. Definitely the most independent woman he'd ever known. After parking the buggy, he removed the tack, released Sage to the pasture, and headed toward the dark house.

Had there been a light on in Amos's room when he passed by it, he would've stopped to check on his brother-in-law. But there wasn't. Just as well—his thoughts were stalled on Katie. What woman, besides her, would think she could climb a ladder and repair her own roof? He slipped his suspenders over his shoulders, then unfastened the eye hooks on his shirt. Maybe tomorrow he could finish work early and surprise her by fixing the porch. Easing his head onto the feathered pillow, he smiled. *Jah*, no woman needed to repair a roof.

Early the next morning Seth shoved his feet into his boots and grabbed his hat on the hook next to the door. He trekked to the barn, hoping Amos would send him away. If he worked with the building crew, there was a chance he would see Katie when the women delivered the noon meal.

Swinging the door open, Seth startled Alend. The growling dog charged, showing his teeth.

"Down!" Seth stood still until the dog obeyed. The dog's name, a *Deitsch* word for "trouble," seemed appropriate. "That's the first time he's done that," Seth said to Thomas, who was milking the cow.

"He's acted weird since *Daed* fell off the ladder," his nephew said.

"Where is your *daed?*" He glanced toward the grain bin, then up at the hayloft.

"He sent us out to start the chores. He said he's stiff and having a hard time moving around this morning."

Paul poked his head around the wall that divided the milking area from the calf pens. "I heard him up during the *nacht*. When I went out to see what the noise was, I noticed the kitchen chair lying on its side. He told me to go back to bed. But I could tell he wasn't feeling very *gut*. He was holding his head."

Seth jammed the old coffee can into the grain bin. "I'll be back to help you boys in a few minutes. I'm going to check on your *daed*." He set the feed bucket down next to the barrel of oats and headed to the house. He wished now he had checked on Amos last night.

Seth entered the house and looked in the kitchen. Empty. Even his nieces were not up yet, and that was unusual. He checked the sitting room and, not seeing anyone, walked down the hall toward the bedrooms. He knocked on Amos's door and waited.

"Go away."

"It's Seth. Is everything all right?"

"I'm fine."

His snappy tone indicated the opposite. The man wasn't fine. Seth waited a moment before asking, "Can I get you anything?"

"What's going on with Leah? Why isn't she cooking breakfast?"

He supposed Amos's being hungry was a good sign.

"I haven't seen her yet. Should I wake her?"

"She can't sleep the day away."

Amos's voice rose, and Seth figured it wasn't helping to talk through the closed door. When Amos was ready to come out, he would.

"I'll let you know when it's time to eat," Seth said. He passed the boys' room and stopped in front of Leah's bedroom and knocked on the door.

"Leah?"

No answer.

He knocked again. Still no answer. Seth paused for a moment, then twisted the knob and eased the door open. "Leah, are you awake?" When no response came, he stepped into the room.

The bed was empty and on her pillow lay a sheet of paper. Seth picked up the note. Although the wording was brief, he still stumbled over the handwriting.

> Dear *Daed*,
>
> I hope you will forgive me for starting my *rumschpringe* a few weeks early. I hope someday you will understand why I had to go. Please tell Thomas, Paul, and Annie I will miss them.
>
> > > Love, Leah

Rumschpringe now? Seth stared at the note in disbelief. This family was falling apart. If his sister were still alive, she'd be heartbroken to think one of her children left home on their *rumschpringe*. Sure, part of their custom was to allow every youth to make their own choice of continuing in the faith or going their own way in the world. But the vast majority of the youth, at least while he was growing up, spent their *rumschpringe* at home attending get-togethers and singings.

What had happened to Leah to pull her into the world?

This wasn't something he wanted to tell Amos. The man would be beside himself with worry, as any parent would. But someone had to inform him of his daughter's absence. He plodded toward Amos's room, praying with each step.

"God, help me find the words. I pray you will continue to watch over Leah. Please don't let her stray too far from the fold."

Seth paused to draw a breath, then knocked on Amos's door.

"What *nau?*" Amos shouted.

He didn't know an easier way of breaking the news, so he just blurted out the information. "Leah's gone. She left you a note."

"What do you mean, gone?"

There was a loud thud behind the door and Amos grunted.

"Are you okay?" Seth placed his hand on the knob when Amos didn't reply immediately. Either Amos had fallen or something heavy had hit the floor.

"Amos?" Seth leaned closer to the door.

Now it sounded as if Amos was patting the door in search of something.

The door jerked open.

"What did she say?" Amos held on to the doorknob with one hand and the wooden door frame with his other.

Seth tried to hand him the note, but Amos refused to take it. "Don't you want it?"

"Read it for me, will you?"

Seth cleared his throat. Normally he refused to read aloud, but Amos wouldn't understand his inability to unscramble the words on a page. Besides, it wasn't a long note and he had read it once to himself. He unfolded the paper and read each word.

Amos sighed. "She didn't say where she was going?"

Seth shook his head. They both knew the odds. When a youth left the house, most likely they had left the faith.

Amos covered his hands over his eyes and swayed.

"Are you okay?"

"*Jah.*" He leaned against the door frame.

It was only too clear he wasn't okay. "I'll take you to the *dokta.*"

"*Nay.*" He slammed the door in Seth's face.

Seth shook his head. He'd meant to deliver the beehives and leave. How had everything gotten so complicated?

Katie paced the kitchen floor. She'd been awake for hours, unable to calm her nerves. Prompted several times during the night to pray, she did so in obedience. Still, her spirit was restless. Only, now, God seemed nowhere near.

She walked to the window. The sun was making its appearance. She'd hoped for some sort of resolution by this time. Mentally, she reviewed those she'd prayed for during the night. Bishop Lapp was first. Leah, of course, consumed a lot of her effort. It wasn't long after praying for Leah that Katie was reminded of the same scripture in Matthew that had impelled her before.

Katie moved away from the window and sat at the table in front of her Bible. The book already opened to the fifth chapter in Matthew, she read it again. "But I say to you, love your enemies, bless those who curse you, do good to those who hate you, and pray for those who spitefully use you and persecute you."

She closed her eyes—tried to concentrate—tried to meditate on the words of the verse.

Amos came to mind.

He certainly needed God to intervene in his life. According to Leah, her father had practically disowned her. The man's heart must have turned to stone to drive a child away. How could he be that cold?

"You are not meditating on the Living Truth. You're allowing your flesh to lead you, child," Elias said. But Leah entered the room before he could gain Katie's attention.

Startled by a noise behind her, Katie clutched her Bible.

"I'm sorry," Leah said, walking farther into the kitchen. "Did I frighten you?"

Katie released her grip and hand-ironed the pages she'd crinkled. "I guess I'm *nett* used to having anyone in my *haus*." She wasn't used to having voices in her head all night, prompting her to pray, either.

"I think we need to talk." Katie motioned Leah to the table. "Have a seat. I'll make us a cup of tea. The water should still be hot." She needed a moment to compose her thoughts. Amos needed to know about his daughter, but she wasn't sure how to convince Leah. Hopefully the girl would see more clearly now that she'd had some sleep.

Katie dipped the tea bag in the cups of hot water a few times, then carried them to the table.

Leah sat with her hands folded on the table, her head bowed. *Gut*, the girl was praying. Katie waited until Leah lifted her head before setting the cups on the table.

"So what happened at home?" Katie blurted.

Leah stared into her cup, her lips quivering. "I'll be seventeen in a few weeks."

"I know." In Katie's first year of teaching, Leah was in eighth grade and a bright student, always willing to help the other children with their lessons.

"This is *mei rumschpringe.*"

"She is hurting," Elias said. "Look beyond her words and see her heart." He moved closer to Katie. "Ask for wisdom, for God will freely direct your steps."

"I think there's something more," Katie said softly.

Leah's eyes brimmed with tears. "Things haven't been the same since *Mamm* passed away. *Daed* is so . . . angry." She used the back of her hand to swipe the tears from her eyes. "He's angry with the settlement, with God, and he's angry with me. I had to leave." Leah's shoulders shook as she sobbed. "I couldn't stay there any longer."

Katie pondered Leah's words and held her immediate response. She, too, had seen the change in Amos since Erma died. He'd fed his bitterness and now it grew like a stubborn weed. If his sin hadn't already, it would soon choke his life—his children's too.

Leah continued, "He only wants me around to take care of the *haus* and look after Annie and the boys. That's all he cares about."

"That isn't so." Katie reached across the table and grasped Leah's hand. "He loves you. You're his daughter."

Leah cried harder.

"I'll drive you home, and if you would like, I'll talk with him."

"Nay!" She shook her head hard. *"Nay.* I won't go back. I wouldn't be *wilkom.*"

"He wouldn't—"

"You don't know him."

True. It seemed lately everything she learned about Amos, she didn't like.

"This is *mei rumschpringe*. Others *mei* age leave the community to live in the world." Leah tapped her chest. "I want to live in the settlement. I want to be a part of the church body. If I return home, *Daed* will forbid me to fellowship."

Erma would be proud that her daughter wasn't fleeing the faith but had chosen to embrace it. Still, Katie wasn't sure how Amos would handle his daughter staying with her. He despised her. Surely Leah knew that.

Without any prompting, Leah continued, "I don't think *Daed* prays. I haven't seen him read the Scriptures since he left the church." She sucked in a ragged breath. "He's changed so much."

Katie's throat tightened. The child had gone through so much with her mother dying and now was caught in the middle of her father's spiritual battle.

"You're *wilkom* to stay here, but I need to ask you something."

Leah lifted her head. "Anything."

"You must know how your father feels about me. Why did you *kumm* here?"

Leah's face whitened and she dropped her gaze to the table. "I knew this would be the last place he would look."

Katie drew a deep breath. "He needs to know where you are."

"He doesn't care. Promise me you won't tell him."

"I can't make that promise." She couldn't knowingly hide someone's child.

Leah's eyes bored into hers. "I just need some time away. Time to think. Besides, even if you brought up my name, he wouldn't care."

"I have to talk with him."

"But what if he refuses? Will you promise me not to tell him where I am unless he asks?"

Katie couldn't imagine a father not asking about his daughter.

"Will you promise me that much? If *nett*, I'll just run away again."

Katie sighed. "*Jah*, I promise. But if he asks, I'm telling him."

Elias extended his wings, spreading his radiance throughout the room in the form of the morning's golden glow.

"Katie, this child is here for a purpose. She needs your guidance. Why else would God have directed her into your path? Remember when I called you to pray? Amos still needs your prayers."

༉

Seth only knew how to cook eggs one way. Scrambled. He added a splash of milk to the mixing bowl and whisked the eggs with a fork.

Annie stood on her tiptoes and craned her neck. "What's that?"

"Eggs." He dumped the mixture into a heated skillet, then sprinkled it with salt and pepper.

"Can I help?" She pulled a chair out from the table.

Seth needed help, but having a four-year-old by the stove was never a good idea. "You can put the butter on the table." He grabbed the butter bowl from the counter and handed it to his niece.

Annie scrunched her nose. "Where's Leah?"

"I'm *nett* sure." He wasn't sure how much to say either. He wished Amos would come out to the kitchen so he could answer the questions. Once the boys finished the chores and came inside to eat, they would wonder about Leah too.

"Isn't Leah hungry?"

With her so persistent, he needed to distract her somehow. He grabbed the salt and pepper shakers and handed them to his niece. "It would be a big help if you would put these on the table."

The puffy eggs' edges turned brown. He slid the spatula under the eggs and scraped the bottom of the pan, then gave them another minute to cook. Thomas and Paul entered the kitchen as Seth unloaded the eggs from the pan onto one of the plates.

"Just in time. Wash your hands."

The boys scurried over to the sink while Annie climbed up on the kitchen chair.

"Where's Leah?" Thomas wiped his hands on the dish towel and pulled a chair out from the table.

Seth glanced at Annie, who blinked a few times and puckered her bottom lip. "Let's pray so we can eat," he said, hoping the boys would see how upset Annie had become and not ask any more questions. Calming a crying child wasn't something that came naturally to him, and by the looks of it, Seth would be the one having to do just that if Amos didn't come out of his room.

He slipped some eggs onto a plate and buttered two pieces of bread. "Here, take this to your *daed*." He handed the plate to Paul, who had just finished drying his hands on the dish towel.

Paul wasn't gone long before he returned to the kitchen, the untouched plate in his hands. "He's *nett* hungry."

"Sit down and eat," Seth said, motioning to the empty chair. "We can save him something to eat later."

He waited for everyone to take their places at the table, then bowed his head. In his silent prayer, he asked God to watch over Leah and keep her safe, heal Amos, and give himself guidance.

He said *aemen*, lifted his head, and then, realizing he hadn't said grace for the food, closed his eyes once again and added the part about blessing the meal.

Seth glanced across the table at his niece. She jammed a forkful of eggs into her mouth, then looked at him and smiled.

The boys practically inhaled their breakfast. Apparently his cooking wasn't too bad.

With Leah gone, someone needed to care for Annie. Certainly this wasn't something he could do. Even if he didn't work with the building crew, he could list several things he needed to work on, and none of them involved child care.

Annie looked up from her plate, pieces of egg on her face. Her broad smile was hard to resist.

Thomas and Paul cleaned their plates, then shot up from their chairs and headed for the door.

"Where are you two going?" Seth wasn't sure he wanted sole responsibility for Annie should Amos decide to stay in his room.

"*Daed* wanted us to clean the stalls."

Seth nodded.

Annie scooted away from the table, her plate clean. She trotted down the hall toward the bedrooms.

Seth stared at the dirty dishes on the table. He still had beehive boxes to set up, and it looked as though he was stuck in the kitchen. He gathered the dishes and walked them to the sink. He had his hands immersed in sudsy water when Annie padded back into the kitchen.

"Will you fix this?"

He glanced over his shoulder. The child held up her prayer *kapp*. "Leah always fixes *mei* hair." Her lower lip trembled.

Seth shook the suds from his hands and dried them on a towel. What did he know about taking care of a child?

Chapter Sixteen

S eth hadn't managed to get anything done and it was already after noon. Annie had kept him busy all morning answering silly questions, and he hadn't seen the boys since breakfast. The longer Amos stayed closed up in his room, the more frustrated Seth became.

Alend barked nonstop when a buggy pulled into the yard. Seth craned his neck to look out the window but was unable to get a good view. He headed for the door, but Amos surprised him in the hallway.

"Who is it?" Amos ambled down the hallway. His hand spread against the wall, he looked to be leaning against it for balance. His gait looked askew. His socked feet glided and didn't leave the wood floor.

"Are you okay?" He took a step toward Amos.

The dog continued to bark.

"What's wrong with that dog? Find out who just arrived."

Seth circled back to the door. He couldn't imagine the dog would create such a ruckus if it were Leah, but he whispered a prayer anyway. He pushed the screen door open and bounded down the steps.

It wasn't Leah. He recognized the horse—Peaches.

"Alend, *kumm*," Thomas called.

Katie remained in her buggy until Thomas had the dog by the collar. "Hello, Thomas." Her smile never faltered, even when Thomas ignored her. "I'm looking for your *daed*. Is he home?"

"He's in the *haus*." Thomas jerked the dog's collar and led him toward the barn.

Seth wasn't at all pleased with his nephew's rudeness. He made a mental note to have a word with the boy.

"Sorry about that," Seth said, jogging up to her.

She lifted one shoulder into a shrug. "*Teetshahs* are *nett* always the most *wilkomed* guests." She glanced at the barn. "*Nett* that Thomas is still one of *mei* students." She faced Seth and smiled. "I didn't expect you to be here. I figured you were working with the men."

The comment caught him off guard. Why had he thought she wanted to see him? Standing beside her, an odd sensation crept over him. Was she so bold that she planned to approach Amos again about moving the bees? The woman was relentless. No way was she going to convince him to talk with Amos about that subject. In fact, Seth decided, he would be the one to steer this conversation.

"Any word about how your bishop is doing?" he asked.

Her eyes dulled. "I haven't heard anything. But after I talk with Amos, I plan to check on him," she said, moving past him.

"*Nay.*" He reached for her arm and stopped her. "I mean . . ."

She looked at his hand clutching her forearm, then quirked her brows, staring up at him.

Seth released her arm. "He's . . . *nett* in the best mood." That was the truth. Amos wasn't in a mood to see anyone.

"Is he ever?" She continued on her way.

He followed her across the drive and up the steps but cut her off at the door. "Really, you don't want to speak with him *nau.*"

"*Jah,*" she said with a short nod. "I must." She reached around him for the handle on the screen door.

He caught hold of her hand and didn't release it. "Katie, this isn't the time to talk about those bees." Even using a firm tone didn't seem to faze the headstrong woman.

"What's the commotion?" Amos yelled from inside. "Is someone here or *nett?*"

Seth stared hard at Katie. She didn't budge.

He opened the screen door. "You're on your own in there. I'm *nett* talking with him about the bees," he said sharply.

"I'm a big girl," Katie told Seth. She was well aware of Amos's personality issues and she didn't need Seth trying to smooth things over. Besides, she had no plans to talk about where he kept his beehives. This was about Leah.

She headed inside and craned her neck to look in the sitting room. Not finding Amos, she moved toward the kitchen.

"Leah?" Amos called.

She planted a smile and forced a chipper tone. "*Nay,* it's Katie Bender." She rounded the corner of the kitchen and found him seated at the table, his back facing her.

His shoulders sagged, and he muttered something undetectable under his breath.

She stood before one of the side chairs and waited, thinking he would invite her to sit down. When he didn't, she cleared her throat. "I was hoping we could talk."

The late afternoon's sunlight spilled into the room and highlighted Amos's sober expression.

"About what?"

She tapped the back of the wooden chair, but he didn't invite her to sit.

His blank stare aimed straight ahead and never veered her direction.

She pulled the chair away from the table. "Do you mind if I sit down?" Perhaps Seth was right about this not being the right time to talk with Amos. Still, she had to let him know his daughter wasn't in danger.

Katie sat. She folded her hands together and placed them on her lap. Inwardly she trembled. But so far he hadn't seemed to notice.

A brief period of silence passed before he barked, "What do you want?"

She stiffened. He was even crabbier than the last time she had attempted a conversation with him. "I want to talk to you about Leah."

"I won't discuss her with you." His tone hadn't changed, nor had the direction of his gaze.

"Well, you don't seem very worried." She waited for some type of response—even a blink. But the coldhearted man continued to stare into space. Leah was right. Amos had shut the girl out of his life. There had to be something more. "Do you even know where your daughter is?" She suspected he didn't but had hoped the question would stir his curiosity.

Amos pounded his fist on the table. "Get out of *mei haus*."

Katie stood. "Apparently this isn't a *gut* time." Maybe in time he would be worried enough to want to hear about his daughter.

She took a few steps toward the entrance before a loud commotion behind her caused her to spin around and reface Amos.

His chair lay sprawled on the floor and he flailed, fighting to maintain his balance, his face a study in horror. He groped the air until he grasped the edge of the table. It steadied him, and he grew calmer. Even then he nearly stumbled over the fallen chair.

"Are you okay?" She rushed to his side and reached for his elbow.

He jerked his elbow away. "Leave me be. I don't need any help." He continued to clutch the edge of the table.

"Are you sure?"

His glare spoke for him. With one hand still holding the table, he bent down, righted the chair on all four legs, then patted the wooden seat before he sat.

Katie backed out of the room on her tiptoes. The screen door creaked as she pushed it open, and when her foot hit the porch landing, she stumbled over Seth in the doorway.

He reached out and steadied her, then immediately dropped his hands from her arms.

"I didn't see you." She clutched her pounding chest and took a few calming breaths.

"I gathered that." He smirked and leaned toward her. "I told you he wasn't in a *gut* mood."

She narrowed her eyes. "You could've warned me. How long has he been blind?"

"Blind?" Seth pulled back, a growing scowl on his face. "What are you talking about?"

"You didn't know?" She cocked her head sideways.

"He must have been ignoring you."

"He tripped over a chair."

Seth turned her away from the door and guided her by the

elbow over to the porch banister. Leaning close, he whispered, "What did you say to him?"

She squared her shoulders. "I didn't upset him, if that's what you're asking." She didn't think she had. Okay, she had, but not any more than usual. "*Nett* purposefully anyway."

He trained his eye on her. "So you really think he's blind?"

She nodded. "Something is wrong."

Seth slid his hat off his head, pushed his damp hair away from his forehead, then shoved the straw hat back in place. He placed his hand on the door handle. "Let's both go inside."

Everything within her screamed, *Run!* but a gentle inner prompting urged her to go. "O-Okay." She wrung her hands, clasped them together, then wrung them some more. At this rate, her hands would be raw before she could settle her nerves.

He lifted a finger and pressed it over his closed lips, then motioned for her to follow.

"I noticed Katie Bender's buggy outside," Seth said, entering the kitchen.

She wasn't sure why Seth wanted to include her. He knew as well as she that Amos wouldn't speak to her. But she stood silent at the kitchen entrance.

"Did she say what she wanted?" Seth went to the cupboard and grabbed a cup, then picked up the kettle from the wire cooling rack.

"She never gets to her point."

Katie slapped her hands on her hips, leaned forward with her mouth open to rebuke Amos, but caught a glimpse of Seth shaking his head at her. She clamped her mouth closed.

"How are you feeling? I haven't seen you since you fell off the ladder."

Amos fell off a ladder. Why hadn't Seth told her?

"I have a headache."

No doubt the man had a headache—he was blind.

"You should see a *dokta*. I'll get the buggy—"

"*Nay*. It'll pass."

"Do you want a cup of *kaffi*?" He picked up the cup and held it just outside Amos's reach. "Here you go."

Amos started to lift his hand but dropped it as quick on his lap. "Set it on the table. It needs to cool."

Katie turned. She wasn't going to talk with Amos today and there was no point in staying any longer. She quietly slipped outside and was down the porch steps when the screen door snapped and she looked over her shoulder.

"Wait," Seth said. "Don't leave. I need your help."

"To do what? Tell him what he already knows?" She folded her arms in front of her. "You might *nett* believe this, but I'm *nett* a cruel person. I feel sorry for Amos." She narrowed her eyes at him. "You poured him a cup of hot water. That wasn't *kaffi*."

He lowered his head and pushed some gravel with the toe of his boot. "I wanted to see for myself." He looked up. "I need your help."

She stared at him a moment. His eyes bored into hers. "There isn't anything I can do." She continued toward her buggy. "That man would never accept help from me."

"But I will."

He kept her pace, and when she reached for Peaches's reins to untie them, his hand stopped hers. "I want your help."

Her heart sputtered with a few extra beats when he gave her hand a gentle squeeze.

"Please. Someone's got to care for Annie—and—and I don't even know how it is you women fasten that prayer *kapp* in place."

A vision flashed before her of Seth trying to shove Annie's tangled hair up under the head covering. She suppressed a smile. Under the circumstances, none of this was funny.

"I guess I should explain. Leah's gone. She left a note."

She opened her mouth to tell him what she knew, but he continued rambling, barely taking a breath between sentences.

"I can't take care of three children. I don't cook. I know, as old as I am and the fact that I'm *nett* married and have never been married, I probably should be able to prepare something more than an egg. But I can't. I don't do laundry. I mean, I can, and have, but——" He tipped his thumb over his shoulder to the smaller of the two barns. "I need to repair that calving barn before Amos decides to give it another try."

Katie waited until he drew a breath, but before she could get a word in, he started again.

"I should've been helping Amos instead of getting those boards at the *schul* ready to reuse at the Planks' place. That's what I should've been doing. I told Amos I would help him."

"Okay," she said.

"Amos has a sister in Ohio, but even if she could *kumm*, it wouldn't be right away. What a mess. This is all *mei* fault. I should've been here." He stopped and looked at her. "Okay? You said okay? You'll help me with Annie?"

She nodded. "*Jah.*"

He sighed, and the lines in his forehead as well as the tension creases around his eyes relaxed. "Really?"

"*Jah.*" She smiled.

"*Denki.*" He blew out another breath. A pink shade spread over his face and he sheepishly grinned. "I guess I rambled on a little, ain't so?"

"On and on." She huffed jokingly and rolled her eyes. "And you men complain about how much women talk." She chuckled.

For an unguarded moment, he laughed with her. Then his expression sobered and he looked toward the house. "*Nau* we just need to tell Amos."

Chapter Seventeen

"What did *mei daed* say?"

For a girl who had run away from home, Leah seemed unexpectedly anxious to hear news of her family. She practically pounced on Katie the moment she entered the house.

"Let's go into the kitchen where we can talk." Katie shucked her cape and hung it on the wall hook. She'd prayed on her way home from Amos's house about how to break the news to Leah.

"He didn't even ask about me, did he?"

Katie wrapped her arm around Leah's waist and gave her a reassuring hug. "Let's make a cup of tea." She motioned to the kitchen while silently whispering a prayer for wisdom. Once in the room, Katie filled the kettle with water and prepared the cups.

Leah slumped into a chair at the table. She traced the wood

grain knot on the table's surface with her finger. "I told you he wouldn't care." She shifted in the chair, facing Katie's direction at the counter. "You kept your promise and didn't tell him I'm staying with you, right?"

Katie nodded. Not because she hadn't tried. Leah was right; her father had closed off his heart to her. She would pray for the right opportunity and trust God to open the door of communication. In the meantime, Leah needed love and support.

She touched the cast-iron kettle with her fingertips. Still not hot enough for tea. Katie looked at Leah. "Something's happened . . . an accident."

"Is Annie all right? What about the boys?" Leah lifted her hand to cover her mouth. Her eyes filled with tears.

"The children are fine," she reassured her. "But your father isn't . . ."

"What do you mean?"

She didn't know how else to tell the girl other than to be straightforward. "He's blind, Leah."

Leah shook her head. *"Nay. Nay,"* she repeated a bit stronger. She blinked, releasing a string of tears.

Katie's throat tightened. With the exception of Annie, who probably hadn't fully comprehended the news, Leah responded with the same disbelief as the boys did when Seth told them.

"Apparently he fell off a ladder. The boys seem to think he was struck in the head by a board that had *kumm* loose."

Leah's shoulders shook as she sobbed. "It's *mei* fault."

"Nay, honey." Katie drew her into an embrace as she searched for comforting words to calm the girl. "It was *nett* your fault." After a few moments, when Leah had collected herself, Katie pulled her back to arm's length. "He fell off the ladder. It was an accident."

Leah hung her head low and her shoulders sagged. She backed

away from Katie, slumped into a chair, and buried her face in her hands.

Wanting to give her a few minutes of privacy, Katie grabbed the kettle from the stove and concentrated on preparing their tea. Her mother used to say that a cup of tea would help ease the blues. At the time, Katie wasn't so sure the tea had anything to do with making her feel better, but now any memory of her mother offered some form of comfort. Katie didn't have her *mamm's* experience with soothing painful situations. Even *Mamm* used to say everyone's heartache was different.

Katie grabbed the jar of cookies, stacked a few on a plate, and placed them on the table. When the water was heated, she filled two cups, then sank a tea bag into each one, dunking it up and down as it steeped.

"*Mei mamm* used to say a cup of tea could soothe one's soul." She set a cup of steeped black tea in front of Leah. "Of course, I didn't always believe that myself growing up."

Leah stared at her cup while circling her fingertip around the rim. "*Mei mamm's* cinnamon rolls usually worked for all of us. Even *Onkel* Seth said while he was growing up, before *Mamm* got married and moved to this district with *Daed*, she used to make him rolls too." She grimaced. "Sometimes I fear I'll forget everything about her."

Katie's eyes welled. "I had those same thoughts about *mei mamm*."

Leah cleared her throat. "I barely remember the sound of her voice."

Katie reached across the table and clasped Leah's hand. "You won't forget her. She will always be in your heart and a part of you. I never told you this, but when you laugh, you sound like your *mamm*."

"I do?"

"*Jah*, you do. Your voice is soft and sweet just like hers." Katie dabbed her eyes with the corner of her dress sleeve, remembering how she worried over the same issues when her mother passed away.

Tears rolled down Leah's cheeks and she swiped at them with the back of her hand.

Katie stood. "I'll be right back." She scooted into the bedroom, grabbed a couple of hankies from the top drawer of her dresser, and returned to the kitchen.

Katie handed one of the hankies to Leah and waited for her to blow her nose before speaking again. "Seth plans to take your *daed* to the *dokta* first thing in the morning. I told him I would watch Annie and the boys. Would you like to go with me?"

Leah shook her head. "It would only serve to provoke *mei* father. Besides, to him, I'm *nay* longer his daughter."

Her words struck Katie like a blow to the head with a rolling pin. Last night she thought Leah had overreacted.

"Perhaps you could try to mend things. He needs you."

"You don't know him like I do." Leah tucked a stray strand of hair back under her *kapp*. "I've disgraced him." She dotted her eyes with the cloth. "Right before he fell off the ladder, I was kissing Jacob Fischer. We were behind the barn . . . and Jacob asked me to run away with him."

Katie covered her hand over her mouth, stifling a gasp.

"*Nett* right away," Leah was quick to clarify. "Jacob thought if we moved to another state, we could join a district where no one knew us. They would assume we were married and we could be together." She bowed her head. "Silly, isn't it?"

She didn't need to remind the girl how public kissing, no matter the age, was frowned upon within the settlement. This was beyond even that. Katie bit her tongue until it throbbed.

"You planned to lie about such important matters? Marriage is a commitment before God. How do you think he would view your actions?"

Leah shrugged.

"You know that answer, Leah." Katie's harsh rebuke caused Leah to flinch.

"I know *nau*." Her eyes pooled with tears. "*Mei daed* must have heard us talking about it." She swiped the back of her hand over her wet face. "He yelled *mei* name as he fell."

Katie cringed.

"I didn't mean for my actions to cause harm."

"I believe you." Katie reached across the table for Leah's hand. "Please tell me you and Jacob are *nett* still planning to move away together."

Leah shook her head. "I haven't even told him I left home yet. I didn't want him to get into trouble. It was silly talk. Really, it was. All I want is to attend the youth frolics and church functions when I turn seventeen. That's what Jacob wants too, only . . . *Daed* already said I wouldn't be allowed."

"Maybe if you *kumm* with me tomorrow—"

"Please don't make me. It won't do any *gut*, especially *nett nau*." She straightened her shoulders. "If you make me go, I won't stay. I'll run away again."

As determined as Leah sounded, she would wander the countryside before she went back home. Katie refused to let her fall into that danger. "I won't make you go." She sipped her tea. *Lord, I need your wisdom.*

Elias unfurled his wings and soared in a sheet of light into the throne room of grace. There he laid the petitions of his charge at the King's feet. In a harmonic chanting of praise, Elias waited for his Master's reply.

A knock sounded at the door, and Katie and Leah exchanged startled glances.

"It's just me," Abigail called from the entry. "I thought I would have seen you at noon when I delivered sandwiches—" Abigail reached the kitchen and halted. "Hello, Leah."

Katie stood. "Have a seat and I'll make you a cup of tea."

"*Nay*, I can't stay." She glanced at Leah again but then continued, "I agreed to collect and deliver the housewares. Did you have things to donate?"

Katie nodded. "The boxes are in the spare bedroom." She glanced at Leah. No wonder the girl caught Abigail off guard. The girl's eyes were blotchy from crying. "I'll be right back, Leah."

Abigail sidled beside Katie. "That's Amos Mast's daughter."

Katie smiled. "*Jah*, I know."

Abigail tipped her head slightly sideways, then wagged her head as though disregarding any more thought on the subject.

Katie was grateful.

"I thought Seth enjoyed himself at supper." Abigail elbowed Katie's ribs. "Despite you hammering him about those bees."

"You think so? I couldn't tell." Katie pushed the spare room's door open. She hoped that if she acted uninterested, her sister-in-law would stop trying so hard to find her a husband.

"Isaac said *nett* to push things, but I'm going to have Seth over for another supper. I would've invited him today, but I didn't see him working with the men."

Katie picked up a box loaded with items to donate and handed it to Abigail. "You should listen to your wise husband and *nett* push things." She stooped down and grabbed the other box. "Besides, Seth isn't from our district."

"He can build beehives anywhere."

"Well, first he needs to move the ones near the *schul*." Katie headed out the door. She walked fast through the sitting room and hoped to get outside before Abigail continued. She didn't want Leah overhearing them talk about her uncle.

"You need to get it in your head the *schul* isn't going to be rebuilt. You have to move on," Abigail said once they were outside. She opened the back hatch of the buggy. "Get married. You're *nett* too old yet. You can have children."

Katie lowered the box onto the floorboard. Her sister-in-law wasn't about to stop. If she thought Katie wasn't interested in Seth, Abigail would fix her up with one of the other men who came to help with the rebuilding.

Abigail reached into the buggy. "You forgot to take the *Budget*," she said, handing the paper to Katie. "Your storm article was exceptional."

"*Denki,*" she said, cautious not to let the compliment go to her head. Not the way she allowed pride to overrule sound judgment when she wrote the articles about the angel sighting. She would rather change the subject than risk talking too much about writing. "Have you heard anything about the bishop?"

Abigail frowned. "I thought Isaac stopped by earlier and told you. Bishop Lapp had a stroke."

Katie gasped. "How is Mary taking it?"

Abigail shook her head. "*Nett* well. I plan to spend the next few days with her."

"Let me know if there's something I can do."

"Keep him in your prayers." Abigail crawled into the buggy. "*Jah*, I'll be sure to."

⁂

Seth wielded the ax, splitting the slab of wood in two. He'd purposely chopped more wood than what was needed for the cookstove so he could be outside when Katie arrived. Since telling Amos about arranging for Katie to help, Seth worried how Amos would treat her. He didn't want his brother-in-law's rude behavior to hurt her in any way.

He readied another log on the stump and swung the ax. She was certainly brave. He'd never known anyone like her. Amos might not ever admit it, but he needed Katie's help. They all did. She had a good heart and was good with children, even if she was somewhat meddlesome.

Seth had fumbled trying to get Annie's hair pulled up under her *kapp* again today. She cried, wanting to know why Leah wasn't home, and Seth found it impossible to reason with the child. About anything. He'd finally convinced her that God wouldn't be upset if she wore her hair down for the day when Thomas sat down at the table and pointed out his sister's shortcomings. Thomas had his little sister in tears in minutes. She refused to eat breakfast, and for a split second, Seth considered thumping his nephew over the head. Instead, he assigned him extra chores that should keep the boy busy in the barn most of the day. When Thomas opened his mouth, Seth threatened him with doing the breakfast dishes if he said one negative word. At least he had enough sense to keep his mouth shut.

Jah, they all needed Katie's help.

Seth finished splitting the last piece of wood as Katie pulled into the driveway. He leaned the ax against the side of the woodshed and met her at the hitching post.

Katie looped the reins through the metal ring. "Are you ready for this?"

Apparently she came prepared with a cheerful tone and sweet smile. If she felt the same uncertainty he'd struggled with during the night, she hid it well now. After she'd left yesterday, he wondered if he had asked too much of her. Asking her to care for Amos's children was like leading an innocent lamb into a lion's den. He cared more than he wanted to about her and worried he wouldn't always be able to protect her from Amos's comments.

"I'm *nett* sure this was a smart plan," he said.

She eyed him closely. "Have you changed your mind? Should I leave?"

"*Nay*. I mean, unless you want to. I wouldn't blame you. Dealing with Amos will be a challenge."

"I don't back down that easily."

He smiled. For once, he saw her strong-mindedness as a *gut* thing. "Then I think Amos has met his match."

"I'm *nett* sure I agree with that." She finished tying the reins, then reached into her buggy and removed a brown paper bag.

Seth raised his brows.

"Things to keep Annie busy."

He extended his hands and she released the bag into his arms. Surprised by the weight, he peeked inside the bag. "How many books do you have in here?"

"I brought some *schulwork* for the boys too."

"*Ach.*" Seth wasn't about to remind her that school was out for the summer, although he inwardly flinched at the idea. "Well, *teetshah*, I suppose you better meet your students then." He motioned toward the house and grinned when he saw her take in a deep breath.

"I won't let him give you a rough time," he said, bringing a smile to her face.

"He won't break me that easily." She squared her shoulders and tilted her chin.

He wished he had even a portion of her resolve. Instead,

dread blanketed him. He not only had to convince Amos to accept Katie's help, he had to persuade him to see the doctor. Both were impossible feats unless God intervened.

Lord, please soften Amos's heart. Protect Katie . . . He wished he could pray more elaborately, but God knew what was truly needed.

He opened the door and waited for Katie. When she hesitated, he reached for her hand. He hadn't expected the simple gesture of encouragement to shoot fire through his veins, but it did. When she gazed at him with those trusting eyes, he dropped his hand and shoved it into his pocket.

Her hand might naturally fit with his, but he needed to be mindful of his actions. But even as he tried to train his mind, his thoughts lingered on the soft texture of her skin.

"Who's there?" Amos craned his neck in their direction as they entered the sitting room.

Katie halted midstep.

Seth set the bag of school supplies on the floor and edged closer to Amos. "I need to talk with you." He looked over his shoulder. She hadn't moved forward. "I've asked Katie Bender to help with the children and she's agreed."

Amos shook his head. "*Nay!* I don't want that woman inside *mei haus.*"

Behind him the plank floor squeaked. *Katie.* Seth pivoted, took a long stride, and reached her before she tiptoed from the room.

"Don't leave," he whispered.

She lifted her somber gaze and met his stare. Neither spoke. The silence was broken by Alend barking. He sounded unusually vicious.

"Why is the dog upset?" Amos asked.

Seth moved toward the front window but didn't see anything out of the ordinary.

"If that's Katie, send her away."

"I won't do that." Seth glanced over his shoulder at Katie. "She's *mei* guest and I expect you to treat her nice. She's going to help. Annie especially needs a—" He almost said a *mamm*, but caught his words.

The dog's barking created such a ruckus Seth wasn't sure Amos had heard his near slip.

Amos grunted. "Can you see what's bothering Alend?"

"*Jah*, and after I do, I'm going to get the buggy ready to take you to the *dokta* so your eyes can get checked out." He didn't wait for Amos to refuse. Alend charged toward the back of the barn.

He smiled apologetically at Katie as he bolted from the house. He hated leaving her alone with Amos, but he needed to find out what had the dog worked up.

Chapter Eighteen

K atie thought if she stood still, she could keep the
floorboard from creaking and maybe Amos wouldn't
discover her in his sitting room.

She was wrong.

The moment Annie noticed Katie, the child's face lit and she
called, "Katie!" as she ran to her and wrapped her arms around
her legs in a hug.

The warm welcome was short-lived when Amos grunted.

"How long have you been in here?" he snapped.

Too long. She should've left the room when Seth had.

"Katie's going to take care of me," Annie said.

She reached for the child's hand. "If you need anything,
Amos, I'll be in the kitchen." She gave Annie's hand a slight tug,
then stooped down and picked up the bag of school supplies. "I
hope you like to color." She motioned toward the bagful of stuff.
"I brought lots of things for us to do."

"Really?" Annie didn't try to contain her high-pitched squeal.

Katie caught a glimpse of Amos's grumpy expression and hustled Annie out of the room, wishing she wouldn't have said anything until after they were in the kitchen.

This was more awkward than she'd expected. It didn't help that Seth ran out of the house to chase after the dog. She set the supply bag on the counter and walked over to the window. Seth wasn't anywhere within view and neither was the dog. But the barking had stopped and she supposed that was good news. She wrung her hands and sighed. Earlier when he tucked her hand into his, she thought she might melt like candle wax.

"Can I color a picture *nau?*"

Katie moved away from the window and over to the bag she'd brought.

Annie crawled up and sat on a chair.

Digging her hand into the bag, Katie pulled out a package of crayons and a thick tablet of paper. This should keep Annie busy and hopefully quiet. Katie wanted to keep the chatter to a minimum. Once she established some sort of order and created a workflow for the household chores, maybe then Amos would see her as a help rather than a thorn in his side.

Seth inched closer to the barn and the muffled sounds of someone greeting Alend, who had stopped barking. He had an idea of who might be sneaking around the barn, but if his suspicions were accurate, Leah's young suitor had some explaining to do.

Seth rounded the corner, and sure enough, Jacob Fischer was on the other side. Alend's ears perked and he wagged his tail. But Seth focused on the young man leaning against the barn and chewing a stem of wheat with his legs crossed at the ankles.

"Do you have a reason to loiter around the back of *mei* brother-in-law's barn?"

Jacob jerked upright, pulled the strand of wheat from his mouth, and tossed it on the ground.

"I asked you a question. What are you doing here?" Seth scanned the area. "Did Leah *kumm* with you?"

Jacob's brows furrowed. "What?"

"Where's Leah?" Seth folded his arms across his chest.

"I don't know." He shook his head. "Really, I don't know."

Seth eyed him. The kid shifted his weight from one foot to the other.

"Leah and I usually meet here twice a week." He dug his heel into the dirt. "I know it's wrong." He glanced up. "But she's going to be seventeen soon."

Seth nodded. "You told me. Four weeks two days."

"Three weeks four days," Jacob corrected.

"Young man, as a general rule, when a man is interested in a girl, he waits until there's a Sunday evening singing, and then he asks to drive her home." Seth didn't need to lecture him. All young men knew the custom—it didn't matter which district they lived in.

"I know." He lifted his eyes to meet Seth's. "I'm in love with Leah."

He'd gathered that much. Not many young men were willing to break the rules and risk chastisement.

Jacob held his gaze. "Once her father stopped attending services, I never got to see her. She wasn't allowed to go to any of the frolics, and even when she does turn seventeen, she said her father wouldn't allow her to attend any of the singings."

"So you sneak off together." Seth drew in a deep breath and exhaled slowly. "Did it ever cross your mind you might destroy her reputation?"

Jacob paced to the end of the barn and back. "I want to marry her and she wants to marry me. We've talked about it."

"Neither one of you are old enough."

Jacob made another pass, only this time he stopped when he reached the corner of the barn. He gazed toward the house a long moment, then turned. "Will you at least tell her that I came to see her?"

"She's gone."

Jacob's brows lifted. "What? Where is she?"

Seth shrugged. "I thought maybe you knew." He studied the boy's reaction. He seemed genuinely surprised. "Does she have any *Englisch* friends that she might be staying with?"

"*Nay*, none. I'll find out if any of her friends in the settlement know anything."

"*Denki.*" Seth blew out a breath. Jacob's offer to help eased some of his stress. If anyone could find her, it would be him. Seth would be able to focus on Amos and getting him into town to see a doctor.

"I'll start asking around *nau*," Jacob said, in a hurry to leave.

"And you'll let me know the minute you hear anything?"

"Of course," Jacob spoke over his shoulder.

Seth trekked to the fence and whistled, and the gelding trotted to the gate. Thomas met him as he tied Sage to the hitching post.

Thomas motioned to Katie's buggy. "She's here again?"

"Katie has offered to help." He eased the harness into place.

"*Daed* says the *teetshah* don't know her rightful place. He won't like that she's here."

"He'll *kumm* around to the idea." Seth fed the leather strap through the buckle.

"Is she going to make us do *schulwork*?"

"We'll see." Seth secured the girth strap. The boys, most likely, would volunteer to do more chores just to stay clear of the house—of the *teetshah*. He could relate. He wasn't fond of his teacher at his nephews' ages either. His teacher embarrassed him in front of the other students when he made simple spelling errors. He struggled through all eight grades, mocked by other classmates, to get his letters and numbers in the correct order. Something he still struggled with to this day.

He fed the reins through the terret and handed them to Thomas.

"Pull the buggy around. I'm going to get your *daed*." He plodded to the house, whispering a prayer that Amos wouldn't put up a fuss.

At the top of the porch steps, he kicked the mud from the bottom of his boots. Entering the house, he headed to the kitchen. He wanted to check on Katie before he approached Amos about going into town.

Annie sat quietly on the kitchen chair as Katie stood behind her, brushing the knots from her hair. He leaned against the counter and quietly watched. Katie set the brush on the table, then twisted the long, stringy hair into a tight bun. She glanced at him but, with her mouth loaded with pins to fasten the prayer *kapp* in place, couldn't say anything. Within a few seconds, she had effortlessly managed to make Annie presentable, something he hadn't been able to do.

"All done," Katie said.

Annie looked up at her and smiled. "*Denki*. Can I color some more?"

Katie nodded.

"It looks like you have everything under control," he said.

"I need to plan when to start the meals, but I haven't seen a clock. Do you have the time?"

Until she lifted her brows, he hadn't realized he was staring. He dug his hand into his pocket and fished out the bronze pocket watch. He studied the placement of the hands.

She leaned closer. *"Ach,* did it stop working?"

He handed her the watch, nervous he might get his numbers mixed up and say the wrong time.

She took a quick look. "I have plenty of time." She extended her hand toward him. *"Denki."*

"You can use it." He glanced around the room. "If I have a chance when I'm in town, I'll get a battery wall clock."

"That isn't necessary."

It was to him. He didn't want to chance being asked the time again. He glanced out the window as Thomas stopped the buggy next to the porch.

"I'll take the boys into town with me and Amos. I'm *nett* sure how long we will be gone."

"Should I make some sandwiches for you to take along?" She moved to the cabinet and reached for the loaf of bread.

Thoughtful and kind, she was easy to like. Too easy. And the longer he stayed in the same room with her, the greater the likelihood that he'd compile a list of all her fine qualities. His heart couldn't risk that.

"Nay. I mean, don't bother making sandwiches. We can eat something later." He took a few steps away, then paused. *"Denki* again, Katie."

Katie stood at the window and marveled at the amount of gentleness Seth used helping Amos down the porch steps. He must have coaxed him out of the house with some of the same skills. After Amos refused earlier, she figured the stubborn man would create some sort of commotion, but he went quietly. Seth helped Amos into the buggy, then climbed onto the bench.

Katie looked away from the window and peered down at Seth's pocket watch in her hand. She glided her fingers over the soft metal casing. She'd seen some pocket watches that were shiny and had fancy carvings etched on the front, but this one was plain with a lackluster finish and worn clasp. Functional, just what she would expect him to carry. She lifted it to her ear and listened to the rhythmic ticking. Steady. She recalled how long Seth stared at the watch as though trying to calculate the time.

"See what I colored?" Annie picked up the picture for Katie to see.

"That's really *schee*." She set the watch on the counter, then pulled out a chair from under the table and sat beside Annie.

"*Denki.*" She lowered the paper to the table and resumed scribbling.

Katie reached for the blue crayon. "*Bloh*. Blue."

Annie looked up from her paper and repeated both the Pennsylvania *Deitsch* and English words back. Excited by the child's enthusiasm to learn, Katie spent the next few hours coloring with Annie and teaching her more colors.

Most children didn't learn English until they started school, but Katie found no harm in teaching Annie a few words while she watched her. Besides, the child seemed receptive to any form of attention—unlike the boys, who avoided her. She suspected since they were removed from school, they hadn't done any formal arithmetic.

She was curious if Thomas still mixed up his numbers and if simple additions still frustrated him. She wished Amos had given her a chance to work with the boy after she discovered his real problem. Erma had agreed, but Amos refused. Even after the librarian in Hope Falls had found Katie several books on dyslexia, Amos didn't see any point in even trying the suggestions in them. Katie had no doubt that Thomas's reading would improve if he applied some of the tools to decode the words. She smiled. Perhaps God had sent her here to do more than cook, clean, and look after Annie. She was a teacher after all.

Razzen pushed off the wall and sidled up beside Katie to murmur in her ear. "You're the only one who believes in your teaching ability. Your family and friends don't. Otherwise they would have rebuilt the school, wouldn't they?"

Katie slumped in the chair as memories flooded her mind of how useless her life was before teaching. She thought she would never get over James dying. But through God's mercy, the teaching position had opened, giving her a reason to celebrate each new day.

Lord, I feel useless. I thought I accepted that I would never get married or have children. I thought I was content as a teacher . . . Wasn't I grateful for all you had given me? What am I supposed to do with my life now? She sighed. "I will trust you," she whispered.

As she made her declaration, she caught sight of the *Budget* paper sticking out of the supply bag she'd brought. She'd hoped once Annie was taking a nap, she would have a chance to read the news. She grabbed the paper and unfolded it, and while Annie continued to color, Katie scanned the pages. She skipped to the Michigan section of the paper. Many of the districts mentioned their sadness over the news of the tornado. Some listed the number of men who were coming to help rebuild. Katie roamed the other district's articles. Oscoda's school had closed early after the teacher of forty-five years passed away.

"How do you like *mei* picture?" Annie picked up her paper. "It's a garden."

Katie pushed the newspaper aside and studied the child's artwork. "It's beautiful."

"Do you want to color with me?"

Katie smiled. It would be easy to spend the remainder of the day coloring with Annie, but she needed to check the time. She glanced at the pocket watch. Where had the time gone? She should be preparing supper and Annie hadn't eaten lunch yet. "We can color tomorrow," she said. She didn't want Seth and Amos returning without something in the oven for them to eat.

"He has a closed head injury," the doctor explained.

Seth shook his head. "What does that mean?"

"The MRI doesn't show signs of an intracranial bleed. However, there is some swelling. That's probably what's putting pressure on the optic nerve."

"So will he regain his sight?" Seth moved aside as a hospital worker pushed a patient on a stretcher down the hall.

"I don't have that answer. I've made arrangements for him to see an ophthalmologist. We need to rule out a detached retina."

"Okay," Seth said, although none of it made much sense. "Did you explain this to Amos?"

"He refused to be admitted for observation, but he has agreed to see the ophthalmologist."

Seth breathed easier.

The doctor tore a sheet from his clipboard. "These are the

specific instructions. He shouldn't lift anything. He needs to rest as much as possible. His blood pressure is within normal limits, but he should avoid any stress."

Seth grimaced. That meant Katie.

Chapter Nineteen

Katie pulled into Amos's driveway the following morning and spotted Seth near the pasture gate. Leaning against the fence with one foot hiked up on the lower board, he gazed in the direction of the rising sun. He looked like he had a lot on his mind.

By the time they returned from seeing the doctor yesterday, the sun was setting. She stayed long enough to put the meat loaf back in the oven to reheat it and to explain how long he should wait before taking it out. Amos had grumbled something about not being hungry, and Seth helped him into the rocking chair in the sitting room. Seth hadn't offered any news about Amos's condition, probably because Amos was in earshot. Katie didn't ask.

She halted Peaches next to the hitching post and set the brake. Seth was walking her way as she climbed out of the buggy.

"Guder mariye." He reached for the reins. Without a hat, his ruffled hair looked as if he'd used his fingers to comb it.

"Mariye." She pulled her shawl tighter around her shoulders. Even for this being the last week in May, the early hours were still chilly. She glanced at the house. A small flicker of lamplight illuminated the kitchen. "Is everyone up?" She was more interested in Amos's mood, but she didn't want to be so blunt as to ask.

"Everyone except Annie. I let her sleep in." He grinned. "I didn't want to mess with trying to put her hair up again."

"That's probably smart," she replied, remembering the struggle to get the knots out of Annie's hair.

He motioned to the house. "Should I go inside with you?"

"To protect me from Amos?" she joked, hoping it disguised some of her worry. Yesterday went well because Amos was gone the entire day. Today she wasn't sure what to expect.

"I won't let him give you a hard time."

"I'll be fine." She couldn't deny liking the idea of his support, but he had work to do and couldn't protect her all day. Either she and Amos would work out their differences—or she would learn to stay out of the man's way.

"I suppose I'm worrying for nothing." Seth eyed her with a smile. "You'll hold your own."

Heat spiraled along her nerves and generated a trail of goose bumps in its wake. At a loss for a quick response, she rubbed her dress sleeve over her arm, but that didn't prevent the tingling sensation from spreading. "I should go inside before Annie wakes up." Walking away, she was surprised to find him at her side.

He shrugged at her lifted brows. "I want to get a glass of water."

She held her smile until they were inside the house. Amos

sat rigid in the rocking chair in the sitting room. If he had heard them enter the room, he made no indication.

"Katie's here," Seth said.

Amos mumbled something inaudible, which Katie assumed went along with his unwelcoming expression.

Seth elbowed her arm and motioned with a head nod toward the kitchen.

"Let me know if you need anything, Amos," she said, then without waiting for a response, followed Seth into the kitchen.

"I should help the boys with the barn chores," he said, turning.

Katie cleared her throat. When he glanced over his shoulder, she pointed at the sink. "You didn't get your glass of water."

By noontime, Katie had swept and mopped the kitchen floor, had a noodle casserole in the oven, and she and Annie were headed outside to pick some peas in the garden. She snapped the pods from the vine and tossed them into a bowl. Meandering along the row, she reached for more to pluck. She stole a glance at Seth as he inspected the damaged barn. He'd walked around the perimeter at least a dozen times, taken multiple measurements, but didn't seem anxious to get started on the repairs.

Annie plopped some pea pods, most still attached to their tendrils, into the bowl Katie was holding.

"*Denki*, I think we have enough *nau*," she told the child. "Let's go inside and wash them."

Annie skipped up the porch steps and waited for Katie at the door.

Once inside, Katie poked her head into the sitting room. "I'll have lunch ready in a few minutes," she told Amos.

"I don't want anything."

She wasn't about to argue with the man in front of his daughter. Besides, after she brought him a plate of food, he might change his mind.

"We picked peas," Annie said, oblivious that her excitement hadn't softened Amos's expression. "Show him, Katie."

She grasped Annie's hand and steered her away from the sitting room. "We need to wash them first. *Kumm*, let's take them into the kitchen." Her distraction worked. Annie skipped ahead into the kitchen.

A chair scraped against the wooden floor as Annie pushed it in front of the sink. Together they washed the peas and placed them in a pan of water. Then Katie sprinkled a dash of salt over them. She removed the noodle casserole from the oven and set it on the cooling rack. After counting the correct number of spoons and forks, she handed them to Annie to place on the table. Meanwhile, she scooped a serving of casserole for Amos. She wanted to make sure his food had enough time to cool.

Seth entered the kitchen, his nose tipped upward. "Smells *gut*." He grabbed the *Budget* from the counter and sat at the table.

She glanced over her shoulder and caught him holding the paper up but looking over the pages at her. "Lots going on, ain't so?"

"Uh . . . *jah*." He raised the paper, shielding his eyes.

Thomas burst through the door, Paul behind him. They both pulled their chairs out from the table.

Seth folded the paper and tossed it on the chair beside him.

Katie cleared her throat. "Wash your hands, boys."

Annie climbed up on her chair and showed Katie her clean hands.

She glanced at Seth, who was looking at his hands. "If you have to look, then they're *nett* washed." Katie flipped her thumb over her shoulder at the sink.

Seth rolled his eyes but stood. He pushed one shirtsleeve to his elbow, then did the other one as he waited for the boys to finish washing.

The moment Thomas dried his hands, Katie handed him Amos's plate. "Take this to your *daed*, please."

Seth held up his wet hands. "Do they pass?"

Katie smiled. "*Jah*, you may take your seat."

"*Denki.*"

"Katie and I picked peas," Annie said.

"I know. I saw you in the garden." He looked at Katie but darted his eyes away.

Thomas returned to the kitchen. "He didn't want it," he said, placing the plate on the counter.

Katie opened her mouth, but Seth spoke first.

"Let's pray." He closed his eyes and bowed his head.

Katie thanked God for the food in her silent grace.

Seth opened his eyes and reached for the pepper shaker. "I didn't know you wrote for the paper," he said.

"Nearly eight years. Well, *nett* the entire eight years; I stopped for a while."

"Why?" He peppered his noodles, then set the shaker on the table.

"It's a long story." And not one she could easily explain. She sipped her coffee and, looking over the brim of her cup, noticed he'd stopped twirling the noodles onto his fork.

"I'd like to hear about it," he said.

She glanced at the boys and Annie sitting next to her. The children hadn't paid much attention to anything except eating, but this wasn't the time to talk about her writing, especially why she stopped. James's drowning was too painful to discuss; besides, if she told him about the accident, it would lead to having to explain the angel's visitation at the river—a topic best left unmentioned in front of the children.

Seth resumed curling his noodles around his fork. "I noticed you've made a mark next to the Oscoda section."

She nodded. "They lost their *teetshah*." It probably sounded silly, but she was considering writing to the Oscoda bishop and asking about the position. She had to do something, even short term, until the school here was rebuilt. She smiled at the boys. "I brought some math assignments for you boys to work on."

In unison, their eyes widened.

"We, uh—that is . . ." Thomas tried doing the talking for the two of them, but his words stammered and he pivoted on his seat to cast pleading eyes at his *onkel*.

Seth cleared his throat. "They were going to work with me on the calving barn."

"Maybe the studies can start tomorrow." She didn't want to say it, but they had spent all morning on the barn and hadn't done a thing. The boys merely stood by and watched Seth measure and remeasure it.

The boys shoveled the food into their mouths, their forks scraping against the plates.

Seth scowled at them. "If you two are finished eating, go out to the barn."

"Me too?" Annie asked.

"You need to take a short nap," Katie said.

The boys pushed their chairs back, stood, and practically

raced to the door. Annie slid off the chair, and with her shoulders slumped and head turned down, she walked toward the bedroom.

He looked around at the empty table. "That was easy to shoo them out."

"Mentioning *schulwork* has a strong effect."

"Ach, jah!" His eyes widened, and he turned to cough into his hand.

"I'm used to it." She stood and gathered an armload of dirty dishes.

Seth followed her to the sink. "Let's take a walk."

Surprised by his request, she nearly dropped the dishes. He reached out and stabilized the plates, but that only jolted her heart to race faster. Lowering the dishes into the sink, she drew in a long, calming breath. She'd never been asked to take a walk in the middle of the day.

He leaned closer to her. "I didn't want to talk about Amos's condition inside."

That explained his request. She forced a smile. "Give me a minute to get these soaking and I'll be ready." She hoped her tone didn't sound too laced with disappointment. Why had she allowed her mind to run with such silly notions?

She poured the hot water from the kettle into the sink and added the soap. "Okay," she said, wiping her hands on the dish towel. "We can go talk."

Outside, she squinted and lifted her hand to shield her eyes from the bright sunlight.

Seth motioned for her to follow him to a shady area where a large maple tree canopied its green leaves over the far end of the porch. It was a relief from the heat, but now they were standing near the sitting room's open window. He glanced over his shoulder, then reached for her elbow. "Let's go somewhere else."

She let him lead the way.

He seemed a bit confused. He took a few steps toward the main barn, then probably remembering he'd sent the boys to start chores, redirected her toward the damaged one. But he didn't seem to like that location either, because he moved them away from the building and stopped at the woodshed.

"I didn't want to talk in front of the window," he said.

"Is the news bad?"

Seth shrugged. "The *dokta* doesn't even know how bad it is."

Her expression must've mirrored her confusion. He gave her a sympathetic frown and then continued, "Apparently the injury caused swelling and it's putting pressure on the optical nerve. But at least the retina wasn't detached." He shrugged. "The *dokta* seemed pleased about that."

"Can anything be done?"

"They gave him medicine to reduce the swelling and said he shouldn't have waited so long before coming in for treatment. The blindness might be permanent." He fell silent and looked down at the ground.

Seth was no doubt battling guilt over not insisting Amos go to the doctor sooner. She wished she could offer something encouraging. "I'll keep him in *mei* prayers." Her words sounded hollow.

Seth nodded without lifting his head.

She waited a moment, not sure if he had more to say, but she wasn't sure how to bring it up or if he wanted to be alone. "I should go back inside." She turned toward the house.

"Why?"

Surprised, Katie circled around. "Did you want to talk more?"

He cracked a smile. "I saw you wrote about the tornado in the *Budget*."

"What did you think of the article?" Earlier at the table, she thought he'd used the paper to hide behind, not to read. His half shrug looked a lot like one of her student's when they hadn't finished their homework assignment. "The part where I wrote about us trapped in the cellar didn't bother you?"

His eyes widened for an instant. *"Nay,"* he replied with some reserve. "Should it?"

She smiled. "You didn't read the article, did you?"

A sheepish grin spilled over his face. "I scanned the headline."

Something one of her students would do. Why did that not surprise her? She suppressed a smile and looked away. A squirrel shimmied up a nearby tree and vaulted from one limb to another, then disappeared among the leaves.

"So . . . are you going to tell me what you said about us being trapped?"

"I was joking. I wouldn't write about that." Just the memory of his hands around her waist sent a quiver over her nerves. Her muscles tensed and she squared her shoulders. Too much teasing had inadvertently given him the wrong impression. She wrote only about the weather now and the damages the tornado had caused.

"I didn't think you did." He lifted his hand to block his grin, but his eyes sparked with mischief.

She shifted her stance and relaxed her muscles.

"You said you had stopped writing. Why?"

Katie hadn't expected him to probe that issue again. Her writing about Samuel Fischer falling off the barn roof and his sister Judith's visitation with the angel at the river had certainly ignited a lot of commentary over the years. It also sent an uproar through the settlement. Their tiny community suddenly crawled with tourists searching for their own angel sightings. Strangers camped by the river and hunted for clues like they were on a scavenger hunt. If he hadn't heard about it already, she certainly didn't want to reopen the painful subject.

"I have time for a long story," he said, breaking the silence.

She pinned a smile on her face and motioned with her head at the damaged barn. "I thought you planned to start working on that barn. The only thing I've seen you do is take a dozen measurements."

Seth's face contorted. "A dozen, you say?" He pulled the hem of his shirt collar away from his neck like the heat had gotten to him and turned his head from side to side. "I didn't know I had an audience monitoring *mei* work."

Katie winced. "I was thinking maybe you needed help."

His brows rose.

"I didn't know you did structural repairs. Why weren't you working with the men—I mean, I know you were pulling out nails, but—" She cut herself off, seeing him shift his weight from foot to foot.

Seth grew silent.

She opened her mouth to apologize, but he cut in.

"I need to see how the boys are doing with the chores." He walked away, kicking up clouds of dust behind his boots.

Returning to the house, she looked over her shoulder at him. His thick shoulders were squared and his spine straight. She could imagine the set of his jaw and the tension in his face. It was probably for the best that she couldn't see the chill in his eyes. She hadn't meant to upset him.

Katie pulled the handle on the screen door and stepped inside. She peeked into the sitting room at Amos, sitting stiffly in the rocking chair and staring forward. He looked old. The man needed his strength. He needed to eat.

She went into the kitchen. The lunch plate she'd prepared for him earlier still sat on the counter. Katie scraped the noodle casserole back into the pan and slid it into the oven to reheat. After a few minutes, she scooped it onto a plate and brought it into the sitting room.

"Where should I set your lunch?"

Amos grunted. "I don't want anything."

"Hold out your hands. I'm *nett* leaving until you take the plate. You need your strength."

His hands remained in his lap and he stared straight ahead.

She shifted her weight to the other hip and waited.

Finally, growling under his breath, he accepted the plate.

"I'll be back to collect your dish in a little while." She left the room, smiling. Getting him to accept the food was a good start. Hopefully, once he ate, his mood would improve.

Katie rolled her dress sleeves up to her elbows and dipped her hands into the sudsy washbasin, searching for the dishrag. The water was tepid, but at least she hadn't been outside so long that it needed to be reheated. She picked up a plate and dragged the dishrag over it as she peered out the kitchen window. Seth wasn't anywhere in view, even when she craned her neck to see a different angle.

She made several more attempts to look for him in between washing, drying, and putting the dishes away. She looked for him again while she cleaned and prepared a pot of vegetables to simmer for soup. He remained out of sight even though the sounds of sporadic hammering filtered through the open window.

Katie paced the kitchen. She needed to think of something to lift the mood around here. It didn't take more than a few tracks from one end of the room to the other before she developed a plan.

Leah had mentioned her *mamm's* cinnamon rolls had a soothing effect. Katie pawed through the pantry in search of the items
needed, then went to work preparing them.

She couldn't have asked for better timing. The back door
opened just as she finished drizzling the frosting over the top of
the rolls.

Seth rushed into the kitchen and halted when his eyes connected with hers. His smile faded as he scanned the room.

Thomas and Paul plowed into the kitchen, no doubt responding to the same scent.

Paul elbowed Thomas to get closer to the counter. "Can I—
may I lick the spoon?"

"I want the bowl," Thomas added.

Katie handed the spoon to Paul and the bowl to Thomas,
then used a spatula to lift a roll out of the pan. She placed it on a
plate and handed it to Seth.

"Denki." He sat at the table and finished the roll in a few
quick bites. He smiled when he placed the plate into the sink.
"That was a nice treat."

"I'm glad you liked them." She wasn't about to ask if they
tasted like his sister's. But she couldn't help but feel some relief
that they seemed to have served the purpose.

"I have more to do outside," he said.

The boys devoured their rolls and trailed Seth to the door.

Katie sighed. She hoped the sweet treat would serve another
purpose: remind Amos of Leah. She placed a roll on the plate
and headed to the sitting room.

"Who is it?"

"Me, Katie." She moved closer. "I wanted to bring you—"
The plate of untouched food resting on his lap caught her off
guard. He hadn't eaten a thing.

"Don't bring me any of those cinnamon rolls I smelled cooking."

"Is there something wrong with the food?" She bit her tongue but then couldn't hold on to her thoughts. "I know you're used to Leah's cooking and probably miss—"

"Don't mention that name in *mei haus* again."

"She's your daughter," she said softly. "She's hurting too. I thought maybe—"

"Enough!" His brows formed a straight line. "I don't need to hear the thoughts of some meddling woman. You've caused enough damage in *mei* life. *Nau* leave me alone."

Katie squeezed her eyes closed. He'd spouted those same accusations shortly after Erma died. Just as when he lashed out at her then, she still wasn't sure how she'd damaged his life.

Lord, Amos needs to experience your love. His heart is bitter and I'm nett *sure if he will ever forgive his daughter. I don't want to be meddlesome. I only want him to forgive as your Word instructs your children to do.*

"Why are you still in here? Get out!"

Katie lowered her head and walked away praying. *Forgive him, Lord. Amos is lost. He has no idea how far he's fallen away from you.*

As she set the plate with the roll on the counter in the kitchen, something shattered in the other room. She rushed into the sitting room. "What happened?"

But he didn't need to answer. The broken plate and the mound of food lay in a heap on the plank floor. She knelt beside the chair and started to pick up the broken pieces of the glass plate, then decided it'd be faster with a broom. She rose off the floor and scooted into the kitchen. She wished now she would've thought to grab the plate earlier. When she returned with the broom, Amos had his hand lifted to his forehead and his eyes closed.

"Are you feeling okay?"

"Where's Seth? I've heard very little hammering today."

Her back stiffened. What did he expect out of Seth? The damaged barn needed a lot of work. "It takes time to figure out what needs to be done," she said, making a pass under his chair with the broom.

"He knows construction inside and out—he's a master builder."

Amos grumbled something more under his breath about how minor his calving barn was compared to the oversized pole barns Seth had put up, but Katie was still trying to wrap her mind around Seth being a master builder. A master builder— building beehives? It made no sense at all.

Unable to reach all the glass, she asked, "Can you lift your feet for me, please?"

"I'm blind, *nett* crippled," Amos huffed.

"Then lift your feet. I need to sweep under the chair." She was losing patience with the man.

Once he lifted his feet a few inches off the floor, she swept everything into a pile. "Okay, you can put your feet back down." She would come back and mop up the creamy remnant smeared over the floor from the noodles after she scooped this stuff into the dustpan.

Above her, something tapped against the surface of the lamp table. She glanced up just as Amos's hand connected with the water glass. Only the condensation dripping from the glass surface made it difficult to grip. The glass slipped though his hand and smashed on the floor, sending water and shards of glass flying.

Amos gripped the arms of the chair. His white knuckles were a bold contrast to the red shade his face turned. He looked like he was about to explode from the way the cords in his neck protruded.

She didn't want to set him off by saying anything, but she needed to empty the dustpan in the trash before she could clean up the new mess. "I'll clean that up in a minute." She set the broom down and carried the filled dustpan into the kitchen.

A loud thump came from the sitting room. Katie vaulted into the other room and gasped. Amos was sprawled over the floor, the broom at his feet. She hurried to his side and dropped to her knees.

"Give me your hand and I'll help you up."

His lip curled into a sneer. "Get away from me!"

"But there's glass all over the floor," she said, reaching for his hand.

He shoved her hand away.

The man hadn't lost any of his pride. She bit her tongue to keep from quoting what the Bible says about pride. He would recognize the Proverbs scripture, but she doubted his heart was pliable to follow its teaching.

"I didn't think to move the broom. I'm sorry."

"That's right. You didn't think." He patted the floor and she scrambled to get out of his reach. His hand stopped searching when he touched the broom handle. Amos slung it to the other end of the room.

Katie fled the house. This wasn't going to work. His animosity toward her ran too deep for him to accept her help.

Seth craned his neck to look around the side of the barn when the screen door slammed.

Katie stomped off the porch steps, talking to herself. "He's stubborn. Mean. Coldhearted."

Seth dropped his hammer and jogged, meeting her in the middle of the driveway.

"What happened?"

"Amos is . . ." Her face contorted.

"I heard you ranting. Stubborn, mean, and I think you said coldhearted." He laughed. Watching her conflicting expressions was entertaining.

"Ranting? Me?" She aimed her pointed finger at the house. "You should have heard him."

He didn't doubt that his brother-in-law had said something that set her on fire.

"I need to—leave." Her words sounded choked.

"Why?" He cocked his head to one side, his eyes meeting hers. Sunlight flickered over her watery eyes. "I'm sorry. I wouldn't have laughed if I knew you were crying. Tell me what happened."

She wiped her cheeks with the back side of her hand. "You better check on Amos. He tripped over the broom."

"And he fell?"

She nodded.

The doctor's instruction to keep Amos calm replayed in his mind. "Don't leave. I'll be right back," he called over his shoulder, sprinting to the house. He took the porch steps two at a time, flung the door open, and rushed inside. "Amos?"

Rounding the corner into the sitting room, Seth stopped. Amos was seated in the rocking chair, the floor around him wet and sparkling from the afternoon sun reflecting on the broken glass.

"Katie said you fell." He crossed the room. "Are you all right?"

"Is she gone?"

"She's outside." Amos certainly didn't sound or even appear in distress. "Did you hit your head?"

"I'm fine."

Annie walked into the room whimpering and rubbing her balled hands over her eyes. "Where's Katie?"

Seth gathered Annie into his arms so she didn't walk barefooted over the glass. "Did you have a *gut* sleep?"

"Nay." She shook her head, and golden curls escaped her *kapp* and draped over her shoulder.

"Are you still tired?"

She puckered her bottom lip and nodded. "Is Katie going to be here when I wake up?"

"I hope so." He carried her to the bedroom and lowered her onto the bed. "Sleep some more." He kissed the top of her head, then pulled the quilt up around her neck.

"Guder nacht, Onkel Seth." Her eyes closed.

Seth continued past the sitting room. He would talk more with Amos later, but first he needed to convince Katie to stay. He stepped outside and, looking across the yard, spotted Katie leading her mare to the hitching post.

"Amos is all right," he said, coming up beside her.

"That's *gut*." She pulled the harness off the rail and positioned the equipment on the horse.

"Do you have to leave this early? I was hoping you would stay for supper."

"I made a pot of vegetable soup. You'll need to heat it." Her fingers fumbled, working at a quick pace.

"I didn't say I was hoping you would stay to cook." He reached for her hand and stopped her from feeding the leather through the loop. "I want you to stay for supper."

"It'll be dark soon." She kept her head bowed.

"I'll drive you home."

"Nay—I mean—It's just that . . ."

He faced the horse and buckled the strap, then handed her the reins.

"Tomorrow is a special church Sunday and I have to pre-pare a dish to take. There wasn't anyone to host services on the other side of the district on account of the storm damages being greater, so service is on our side again."

"What about Monday?"

She sighed. "Amos doesn't want me here."

"I do." Surprised by his automatic response, his heart thrummed against his ribs. "Annie wants you here," he said, trying to defuse his unguarded statement. Not that it wasn't true. He hadn't realized before just how much he wanted her to stay. He couldn't recall ever having these strong feelings for Diana.

"Can I ask you a question?" she asked.

"*Jah*, anything." He lifted his brows.

"Are you reading the Scriptures to the children at *nacht*?"

He lowered his head and pushed a stone with the toe of his boot. He'd already exposed more of his heart than he wanted. Still, he couldn't bring himself to tell her about his reading problem. The jumbled words on the page moved and made it impossible to read aloud.

"Seth," she said, summoning his attention. "You have to take on some of the duties as head of the *haus*. Amos isn't able."

Neither was he. If he tried to read aloud, he would stammer like a fool. He hadn't thought about the duties required by the head of the house.

"Well, something for you to consider. I'm sure it would do Amos *gut* to hear the Word." She climbed onto the buggy bench. "I'll be here Monday." She released the buggy brake. "And maybe after supper, you'll start devotions."

Seth forced a smile until her buggy rolled away. He hoped God would extend a bit of grace. He wanted her help with the children, but couldn't read in front of her—ever.

Chapter Twenty

En route home, Katie's heart drummed at a steady beat with thoughts of Seth. His adamant tone when he said he wanted her to return weakened her knees. He certainly had an effect on her senses. She was growing fonder of him by the day—the hour.

Peaches whinnied. The mare swung her head as far as the equipment allowed, like a young horse pulling a buggy for the first time.

"Easy, girl." Katie slowed the horse's pace. There wasn't any need to rush, and something had the horse on edge. Peaches stopped suddenly with no signal from Katie. She jerked her head up and down, then lurched forward only to stop again.

"What is it, girl?" Katie climbed out of the buggy. Maybe something was wrong with the harness and it was rubbing Peaches. She eased up to the horse and patted her neck.

"Is something wrong?" Elias asked, appearing at her side.

She jumped, clutching her hand to her chest. "I didn't see you."

"I'm sorry I frightened you." He motioned to the patch of birch trees. "I was sitting on the stump."

"Are you waiting for someone? I can give you a ride somewhere if you need one."

"That's very kind." He reached out and stroked Peaches's neck. "I think she's calm now."

Katie studied her horse. Peaches's nostrils weren't flared as they normally were after trotting this distance. "That's odd."

Elias smiled. "Sometimes animals have a better sense of their surroundings."

She nodded, remembering her father tell about the time his grandfather was clearing the land where her barn was now and his horse sensed danger prior to him spotting a coyote. She scanned the area but couldn't see too many feet away with the sun falling behind the dense line of pines.

"How is Amos?"

"The *dokta* isn't sure if the blindness is permanent."

"The darkness reaches beyond the physical. Don't stop praying for him," Elias said.

She nodded and looked down at the gravel road.

"There is death in darkness. The Word of God is life. It is an everlasting lamp in the darkness."

"I believe that too. I even suggested that to Seth before I left." She wasn't sure what prompted her to continue. "I tried to tell him that it was important for Amos and the children to hear the Scriptures."

"It is equally important for Seth that he reads." He pointed to the wooded trail off to the side of the road. "Some obstacles, like that fallen tree blocking the path, are too overwhelming for one to move alone." He sighed. "But a certain helpmate alongside him could work with him to move that obstacle out of his path."

She wasn't sure if the man intended to flip the conversation from Seth reading to a fallen tree, but she nodded like she was following along with his thoughts. "Ah . . . do you need a ride somewhere?"

"No," he said, walking down the slope of the ditch. "I'm still staying, for the time, by the river." He crossed the gully and disappeared through the woods.

Katie climbed into her buggy. She waited a moment, then signaled Peaches forward.

It didn't take long to reach the house, and when she stepped inside, the wonderful scent of baked *yummasetti* surprised her. For the brief moment she paused to take in the aroma, her thoughts filled with fond childhood memories of her mother's cooking.

"How's *mei daed*?" Leah asked the moment Katie entered the kitchen.

"The *dokta* isn't sure if he'll recover his sight. It will depend on what happens after the swelling goes down."

Leah's hopeful smile faded and she pointed toward the stove. "I made *yummasetti*." She grabbed two pot holders from the counter and opened the oven. "And cinnamon rolls for dessert."

Katie inhaled. "I thought it smelled sweeter in here than usual." She peeked into the oven at the rising rolls. "I made some today too."

"*Onkel* Seth loved them, didn't he?"

Katie's face warmed, and not just from the oven heat.

"He likes *yummasetti* too . . . in case you're wondering," Leah said, pulling the pan out of the oven and setting it on top of the stove.

"*Nau* who said I was wondering?" She planted her fists on her hips.

"It's true," Leah said, pulling two plates out of the cabinet. She sent a sidelong glance at Katie. "You know, Katie, my *onkel* can build beehives in any district."

Katie narrowed her eyes. "Was Abigail here today?" She planned to have a word with her sister-in-law if she filled Leah's mind with crazy notions.

Leah shook her head. "*Nay.*" A sheepish smile spread over her face. "I overheard her the day she picked up the donations."

Katie debated whether to mention anything about Seth's supper invitation. "I suppose I should tell you—since you're staying here. I won't be home for supper Monday *nacht.*" She wagged her finger at Leah. "And don't you dare tell *mei* sister-in-law that bit of news. She will turn it into something that it's *nett.*"

"*Nett* yet," Leah teased. "You'd make a *gut Aenti* Katie."

Unexpected heat rushed to Katie's cheeks; she reached for the handle on the cabinet containing cups. "I'll make some tea."

"It's already made and on the table."

Katie looked over her shoulder at the set table. Steam curled up from the cups.

Leah placed the food on the table and motioned to the chair, grinning. "Everything is ready, *Aenti.*"

She'd wait until after the blessing before she set the girl straight. Leah's teasing had distracted her, and it took an extra minute before she could say her silent grace. When she looked up, the corners of Leah's mouth had turned down. "Is something wrong?"

"*Daed* didn't ask about me, did he?"

Katie reached for Leah's hand and gave it a gentle squeeze. "Take the first step and go to him. Don't let pride stand in your way."

She shook her head slowly. "I'll pray for him, but I'm *nett* going back home."

Katie sighed. She'd been praying and trusting God to change both Amos's and Leah's hearts.

"You kept your promise, ain't so? You didn't tell anyone, including *Onkel* Seth, I was staying with you."

Katie shook her head. She wished she hadn't made the promise, but she also feared that Leah would run away as she'd threatened, and she couldn't allow that either. *God, I need wisdom. Please use this situation for your glory.*

Seth waited until the children and Amos had gone to bed before he cleaned up the supper dishes. He pulled the drain plug when someone tapped on the back door. Seth wiped his hands on the dish towel as he went to the door.

Standing on the stoop, Jacob Fischer swayed back and forth, his hands clutching a piece of paper. "I got a letter today." He unfolded the rumpled paper and held it against his leg to press it with his hand. "Leah said she would see me in church tomorrow."

"Where is she? She must be close to know that services got changed to this side of the district again."

Jacob shook his head. "She didn't say." He thrust the letter toward Seth. "Do you want to read it?"

Seth appreciated the young man's wiliness. He glanced at the fancy writing and handed it back to Jacob. "This is your private message. You said she plans to attend church, so I'll talk with her tomorrow."

Jacob refolded the letter and stuffed it in his pocket. "I wanted to be sure to tell you."

"*Denki*, I appreciate it." He clapped the young man's shoulder. "Things will work out just fine."

Jacob jerked his head in a nervous nod.

"Go home and get some sleep," Seth said.

After Jacob left, Seth tried to take his own advice, but instead of sleeping, he tossed in his bed most of the night.

The next morning Seth arrived early at the Hartzlers' farm, the family hosting the Sunday service. He stood off from the crowd but kept a keen eye on Jacob Fischer. The antsy young man stood with several other unmarried youths his age, but instead of interacting with them, Jacob had his eye trained on every buggy that pulled into the drive.

Behind him, the gravel crunched under footsteps and Seth swiveled to his left as Isaac Bender approached.

Isaac clapped Seth's shoulder. "*Mei fraa* wanted me to invite you to supper." He paused and kicked at the ground. "Katie too."

Seth smiled. "I'd like that."

Isaac lifted his head, brows crinkled. "You want to *kumm*?"

"You sound surprised."

"I didn't think the last supper went so well." He shrugged. "Okay, I'll tell Abigail." He glanced over his shoulder at the barn. "I should go inside. I'm doing the first reading," Isaac said before walking away.

Seth tugged at his collar, moving it away from his neck. But it wasn't just the warm weather that had caused him to sweat. Isaac hadn't seemed concerned about his upcoming scripture reading during the service, but the thought sent a shudder through Seth. Another reason he should never marry. Once a man married, he was eligible for ministry. Eventually his name would be added to the lot when a minister's position opened, and part of that responsibility included reading during the services.

Now he wasn't sure he should have accepted the supper invitation. Since he could never marry Katie, it'd be wrong to give any false hope by courting her.

Seth dug his hand into his pocket and pulled out his watch. Not that the time mattered; the service would start once everyone arrived.

Jacob crossed the lawn with the other youth, but instead of going into the service with his friends, he stopped and stood with Seth.

"I haven't seen her yet," Jacob said, a glum look overshadowing his face.

"There's still time," Seth said, keeping his voice even. "The service won't start for a little while yet."

Jacob knew as well as he did that most of the members had arrived, but he nodded.

A lone buggy cornered the drive. *Peaches.* Seth's heart skipped a beat.

Katie parked the buggy next to the other church members' buggies and set the brake. If they didn't hurry, they would walk into service late. She didn't want to bring that attention to herself or Leah.

"There's Jacob," Leah said, her voice shaky.

Katie looked out the window opening at the two men headed their direction. But she wasn't watching Jacob. She eased off the bench.

Seth walked past Katie to reach Leah. "Where have you been?"

"*Jah,*" Jacob said, coming up beside Seth. "I've been worried about you."

"So has your family," Seth added sternly.

Leah bowed her head.

Katie looped the reins over the rail, then moved next to Leah's side and placed her arm around the girl's shoulder. "She's been staying with me."

"You!" Seth glared.

Katie flinched.

"How long has she been there?" His jaw tightened and he folded his arms across his chest. "How long, Katie?"

"*Onkel* Seth, I had nowhere else to go." Leah curled into Katie's arms.

"That isn't the point." He stared at Katie a long moment, shook his head, then turned and walked toward the barn.

"I'm glad to see you," Jacob said softly.

Leah lifted her head off Katie's shoulder. "*Denki*, Jacob. I've missed you too." She smiled.

Katie wished Seth wasn't walking so quickly; she wanted to talk with him privately but couldn't risk being overheard so close to the entrance. Truth was, she couldn't risk him scolding her in front of the congregation. He entered the building without looking back once.

Katie motioned to Leah. "We should go inside. You two can catch up after the service."

Leah and Jacob exchanged sheepish smiles.

"*Geh* on, I'll wait and walk in after you," he said.

Leah tucked a strand of stray hair under her prayer *kapp* as she walked beside Katie. "I've been away from services so long, this is going to seem strange," she whispered.

Katie wanted to say she hoped Leah's friends greeted her better than her *onkel* had, but she held her tongue. His sour expression clearly indicated he was upset with Katie and hopefully not so much with his niece.

Inside the barn, Katie sat in her usual spot next to Abigail. Katie had moved to the married women's section a few years after everyone her age had married. Sitting with the young unmarried girls, many former students, made her feel uncomfortable. In many ways, the bench move signified her acceptance of remaining unmarried—taking herself out of the pool of those wishing to court.

Leah walked past them and sat with the unmarried women on the back rows of benches. The soft welcoming whispers hushed immediately once the service began.

Three hours seemed more like six. Katie only dared to glance once at the men's side of the room. Seth held his head down. His shoulders rolled inward.

Lord, I don't know how to fix this.

When the service concluded, Katie stood with the women, but her attention drifted to the other side of the room. She caught Seth's eye, but he looked away immediately. Katie's throat dried. She swallowed hard, but it only made it feel scratchy.

Abigail elbowed her. "Why were you late?"

She shrugged, fearing that if she spoke, her voice would squeak.

"Are you okay?"

She wasn't, but she nodded anyway. With her sister-in-law, sometimes it was easier to pretend all was well even when life was falling apart. Like now.

Abigail grabbed her arm and led her outside. "What is going on?"

Katie leaned closer. "Don't ask me *nau*, please."

"This is about Seth, ain't so?"

Katie forced a smile as Leah glided past them, her arms locked with two of her close friends. At least Leah easily fit back in with her buddy bunch. The threesome headed toward the larger group of unmarried youth, and Katie couldn't help but notice Jacob's beaming smile.

Katie caught a glimpse of Seth as he headed toward the parked buggies.

Abigail leaned close to Katie and whispered, "He's *nett* staying for the meal?"

"So it appears." She hoped her monotone voice masked her disappointment. She motioned to the house. "Let's go inside and help get the meal ready."

Katie sacrificed her entire Sunday afternoon so Leah could spend some extra time with Jacob. She usually enjoyed the meal fellowship and helping to *redd-up* afterward, but she'd never had to dodge a conversation with Abigail to this extent. It was work, too, constantly trying to aim the conversation in different directions. Talking with the bishop's *fraa* helped.

Mary updated the women on the bishop's condition, even though it was quite clear by looking at him seated beside Andrew at an adjacent table that the bishop had turned frail since his stroke. Still, Katie marveled at how determined Bishop Lapp was not to miss the Sunday service.

The bishop's wife stood. "I think Zechariah is trying to get *mei* attention. He must be ready to go." Mary scooted away to join her husband.

"A *wundebaar* thing," Abigail said.

"What's that?"

"Finding a *gut* man to love." Abigail winked.

Ach, she should have known her sister-in-law had baited her. This topic needed to change immediately.

"I think I'll get started on the kitchen duties." Katie collected a stack of dirty dishes, Abigail at her side doing the same.

"I asked Isaac to invite Seth for supper."

Katie carried the load of dishes inside the house and placed them on the counter next to the sink, then started filling the basin with water. She didn't want to discuss supper with Seth. That wouldn't happen anytime soon. She had mixed thoughts about seeing him tomorrow at Amos's house.

"I was thinking Wednesday would be a *gut nacht* for supper. What do you think?"

Katie thought the idea was crazy. But she was pressed between two immovable objects—Abigail and the kitchen sink—so she had to work faster.

Humming hymns helped. So did the other women joining in the cleanup. The chatter in the kitchen rose.

Katie kept Abigail at bay by handing her one clean dish after another to rinse. After washing the last dish, she pulled the drain plug, cleaned off the soapy residue on the basin, and dried her hands with a spare dish towel.

She grabbed the dish she'd brought for the meal, said her good-byes to the women, and even told Abigail she would talk with her before Wednesday. Then she trekked across the lawn to the buggies.

Leah walked up as Katie unfastened Peaches from the hitching rail.

"Did you have a nice visit?" Katie asked, even though the answer was clear in Leah's smile.

"*Jah*, it's *gut* to be back." Leah climbed onto the bench, then pivoted on the bench to face Katie. "In a few weeks I'll be seventeen," she said.

Katie suspected that was the main topic among the youth. Seventeen was an important marker in one's life in their district. The youth always looked forward to attending the Sunday evening singings.

Katie sighed. She remembered it took James three singings before he'd rallied the nerve and asked to drive her home. Now, at twenty-nine, those days seemed so long ago.

"Jacob's already asked to drive me home. Once I turn seventeen," she was quick to add.

Leah continued talking, but her words became a blur in the background of Katie's thoughts. She spent the remaining drive home thinking over her options. She only came up with one if she didn't want to grow old working the rest of her life at Abigail's vegetable stand—send a letter to the Oscoda bishop and request the teacher's position. It made perfect sense. She needed a job. As it was, she'd depleted her savings to donate to the settlement's rebuilding fund.

Once they were home, Leah offered to put the buggy away and feed Peaches. Katie was grateful for a few minutes alone to write her letter. She listed her years of experience and explained the situation after the storm. The Oscoda district had sent men to help with the rebuilding, so the bishop would know about the tornado damages, but he probably had not heard how the school had been destroyed.

Leah fixed a cup of tea and sat across the table from Katie. "Am I interrupting you?"

"*Nay.*" Katie signed her name and folded the paper. "I'm writing to the Oscoda bishop to request the teaching position they have available."

"You're going to move?"

"I'd have to. But it's only a few hours away. I'll be back to visit."

Leah stared at her cup. After a long moment of silence, she asked, "Where will I go?"

Katie drew a deep breath. "I think you need to consider going back home." Katie's words brought tears to Leah's eyes. She reached across the table for her hand. "Don't you?"

෴

Since leaving church earlier, Seth had stopped himself twice from driving to Katie's house to talk with Leah. But now that the barn chores were finished, the children fed, and Annie in bed, there wasn't much to keep his mind occupied. Besides, he wouldn't be gone long—he didn't have much to say.

He tossed the dish towel on the counter and went to the sitting room. "Amos," he said, shoving his foot into his boot. "Will you be okay for a little while? I need to take care of something."

"This late?"

"*Jah.*" Perhaps this wasn't the right time. Then again, he wasn't going to sleep tonight without talking with her. He yanked the door open. "I won't be long."

Seth trekked out to the barn. He coaxed the horse out of the stall, leading the gelding out by his halter. Threading the leather strap of the harness through the buckle, his thoughts competed against one another, but the goal of convincing Leah to return home won out. Her father needed her. So did Annie. He needed her to return—so he could go back home. It would only take a day or two to train Thomas how to take care of the bees, and he would pay someone to rebuild Amos's barn.

By the time Seth covered the distance between Amos's house and Katie's, he had a plan. He tied the horse. Black smoke curled from the stovepipe.

Wiping his hands down the sides of his pants, he climbed the porch steps, paused for a moment to take a deep breath, then knocked on the door. The moment he did, he wished he would've paused longer and prayed.

Seth on edge—primed for manipulation—just where Razzen wanted him.

The door opened and Katie stood at the entrance. "Seth? What are you doing here? Is something wrong?"

"Really? She had to ask if something was wrong? Now you know why Amos despises the woman. She's heartless," Razzen said.

Seth closed his eyes. One wagon wheel—two wagon wheels—three—this wasn't working. "May I speak with Leah?"

"Please *kumm* in."

"The spider calls you into her web. She has a lot of nerve," Razzen said.

"I'd just as well stay out here." He needed to distance himself from Katie.

She didn't move.

Seth shifted his weight to his other foot.

"I'll get her," she said, and disappeared behind the door.

He glanced up at the porch overhang. The roof damages from the limb hadn't been repaired yet.

The door creaked open and Leah stepped outside. "*Onkel* Seth? You wanted to speak with me?"

"*Jah.*" He crossed his arms in front of him and leaned against the banister. "When did you plan to tell your family where you're staying?"

She shrugged.

"Have you been here all along?"

She lowered her head. "*Jah.*"

"Your father is blind."

She said nothing.

"Did you hear me, Leah?" His words were harsh enough. Surely she heard.

She nodded, her shoulders shaking.

Seth pushed off the banister. He wasn't trying to make her cry. He placed his hand firmly on her shoulder. "Your *aenti* Lilly sent word that she can help, but she won't be able to leave Ohio until the end of the month. You need to *kumm* home."

She lifted her teary eyes. "Katie and I were just discussing that."

Perhaps Katie was insightful enough to know where the girl belonged. "Go get your things. I'll wait for you in the buggy."

"*Nay. Onkel* Seth, I can't go home."

Chapter Twenty-One

The small morsel of sleep Seth devoured last night did little to alleviate his disappointment in Katie. He'd never felt so much dread as when her buggy pulled into the drive at daybreak. As he did every morning, he met her at the hitching post, took hold of Peaches's reins, and waited for her to step down from the buggy.

Pivoting to face the mare, he grasped the leather strap and loosened the harness.

"*Guder mariye,*" she chirped.

His fingers froze and he glanced sideways at her. She pulled a shawl out of her buggy, then turned toward him and boasted a broad—fake—smile.

"*Mariye,*" he said, rejecting the part about it being good. Seth forged a similar smile, only his best was lopsided and developed into a snarl.

He resumed unlatching Peaches's equipment. His peripheral vision caught the sashayed swing of her dress hem as she spun to leave. The song she hummed while walking away replayed longer in his mind than he cared to hear. At this particular moment, he'd rather drink curdled milk than be forced to listen to that honey-sweet tune.

Seth left the horse tethered at the post and charged after her. He caught up to her before she reached the porch, snatched hold of her arm, and twirled her toward him. When she opened her mouth to object, his hands cupped her jaw and he pressed his thumbs against her mouth to prevent her from speaking.

Her eyes narrowed.

"I want to say some things without you interrupting me." Her skin soft against his hands, he released his hold. "Do you have to gloat with all that humming?"

"What?"

"You're coldhearted. You *kumm* here humming as though nothing happened."

"I'm sorry."

"Sorry," he snorted, crossing his arms over his chest. "What about Leah? Are you sorry about keeping that hidden from me—from Amos? His daughter was missing and you didn't tell him. Have you any remorse about that?"

"*Jah*, I should've told him," she muttered under her breath. "I'm sorry."

"*Gut*, I'm glad we agree." He reached for her elbow and in one brisk move had her turned and heading toward the porch steps.

"Wait!"

She planted her feet, and Seth wasn't about to drag a woman. He had no choice but to stop.

"Hasn't Leah talked with him?" Her brows crinkled. "She is home . . . ain't so?" A horrified expression spread over her face.

"*Nay.*" He shook his head. "She's at your *haus.*"

Katie bit her bottom lip and closed her eyes. He felt her body tremble.

"What's wrong?"

She groaned. "I woke up this morning and she was gone. She left a note thanking me and said she didn't want to cause any more trouble. I assumed she came home."

Cold fear shot through him. He shook his head, drew a deep breath. He had to find her. Seth headed to the barn.

"I'm going too," Katie said, jogging up to his side.

"I'd rather you *nett.*"

"Seth, you don't know this area. I do."

He stopped. She had a point. He glanced at the house, then faced her. "I need to tell Thomas to listen for Annie to wake up so he can keep an eye on her." He hoped Katie going with him wasn't a mistake.

Katie didn't wait for Seth to pull the buggy up to the house. Peaches was still tied to the post, so it didn't take long to fasten a few straps. She handed Seth the reins once he climbed onto the bench, and he signaled to Peaches.

"Which direction is the Fischers' *haus?*" he asked once they reached the end of the driveway.

"Turn right."

He did.

"You have to go past *mei* place."

An uncomfortable silence fell between them. He stared at the road ahead. She alternated between glancing at him and peering out the window at the hilly green pasture. Peaches started acting skittish, making lunging spurts, like she did the other night when they reached the wooded area.

"Easy, girl," Seth said, working the reins to pull Peaches back.

"She did this the other *nacht* when I passed through here." Katie sat straighter and stretched her neck to get a better view. "Stop!"

Seth yanked on the reins. "What's wrong?"

"You didn't see someone? I think it was Elias."

"Where?"

"I don't see him *nau*." She opened the buggy door, but Seth caught her arm. She pulled away from him, straining to leave the buggy. "Something might be wrong."

"Well, wait until I find a place to park off the road." He steered the horse onto the path and stopped the buggy in front of the fallen tree. He climbed out, scanned the area, then tied Peaches to a branch.

Katie stood at his side. "I know this is taking time away from finding Leah, but I would feel awful if Elias needed help and we didn't stop."

"I'm still trying to figure out how you saw him and I didn't." He climbed over the massive oak and reached for her hand.

Shielded from the sun, the dew was still heavy on the bark, making it slippery. She teetered, but he kept her from falling. *"Denki,"* she said once she was on firm ground. She swept the pieces of bark off her dress as they headed down the sandy trail.

She heard the sound of rushing water, and the scent of the river registered, and then the clearing opened before her.

On the bank of the river, seated on a large rock, was Leah.

Seth rushed over to his niece.

Katie froze, staring at the foamy water. She hadn't been to the river in years. Not this close. Not since she jumped in to try to save James. Memories clawed at her throat, making it difficult to breathe. A high-pitched ringing in her ears drowned out the sound of the rushing water and skewed her balance. Too dizzy to stand any longer, she dropped to her knees, then sat on the sandy soil and rested her head in her hands.

Breathe.

A vision of James going under the water flashed before her eyes. Her focus blurred.

"Katie," Seth said, squatting next to her.

She lifted her head. Even that small motion made her think she might vomit.

"You're as pale as a sheet. Are you sick?"

Leah dropped next to her. "You don't look well."

Her eyes stung, pooled with tears. "I'll be all right. I just—I just need a few minutes, is all."

Seth stood and went toward the river.

"I'm glad we found you, Leah," Katie said. She was breathing easier, but she didn't dare stand just yet; the ringing in her ears hadn't disappeared.

"I'm sorry," Leah said. "I left because I didn't want *Onkel* Seth upset with you."

Seth returned and bent to his knee. "She's agreed to go back to your *haus*," he said, handing Katie his wet hankie. "Wipe your face with it. The cold water will make you feel better."

"Is that okay with you?" Leah asked.

"Let her get her wind back." He focused on Katie, his eyes searching her. "Your color looks better."

She handed him the hankie. *"Denki."*

Seth reached for her hand and helped her up.

One glimpse at the river and Katie couldn't hold back the tears from rolling down her face.

"Leah, would you wait for us in the buggy?" Seth motioned to the path. "It's parked at the foot of the path. We won't be long."

Leah nodded and shot down the trail.

Seth waited until Leah was no longer in sight, then asked, "What's wrong? I don't think you'd be crying if you were sick."

Katie wiped her face with her dress sleeve. "It's a long story."

"You always say that." He tugged her elbow. "Let's sit on that rock. I want to hear the story."

Kate shook her head. "I can't. I don't want to go any closer to the river. I can't— James—James died in the river."

"We don't have to stay." Seth placed his arm around her shoulder and directed her toward the path.

A few feet down the path she broke the silence. "You asked why I stopped writing for the *Budget*." She didn't know any other place to start but at the beginning. "A few years back Samuel Fischer, one of *mei* students, fell off the barn roof. About the same time, his sister Judith saw an angel at the river." She knew by his wrinkled forehead he was confused, but he kept silent and she continued, "I wrote so much about it that the entire settlement was flooded with visitors, mostly *Englischers* with cameras."

"I can see where that would become an issue," he said.

"That wasn't all. James's sister, Rachel, hadn't been asked home from any of the singings, and I suggested she look for the angel at the river and ask him why."

Seth opened his mouth but closed it just as fast.

"I know that was wrong."

He cracked a smile. "Go on."

"Well, she took my advice. Only, she rushed through chores

and left the sheep gate open by accident . . . James tried rescuing one from the river, but . . . the current swept him under." Her words were garbled from sobbing.

Seth pulled her into his arms and hugged her tight. "I'm sorry," he whispered in her ear.

Nestled against his chest, she listened to the steady beat of his heart and breathed in the scent of hay embedded in the fabric of his shirt. She lifted her head and their gazes held. He brushed her cheek with the tips of his fingers, sending a tingling sensation down to her toes.

She broke from the embrace. "We shouldn't leave Leah waiting too long."

He nodded.

As they continued on the path, Seth's attention flipped from one area of the woods to another. Either he was uncomfortable about the closeness they'd just shared, or he'd turned jumpy about walking through the woods. A swift breeze rustled the leaves, but Katie focused on the shimmering shades of green against the blue sky. Seth appeared more concerned about the movement of the ferns. The foliage, near to the ground, usually didn't move unless a rabbit or other wildlife was in it.

Now anxiousness rose inside of her. She would rather talk than hear creepy sounds of nature. "I should've told you about Leah showing up in *mei* barn that *nacht*. I'm sorry I didn't. I mentioned her name to Amos and he forbade me to speak it in the *haus* again."

"I'm glad she's safe and staying with you," he said.

"Her *rumschpringe* isn't typical. She's *nett* running from the church, she's returning to the fold."

"Maybe once Amos's sister arrives from Ohio, she can convince him to turn back to God." Seth shrugged. "He is stubborn and he doesn't listen to me. We need to keep him in our prayers."

Katie nodded.

"Let's talk about this later," he said, reaching for her hand to help her over the fallen tree.

She understood. The buggy so close, Leah would be able to hear their conversation. Grateful for the peace between them, Katie whispered a prayer of thanks. She never wanted to make him that upset again.

He had almost kissed her—what was he thinking? Seth stared at the road ahead. The rhythmic clip-clopping of the horse's hooves wasn't doing anything to settle the growing knot in his stomach.

Around the bend of the road, rolling green pastures and Katie's whitewashed clapboard farmhouse came into view. Katie and Leah chatted about Katie's garden as he pulled into the drive. He learned Katie didn't like green peppers but loved zucchini and peas. He stopped Peaches near the door.

Katie climbed out and Leah followed. "I'll just be a minute," Katie told Seth.

Seth assumed Katie wanted to give Leah some household instructions for while she was gone. He looked at the barn, a simple post-and-beam with a gambrel roof. The timber structure looked older than the house, but it wasn't uncommon for the Amish to put up a barn first.

"Okay, I'm ready." Katie climbed into the buggy and plopped down beside him on the bench, an envelope clutched in her hand.

"What's that?"

"A letter I need to mail."

"Which direction is the post office?"

"I have a stamp on it. I can leave it in the box for the carrier to pick up. Besides, we need to get back to check on Annie and the boys."

We. He liked how that word sounded. He clicked his tongue and Peaches lurched forward. His thoughts drifted to ways to spend more time with Katie, and this time his stomach didn't roll.

"I wonder where Elias went. I didn't see him," Seth said.

"*Jah*, that's strange." Katie grew quiet and gazed out the window as if lost in her thoughts. Then she pivoted on the bench and faced him with a wide smile. "Did you have devotional time with the family and read the Scriptures?"

He shook his head, then shifted his focus to the road when her smile dropped and her eyes saddened with disappointment. He was disgusted with himself. How could he have fallen in love with another woman who would never accept him? Only this time the pain now reached his core. He was more annoyed with Diana than hurt by her when she voiced her dissatisfaction with his decision to build beehives. With Katie, it felt entirely different. He would give anything to be the man she wanted him to be.

Seth stopped at the end of the driveway. "Give me your letter and I'll put it in the mailbox."

"*Denki,*" she said, handing it to him.

Seth slid off the bench, gazing at the envelope. Jonas Yoder. Big Creek Township. He recognized it as one of the Oscoda County districts.

She cleared her throat. "Don't forget to put the flag up on the box."

He shoved the letter inside, made sure to lift the red flag, then climbed onto the bench. Proud of himself for not asking who Jonas was, he signaled the horse and stopped near the porch to let her get out. "Will you send the boys out to the barn?"

"Jah." Katie glanced at the sun, then at him. "Will you tell me the time? I'm wondering if I should get lunch started."

He lifted his hip and reached into his pocket for his watch. Without glancing at it, he handed it to her. "I'll get it from you later." He waited for her to step away from the buggy, then continued to the hitching post.

Seth struggled to shift his thoughts away from Katie as he removed the horse's harness and led the mare to the pasture gate. Peaches lowered her head and snorted, lifting a layer of dust from the dry ground. Seth leaned against the fence and lifted one boot, resting it on the bottom board. Peaches dipped her head into the water trough, took a long drink, then lifted her head and perked her ears at the snap of the screen door closing.

Seth turned.

Thomas and Paul walked side by side, hands in their pockets and scuffing their feet over the gravel drive.

"Why the long faces?"

"I don't understand why she has to bring *schulwork* with her when she *kumms* over," Thomas said, kicking at a stone and sending it skipping over the lawn.

"We looked through the bag she brought," Paul said.

"It's math." Thomas scowled.

"And reading," Paul added.

"You had no business looking through her stuff." Seth related to their dread of schoolwork, but he couldn't let them get away with invading Katie's privacy. It'd probably do them both some good for Katie to help them with a few lessons. After all, they'd missed plenty of school from Amos removing them. "She means well. Besides, that's what *teetshahs* do."

"Jah, at *schul.* But we're *nett* in *schul."* Thomas huffed. "When is *Daed* going to get better?"

"I hope soon." Seth glanced at the house. Katie had certainly gotten under the boys' skin. His too, but in a much different way. He hoped Amos's swelling went down soon. Things would be easier once Seth could return home and get back to building hives. As it was, he had several orders to fill to keep him busy. In recent years, his business had grown. Once the *Englischers* learned his beehives were cheaper than his competitors' hives, he had more orders than he could handle without hiring help.

Katie's comment flashed through his mind. How did she know he was bored building hives? He should be thrilled that God had allowed him to prosper despite all his past mistakes. He shipped his products out of state and even into Canada. Perhaps if Katie knew how successful his business was, she would think differently.

Later that afternoon, while Annie napped, Katie gazed out the window as the sink filled with soapy water to scrub the cabinets and walls.

When Seth leaned a ladder against the damaged barn, her breath seized. He took the first step and paused. She hoped he was checking the ladder's stability. Amos's injuries were a result of falling off the ladder. Seth climbed higher, the boys holding the base of the ladder below. He spent a few minutes at the top of the ladder studying the structure, then climbed down.

Katie blew out a pent-up breath.

Water gushed over the lip of the sink. She snapped to attention and turned off the tap. She rolled up her sleeves and reached into the bottom of the deep cast-iron sink to pull the plug. More water cascaded over the rim this time, soaking the front of her dress and spilling onto her shoes. She should've been paying attention and not gawking like a teenager out the window. She looked at the puddle on the floor. At least she'd planned to give the floor a good scrubbing sometime today.

Katie wiped her hands on a dish towel and grabbed the mop. The walls and windows could wait until after the floor dried. By the time she had finished scrubbing, she was wet and exhausted. She couldn't very easily wait in the sitting room for the floor to dry, so she went out to the porch and sat on the top step. She wasn't there long before Seth meandered her way.

"Is Amos giving you a hard time?"

"*Nay*, I scrubbed the floors and I'm waiting for them to dry." She glanced at the boys moving the ladder away from the building and thought it was odd. No work had been done on the barn. But the sky had turned gray, and Seth probably figured it would rain.

"I can't do anything without supplies," he said as though responding to her puzzlement. "I made a list of the materials, but it's too late to go into town today."

"Are the boys finished?" she asked, intentionally changing the subject.

"*Jah.*"

"*Gut.*" She stood. "Please send them inside. I want to work with them on math."

Seth had chopped a nice-sized pile of kindling by the time Paul shot out of the house. Something had happened. Paul was holding his belly laughing.

Seth lowered the ax. "What's so funny?"

Paul flipped his thumb over his shoulder. "The *teetshah* is giving Thomas a hard time about his numbers."

"What about them?"

"He writes most of them backward. He always did." He bent down to pick up some pieces of wood.

Seth groaned. "Stay here. I'll take the wood inside."

"Thomas should just do the work," Paul said, handing Seth the wood. "They're *nett* hard, even for me, and I'm younger."

Seth understood too well. He trekked to the house.

"Thomas, all I'm asking is that you try it this new way," Katie was saying.

"I still won't remember them in the right order," he said.

The familiar words stung like darts. Seth had said the same thing to his teacher when he was Thomas's age. He wished he had a nickel for every time his teacher told him to try harder.

Seth tossed the wood into the box beside the stove, then wiped the bark from his hands.

"That's a little better," Katie said, studying Thomas's paper.

Seth patted his nephew's shoulder. "Sounds like a *gut* stopping point."

Thomas sprang out of the chair.

Katie shook her head. "He's *nett* finished."

Seth furrowed his brow at her, but she didn't take the hint. "He can work on the problems later."

"Can we have a word outside, please?"

Seth nodded and followed her out to the back porch.

"He's further behind than most boys even Paul's age," she said once the door closed.

"He'll catch up."

"*Jah*, I believe he will, but I need time to work with him on some new ways—"

"*Schul's* out, Katie." Seth stressed each word.

She squared her shoulders and opened her mouth, but Seth spoke first.

"Let the boy be." His harsh tone drove home his point.

Katie looked away for a brief moment, then with regained composure turned back to him. "Keep your ear open for Annie. She should wake from her nap soon." She stepped off the porch. "I think I need to take a walk."

Chapter Twenty-Two

Seth's arms quivered under the weight of the ax. He stopped and swiped his shirtsleeve over his forehead. Dark clouds had rolled in and Katie still hadn't returned from her walk. He hurled another swing.

He should have stopped her from storming off.

Thunder boomed. That was enough reason to go find her. He leaned the ax against the woodshed and sprinted to the house. After telling Thomas and Paul to stay inside with Annie, Seth bolted in the same direction as Katie had gone.

As he tromped across the furrowed field, it began to rain. A downpour drenched his clothes by the time he reached the school yard.

"Katie?" A steady stream of rain drained off the brim of his hat and ran down the middle of his back. "Katie," he called louder, scanning the area. He thought for sure she would have come here.

Except for the concrete stoop that once led to the school and the planks covering the cellar so no one would accidently fall into the pit, the area was bare. He hoped she had enough sense not to go in there but figured he'd better check. Seth climbed on the planks and lowered himself through the escape hatch.

"Katie?"

"Over here," she said.

"What are you doing in here?" He moved closer to the corner where she huddled and sat beside her. Regretting the harsh tone he'd used that drove her away, this time he intentionally spoke gently. "This place isn't safe. These walls could collapse at any time."

"I don't plan to stay long."

He sighed. "I hope you don't mind if I wait in here with you."

"I suppose you have the right to get out of the rain."

They weren't totally clear of the rain. Water streamed between the planks, creating a puddle on the cellar's dirt floor. At least they were away from the direct flow. Besides a few drips on his shoulder, the corner was dry.

"How did you know where to find me?" She scooted closer to the wall, giving him more room to get away from the leak.

"This is the first place where we met." He squeezed closer, his shoulder brushing against hers.

She snorted.

"*Jah*, I suppose you didn't *kumm* here to reminisce about me." He thought better than to chuckle. His dry humor wasn't what she needed. "I do think this was the last place you felt some stability in your life." Her silence loomed and he sensed his assumption was correct. "I have a place at home where I go . . . but I have yet to sort everything out."

"*Ach*, and here I thought you had all the answers."

He didn't mind her snide remark. Although he hated to think that was her true belief. He had no answers, about his life or anyone's for that matter.

"Have you always wanted to be a *teetshah*?"

"*Nay*," she whispered.

Not expecting that reply, he was at a loss for words. He thought she lived and breathed grading papers.

She continued without any prompting from him. "I suppose you were right about me finding some form of stability here." She forced a smile. "I had everything I wanted . . . then James died and *mei* life became meaningless. Being a *teetshah* gave me a purpose." She nodded. "So, *jah*, I found stability here."

At the river, when she had mentioned James, Seth could tell the man had been special to her. But she hadn't explained their relationship at that time, and he hadn't wanted to pry. But now he needed to know.

"You never did say who James was to you."

"We were engaged. Just published in the church."

"You never fell in love again?" Normally he wasn't so inquisitive. He didn't care to know the answers to these personal questions—until now. He especially wanted to know about Jonas Yoder, the man she sent a letter to.

She shook her head. "I believe teaching is God's will for me." Her eyes darted up to the overhead planks. "At least, that's what I believed before the tornado." She blew out a breath. "I'm *nett* sure about anything anymore."

He wasn't either.

He looked around the opening. With more light than the last time they shared this space, he had a better view of the stone-wall-structure. He eyed the wood stacked in the corner—it supported the wall better than he expected.

He couldn't stand the silence any longer.

"Who is Jonas Yoder?"

Her brows crinkled.

"You mailed a letter to him. Who is he?"

"You shouldn't be reading other people's mail." She tapped her chest. "*Mei* mail."

Jah, and he shouldn't be thinking about kissing her, but he was.

"I think the rain has let up *nau*."

It hadn't, but when she stood, Seth rose to his feet. He knocked his head hard on a plank.

"Are you okay?"

"*Jah*—*nay*, I'm *nett* okay." She had him half crazed. "Never mind." He had to get out of this tomb.

She reached up, grabbed hold of the plank at the opening, and tried to climb out. Her shoe slipped on the wet stones.

Seth came up behind her and placed his hands around her waist, but instead of lifting her, he spun her to face him. He lowered his mouth inches from hers. "Tell me Jonas is *nett* your *bu*," he whispered hoarsely.

"He's *nett*."

Her words barely audible, he wasn't even sure he heard her right as his mouth moved over hers, parting her lips and capturing everything he wanted in the moment. Pressing his hand against her back, he brought her closer to him. Then he stopped. In speechless wonderment, he gazed into her eyes until he couldn't stop from kissing her again.

This time she pushed away. "It's stopped raining." She pivoted around.

He placed his hands around her waist, hesitated a moment, then lifted her out of the hole. Once she was safely out, he grasped the planks and pulled himself up.

She hadn't waited. Katie scurried over to the edge of the plank and jumped off, landing in a puddle. Muddy water splattered her dress. She glanced at her soaked shoes and frowned.

His long stride easily cleared the water. He came up beside her. "You never said why you sent a letter to Jonas Yoder."

"He's the bishop of the district in Oscoda County whose *teetshah* died."

"So you were sending your condolences?" His foot sank into the loose ground as he tried to walk beside her.

"*Nay*, I was applying for the position."

He loped alongside her as they skirted the drenched field's border to avoid some of the mud. "It seems like it was just yesterday when we were stuck in the cellar."

"I think you promised the students and me ice cream."

"So I did." He smiled, until a few steps from the yard his foot sank again, this time past the ankle. He yanked it out and gave it a shake.

She continued walking, making it to the driveway.

He caught up with her. "They sell ice cream in town . . . We could . . . take a buggy ride."

"I think I will have to pass." She smiled and kept walking. With a pang, Seth noticed she wasn't headed toward the house but in the direction of her buggy.

"Are you leaving so soon?"

She lowered her head and nodded.

His shoulders slumped. "I'll get your buggy ready." He never really knew what to expect from her, but this reaction wasn't it. He harnessed the horse without commenting about her silence. Then before she climbed onto the bench, she paused.

"Did you just kiss me because you felt sorry for me? Because I said I had everything I wanted and then lost it all?"

He cleared his throat. *"Nay."* Seth leaned over and kissed her cheek. "And it wasn't because we were alone in a dark cellar. I'll kiss you right here in the open if that will make you happy."

She gave him a sheepish grin. That was enough for him. He tipped her chin and kissed her lips lightly.

Peaches trotted slightly faster than her normal pace in the rain. Katie wasn't sure if the horse had turned skittish after surviving a tornado, or if the overcast sky shielding the sun's heat gave the mare more energy. Either way, Katie was relieved to have left Amos's house with her heart still intact.

Intact, but it felt hung by a pendulum. Swinging through every imaginable emotion after Seth's kiss. She'd never experienced tingling at the roots of her hair, or her whole body wanting to dance as she did when his mouth came over hers and suspended her breath. Now she could barely hold Peaches's reins, her hands trembled so much.

Katie drew in a lungful of fresh air, then blew it out. She needed to redirect these thoughts. All this fuss about a kiss had her hoping for too much.

Without warning, the pendulum stopped. The rushing sounds of the river grew louder, and her emotions numbed with thoughts of James. Katie pulled back on the reins and stopped Peaches. Maybe it was guilt after kissing Seth, but something had drawn her to the river again. She tied Peaches to an overhanging branch and sped down the sandy, fern-laden path.

Reaching the clearing, she slammed to a halt.

Elias was squatted next to a small bed of embers. "You can dry by the fire," he said without looking her direction.

She glanced down at her clinging, wet dress. A sudden chill seeped over her body. She stepped closer with caution. The ground wasn't wet, neither was Elias.

"I thought you might stop by the river again." His smile reached her core.

"This morning was the first time I've been back in years. I used to spend a lot of time here."

"Yes, I know." He pointed upstream. "Around that bend, you used to sit on the riverbank and watch James fly-fish."

"*Jah.*" Her insides trembled. James loved to fish. That was common knowledge for those in their settlement, but Elias hadn't lived in their district for long.

"So you've come to the river to search for answers." He motioned to the campfire. "Would you like to sit for a while?"

She inched a few steps closer, heat penetrating her insides from the flameless fire. Mesmerized by the glowing cinders, her thoughts slipped away, then she glanced at Elias.

"Remember the other day when you said something about obstacles needing to be removed?"

He smiled. "You were listening—that's good."

"But I still don't understand what it all means."

He shifted his gaze toward the warmth, and after a moment of holding his focus elsewhere, he faced her. "Why do you empty the ash pan on your woodstove?"

She crinkled her brows. "So there's airflow. So the wood can burn. Because the ashes would overflow the pan. I don't know."

"You are right. The ashes become an obstacle."

"*Jah,* but I still don't understand how that's supposed to relate to me."

"Sometimes the past becomes an obstacle to reaching your future. The future God planned for you."

Since the tornado destroyed the school, that future seemed dim.

"Each step you've taken serves a purpose. It prepares you to fulfill your destiny." He stood. "I'll give you time to pray. There is more reason you've come to the river beyond talking with me." He ambled away.

Katie pushed off the ground and walked to the riverbank. Three large rocks evenly spaced across the river diverted the water flow, creating enough drop that foamy water pooled below. She closed her eyes. "God, I believe you've called me to become a *teetshah*. I love teaching. I was content to do that *mei* entire life." She drew a deep breath. "But I'm falling in love with Seth. Now I'm confused." There, she said it. Katie dropped to her knees. "I want your will for *mei* life . . . whatever that may be. I'll follow you."

She remained stationary, waiting to hear from God so long that her legs turned numb. Finally, she rose. Her mind was set. She would trust that if God wanted her to teach, he would provide her with students.

The following morning Katie tried to pretend the kiss never happened, and apparently Seth was trying too. He hadn't spoken more than a few words at breakfast, then dashed outside the moment he drained his coffee cup.

She didn't see him again until a few hours later when she was preparing sandwiches for lunch and he came back inside. "I need to go into town and pick up some building supplies," he said.

"Don't you want to eat lunch first?"

"I'm *nett* sure how long this will take, so I'll eat something later."

"Can you buy a few grocery items? I made a list." She licked the peanut butter off her fingers. After pawing through a stack of Annie's coloring, she produced the sheet and handed it to him.

Seth scanned the list. "You need all this?"

"If you want to eat." She leaned closer, peering at the list with him. "Can you think of anything I forgot?"

"I doubt it." He folded the paper, then shoved it into his pocket.

"*Ach*, I didn't even think. If you're going after building supplies, do you have enough money for groceries?" She extended her hand. "Let me have the list. I can find some things to remove."

"Beehive builders do bring in an income."

"But you haven't been home."

"Katie, I have money."

"Can Paul and I *kumm*?" A hopeful smile spread across Thomas's face as he waited for the answer.

"Sure. Go harness the buggy."

The boys practically tripped over themselves to get to the door.

Seth caught Paul by the back of his suspenders and stopped him before he knocked over a kitchen chair. "Slow down. You're stampeding like a herd of crazed animals."

"Sorry." Paul shook his shoulders to get his suspenders back into place.

Seth motioned to the door. "*Geh* on with your business, then."

"I suppose they're trying to get away from me." Katie tried to make light of the fact.

He grinned. "I was never fond of *schul teetshahs*." He headed for the entrance, paused, then looked over his shoulder at her and winked. "At least, I wasn't at their age anyway."

Chapter Twenty-Three

Seth made a second lap down the pasta aisle in the IGA store searching for the last item on Katie's list: noodles for baked ziti casserole. He figured noodles were noodles. But this store had a huge selection. His mother cooked mostly with egg noodles, and only with ones she'd made herself.

"All these different noodles and they probably taste the same," he mumbled as his gaze darted over the various types.

"Need help?" a woman asked.

He started to say no but caught a glimpse of the hem of an Amish dress in his peripheral vision. He turned and greeted Abigail Bender with a smile. "Katie sent me into the store for this." He handed Katie's sister-in-law the list.

"Hmm." Her mouth creased into a smile the longer she studied the page. "Long list, ain't so?"

Seth shrugged.

"Katie makes really *gut* baked ziti casserole." Abigail reached for a box of noodles and handed it to him. "Only she uses penne noodles in hers. *Nett* that it matters in the recipe."

"Denki." Seth put the box in the cart with the other items.

"So why are you doing Katie's grocery shopping?" Her brows wiggled as if she had some sort of tic. She pointed at the paper. "You said this was Katie's list, *jah?*"

"Ach." He laughed, hoping it hid some of his nervousness. "She's helping out at Amos Mast's *haus.*" Before she could ask, he explained in one long-winded, rambling summary. "Amos had an accident and I needed help with Annie . . . Katie didn't tell you any of this?"

Her brows puckered and her mouth fell slightly ajar. She nodded in an absentminded manner.

"She's very *gut* with children," he added. He wasn't sure what prompted him to defend Katie's ability to care for children. After all, she was the district's schoolteacher. Her sister-in-law should already know this about Katie.

"How serious was Amos's accident?"

"Bad. He fell off a ladder and hit his head. He lost his sight."

Abigail covered her mouth with her hand to restrain her gasp. "That's awful news."

"I'm surprised Katie hadn't said something to you. She's been helping out over a week *nau.*"

"Are you working on building more beehives?"

"Other than the ones I put up for Amos, *nay*, I haven't had time." He listened for the sound of disapproval in her tone but couldn't detect anything that suggested she was as disappointed in his form of business as Katie was.

"I know Katie gave you a rough time about setting up Amos's hives near the school, but it seems to me you could move your business anywhere—if you decide to stay in Hope Falls."

He smiled. "I think I'll be too busy with repairing Amos's barn to think about that."

"I take it Katie and Amos are getting along."

He hoped.

"Is something wrong?" she asked.

Probably. He'd spent more time than anyone should searching the grocery aisles. He'd left Katie alone with Amos longer than expected. And the boys. It dawned on him then that he'd left the boys with the buggy and building supplies to run in for what he thought wouldn't be more than a few minutes.

"I shouldn't hold you up any longer," he said, a hint of panic tingeing his words. He pushed the cart toward the register. Isaac's *fraa* probably thought he was scatter-minded. Standing in line with three shoppers ahead of him, he dug his hand into his pocket and pulled out his watch. She would be preparing the supper meal about now. He hoped she wasn't waiting for anything on this grocery list.

"Is someone there?" Amos's voice rang out from the other room.

Katie stopped peeling potatoes and set the paring knife on the table. She went into the sitting room to check on him.

"Do you need something, Amos?"

"Who else is here?" He turned his head one direction, paused, then craned in the opposite direction. "I heard someone."

She glanced around the room. "There isn't anyone here but Annie and me, and we've been working in the kitchen." Since she'd agreed to have supper with them tonight, she had spent most of the afternoon planning a nice meal out of the sparse sup-plies from the pantry.

"Seth and the boys aren't back?" He snapped his head in the opposite direction and shifted on his chair to face the wall.

Sitting so long by himself, he must be going stir-crazy. She walked over to the front window and gazed outside. "I don't see the buggy. They're *nett* back yet." Turning to face him, she paused to study his expression—a tense mixture of fear and bewilderment.

He gripped the arms of the rocker so tight his knuckles turned white. His brows creased and he craned his head one direction and then the other, as if listening for something.

"Do you want me to sit in here and keep you company for a while?"

"Why? To stare at me? Take pity on the blind man?"

"I thought you could use some company, is all."

Razzen whooshed again from Amos's left side to his right and then back to his left side. The breeze he caused disturbed the man. Mind games—Razzen loved them. Unable to see, Amos relied heavily on his hearing. But as Amos was finding out, he could never pinpoint Razzen's location. Stupid fool. Did he really believe he could outwit the master deceiver?

"It's hot in here," Amos said. "Is the window open?" He fanned his face as beads of perspiration welled along his forehead.

Razzen blanketed himself around Amos in the form of fog. Adding an ever-increasing burden of oppression, the demon hadn't left the man alone. Now that he'd niggled Amos into summoning the woman into the room, he could torment them both.

"The windows are open." She studied Amos. Hunched over in the rocking chair, he looked twice his age. A shriveled prune is what he reminded her of. "What if I set a chair under the shade tree—would you like to sit outside?"

"*Nay.*"

She should've expected that answer. "Would you like me to move your chair closer to the window?"

"What for? It's *nett* like I can see outside."

"But you could feel the breeze and smell the fresh air." She slipped behind his chair. "Pick your feet up." She pushed, but the chair only inched forward.

"I didn't say I wanted to move."

"It'll be a *gut* change." She groaned as she tried to push harder. The chair wouldn't budge.

"Okay, stop!" Amos insisted.

She removed her hands from the back of the chair, and he surprised her by standing. "Stay right there," Katie said. She maneuvered the chair around him and quickly pushed it in front of the window.

"Where did you put *mei* chair?" His hands groped the air.

Katie came up beside him and weaved her arm around his. Amos flinched.

"I'm going to help you," she said. "Take a few steps forward."

He mumbled under his breath something she couldn't decipher, but he took a step. With a few simple instructions, she guided him to the chair. "This is much better in front of the window, ain't so?"

Amos huffed.

"It's a beautiful summer day."

"How would I know? I'm blind."

Katie frowned. If he continued in this downward spiral, he

might never get back on his feet. "Amos," she said softly. "God gave you more senses than just sight. Listen to the birds. Smell the grass. Feel the breeze on your face. There's so much for you to enjoy, you don't have to let life pass you by."

He didn't respond.

"I'll be in the kitchen if you need anything." Katie took a few steps away but paused. "Lord, what does it take to reach him?" she whispered.

"Katie, are you still in here?"

She walked toward him. "Did you need something?"

"No wonder I'm hearing things. Stop spying on me."

She left the room. "Lord, have mercy on his wayward mind. You're the only one who can reach him."

Seth squinted into the late afternoon sun, trying to focus on the object several hundred feet down the road. As he lessened the distance between them, he recognized the elderly man ambling along the shoulder of the road. Elias was certainly right when he said he liked walking. From where they were, the nearest Amish farm was over ten miles away. He'd never known anyone who traveled so far walking with a cane. Yet the closer he came to Elias, the easier it was to see the man had a steady gait.

"Whoa," he called as he reined the horse to a stop. "Would you like a ride?"

Elias looked Seth's direction and smiled. *"Jah, denki."*

Seth motioned with his thumb over his shoulder to Thomas and Paul. "Jump in the back, boys, so Elias has a place to sit."

Without hesitating, Thomas and Paul climbed into the market buggy's cargo area with the supplies.

"Awfully thoughtful of you to give me a ride," Elias said, using the bench to pull himself up to the seat. He glanced behind him at Thomas and Paul. "Working with your *onkel* today?"

Thomas nodded.

"We just *kumm* from town to pick up supplies," Seth said. "I haven't had a chance to help more with the needs of the settlement, but I hope to soon."

"I heard today they expect more workers to arrive tomorrow. I'm *nett* sure how long they will be here, but some of the elders were making arrangements for places they could stay."

"I'm glad to hear more help is arriving." Seth wished he could do more, but as it was, the work that needed done at Amos's house would consume his next few weeks.

Elias looked over his shoulder. "You didn't need many supplies, I see."

"Couldn't find much. It seems there isn't any building material left in Hope Falls. The lumberyard is dry of both lumber and roofing material."

"I heard that today too."

"I didn't realize how hard the *Englisch* were hit until I went into town. I feel bad. Normally the Amish are quick to help in a crisis. In *mei* district last fall, we put up a new barn for an *Englisch* neighbor who lost his in a fire. But here, with so much destruction throughout this settlement, every man is needed to rebuild the Amish farms. Planting time has already been pushed back, and the barns will be needed before harvesttime."

Elias nodded. "I heard the government stepped in and provided the *Englisch* with temporary houses and drinking water."

"*Jah,* some county representatives asked the bishop if the Amish needed government assistance. Every Amish man understands why the bishop turned them down." He chuckled. "But

I'm sure the representatives were confused that we would still wish to maintain separation from the world even in the most desperate times. Perhaps they won't ever understand our plain living and that we can make do with what we have." Seth wagged his head. "I'm *nett* so sure the *Englischers* can cope long without what they believe are necessities, ain't so?"

"God's provision comes from an unlimited source. But there are so many people who hoard their possessions as if they had some sort of control over their future."

Seth opened his mouth to agree but held his comment. Elias fixed his gaze upward. Only he seemed to be looking at something beyond the buggy roof.

The man's eyes closed. "Jehovah-Jireh," Elias said in almost a whisper. After a moment of silence, he opened his eyes and looked at Seth. "If only people could truly see that the hand that feeds them also provides for them in every other way."

Seth nodded.

"It's unnecessary to worry or be anxious about anything," the elderly man added.

Seth swallowed hard as a shudder sped through him. Elias seemed to be speaking directly to him. He suspected Elias's comment held a deeper meaning, but he hesitated to ask. He wasn't prepared to face correction if, in fact, Elias's word was directed at Seth.

Elias continued anyway without any prompting. "You might believe you lack certain abilities, but be of good cheer, God has equipped you to accomplish his will."

"Equipped you . . ." Elias's words echoed in Seth's suspended state of consciousness. For a dazed moment, he felt removed from the natural realm as voices rang out, *"Be of good cheer."*

Seth shook his head. No one in this settlement, except for

Amos, knew about Seth's past. How he had vowed never to build anything besides beehives again. How would Elias know he lacked confidence? Or that he worried his building abilities were severely deficient?

Elias pointed to the woodsy area up ahead. "You can drop me off there."

Seth slowed Sage. He recognized the spot near the river where they had found Leah. "It was nice talking with you," he said as he pulled the horse to a stop.

"If it's okay, I would like to help you repair Amos's barn."

Seth smiled. He appreciated any help he could get. "Would you like me to pick you up in the morning?"

Elias smiled. "It's going to rain for four days. I'll see you after that."

Seth glanced at the clear sky. It sure didn't look like rain to him.

Chapter Twenty-Four

Katie positioned herself at the clothesline so she could see anyone who entered Amos's drive, particularly Seth. He and the boys had been gone a long time. She wanted to time supper so they wouldn't have to wait long to eat. She placed the folded towel on top of the others and picked up the laundry basket as Seth pulled into the drive. He parked the buggy close to the house and the boys piled out the back end.

"Don't run off," Seth said, stopping Thomas and Paul, who had their sights set on the barn and had turned in that direction. "The groceries need to be taken inside."

The boys doubled back without a word and joined Seth at the back of the buggy. Katie walked up, basket in hand, as Seth handed two bags to Thomas and another two to Paul.

"Did you find everything you needed for the barn?"

"The lumberyard was practically empty." Seth loaded his

arms with the remaining bags. "Sorry we're late. I hope you weren't waiting for any of these items to start supper."

She shook her head. "I just slipped it into the oven."

They climbed the porch steps, and Seth juggled the bags to one side in order to reach for the doorknob.

"I'll get the door." It was easier for her to shift the laundry basket over one hip. She weaved her arm between him and the house. Standing close enough to detect the variation of blues in his eyes, her breath caught. No wonder his eyes mesmerized her. A lighter shade surrounded his pupil and a darker blue outlined the iris. She hadn't ever seen anyone with such vibrant coloration.

"Your eyes sparkle," he said.

"Mine?" She was thinking the same of his. She jiggled the handle, but he hadn't seemed to notice the door was stuck. She gave the door a bump with her hip. He was still gazing at her eyes.

The door opened. Thomas looked at her, then at his *onkel*, and crinkled his face.

With his weight off balance, Seth nearly dropped the groceries, thrusting the bags into Thomas's arms. "Take these into the kitchen, please."

"Sure." Thomas took another puzzled look at the two of them before shaking his head and walking away.

Seth grinned. "Sorry if I embarrassed you." Now that his hands were free, he reached for the laundry basket. "I'll take this inside for you." He opened the door wider for her to enter.

She scooted past him and headed into the kitchen.

Seth followed and set the basket on the table.

Standing near the sink, Thomas nudged Paul in the ribs. "Let's go outside."

"Me too." Annie left her crayon on the table and scooted off the chair. She ran across the room, following the boys.

He motioned to the bags. "I think I found most of the stuff on your list."

"*Denki*." She grabbed an armful of groceries and placed them on the pantry shelf. The penne noodles took her by surprise. She'd thought about her list after Seth had left for town, and remembered only writing "noodles for ziti." It was strange for him to think to buy penne noodles. As far as she knew, she was the only one in her district who made that particular casserole with that type of noodles.

"I ran into your sister-in-law at the store."

That explained the noodles.

"She seemed surprised you hadn't mentioned helping here." He raised his brows.

Katie removed more items from the bag. "Abigail sometimes jumps to the wrong conclusions."

"Hmm . . . Is that why she asked if I had moved my beehive business to Hope Falls?"

Katie froze. Even for Abigail it was bold to plant that suggestion. "What did you tell her?"

"That I had enough work with Amos's barn to keep me busy." He took a few steps toward the door, then stopped. "How was Amos?"

"I'm worried about him. He seemed skittish today."

"What you mean?"

"He kept rotating his head from side to side. He was hearing things. Seth, he needs to hear the Scriptures. You have to start reading the Word."

His face sobered. "*Jah*, you're probably right." He motioned with a head nod to the door. "I need to unload the supplies."

Elias sheathed his charge. "He struggles to keep his pain buried."
Then added, "But the Master sheds light on the darkness to bring forth
his perfect will."

For a moment Katie wasn't sure what to make of Seth's expression, but she was pleased he agreed about reading. The wagon wouldn't take long to unload, so she needed to finish preparing the meal. She jumped into motion and opened a jar of green beans to heat, chopped some celery she'd cut earlier from the garden, and put together a pan of rhubarb crisp.

Annie returned, her lips protruding in a pucker.

"Why the long face?"

"They said I couldn't help unload the wagon."

"You can set the table for me," Katie said.

Annie nodded and the two worked together.

The closer it came to supper time, the harder it was to settle her jitters. She grabbed a pot holder and checked the roast one more time, stabbed a fork into a few of the red potatoes, then placed the lid back on the roasting pan. Not much longer now. She scanned the place settings on the table. Thomas and Paul would sit on one side of the table, opposite her and Annie, and Seth would sit at the head. *Ach*, what was wrong with her? Everyone would sit in the same spot as breakfast and lunch. Her heart was pounding and her hands were moist. What was wrong with her?

It was only supper—a family supper.

It wasn't like she was dining alone with Seth. So why was her spine tickling like it had last night when he asked her to stay?

She was too old for these girlish feelings. But she couldn't pull herself away from looking out the window to check Seth and the boys' work flow. They piled the last of the lumber from the wagon next to the barn.

Katie hurried to grab a pot holder. They would be inside soon. She opened the oven and lifted the lid on the roaster. The scent of beef roast engulfed her senses. She hoped Seth liked roast as much as she did. It was brown and falling-off-the-fork tender as she transferred it to a platter. The potatoes and green beans she put into serving bowls and set on the table.

The door opened, and Thomas and Paul entered the kitchen. Thomas went to the sink and turned on the water. "*Onkel* Seth is hitching your buggy," he said, lathering his hands with soap.

"*Nau?*" She peeked out the window. Sure enough, he had Peaches tethered to the post and was buckling the mare's harness. Had it slipped his mind that he had invited her to stay for supper?

Inside, Katie wanted to crumble. She squared her shoulders instead. "Be mindful of your sister," she instructed Thomas.

Katie removed her shawl from the hook and wrapped it around her shoulders. Not that she needed her shawl for warmth. She couldn't ask for a more pleasant warm summer evening. A night like tonight was perfect for sitting on the porch and listening to the bullfrogs. But that didn't matter now.

She walked across the lawn and met Seth near the hitching post.

He glanced sideways at her. "*Denki* for waiting until the wagon was unloaded."

"That's okay. I made pot roast . . . for supper."

"That sounds *gut*. *Denki*." He untied Peaches.

She stared at him a moment, then realizing how foolish she looked loitering, she climbed up on the bench, wishing she had the courage to ask what she'd done wrong.

Seth wanted to call out and stop Katie from leaving, but he couldn't. If she stayed for supper, she would expect him to read the family devotions aloud. He wasn't ready for that humiliation. He lowered his head and shuffled gravel with his foot until he no longer heard her buggy wheels crunching over the driveway. Then he turned and went inside. He had to stop these feelings from growing before they developed into something he couldn't control. He already had no control over the consequences of past mistakes, nor could he change the fact that he would never measure up to her expectations. Seth sighed. Inhaling the aroma of pot roast didn't help his conscience.

A clean plate sat in front of the chair where Katie had sat during lunch. Feasting on guilt, Seth lost his appetite. When he bowed his head to say silent grace, he asked God to forgive him for hurting her.

"Where's Katie?" Annie asked the moment everyone finished their prayers.

"She went home," Thomas said.

Annie pointed to the plate. "She's supposed to be right there."

"She'll be back tomorrow." Seth took a spoonful of beans and passed them to Paul on his left. The roast practically dissolved in his mouth, it was so tender. The best he'd ever eaten. He took another bite, then pushed away from the table. He couldn't eat any more. Not without settling things with Katie.

"I need to run an errand. You boys *redd-up* the kitchen after you eat and keep your eye on Annie." He grabbed his hat off the wall hook. "Leave *mei* plate on the table. I'll eat when I get back." Before he changed his mind, he fled the house.

He had Sage hitched in no time and was headed to Katie's house without a clue as to what he would say to her. He only knew he wouldn't get any sleep tonight if he didn't see her.

"Lord, please help me with my words . . ." He couldn't even find the right words to pray. Was this a mistake? But despite the risk of humiliation, he continued.

Sage hadn't come to a complete stop before he jumped out of the buggy. He knocked hard on the door, then impatiently knocked again.

Stomach acid burned the back of his throat. He swallowed, but that didn't dilute the bitter taste.

He knocked again. This time the door opened before he pulled his hand away.

"*Onkel* Seth? Is something wrong?"

"*Jah*, I need to talk to Katie," he said.

"She's *nett* here. But you can wait for her."

His stomach dropped as if he'd jumped off the barn loft into a stack of hay. "Where is she?"

Leah opened the door wider and shook her head. "I don't know." She motioned for him to enter. "She told me the other day that you invited her for supper. Did she change her mind?"

Emotionally drained, Katie stared into her cup of tepid tea. She now feared her impulsive decision to stop at her brother's house wasn't so smart. Abigail zoomed in on her gloomy mood.

"I don't want you to move away," Abigail said.

"I just mailed the letter. I don't even know if I'll get the job." She hoped that was the case. She needed a source of income.

"Are you sure you've prayed about the matter?"

Katie nodded. "You were the one who helped me decide to become a *teetshah*."

"I know."

Isaac entered the kitchen with the milking bucket and set it on the counter. He glanced at them, his attention split between Abigail and Katie. "Did someone die?"

Katie shook her head.

"She wrote a letter to the bishop in Oscoda County about the *teetshah* position," Abigail said.

"Where did you hear about the *teetshah* job?"

"The *Budget* had an article about their *schul* closing early because the *teetshah* passed away." Katie sipped her tea.

"They wouldn't need anyone until next fall," he said.

Katie nodded. "I would have to make living arrangements and . . ."

"This isn't what you want." Abigail reached across the table for Katie's hand. "Be truthful with yourself."

"What I want is for us to rebuild our *schul*." She looked at Isaac. "Do you think there is any chance of it being rebuilt?"

He shook his head. "The members are all struggling. Either they've had damages from the storm or their crops are in jeopardy from so much rain. We won't raise enough funds for a *schul*. *Nett* by fall. A disaster like we've had will take years to recover from."

Katie slumped in the chair. She understood the members' limited resources. She'd depleted her savings to help also.

Isaac took a few steps toward the door but paused at the kitchen's entrance. "With the building materials in short supply, I know of a few men looking to buy a farm instead of rebuilding. I'll talk with them and see if someone is interested in purchasing the farm."

Katie's jaw dropped. "You want to sell the family farm?"

"We wouldn't be *gut* stewards if it sat unoccupied," he said.

"What happens if I don't get the job?"

266

"You can live here. The *grossdaadi haus* is empty. It's something we need to consider since our finances will be upside down along with everyone else's if we lose the crops."

It sounded as though Isaac had already given the idea thought. If she knew her brother, he'd already made up his mind on the matter.

"Can't we wait and pray about this?" Katie glanced at Abigail for her agreement.

"We can't wait too long," Isaac said. "Would that be God's will when so many people are in hard times from the storm?"

Katie wasn't sure what God's will was about anything.

Isaac walked out of the room.

"It'll work out. Trust God." Abigail patted her hand and sighed. "Let's talk about something else. I saw Seth in the store buying groceries. Why didn't you tell me about Amos's accident or that you were helping them?"

Katie shrugged. "You were busy helping Mary. How is Bishop Lapp?"

"He's making small improvements, or at least he's learning to cope with his limitations."

"That's *gut*." Katie stood. She had more thoughts to sort out now that Isaac wanted to sell the family farm.

Abigail followed her to the door. "Seth seemed very pleased you were helping him." She lifted her brows. "Very pleased," she restated. "Does he know about you requesting the position in Oscoda?"

Katie nodded. "He mailed the letter."

Abigail's smile plummeted. "And here I thought you two were secretly courting."

"I'll talk with you soon." Katie slipped out the door before her sister-in-law drilled her with more questions.

☙

Seth drummed his fingers on Katie's kitchen table. She should've been home by now. He wasn't sure if he should start looking for her, but he couldn't sit still any longer. He jumped to his feet.

"You're *nett* leaving before she *kumms* home, are you?" Leah asked. "She probably stopped at a store."

"It's dark. She shouldn't be shopping at this hour." He remembered how antsy Peaches was the other day and how difficult the mare was to hold back. "I'm going to look for her." He crossed the room, opened the door, and stood face-to-face with Katie. He hadn't even heard her buggy pull into the drive, which was unusual.

"Seth? What are you doing here?"

"Can we talk out here? I won't stay long." He stepped outside and closed the door behind him.

"*Jah.*" She moved past him and opened the door. "Give me a minute to get a lantern." She disappeared inside.

Seth rubbed his hands on the sides of his pants.

The door creaked and Katie stepped out, a lit lamp in hand. "What did you want to talk about?"

"I, ah . . ." He jammed his hands into his pockets, then pulled one out to motion toward the steps. "Do you want to sit for a few minutes?"

She nodded and set the lantern on the banister sill, then sat beside him on the top step.

Crickets sang in the background of their silence. Seth gazed out in the darkness, his mind groping for the right words to say.

"It's a nice *nacht*, ain't so?" she said.

"*Jah. Nett* hot or cold." He blew out a breath.

"The rain helped yesterday."

He looked at the moon. Full. Bright. His chest ached, and if he didn't release the pressure, he thought he might burst.

"There're a lot of stars out tonight," she said.

"I shouldn't have snapped at you about Thomas. I didn't mean to insult your teaching. That's why I went looking for you. I wanted to apologize, but I . . . I guess I got sidetracked while we were in the cellar. I'm sorry."

She took a moment before responding. "You were right. *Schul* is out. Besides, I hadn't had Thomas as a student in a long time."

"Amos was wrong to remove them from *schul*." Seth swatted at a mosquito buzzing next to his ear.

"I agree." Distracted, she chased a pesky mosquito off her arm. "I had a long talk with your sister about Thomas before she passed away . . . before I knew she was sick."

"Thomas mixes up his words and numbers. They appear backward to him," he added.

"Erma told you?"

He shook his head. "He's probably a slow reader and gets poor grades, ain't so?"

"*Jah*." Her expression hardened. "He isn't stupid."

"I didn't say he was stupid."

Her stern defense of his nephew surprised him.

She relaxed a little. "Amos wasn't supportive of Thomas receiving extra help."

"And Erma was?" His sister had been so timid he couldn't imagine her going against her husband in something.

"She asked me to do everything I could." She smiled proudly. "That's why I know he is a smart child. I tested him differently."

"What do you mean? How?"

"Well, first I spent a Saturday at the library, talking with the librarian. I explained the backward numbers and letters and asked if she had ever heard of such a condition."

"And she knew about it?" Until he found out about Thomas, Seth didn't know anyone was like him.

"*Jah*, she spent some time on her computer and within minutes had a list of books for me to read. It's called dyslexia."

Dyslexia . . . There was actually a term associated with reading letters and numbers backward. Even books about it too. For years he had struggled to hide his shame.

"Erma was going to talk with Amos and convince him Thomas needed extra help, but then she got sick and . . ." She dabbed the corner of her eye with the hem of her dress sleeve.

"I have a confession." The words spilled out. This was difficult enough without her crinkling her brows questioningly at him. Still, he knew if he didn't say something now, he might never find the courage again. He swallowed hard and continued, "I tried to protect Thomas because I have the same problem."

The line between her brows deepened and she tilted her head slightly sideways.

He reached into his pocket and pulled out his watch. "I remember numbers by the position of the clock hands. You said Thomas gets his twos and fives and the sixes and nines mixed up. So do I." There, he said it. He wished the confession supplied some sort of balm of relief, but it didn't. Instead of feeling peace, his nerves fired even more sporadically.

"Did you know you have dyslexia?"

Unable to face her, he closed his eyes and shook his head. "I didn't even know it had a name until you said so just now. I knew I had a problem. That's why I didn't want to read the Scriptures. Why I hitched your buggy before supper."

"You practically shooed me off too."

He smiled. "*Jah*, I suppose I did do that."

She sighed. "I'm glad you told me."

"I didn't want you to think you did something wrong."

She sounded surprised or relieved, he didn't know which. Either way, the truth was out in the open. She knew his shortcomings—most of them.

Another mosquito landed on her, this time on her cheek. Seth shooed it away. "I suppose I should go before we get eaten alive out here."

She nodded. "*Denki* for stopping over."

"I'll see you tomorrow." He walked down the steps and was near his buggy when he heard her call his name. He turned as she was coming down the steps.

"Would you let me help you?"

"You want me to be your student?" He sighed. He should've anticipated her offer and had an answer prepared. Looking in her eyes now made it difficult to refuse.

"On a trial basis?"

"Am I going to have to raise *mei* hand and call you *teetshah*?"

She laughed. "*Nay*, silly."

Ach, why did he think he would regret this? "We can try it—for a short time."

Chapter Twenty-Five

The next morning Katie arrived at Amos's house prepared for her new student. She'd stayed up late to read through the notes she'd taken in the library about dyslexia, and to jot down a few scriptures on some index cards.

"You're early." Seth's smile dropped when he reached for the bag of supplies in her hand. He led the way to the kitchen, muttering something about needing more coffee before he dared to ask what she'd brought with her. He placed the bag on the counter and, without asking, poured her a cup of coffee.

He handed her the drink, then motioned to the chairs.

"Denki." She sat.

"All right, how hard are you going to make this on me?"

She blew into her cup. "I thought you needed to finish your *kaffi* first."

"I'm just trying to get an idea if I should *kumm* back in after chores or hide out in the barn for the rest of the day."

She shrugged. "I suppose that depends on if you want a treat or not."

His eyes widened. "So you're saying there's food in that bag?" He set his cup on the table and pushed back his chair, the legs scraping against the wooden floor.

"Ach, nay." Katie lurched for the bag and snatched it before he could look inside. "You'll find out soon enough."

"I suppose I will." He rubbed his jaw. "All kidding aside, I am nervous about this. I haven't been in *schul* in over fifteen years."

"I promise you won't think you're in *schul*." She opened the bag and dug her hand inside.

He cracked a smile and leaned closer, but groaned when she showed him the index card she'd pulled out. "What's that?"

She returned to the table and sat. He did the same.

"I thought we would start with scriptures." She held the card for him to see as she read the passage of Jeremiah. "'For I know the thoughts that I think toward you, says the LORD, thoughts of peace and not of evil, to give you a future and a hope.'" She handed the card to him. "Now you read it to me."

Seth's hands shook. He cleared his throat, hesitated a moment, then read it, dragging some of the words.

"You have a nice reading voice." She meant it. He wasn't as slow as she'd expected. He needed confidence mostly.

"Some of the words jumped." He held out the card.

"That's for you. Read it over throughout the day and try to memorize it."

"What's next?"

"That's it for *nau*." She sipped her coffee.

273

He tipped his head. "So I'm excused?"

"You do plan to finish your *kaffi, jah?*"

He smiled. *"Jah."*

It wasn't long before Annie padded into the kitchen, prayer *kapp* in hand, and handed it to Katie.

Seth rose from the chair. "I'm going to see what I can get done before it starts raining." He grabbed his hat from the hook and headed outside.

Katie pinned Annie's *kapp* in place, and the two of them worked together preparing pancakes for breakfast.

By noontime it was raining. Hard. It didn't stop the boys from going back out to the barn, but after the meal Seth loitered at the table with Katie. He recited the scripture a few more times, then she gave him another card with a new scripture to work on.

An hour later Seth stood. "I think I'm going to like this," he said, shoving the cards into his pocket.

"I told you it wouldn't be tough."

"I was referring to spending time with you." He winked.

Thankfully, he turned to leave before noticing that her face had heated. She liked spending time with him too, but she wasn't bold enough to make that admission.

Four days of constant rain prevented Seth from working on the calving barn, but it gave him more time to spend with Katie and he wasn't complaining. He would continue to endure the reading assignments because they gave him an excuse to be alone with her. And he was probably learning something. He discovered her smile was contagious and her laughter was a song in his heart.

"Do you think it'll rain tomorrow?" Katie moved away from the window when the kettle hissed.

"I hope so."

She looked at him a moment, then continued pouring the coffee. "You're *nett* a little antsy to start working on the barn?"

"Nope."

She handed him a cup, then circled around the table to sit facing him. He meant it as a compliment since the rain gave him free time to memorize those index cards she made for him. But her quietness indicated something was heavy on her mind.

"Have I taken up too much of your time?"

"*Nay.*" She smiled. "I would think just the opposite. I'm occupying too much of your time."

He shook his head.

"I think Amos is uptight about *nett* hearing any hammering." She looked down at her cup and sighed. "Why do you think he hasn't asked about Leah?"

"He's bullheaded."

"He's beyond that. I cannot imagine *nett* knowing where my child was."

"I agree. He needs our prayers."

She reached for the Bible at the far end of the table, opened it, and gave it to him.

"I'm *nett* ready to read any passages." Nervous, he tapped his fingers on the tabletop. "I can't do it."

"Why *nett*? You've learned more than a dozen scriptures already." She stood and grabbed a rectangular piece of cardboard cut off from a noodle box. She laid it across the page. "Read that line, then move the marker down to read the next line."

He shifted on the chair. His reading hadn't advanced to this level. He leaned over the pages, then looked up at her. "I can't do it."

"*Jah*, you can. Try. I think you'll be surprised."

He blew out a breath and stole another glimpse of her. He should've known she wouldn't back down. He would read it, but once he did, he was heading out to the barn. Seth focused on the page in Jeremiah and began to read. When he reached the end of the line, he uncovered more words. "'. . . I, the LORD, search the heart, I test the mind, even to give every man according to his ways, according to the fruit of his doings.'"

He glanced up. "The words haven't jumped."

She smiled.

"Did you want me to continue?"

"If you want," she said.

He read a few more verses, then stopped. "How did you *kumm* up with the cardboard idea?"

"I read it in a book." She motioned to the Bible. "Amos needs to hear that passage."

"Katie."

"You just read and you did fine."

"*Jah*, with this piece of cardboard holding my spot."

"There's nothing wrong with using it. Besides, if Thomas sees you, maybe he would be willing to try it too."

He let out a muffled groan.

She stood. "You're beginning to sound like Amos, making all those noises."

Distracted by Annie's long face when she entered the kitchen, Seth held his reply. Probably for the best—he'd been about to remark on her ability to stir up Amos with her prodding.

The boys came in from outside, tracking mud from their boots and dripping water on the floor from their clothing and hats.

"You can't remember to leave the boots on the porch so you

don't muddy up the floors?" Seth shook his head. "*Geh* get the mop. You can clean up your own mess."

"That's *nett* necessary," Katie said.

"The calves broke through the pen. Paul and I need help." Seth stood.

Annie moved in between Thomas and Paul. "Me too?"

"*Nay*," Thomas snapped.

Annie's bottom lip puckered. "I miss Leah."

His niece's eyes bore into Seth. He grabbed his hat off the hook and pushed it on his head as Katie told Annie she could work with her.

Seth glanced over his shoulder. "Maybe you two can make some cinnamon rolls." He eyed Katie. "That might soften both the growling men."

"Then we'll make a double batch."

Seth shot outside. Rainwater plunked into the mucky puddles as he held his hat in place and ran for the barn.

A cool breeze lifted the curtains and they flapped over the sink. For the first time in four days, the sun broke from the clouds and cast a soft glow into the kitchen. As Seth suggested, Katie made a batch of cinnamon rolls with Annie's help.

Annie licked the icing from her fingers as Katie slid a roll onto a plate.

"Will you take this in to your *daed*, please?"

Annie nodded, her eyes beaming.

Katie put the coffee kettle on the stove to warm and meanwhile looked out the window. Although the rain had turned into a drizzle, the gutters continued to drain water off the roof, dumping it into a collecting barrel. With the extensive amount of rainfall over the past few days, they wouldn't need to tap that resource to feed the garden anytime soon.

A grackle pecked at the ground for insects, and the iridescent blue on his head reminded Katie of Seth's eyes.

Several minutes had passed and Annie hadn't returned from taking Amos the roll. Katie tiptoed into the sitting room.

Perched on Amos's lap, Annie rested her head on his shoulder. "I miss Leah," the girl said. "When will she *kumm* back home?"

"She might *nett*," Amos replied.

"Like *Mamm*?"

Katie held her breath. *Open your eyes Amos. You're spiritually blind if you don't see that the child is hurting.*

If Amos had a response for Annie, he held it. He gave his daughter a small hug, then eased her off his lap.

Annie's shoulders slumped.

Katie bent to one knee and spread her arms open, and Annie fell into the embrace sobbing. She soothed the child, holding her close and patting her back. Then, after several minutes, she pulled Annie's arms away from clutching her neck and set her down.

"There's a plate on the table with a roll on it for you. I'll be in the kitchen in a few minutes."

Annie padded away.

Katie inhaled a long breath, then released it slowly in an attempt to calm herself. "It stopped raining," she said, approaching Amos. "I'll put the window up so you can enjoy the day."

"There isn't anything to enjoy."

"Nothing at all? How sad for you." She sounded harsher than she intended but continued anyway. "There is plenty to enjoy. I saw a grackle earlier, the first one this summer."

"I can't *see* anything." He stressed each word.

"Then tune your ear and listen for its raspy call. Work those other God-given senses of yours."

He harrumphed.

"You're *nett* just physically blind—you're spiritually blind, and that's something you can change. God will shine his light and give knowledge to those who ask. But how long you stay in the darkness is your choice." She took a few steps away and stopped. "And one more thing. If Job had your outlook, do you think God would've restored all that he'd lost?" She walked away before he barked how she'd talked out of line. True, she shouldn't have spoken so harshly to a man. Perhaps the real sin was the fact she wasn't sorry she had.

Chapter Twenty-Six

Katie, you don't understand how hard it is to read aloud." Seth paced to the end of the porch and back. "And don't tell me how much progress I've made."

He made another lap.

Her arms folded across her chest, she wasn't budging from her spot, nor did she appear to accept his excuse.

"I don't want to risk Amos getting upset." He stopped in front of her. "I never told you, but the *dokta* wanted him to stay calm. He said stress could alter the pressure around his optic nerve."

Katie covered her hand over her gaping mouth.

"This might send him over the edge."

She was silent longer than he liked. Then she smiled and he knew he was in over his head. "Let's pray Amos is receptive."

"Sure, I will."

As if his promise wasn't enough, Katie reached for his hand and nodded.

"What, *nau*?" He planned to pray about the matter tonight. Alone.

She closed her eyes and gave his hand a gentle squeeze when he didn't start praying.

Seth cleared his throat. "Lord, Amos needs to hear your word. We all do. We ask that he is not only receptive but will heed your commands and turn from his wicked ways. In Jesus' name, *aemen*."

Katie opened her eyes. "You sound like you could be one of the ministers."

He shook his head. There was no hope of that, but he didn't want to dampen the moment. He wanted to be someone she admired, if only for this short period.

"Okay," he said, motioning to the door. "I might as well make the suggestion to Amos about reading and see what he says." He hoped the answer was no.

Razzen sidled beside Amos and hissed when Seth and Katie entered the room. The putrid odor that enveloped the two of them sickened Razzen. He positioned himself at Amos's neck in an attempt to gain a stronghold. "The God you serve has allowed you to wallow without direction. Your situation is pitiful and you're losing hope. Have you placed your hope in the Lord? He's disappointed you, hasn't he? Perhaps now the truth shall set you free. He doesn't want you to have the abundant life he speaks about."

Razzen listened with alarm as Seth mentioned reading. "No! What could you possibly gain, Amos, by his reading from the book of Perceived Truth?"

The wicked angel swooped across the room, landing just out of reach of his enemy Elias but near Seth. But before he could spit out a word of deception, Razzen was prodded by the tip of Elias's sword and backed into the corner. Razzen waited until Seth started reading about God searching the heart and testing the mind before he inched toward the man.

Swoosh.

Elias's blade sliced the air. Razzen retracted his steps.

Echoes of chants filled the air and the room filled with angelic hosts from all ranks. Shards of light reflecting their Master's glory forced Razzen to cover his eyes and recoil. He released a shrill cry, but the chorus of angels, singing in one accord, blotted out his attempt. The archfiend covered his ears and vaporized.

Seth closed the Bible and smiled, elated he'd made it through the passage without much stammering. He couldn't explain the warmth that sped through his veins or the strength he discovered when he started the first verse. Katie was right. During the reading, Amos had leaned forward as though hanging on to every word.

"Denki," Amos said. "I . . . I suppose I needed to hear that."

Seth glanced at Katie. She dabbed the hem of her dress sleeve over the corners of her eyes.

"Will you read tomorrow too?" Amos asked.

"Sure." If he hadn't witnessed it himself, he wouldn't have believed Amos could soften.

Katie gave a short wave, then slipped out of the room. Seth left the children with Amos and followed Katie outside.

"Do you have to leave so soon?"

"It's getting late." She smiled. "That was a *wundebaar* reading. I know you don't want to hear this, but you do sound like a minister."

He shook his head. "I still stammered."

"I understood every word and so did everyone else."

A soft breeze tugged at Seth's hat. He pushed it down on his head. "It's a little chilly," he said. "You can wait in the house while I harness Peaches."

"I've been cooped up all day. It's nice to be outside in the fresh air." She drew in a noisy breath and tilted her face to the evening sky. "Maybe the wind will dry up the puddles and you'll be able to start working on the barn damages."

"*Jah*, maybe."

"You like building, don't you?"

He shrugged, then whistled for her horse.

"Maybe after you finish Amos's barn, you can help the other men. I'm sure there is plenty—"

"I have *several* beehive orders to fill." He hated to interrupt her like that and hated to see the corners of her mouth turn downward. But he couldn't let her continue the subject.

She held her tongue the entire time it took to harness her mare. Probably praying.

He held out the reins. "See you in the morning?"

"Bright and early." She climbed on the bench.

The unrelenting sun penetrated Seth's clothing and heated his shoulders and back, and he hadn't even climbed the ladder yet. He'd spent the majority of the morning clearing out the equipment and preparing the barn. His sweat-soaked shirt clung to him, making it miserable to work in. It wasn't even the hottest point of the day and the rain puddles had evaporated.

As Elias had said, after four days of rain, he arrived early that day to help. Seth thought it best not to mention the weather.

It didn't matter how Elias knew it would rain four days; the sky was clear of clouds today and Seth was grateful. He valued Elias's opinion. But when the man suggested the entire side of the barn needed to come down, Seth had to respectfully disagree. Until he poked at the timber with his pocket knife and discovered insect damage. No telling how extensive the tunnel network was, but he wouldn't dare jeopardize safety. He prodded another beam and found dry rot. A musty odor assaulted his nose. That particular beam probably wasn't infested with ants but had decayed over the years from water damage.

He scratched his jaw.

"Do you still want to try and shore up the wall using the steel brackets you bought in town?" Elias asked.

Seth shook his head. "It won't work. Tying into the existing support post in that poor a condition might make the wall plumb for a period, but I'm guessing there's more insect damage than what's visible. I only checked two timbers and both had some signs of ants. It wouldn't be sound enough for me to sleep at night." He sighed. "You're right. The building must come down. There isn't another viable choice." He might as well get the ladder. This would be a long day.

Razzen cloaked Seth as he climbed the ladder. He wheezed, the same haunting sound that could rouse the man from a restful sleep in the middle of the night and incite his mind's eye to play back every morbid detail. Humans were stupid pawns, creatures to manipulate or sacrifice, and Razzen loved to subject them to their own uncanny ability to recall past events.

"You can't escape the man's death. You know deep in your heart that structure should have fallen on you. Instead, you live. A pitiful, tormented life, but you survived, didn't you?" Seth climbed higher, and Razzen

worried his condemnation hadn't worked. "Failures aren't blotted away, are they?"

His target paused and squeezed his eyes closed. His breathing quickened and his hands trembled. At this rate, Razzen was certain Seth wouldn't reach the next rung on the ladder.

"Lord . . . ," Seth cried.

You fool! Razzen goaded himself for leaving the man any time of reprieve. It only took a second to call out to the One who waits patiently. Razzen couldn't risk more silence. The man could prevail and demand him to flee.

Razzen resumed the raspy breath sounds. "Your trusted workmanship—your error—killed the man. You're not expected to forgive yourself. Who could?"

Seth forced through the badgering self-condemnation and called out, "God, forgive me."

Katie looked out the kitchen window. On the top rung of the ladder, Seth removed the crowbar from the loop on his work belt and wedged it between the sideboards. His face grimaced as he pried the sideboard free from its nails. The board dropped to the ground. Thomas and Paul dragged it away from the building and over to Elias, who placed it across the makeshift sawhorses where he could remove the nails. Seth dropped another board.

Why hadn't she noticed his sweaty shirt earlier? He needed a drink. She filled a jug with water, grabbed four glasses, and headed outside.

Water sloshed against the sides of the container and spilled over the rim, soaking her dress apron as she dashed across the yard. She reached the foot of the ladder and peered up at Seth, who clung to the ladder, his eyes closed.

"Seth, are you okay?"

He jerked. Then, opening his eyes, he squinted in her direction. "Katie?"

He sounded disoriented. People could get heatstroke in this weather. She lifted the jug of water. "*Kumm* get something to drink."

He reversed his steps, and when his feet hit the ground, he adjusted his hat. His beet-red face made her wish she would've thought to bring water out earlier. She poured a glassful of the cool liquid and handed it to him.

"*Denki.*"

Seth gulped it down before she had another glass filled for Elias, who had left the boards he'd been working on to join them. She handed Elias a glass and reached for the empty one in Seth's hand. She frowned. He was breathing harder than he should be for the activity he'd been doing.

"You look like you could use more," she said.

He nodded and lifted his arm to brush his forehead with his shirtsleeve.

Katie handed him another full glass and glanced at Elias. "Do you need yours refilled?"

"This is enough, *denki.*" The man was more than twice Seth's age, but he showed none of the signs and symptoms that Seth demonstrated.

She scanned the yard for the boys, then spotted them near the pile of lumber and waved them over. By the time Thomas and Paul ambled across the lawn, she had their drinks poured.

Elias returned the empty glass. "You're very kind," he said before he headed back to the sawhorses.

Katie collected the boys' empty glasses and returned to the house. An hour later she brought them more water. She didn't want any of them dehydrated from working in the heat.

"A cold drink was just what I needed." Seth drained the glass so fast that he coughed.

"Do you need another refill?"

"I'm *gut nau, denki*." He handed her the empty glass.

She gazed at the dismantled building. "I didn't think you planned to take it completely down."

"Have to," Seth said. "The tree had cracked a few roof trusses, but we also found extensive carpenter ant damage on a support post and dry rot on another."

"You know a lot about construction, don't you?" She picked up the inflection in his tone when he first started talking about the barn. But why didn't he speak up at the meeting when the question was raised for another lead builder?

He shrugged. "Elias tapped the post with his cane and detected its hollowness."

Elias walked up and handed Seth a fistful of nails. "I suppose if we're finished for the day, I'll be on my way."

"I can give you a ride," Seth said.

"No. I wish to walk. I'll be here tomorrow," he said, already walking away.

"There isn't any more we can do without supplies," Seth said.

Elias looked over his shoulder and smiled. "Have faith, son."

Seth nodded, though it seemed more a gesture of respect than one of agreement.

Katie elbowed Seth's arm. "Do you think the lumberyard has replenished their supply?"

"Nay." He wagged his head. "But I didn't think it would rain four days in a row either." He motioned to the barn. "I think I'll go into town. The man's been uncannily right about everything else."

Chapter Twenty-Seven

The next morning after the boys had disappeared to the barn, Katie handed Seth a stack of index cards. "You can read these scriptures while I do the breakfast dishes."

"Isn't this more than usual?" He fanned the cards with his thumb, looking at her.

"You can do it."

His reading had improved such that last night he read without any noticeable flaws. His posture had straightened with confidence by the time he finished. More importantly, Amos seemed receptive even knowing Katie was in the room. Not that he'd spoken with her, but last night he hadn't objected when Seth invited her to stay. She believed God's Word had started to soften his stony heart.

Alend's barking brought Seth off his chair. He moved to the

window. "It's probably Elias. I need to tell him the lumberyard hadn't received a new shipment yet." His brow crinkled and he headed for the door.

Katie glanced out the window, spotted her brother's buggy among several that had arrived, and hurried to join Seth outside.

"I wonder what they're here for," Seth mumbled.

She wondered more how Amos would respond. Amos might have warmed a little, but he would turn ugly again if he was confronted about something. Isaac, Andrew, and David—all three of the district ministers—had arrived.

Seth stepped forward. "Is there something I can help you with?"

Isaac crossed the drive and met Seth. "We heard about Amos's accident."

Andrew nodded. "We *kumm* to help put up his barn."

"*Denki*, I appreciate the offer, but I'm afraid you've wasted the trip here. I wasn't able to get all the materials. The lumberyard is sold out." Seth's apologetic smile seemed to greet each man as he joined the group.

"We brought the building supplies." Isaac pointed at a wagon pulling into the drive. A team of draft horses carted the flatbed hay trailer, only it was loaded with stacked lumber.

Seth faced Isaac. "You must have more pressing projects. This is the calving barn, *nett* his main barn."

"We know." Isaac glanced at Katie and smiled.

Seth turned to her. "Did you know about this?"

"*Nay.*" Her sister-in-law had heard about Amos's accident but not through Katie's gossip. Abigail said Seth had told her the news.

"After we discovered we didn't have enough supplies to meet all the settlement's needs, we called a meeting to reprioritize the greatest issues," Andrew said.

"I don't understand." Seth cocked his head sideways. "You mean you're putting Amos ahead of the others in the settlement? Sacrificing your building materials for his barn?"

Andrew glanced at the other men around him and smiled. "*Jah*, that's the decision of the body. We want to be a blessing to Amos and his family."

What a blessing indeed. Katie hoped Amos would view it in the same light.

"You are all so kind. *Denki*. I don't know what else to say." Seth shook his head.

Isaac stepped forward. "*Denki* is plenty." He clapped Seth's shoulder. "Let's get to work."

Seth nodded and the group dispersed. He glanced at her and smiled. "This is what Elias said to have faith for. It had nothing to do with the lumberyard."

This went way beyond her faith. True, the members in her settlement were generous people, but even she knew this was a miracle. Anyone would know a secondary barn wouldn't take priority like this.

Katie scanned the crowd, taking a silent head count. The men would be hungry by noon and she needed an idea of how many workers she would be cooking for today. She'd counted as many as twenty men when Elias appeared at her side.

"It is good when God's people work in unity," he said.

"*Jah*, I agree." She hoped Amos would too. The screen door creaked behind her and Annie poked her head outside. "Stay inside. I'll be in soon." She turned back to finish her count, but the men splitting into different directions made that impossible. She supposed it wasn't necessary to have an exact number. She would make a large pot of chili and some corn bread.

"Thirty-six," Elias said.

Katie lifted her brows.

"You were counting, right?" he said as he meandered away.

The door opened. "Katie," Annie said, leaning outside. "*Daed* is calling for you."

⚭

Seth pulled a rough-cut two-by-four timber post from the back end of the wagon and toted it toward the pile of stacked lumber.

"See what faith can do," Elias said, ambling with his cane closer to Seth.

He dropped the post with others and faced Elias. "I have to confess, I didn't have this much faith, especially after I drove into town and didn't find any supplies."

Elias smiled. "All it takes is a mustard seed."

"True," Seth chuckled. "And that's about all I had driving into town."

"Brother William just found out his *fraa* is in labor." Elias pointed to a lanky young man with his hand pressing his straw hat in place as he hustled toward a buggy. The anxious man rattled several words together as he passed by a group of men.

"His first child," Elias explained.

"*Gut* for him." Seth motioned to the wagon. "I should finish unloading the supplies."

"In a moment there will be a call for someone to take his place as the lead carpenter."

Seth froze in midturn. Why was he telling him? There were plenty of other men more capable for the job.

"You need to accept."

Seth made a quick glance around the area. "There's close to forty men, surely someone—"

Elias shook his head. "You have a gift—use it."

"*Nay.*" He leaned closer. "You don't understand," Seth whispered.

The elderly man's insistent gaze could've driven a wooden peg through petrified wood.

Seth wouldn't dare assume the duties of the lead carpenter's role. He couldn't. Sweat trickled from his forehead down his neck and collected under his collarless shirt, making the fabric scratch against his skin. He tugged at the hem without relief.

"When God entrusted you with a gift, he also equipped you to complete what he's called you to do." Elias's voice sounded gentle enough to calm the wind. "But the choice is yours. I am merely a messenger and cannot force you to accept God's plan."

God's plan? Seth had already accepted his limitations, the facts. He'd prefer not to pick up a hammer, and he wouldn't dare think he could lead the building project. He'd been foolish once and that led to despair.

"Is anyone willing to take the lead?" asked Andrew Lapp as he moved through the crowd.

Seth walked in the opposite direction. In his peripheral vision, he caught a glimpse of Elias keeping stride.

"Don't let doubts and fears cause you to stumble any longer," he said without even a hint of windedness. "This is not the time to be stubborn in your ways, child."

Seth stopped at the wagon. "This is beyond simple stubbornness, and I respect your belief in my abilities, although, for the life of me, I have no idea how you *kumm* to think I'm a lead builder since the only thing you've seen me do is pull out nails and tear down the old barn. I'm *nett* the man. I build beehives and that's all." He hoped he didn't sound disrespectful, but he had to make his point clear. He spotted Andrew Lapp talking with a group of men and Seth's confidence rose that they'd find someone.

"He will be asking you soon," Elias said.

His spine shuddered at the man's peculiar assurance. Seth waited until Thomas pulled a piece of lumber off the wagon and stepped aside before he reached for the next board.

"God wants you to trust him," Elias said.

Seth let the board drop back on the wagon and spun to face him. "I trust God." He kept his tone level, hoping to disguise the sprouting resentment.

"Where is your mustard seed of faith?" Elias didn't wait for Seth to respond. "He wants to restore your dreams."

"And I suppose he sent you here to tell me that." Seth caught his tongue between his teeth and clamped it hard. He'd allowed himself to become offended, a sin he knew to avoid.

Grace radiated from Elias's smile. "God has been known to use a donkey to stop a man on the wrong path, hasn't he?"

"*Jah.*" Seth nodded, recalling the story of Balaam in the Bible. "I always thought it was odd that Balaam didn't recoil hearing his donkey talk, but instead argued with the creature."

Elias smiled. "Some men are more stubborn to convince than others."

"I suppose there are a lot of us like that." Seth turned, reached for a board, and slid it off the wagon. He kept a keen eye on Andrew as he moved through the crowd. He would find someone.

"Andrew," Katie called, "do you have a minute?"

Seth tried not to crane his neck too noticeably as he strained to hear why she stopped Andrew. Once Katie asked about the bishop's health, Seth continued toward the pile with the board.

"Here comes Andrew Lapp for your answer," Elias said.

Katie sent Annie into the kitchen to color while she talked with Amos. She didn't want the child subjected to his wrath.

She cleared her throat and entered the sitting room. "Did you need something?"

"I keep hearing buggies." Amos tilted his head. "There's another one. What's going on?"

"The men have *kumm* to work on your barn." She studied Amos's reaction. The grooves along his forehead deepened and his square jaw appeared set. He growled something, but his distorted words weren't something she could follow. "Did you say something? I didn't understand you." So much for thinking the man's heart had softened.

"Who sent them here?"

"I'm *nett* sure."

He shifted on his chair. "Is Bishop Lapp here?"

"*Nay.* He hasn't recovered from his stroke. Perhaps if you prayed for him, it would take your mind off your own troubles." She had half a notion to quote him the scripture from Matthew about praying for your enemies. Apparently that was how Amos viewed the settlement members. Instead, she closed her eyes and prayed for Amos.

"Are you still in here?"

"*Jah,* would you like me to close your window so you don't have to hear the commotion?"

"*Nay.*"

She risked upsetting him to ask, "Did you ever think that God allowed this darkness just to get your attention?"

He remained silent.

"If you don't need anything, I'll be in the kitchen. I have a lot to prepare. And before you say anything about using your pantry to feed them all, you should know they put off rebuilding the Fischers' barn in order to use the supplies on yours."

"What?"

"There was more damage than Seth originally thought. He had to tear down your barn completely."

"What does *mei* barn have to do with them *nett* rebuilding the Fischers'?"

"The lumberyard is out of material. Supplies are hard to find. Apparently everyone agreed that your place was more important, so they sacrificed their building materials for your barn."

Amos lowered his head.

She hoped it was to pray.

Seth sensed Andrew Lapp's nearness but trained his focus on the lumber pile to avoid eye contact. He wanted Andrew to exhaust all other possible sources. Waiting to decline his request gnawed at Seth until the cords of his muscles tightened. *Just be forthright.*

Someone clapped his shoulder from behind him. He turned and greeted Isaac.

"*Mei fraa* told me about Amos's accident. How is he?"

Seth shook his head. "I haven't seen any changes."

"Abigail said Katie was helping you with the children. That's *gut*—it'll keep her mind off the *schul.*"

Another man stopped beside Isaac. "I am interested in renting or possibly buying your farm," he said. "I talked it over with *mei fraa* and we think it's what we need. Can we get together next week?"

Isaac nodded.

Seth waited until the other man was out of earshot. "Are you moving?"

Isaac shook his head. "Katie is. Well, there's a chance she'll get the *teetshah* position in Oscoda County."

Seth's chest grew heavy. "Does she know about you selling the *haus*?" He winced at his own prying. "I'm sorry. I shouldn't be asking about such private matters." Still, he couldn't see Katie wishing to sell her family *haus*.

"She isn't keen on the idea." Isaac shrugged. "But if she's moving to another county, there isn't much sense in the *haus* standing vacant. Besides, we all know the shortage of building supplies will put a high demand on any new materials. It'll be cheaper for them to buy or even rent for a year or two than to rebuild." Isaac smiled. "But I think it's nice how concerned you are about *mei* sister. She'll be all right. I have an empty *grossdaadi haus* she will move into if the new job doesn't work out."

Someone called Isaac over to the wagon and he walked away.

Seth added the board to the stacked lumber, then focused on the ground as he retraced his steps back to the wagon.

"God wants to restore your dream." Seth couldn't erase Elias's words even though the man was no longer at his side. He wasn't sure what his dream was anymore. It certainly wasn't to have stomach acid climb to the back of his throat at the mere thought of having charge over a building project.

With not many boards left to unload from the wagon, the men would be anxious to start hammering. In his peripheral vision, Seth caught sight of Andrew.

"Brother William had to leave to be with his *fraa*," Andrew said. "We need someone to take the lead."

Seth choked on his reply before the words left his mouth. He shook his head.

"Katie Bender said you're a master builder."

"I couldn't— She said what?" He hadn't breathed a word of that part of his past to her. Who told her?

"She mentioned you head up all of the barn raisings in your district."

Seth rubbed the back of his neck and casually slipped a peek at the house. Katie peered out the kitchen window. Why hadn't she talked with him first? Amos was right. The woman was meddlesome indeed.

"She said you might *nett* step forward and that I should approach you direct."

"*Ach*, she did. Did she happen to say where she learned that piece of information?" He shot another look toward the house, but she had disappeared from the window. Hiding, no doubt.

Andrew smiled as Isaac approached. "I found us a master builder," he said to Isaac, then shifted his attention to address Seth. "Ain't so?"

Chapter Twenty-Eight

Seth stood with the men at the building site and pulled in a long breath, hoping to settle his nagging unease. Outside of helping to remove nails in order to reuse the lumber, he hadn't worked with these men, and yet they asked for direction and seemed eager to follow his lead.

Elias stepped forward and rested his hand on Seth's shoulder. "Where should we start?"

Seth wagged his head in disbelief. He never thought he would be in charge of another barn raising.

"It's okay," Elias said soothingly. "Take a moment to gather your thoughts."

Seth drifted away from the crowd. "I used to think I could do this with *mei* eyes closed," he said under his breath.

"You still can."

Jolted by his response, Seth sucked in a lungful of air. Not only had Elias followed him, but the elderly man heard what he'd said. At least the others continued to mill together unalarmed.

Elias patted Seth's shoulder. "You're not having second thoughts, are you?"

The elderly man's words caught Seth off guard for a second and he almost choked on his repressed breath. "Of course I am. This wasn't ever *mei* idea."

"Your young woman friend sees your potential."

"So I heard," muttered Seth. It still bothered him that Katie's interference placed him in this jam. No wonder she wasn't married.

"You haven't forgotten how to build a barn," Elias said.

Seth dragged his shirtsleeve over his perspiring forehead as images of the last barn he'd built plagued his thoughts.

After a short time, Seth joined the others. He laid a piece of timber between the pair of sawhorses, and Elias handed him a pencil that he withdrew from behind his ear. Seth studied the tape measure. He made a faint mark indicating where he needed to cut the board, then promptly rechecked his work—multiple times. Repeating the same process, the hours crawled by.

"Corner posts are in place and the men are notching out the area you scored on the foundation beams," Isaac said.

One of the men working on the north side of the structure called for Isaac and he walked away.

Seth pulled a hankie from his pocket and wiped his forehead. This was probably the slowest barn raising any of them had worked on, but these things couldn't be rushed. He had to know that his measurements were correct even if it did take twice the time. Usually they built their barns closer to fall, during the cooler season. For the beginning of June, the sun beat down hard, and everyone's progress slowed as the morning wore on.

Seth dabbed the damp cloth over his brow another time before returning it to his pocket. As long as he didn't make a mistake, it didn't matter how long the construction took.

It took several hours before Seth's nerves settled and he didn't feel like he was swimming against the current. He remembered how much he liked working with lumber and seeing the building take form. How much his muscles ached from the repetitive lifting and climbing and swinging a hammer.

"Leah's birthday is in a few days," Seth teased Jacob, then counted to himself how many times the young man missed the nail. But Thomas, holding the next board for Jacob to nail, announced how he'd struck the board five times and hadn't hit the nail.

Seth rested another piece of lumber on the sawhorses. He marked out the length, then paused to scan the area for Elias. Now that the pace had picked up, he didn't want Elias overdoing it in the heat. Not seeing him, Seth returned to measuring the board.

"Seth!"

He glanced over his shoulder, then pivoted around when several men waved him over to the north side of the barn.

He dropped the tape measure and hiked over to where Jacob and Thomas were working.

"Check this out," Jacob said. He tapped his hammer on the board and the iron head went through the wood.

Seth wanted to vomit. All his careful attention and he still made a serious mistake. He eyed the span of the beam. Load bearing too—it must be removed immediately.

"Jacob, *kumm* down from the ladder." He tapped Thomas's shoulder. "Stand away from the barn. We need to clear the area," he told the men.

Seth's stomach rolled as images of the last collapse flashed before him. The man's wheezing echoed.

"What's going on?" Isaac's brows furrowed. "You look pale, Seth. Are you feeling ill?"

He was ill all right. Seth glanced at the crowd. With all eyes on him waiting for instruction, he had to say something.

"Somehow some insect-damaged wood was used." He pointed to the area. "The beam from that post over to the next post needs to be taken down."

Silence fell over the men.

"We have to build a makeshift support to hold the weight," Seth explained. "Until then, everyone should stand clear of the structure." While he had the group's attention, he spat out orders. Then the men dispersed with their own assignments.

Seth had to erect a makeshift support. He'd done it before, but not for something of this magnitude.

Katie strolled into his peripheral vision. She stopped at the first group of men. "Thirsty?" She motioned to a jug of water in her arms.

Seth rubbed his corded neck muscles but couldn't loosen the knot. The last thing he needed was her wandering around on the job site. He shot a glance across the yard at Isaac, hoping he would take the initiative and send his sister back to the house. But Isaac didn't notice his sister's disruption. The tension in Seth's neck balled tighter.

He stared at the roof joist, not that he could concentrate on the needed adjustments. With the constant sawing and hammering in the background, he didn't realize she'd come up beside him until she spoke.

"Would you like something to drink?" She poured water from the pitcher into a cup and held it out.

"Nay, denki."

"You really should drink," she said. "You don't want to get dehydrated in this heat."

This time he accepted the drink. *"Denki."*

"The barn is going up quick, *jah?"*

He drank the water; it gave him a reason not to respond. She didn't know anything about barn raisings.

She gazed at the barn. "A little more complex than a beehive box, ain't so?"

He shot her a sideways glare, but with her focus set on the barn, she didn't notice.

"I think you're doing a fine job. I don't know why you didn't speak up sooner that you're a master—"

"That's right, you don't know." The icy water numbed his throat.

She snapped around to face him, her brows crinkled.

"From *nau* on," he said, handing the empty glass back to her, "I'd like for you to mind your own business."

A bitter taste rose to the back of his throat. He suddenly wished he had more water to force it down. He ought to apologize.

"Katie, I'm *nett* used to . . ." *An interfering . . . meddlesome woman.* His mind reeled, searching for something nicer to say.

She lowered her head.

"I have to get back to work." He left her standing alone and went closer to the structure.

Isaac finished hammering a wooden peg into the drilled beam and looked up at Seth. "The new support is *kumming* along fine, *jah?"*

Seth nodded. "I don't know how I let that timber slip through. I thought the damaged lumber was discarded into a pile for burning."

"We can all learn from our mistakes."

Seth learned never to take on another project like this. Why did he allow Katie to put him in this situation? And she seemed so pleased with herself, pointing out the barn construction was more complex than a beehive box. Of course it was more complex. He didn't need a woman to tell him that. Katie wasn't any different than Diana; they both belittled his choice of trade.

Razzen shelled Katie with lies as she worked to prepare the afternoon meal. His words of discouragement drained her hope and fed her mind with despair. "You thought you were in love. Did you think he could love you? You're intrusive."

The woman's eyes closed. When the child coloring at the table held up her picture, Katie forced a smile. She pushed a tear away with the back of her hand and nodded at the child. Razzen sneered. She was speechless. When Amos called her name from the other room, Katie sucked in a breath. Razzen's chest billowed with pride. He was about to earn two more souls.

"You have not the power to pluck a man's soul from the Master's hand," Elias said, unfurling his wings.

"It only depends which master they choose to serve. Eventually they'll come to my call—obey my voice. The flesh is weak. Soon my reasoning will sound like theirs."

"Leave them be, Razzen!"

The evil fiend shot like a ball of fire through several ethereal dimensions of time and reappeared near Elias's charge.

Elias wielded his sword, slicing the enemy's feathered appendages.

Shrinking back long enough to withdraw his weapon, Razzen armed himself for battle. A venomous miasma escaped his flared nostrils as he waited for the ideal time to pounce.

Razzen jabbed first, nearly skewering Elias.

Elias whirled his sword, cutting through the air and missing his target.

"What are you—a warrior with no aim?" Razzen taunted.

Swords clashed as both fought for an upper hand.

Razzen refused to lose his hold on the blind man's life. Not now, especially since he'd gained access into the man's mind—it wouldn't take long to obtain his soul. Ultimately, the man would bow to him—the woman too—and help promote Razzen to his status of deserved glory.

Whoosh.

Elias's sword came uncomfortably close to Razzen's ear.

Razzen fought back. Through craftiness and swift action, he dodged the challenger's blade and was even able to land some blows himself.

Elias's blade flashed. Razzen felt a piercing pain slice through his chest. He stumbled backward. Pressing his hand over his wound, he gulped air into his burning lungs.

A few relentless slashes and Elias seized dominance.

Razzen slithered into the shadows. His reward might be delayed, but it wasn't denied.

Katie crossed the room. "Do you need something, Amos?"

"Are they about finished with the barn?"

"I'm *nett* sure." Her voice cracked and she cringed, wishing she could have better control.

He shifted on his chair and leaned in her direction. "Are you crying?"

Katie drew in a breath. *Lord, I don't think I can take seeing the satisfaction on his face.* "Did you need something?" Maybe with a firmer tone he would get to the reason he called her into the sitting room.

"Will you bring me a glass of water?"

"Sure." She left the room, filled a glass with water, and

returned to Amos's side. "Do you want it now or do you want me to place it on the lamp table?"

He reached out his hand. "I'll take it."

Once she handed him the glass, she didn't dally. The last batch of corn bread should be ready to come out of the oven.

"Why do you do it?"

Katie pivoted around to face Amos. "Do what?"

"*Kumm* here every day to cook and take care of *mei* family?"

"*Do good for those who hate you,*" she recited silently. "I want to be a blessing and help you." *Because Jesus instructs us to bless those who curse us.*

Katie took a deep breath and stepped closer to his chair. "I also pray for you." She expected one of his noisy snorts, then took full advantage of his silence and continued, "Even if you choose to no longer belong to our district, you are still a neighbor in need." Surely he still held on to some of his Christian values.

Glancing at the table against the far wall, she noticed a Bible. She went to the book and opened it to the thirtieth verse in the twelfth chapter of Mark. She read, "'Love the Lord thy God with all thy heart, and with all thy soul, and with all thy mind, and with all thy strength.'"

"And 'love thy neighbour as thyself,'" Amos completed the passage.

"So you do remember what Jesus said." She bit her tongue and whispered an apology to God for her sarcastic words. This wasn't the time to talk with Amos, not with her emotions on edge from Seth's comment in the yard.

Katie closed the Book and returned it to the stand. "If you need anything, I'll be in the kitchen."

"*Denki*, Katie," Amos said softly. "For everything."

She never predicted Amos would ever thank her for anything. Perhaps God was speaking to his heart. "You're *wilkom*."

Once the food was prepared, she and Annie fed the men.
Since many of them had packed their lunch, there was plenty
of chili for leftovers. Seth took a bowl of chili and a chunk of
buttered corn bread and sat near the barn. Katie had hoped for
a chance to speak with him, but that wasn't likely today. She
headed up the porch steps and Isaac stopped her.

"I just wanted to let you know I think I've rented the *haus*,"
he said.

Unable to speak with the way her throat was constricting,
Katie nodded. She would ask her brother later how long before
she needed to pack up the house.

The following morning Seth managed to avoid Katie. He tin-
kered with arranging tools in the new barn, something that
wasn't necessary other than to give him a place to gather his
thoughts. But his thoughts hadn't changed from last night and
he had to tell her.

"*Onkel* Seth, are you going to show me how to take care of
the bees?" Thomas hung the hammer on the peg.

"*Jah*, after the tools are—"

The door creaked open and daylight spilled into the barn.
Katie stepped inside. She wiped her hands on her apron. "Paul
and Annie are pulling weeds in the garden, and I was hoping . . ." She glanced at Thomas, then redirected her attention to
Seth. "I was hoping—"

He held up his finger to stop her. "Thomas, I need to talk
with Katie a few minutes."

Thomas hung the handsaw on a hook next to the hammer and left the barn.

"I've been waiting all morning for the right time to tell you. And this probably isn't a good time either." Seth knew he was rambling.

"I wanted to talk with you too."

Her smile made this even harder for him. He rubbed his hands on the seams of his pants. "*Nau* that the barn is done, I can take care of the children."

Katie looked as startled as a raccoon caught in the henhouse. "You don't need me?"

She spoke so softly he barely made out the words.

"Amos's sister will be here in a few days."

"I didn't know you had made other arrangements."

He nodded. "She couldn't leave Ohio immediately. Besides, I have to go home. I have a business there. A beehive business."

"I thought when you kissed me—" She pivoted, leaving him to face her back. Her shoulders shook.

Outside the barn, the dog barked.

"I care a great deal about you. I hope you'll forgive me. But it wouldn't work between us." He waited a minute but wasn't sure he would hear her faint response over the dog's obsessive barking. When she hadn't turned to face him or hadn't spoken a word, he pulled on the door latch. "What is that dog barking about?"

He slipped out, expecting to find a visitor, but didn't see anyone. "Hush, Alend," he said. The dog barked at him, ran a few feet toward the field, then returned to Seth. He scanned the perimeter but didn't see anyone.

Katie stepped out of the barn, wiping her sleeve over her wet face.

"Where did you say the children were?"

"The garden"—she looked that direction—"I checked on them just a bit ago."

"Let's split up," he said as the dog nudged his leg and started to bark. "If you look inside the main barn, I'll search around back."

"Sure."

The two sped in opposite directions. Katie headed toward the barn, and Seth followed Alend into the field. He hadn't gone far before he spotted Paul running, arms flailing.

Seth sprinted and met Paul in the pasture.

"It's Annie—she's—" He clutched his side and bent at the waist, gasping for air.

"Where is she?"

"In the pasture." Paul pointed with his thumb over his shoulder.

Seth scanned the pasture just as Thomas crested the hill, running hard with Annie cradled in his arms.

"Ach, nay!" Seth raced toward Thomas. "Have mercy, God. Please let her be okay." He crossed the field and pushed himself to run harder up the incline as Thomas's pace had begun to slow.

Her body was limp, and her face was blotchy and swollen. Bee stings. Seth had heard of allergic reactions to them, but he'd never seen it in person. Cold prickles swarmed his flesh.

"Give her to me." Seth took his unresponsive niece into his arms. "Go to the *Englisch* neighbors. Have them call for an ambulance." Fear giving him energy, he dashed toward the house. Passing Paul, Seth gave him the same instructions to notify the neighbors. There wouldn't be time to harness a buggy and drive her anywhere. As it was, Annie's raspy breathing was barely audible. He was losing time.

"God, please have mercy!"

He reached the yard as Katie raced from the barn to him. "What happened?"

"Get the door," he said. "She's hardly breathing."

She ran ahead of him, flew up the porch steps, and pulled the screen door open.

"Get a towel, sheet, something to drape her with." He went directly into the kitchen and lowered Annie onto the table. He bent to listen for breathing sounds. Shallow rasps.

"What should I do with these?" Katie asked, rushing into the room.

He gathered Annie into his arms and moved closer to the stove. "Unfold the sheet," he said.

She did.

"Tent it over us and help me hold the end over the stove top." Thankfully, the kettle let off a steady flow of steam. He hoped the moist steam would stop her airway passage spasms. The kettle probably didn't produce enough steam, but he had to do something while they waited for an ambulance. He listened closely to Annie's chest. She sounded no different from Abraham when the barn wall collapsed and he lay dying. Suffocating.

Seth fought to sort his niece's rasps from the terrible memories.

"What's going on?" Amos called from the other room.

Seth looked at Katie huddled beside him under the sheet.

"Seth? Katie? Tell me what's going on," Amos demanded.

"Everything's under control," Seth said.

But it wasn't.

Annie's high-pitched wheezing continued with each labored breath.

Then it ceased.

His niece wilted in his arms. "This isn't working." He batted the sheet away. "Pour that boiling water over a paring knife."

Katie gasped.

"Do it!"

Annie's eyes, marked by slits, swelled closed. So had her lips, and when he laid her on the table to open her airway, he realized her tongue was swollen as well.

"Lord, help me." He tilted her head back, covered her mouth with his, and blew air into her lungs. Her lungs never expanded. He repositioned her head and neck and repeated the process. Still, his airflow met resistance. He tried again. And again.

He remembered when the emergency crew took care of Abraham, they'd cut a hole in Abraham's neck and inserted something that looked like part of a PVC pipe to blow air into his lungs. Seth wasn't about to let his niece die without doing everything possible.

"Find me an ink pen," he said, starting to remove the clothing from around the child's neck. Her lips were tinged with blue.

"I got it," Katie said, holding out both the pen and the cleaned knife.

He took the knife. "Remove the ink insert. I only want the plastic casing." He didn't want to make the cut and chance losing where he'd place the hole until he had the plastic sheath ready to place. He would need to cut between the ridges on her larynx. Seth palpated Annie's neck for the right placement.

As Seth prepared to cut, heavy footsteps tromped into the kitchen. His concentration lost, he lifted the knife.

"Stop!" Elias extended his cane, blocking Seth from repositioning the knife. Elias placed his hand on Seth's chest and gently pushed him aside, then he leaned down, covered his mouth over Annie's, and puffed his breath into her.

"I tried that," Seth said.

"Yes, I know." Elias lifted his face heavenward.

Seth clutched the knife's handle. He couldn't wait any longer. "Is Annie breathing?"

"She's *nett* breathing?" This time Amos stumbled into the room.

"Katie, help him out of here," Seth said.

"*Nay!*" Amos groped for something to hold on to. Finding the back of a chair, he steadied himself. "Tell me what's wrong."

"This isn't the time." Seth motioned for Katie.

She came up beside Amos and reached for his arm, but Amos pushed her hand away.

"Amos!" Seth snapped. "Let her help you back to the sitting room."

Amos shook his head. "Tell me what's wrong with *mei* child. I have to know!" He leaned forward, one hand holding the chair, the other stretched out. His hand clasped hold of Annie's foot and he gave it a shake. "Annie!"

A faint but high-pitched noise came from her. Her color had returned.

"Annie," Amos said, wiggling the girl's foot more. His chin was quivering.

"You have to go into the other room." Seth passed the knife to Katie and then placed his hands firmly on Amos's shoulders, but Amos resisted.

"*Daed?*" Annie's small voice squeaked.

Seth froze.

Amos squirmed loose. "*Jah*, I'm here, daughter." He pushed aside the chair and patted the table until he found her foot, then her hand. "I'm here," he said, tears streaming down his face.

Seth moved to the head of the table. The blotchiness had faded and the welts had disappeared. He looked around for Elias, but the old man was no longer standing in the kitchen.

Thomas and Paul both bolted into the kitchen, panting for breath.

"No one was home," Thomas said.

"*Jah*, we went to both neighbors' houses," Paul added.

They moved closer to the table. "How's Annie?"

Seth gingerly touched her cheek. "I think she's going to be okay."

"It's all *mei* fault," Thomas blurted. He faced Seth. "I wanted to show you how I could check for honey, and Annie and Paul followed me."

"It's okay, *sohn*," Amos said.

Katie sniffled as she left the kitchen. Seth wanted to go after her, but it wouldn't be safe to leave Annie on the table. Amos wouldn't be able to catch her if she started to roll.

"She needs to see a *dokta*," Amos said. "Seth, will you take her? I'd only be in the way and slow you down." Amos patted the chair and sat. "Please, take her *nau*."

"*Nay dokta*." Annie whimpered.

Her voice was a hoarse whisper. Amos was right, she needed to see a doctor. "*Jah*," Seth said. "That's a *gut* idea."

"I'll get the buggy hitched," Thomas said.

Paul left the room on his brother's heels.

Seth waited until they returned to gather Annie into his arms. "We'll be back shortly," he told Amos.

The boys held the door as Seth carried Annie outside, then they climbed into the buggy.

Outside on the porch, Katie leaned against the banister, sobbing. She followed him. "Are you taking her to the *dokta*?"

"*Jah*," Seth said, setting Annie on Thomas's lap. "Will you watch Amos?"

She nodded, dabbing her eyes with a hankie.

❧

Katie entered the kitchen as Amos stood. He teetered for balance, then groped the air. Katie came up beside him. "Let me help you," she said.

"I got dizzy," he said, sounding a little winded. "I was afraid I might pass out if I went with them. How does Annie look?"

"Better." She guided him into the sitting room and helped him into the rocking chair. "I'll get you some water." She hurried into the kitchen and filled a glass with water, then brought it to Amos.

He gulped the drink. "More, please," he said, handing her the empty glass.

"You thirst," Elias said. "But you will not satisfy what your soul is thirsty for." He moved closer, allowed his light to warm the side of Amos's face. "Drink from the Living Water and you will thirst no more. Abide in your Savior and he will abide in you."

Well aware of his adversary's presence, Elias continued.

"Amos, the Master is waiting for you to call out to him. Ask him to search your soul and reveal the condition of your heart. For the joy of the Lord and his ever-living abundance are found in a repentant heart."

The man's eyes closed.

"No!" Razzen roared. "Don't you remember? You prayed before and he never answered." His talons extended, he clawed his way closer—shredding Elias's luminosity.

Razor-sharp nails peeled an insulating layer of feathers from Elias's backside, but Elias maintained contact with his charge.

Elias planted his feet firmly, expanded his chest, and refused to move. "My strength comes from the Almighty—the Alpha and Omega—the Great I Am." Elias endured the enemy's penetrating talons, knowing it glorified the Master.

"Amos, hear these words and obey God's command: 'I call heaven and earth as witness today against you, that I have set before you life and death, blessing and cursing; therefore choose life that both you and your descendants may live.'"

Head bowed, Amos called out to the Savior. "Please forgive me. I have sinned and made a mess of my life." Amos slid from the chair to the floor. On bended knees, he cried out for Jesus to be center in his life. The man's body trembled as he emptied his heart before the Lord.

"Katie! Katie, *kumm* quick!"

Katie rushed into the room as Amos pushed off the floor. She set the glass of water on the lamp table, then reached for his hand. "Are you all right?"

"Jah," he said, although he sounded unsure of his own words.

"I was only gone a minute," she said. "I didn't hear you fall."

"I don't know what happened . . . Time stood still," he muttered under his breath.

"Let me help you." She grasped his arm and helped him into his chair. She wished Seth were here. He would know what to do about Amos passing out.

"Katie, I need to talk with Leah. Will you bring her here to me?"

Katie bit her lip. She hadn't been able to convince Leah to return home yet, and she wasn't sure she could talk her into it now.

"She is staying with you, *jah?*"

"You've known about that and you didn't say anything?"

He bowed his head. "*Mei* pride got in the way. But I'm changed *nau*. I asked God to forgive me, and a certain peace flooded *mei* soul. I must ask for Leah's forgiveness too."

Hope bubbled up within Katie. He sounded as though he'd had a life-changing experience. Katie couldn't help but think about Saul on the road to Damascus and how his life-changing experience impacted more than just himself.

"Please bring Leah to me." He paused, his eyes brimming with tears. "I must talk with her. I don't want any more time to pass."

A tap on the front door summoned her attention. "I'll be right back."

Elias stood on the other side of the screen. "How's Annie?"

"Seth's taken her to the *dokta*." She opened the door wider for him to enter. "Where did you go after she started breathing again?"

He smiled. "I had another mission to tend to." He motioned to the sitting room. "I wanted to speak more with Amos," he said.

"Will you tell him I went to take care of the errand that he requested?"

Elias nodded. "Will you and Leah be long?"

Chapter Twenty-Nine

Tact wasn't something Katie naturally possessed. On the ride home from Amos's house, she'd thought about how she would break the news to Leah. When she returned to her house and climbed out of the buggy, Leah looked up from pulling weeds in the garden. Her bright smile faded when she saw Katie.

"What's wrong?" Leah squinted and lifted her hand to shield the sun from her eyes.

"Annie had an allergic reaction and nearly died."

"Wh-what?"

"Annie was stung by bees and . . . she stopped breathing. But she is fine *nau*."

Leah staggered backward. The rake dropped from her hands, prong side up.

"Let's go in the house," Katie said. She didn't want Leah passing out in the heat.

Leah didn't move. Her eyes locked in a vacant, dazed stare.

"I think you've been in the sun too long." Katie reached for Leah's hand and led her into the house. Once inside the kitchen, Leah sat without saying a word. Katie wet a dishrag to make a cool compress, then filled a glass with water and handed it and the cloth to Leah.

"Tell me again how Annie stopped breathing?"

"She had some sort of allergic reaction to bees," Katie explained, unsure if Leah really understood. "Drink the water."

"How is she *nau*?"

"Seth wasn't back from taking her to the *dokta*."

"Then it's bad, ain't so?" Leah's bottom lip quivered.

"I think she'll be fine." She motioned to the glass. "Please drink some water."

"You're holding something back." Leah's voice cracked.

"*Nett* about Annie. It's . . . your father."

Leah's forehead wrinkled with worry. "What's wrong with *Daed*?"

She smiled. "I think God has worked on his heart. He sent me here to get you—to bring you home." She didn't give Leah time to respond. "That's *wundebaar, jah*?"

Leah shrugged. "I suppose if his heart is really changed."

"You can believe it's so." Katie reached for Leah's hand and gave it a squeeze. "Please give him another chance. He doesn't want to lose you."

Leah pushed her tears away, smudging garden dirt from her hands on her face. "I'm scared he will reject me."

"God is in control. I know that to be true." Katie nodded, affirming her statement.

Leah stood. "I'll get *mei* stuff together," she said over her shoulder as she left the room.

Katie sighed. *"Denki,* Lord." She caught a glimpse of the mail stacked on the counter and grabbed the pile. As she waited for Leah, she flipped through the mail. Her hand stopped on the letter from the bishop of Oscoda County.

Annie had fallen asleep shortly after they'd started home from the *dokta's* office. Seth eased her into his arms and carried her into the house. Although he purposely tried to be quiet so Annie didn't wake, he half-expected Katie to meet him at the door.

Katie wasn't in the kitchen, so he peeked into the sitting room and was surprised to find Elias seated beside Amos. Apparently neither heard his buggy pull into the drive or him enter the house.

Seth slipped down the hall to Annie's bedroom and lowered her onto the bed. He paused a moment before leaving the room to gaze at her peaceful expression. *"Denki,* God, for saving her," he whispered, then treaded softly down the hall.

Anxious to thank Elias for his help earlier with Annie, Seth returned to the sitting room. Only Elias was no longer there.

"Annie is asleep," he told Amos. "The *dokta* said to watch her closely over the next few hours. I described the reaction and he said she was lucky to be alive." He also didn't understand how she could've recovered without medications to open her airway, but Seth didn't tell Amos that. He wanted to wait and see Elias's reaction to the comment.

"The Lord was merciful, ain't so?"

"Jah," he said, staring at Amos. It seemed as though another miracle had taken place while he was gone. This wasn't like his

brother-in-law at all. "It's a blessing that God spared her." A blessing God directed Elias to arrive at just the right time. Seth glanced around the room. He wished Elias had stayed.

Seth drifted to the window and scanned the yard, looking for Elias, but discovered instead that Katie's buggy was gone. "Where did Katie go?" He forced an even tone, hoping Amos wouldn't hear the panic in his voice.

Amos smiled wider than what Seth had seen him do in years. "I sent her home."

Seth's stomach pitted. He closed his eyes and took in a deep breath. "What happened?"

Buggy wheels crunched over the driveway gravel and Seth turned to the window. "She's back," he said after spotting Peaches. He studied Amos's face for his reaction.

The man's smile held. He even sat straighter on the chair. "Is Leah with her?"

Seth looked outside again. Sure enough, Leah was heading up the porch steps. *"Jah,"* he said, somewhat stunned. He rushed to the door and met her on the porch.

"Katie told me about Annie," she said, entering the house. "How is she?"

"She's sleeping, but I think she's all right *nau*." He glanced at the bag in her arms. "Do you want me to take that?"

"That's okay." Leah lowered the bag to the floor.

He hoped it held her belongings and that she hadn't purposefully left it by the door expecting to make a quick exit.

She wiped her hands on her dress. "How's *Daed*?"

"Probably a little shook up yet. But in a *gut* way." He placed a hand on her back. "I'll go with you to see him." When she didn't budge, he dropped his hand.

"Perhaps I should see him alone," she said softly.

"Okay." He nodded his head toward the sitting room. "Leah, I'm glad you're here."

"*Denki.*" A faint smile formed before it faded.

As she shuffled toward the sitting room, Seth went to the door. Assuming Katie was still unhitching her horse, he stepped outside, hoping she would fill him in on Leah's return. But Katie had turned the buggy and was already at the end of the drive—leaving.

He ran after the buggy but couldn't catch her before she pulled out on the main road. Seth waited a moment. "It's for the best," he told himself. But the thought didn't ease the heaviness in his chest.

Seth trekked toward the barn. Although the boys could handle doing the chores without his help, he needed something to keep his mind occupied.

The screen door opened just enough for Leah to poke her hand outside and motion. "*Onkel* Seth, *kumm* quick!"

Seth's heart pounded as he raced toward the house.

"It's *Daed*," she said, pointing to the sitting room.

"*Mei* vision is back!" Amos bolted out of his chair. "I can see patches of light."

Seth's jaw fell slack.

Amos was so elated he practically danced around the room. "It's great, ain't so?"

"*Jah* . . . Wow. It's amazing," Seth said.

Leah beamed.

"I still have some blurry spots," Amos explained. "But I can see!" He wrapped his arms around Leah and gazed proudly at his daughter. "You look so much like your *mamm*."

Seth bowed his head. *Denki, God, for the marvelous works of your hand.*

"Where is Annie? Is she still sleeping?" Amos made a tight circle in the room. "And where are Thomas and Paul? I want to see them too."

Leah laughed. "Maybe you should sit down, *Daed.*"

He shook his head. "I've been sitting for too long. I feel like burning that chair."

Seth understood the man's excitement, even knowing Amos would never destroy a perfectly sturdy chair.

"Where are the boys—in the barn? Call them inside." Amos headed for the door. "Never mind, I'll do it."

Seth stopped him. "I'll go get them." He motioned to Amos's socked feet. "You don't have any shoes on."

"I suppose you're right. *Mei* vision is still a little blurry. I might step into something that would surprise me."

"*Jah*, Katie—" He stopped before saying she wouldn't want barn muck on the floor. "I'll go get the boys." He rushed outside. He hoped in time her name wouldn't slip into conversations—but who was he trying to kid? She wouldn't be easy to forget.

Seth entered the barn, but before he could open his mouth, Thomas spoke.

"I was the one who grabbed the wrong lumber the other day," he said.

"What are you talking about?"

Thomas lowered his head. "The bad wood that had to be replaced—I pulled that off the wrong pile."

Seth clapped his nephew's shoulder. "No harm was done."

"But I should've remembered which pile you said needed to be burned. I guess I got my right and left mixed up."

"Does that happen a lot?"

Thomas shrugged. "I guess it does."

"For me too," Seth said. "Where is Paul?"

"I'm up here, in the hayloft."

He waved his younger nephew down. "Your *daed* has some news to share in the *haus*."

Thomas and Paul looked at each other, then at him.

Thomas leaned the pitchfork against the wall. "What's going on?"

Seth shooed them from the barn. "He wants to tell you himself. *Nau geh* on." He wasn't about to spoil Amos's surprise.

Seth stayed behind. After everything Amos had gone through, he needed a few minutes alone with his children. God had certainly given him a second chance to sort out his life. Seth sighed. He hadn't spent so many hours hoping for his own second chance at happiness since he'd met Katie.

"*Denki*, God," Seth said. "You answered *mei* prayers for *mei* sister's family." Seth grabbed the pitchfork from where Thomas had placed it and stabbed the mound of hay. "*Mei* heart is heavy. I don't even know what this empty void is . . . *Jah*, I do. It's Katie. She's messed me up completely."

The sweet scent of apple blossoms filled Katie's buggy. Normally she slowed Peaches through this area to take in the fragrant scent when the orchard was in bloom. Today the simple pleasure held no interest.

Until now she hadn't had time to think about Seth and their conversation in the barn. How he said it wouldn't work between them. The kiss didn't mean anything to him. But she should've figured that out when he not only never mentioned it again, but also didn't ask her to take any long walks or sit on the porch with him.

For years she was content with the idea of never falling in love. Now she wasn't sure if she could ever get over not seeing him. Down deep in her heart she'd secretly wanted him to move to Hope Falls. She'd started to believe that maybe he would want to move his beehive business to their settlement. She was wrong.

Katie stopped at the county-line crossroad and waited for a car to pass. A gray cloud of road dust billowed up from the vehicle's tires, causing Katie to cough. She waited for the dust to settle, then instead of continuing straight to go home, she steered Peaches in the direction of her brother's farm. She needed a cup of tea, a friend.

As hard as Katie tried to mask her dismal mood with her fake smile, Abigail saw through her disguise. "Something's wrong," her sister-in-law said, ushering her into the kitchen.

If she responded verbally, she wouldn't contain her tears, so Katie shrugged. But when her eyes met Abigail's, her feeble efforts failed and she couldn't wipe the tears rolling down her cheeks fast enough.

Abigail disappeared into another room, then returned a moment later with a hankie.

"*Denki.*" Katie dabbed her eyes. "I feel like such a fool."

"Why?"

"I didn't want to fall in love with him and I did."

Abigail smiled. "Seth Stutzman is a *gut* man. Your *bruder* has said so many times." Abigail reached across the table and patted Katie's hand. "There is nothing wrong with falling in love."

"There is when he doesn't feel the same way about me." Her vision clouded with tears. "He told me today that it would never work out."

"Did he say why?"

Katie shook her head. "He didn't say, but it's me. I'm

meddlesome." She paused, reflecting on her life. "I was content as a *teetshah*. Sure, I had moments of envy that I'm *nett* proud about. But I accepted never having children of my own. I accepted that was God's will for my life . . . *Nau* I don't even know what his will is for me."

"Maybe Seth is confused. He must have feelings for you or he wouldn't have given any thought to whether things would work out or *nett*."

"He kissed me. It just happened and we both . . ."

Abigail smiled. "So he does have feelings for you."

"We both understand *nau* it was a moment of weakness . . . on both our parts." She bowed her head. "I forgot how much a broken heart hurts. I don't ever want to feel this way again."

"Maybe things will be different in a day or two. You'll still see him at Amos's *haus*, ain't so?"

"*Nay*. Leah returned home and Amos's sister is *kumming* from Ohio to help. Seth said he planned to leave soon anyway." Katie fell silent, pondering her options, not that she had more than one. "I think moving to Oscoda will be the best thing for me. I just wish it was fall and closer to *schul* starting."

"You want to fill the void in your life with teaching, and it'll never satisfy you again."

"Haven't you heard me?" She blew out a breath, hoping to release some of the pent-up frustration. "Being a *teetshah* is all I have."

The door opened and Isaac stomped his feet on the braided rug. He stepped into the kitchen, looked at his *fraa*, then Katie, then back to Abigail. "Should I leave?"

Abigail stood. "I was going to make some *kaffi*. Would you like a cup too?"

Isaac shook his head. "I saw your buggy, Katie, and I

wanted to let you know I have the *grossdaadi haus* cleared out so it's ready for you to move in."

Katie nodded. She hadn't wanted to think about packing, but the sooner she did, the sooner she would be able to go on with her life. "I don't have much. It shouldn't take me more than a couple of days."

He nodded. "Once you're ready, I'll bring the wagon over to move the boxes and furniture. I know you don't want to hear this, but renting the farm is for the best. It gives the Wyse family a place to stay while they wait to rebuild, and the income will balance some of the recent losses. It's for the best."

"I like the idea of you living in the *grossdaadi haus*," Abigail said, then added, "even if it's only until you move to Oscoda in the fall."

Katie forced a smile. She wished she could embrace the plan. At least the farm wasn't being sold.

Abigail set a cup of coffee in front of Katie. "Have you heard if you got the *teetshah* job yet?"

Katie's eyes widened. "I got a letter! I was in such a hurry and"—she stood—"I have to go home." She sprang from her chair and rushed to the door. "I'll talk with you tomorrow, Abigail," she said over her shoulder.

Driving home, Katie sat on the edge of the bench, urging Peaches to trot faster. When she arrived at the house, she unhitched the buggy, tossed a tin can full of oats into the mare's feed bin, and nearly tripped over her feet rushing inside.

Katie's hands shook as she opened the envelope. She unfolded the paper and scanned the letter. They had found someone within their settlement who wanted the position. Katie slumped in the chair.

After thoughts of Katie interfered with any chance of a restful night, Seth plodded out to the new barn. He lit the wick on the oil lamp and scanned the rafters.

"It's sound."

Seth jolted at the sound of Elias's voice. "Have you stayed in here all *nacht*?"

Elias shook his head. "I've been waiting for you."

How did Elias know he would be out here at this hour? The sun hadn't even risen. Seth scratched his jaw. He hadn't slept enough to think clearly. He couldn't imagine anything so important that the man would come here at this hour. "Is something wrong?"

"You plan to leave Hope Falls before discovering why God has led you here."

"I don't understand," Seth said. "Amos's sight has returned and his barn is built. He doesn't need *mei* help anymore."

"I gave you the message. It's up to you to pray for God to reveal it to your heart. Then you will understand the purpose of coming to Hope Falls," Elias said.

Seth gazed up at the rafters. He'd prayed all night to be able to escape the nagging pull on his heart caused by Katie. He looked to his side as the barn door opened, then closed. Elias was gone. Seth bowed his head and prayed for God's will in his life, for guidance, and finally for forgiveness for the way he had snapped at Katie. "She deserves more than someone like me. Forgive me, please. I was full of pride not to tell her about my past."

Seth lingered in the barn several hours. He'd reached the conclusion he needed to write Katie a letter once he returned home to Saint Joseph County. It would be a chore, but maybe she would appreciate his effort and look beyond his poor spelling.

The sweet scent of cinnamon rolls met him at the door. He rushed to the kitchen.

"*Ach,*" he mumbled. Why did his mind fool him with the thought that Katie might have returned?

Leah smiled. "You were looking for Katie, ain't so?"

He groaned.

"It's a nice day to take a buggy drive," Leah said, then pushed a little more. "Go see her."

He shook his head. "I'm going home tomorrow."

"I know, but don't you want to at least say good-bye?"

"I figured I would write her a letter." Why was he telling his niece all this?

Leah extended him a plate with a cinnamon roll on it. "Wouldn't you rather see her? I know she would want to see you."

Seth cleared his throat. "I'll eat this later." The way his stomach had knotted, he couldn't choke anything down at the moment. He set the plate on the counter.

"I'm going to take a walk."

"*Onkel* Seth?"

He glanced at Leah over his shoulder.

"Take a buggy ride," she said.

"That trip is too hard to make." He continued outside and meandered across the yard to the fence. He propped one foot up on the board and stared out at the field.

Lord, this is hard. How will I get over her? This feels so different from when my engagement to Diana was dissolved.

"Seth?"

He glanced sideways as Amos approached the fence.

"Nice day, ain't so?" Amos sighed as he scanned the property. "I had forgotten how beautiful green grass looks."

Seth nodded.

"I assumed Katie would be here today."

"*Nay* need. Leah is home," Seth said.

"I thought the woman was meddlesome. A jezebel. Do you know how many times she insisted on me sitting in front of that window? Listening to birds and smelling—"

Seth straightened his shoulders. He didn't like what he was hearing.

Amos pressed his hand against Seth's chest. "Let me finish."

Seth relaxed some.

"She tried to get me to see things through my other senses. She called me spiritually blind. I wish I had seen things differently when Erma was alive." He blew out a breath. "*Jah*, I thought Katie was meddlesome. She talked with Erma about Thomas's *schulwork*. I was angry that Katie interfered. Even angrier when she convinced *mei fraa* our son needed more help." He paused and his eyes dulled. "I gave Erma the silent treatment. I thought she would *kumm* around and drop the nonsense . . . but she didn't. That's the week she . . . died." Amos's eyes watered and he looked away. "I blamed Katie for *mei* stubbornness. For robbing me of the last few days I had with Erma."

"I'm sorry," Seth said softly.

Amos peered into the distance. "I used to *kumm* out here after Erma died. I would spend hours telling her how sorry I was. What a fool I had been to give her the cold shoulder." Amos drew a deep breath. "I should've followed the Word. 'Do not let the sun go down on your wrath, nor give place to the devil.' I never thought I wouldn't have the next day with Erma. I never thought *mei* faith would falter and I'd give place to the devil either. It's easier to do than sometimes we think." He tapped the fence board. "Katie helped me see the truth. I was spiritually blind, and I had a meeting with the ministers about that this morning."

Seth smiled. Her persistence had made a measurable difference. "I have the same problems as Thomas. Katie pushed me to read the Scriptures in the evenings. I was a little bullheaded myself since I don't read out loud well."

Amos sighed. "When I stay this long at the fence, it's because I'm grieving over Erma. Your helpmate is *nett* dead."

Seth straightened.

"Katie might try to *help* you too much. But she will make a *gut fraa*."

"And what makes you think—"

"I might have been blind, but I know when two people are falling in love." He smirked. "Besides, you sure didn't like it when I called her a jezebel." Amos motioned to the hitching post. "I left the buggy hitched after I *kumm* back from my talk with the ministers."

Seth stared at him a moment.

He lifted an eyebrow in response. "You made her cry the day the barn was being built."

"She told you?"

Amos shook his head. "I'm telling you, as a blind man I saw a lot. She sounded like a woman who'd lost her best friend."

Seth lowered his head. "*Jah*, she didn't even understand why I snapped at her either."

"There's the buggy," Amos said, pointing to the post. "Ask her to *kumm* for supper and tell her I'm inviting her."

Seth did need to apologize. He couldn't have her believing she did anything wrong. "On one condition," he said. "Don't call her a jezebel again."

Amos smiled. "I'd like to call her *mei* sister-in-law."

Seth chose not to respond to that statement. He turned and headed for the buggy, and as he did, his eye caught on the beehive boxes Amos had him retrieve from the back property earlier.

It didn't take long to disassemble the beehive box and load it into the buggy. Then he jumped on the bench and headed out the driveway. He wasn't far down the road before he spotted Elias walking along the roadside.

"I've been waiting for you," Elias said when Seth brought the buggy to a stop. Without giving Seth time to reply, he pointed at the farm ahead. "Ask the farmer about his barn."

"Why?"

"He's looking for someone to haul off the old wood so he can build his new structure."

Seth furrowed his brows.

"Isaac Bender will be interested in the news. Wasn't someone planning to move into the Bender farm because he couldn't find lumber to rebuild on his own lot?"

Seth nodded. "Do you need a ride somewhere?"

Elias shook his head.

Seth smiled. "You wish to walk so you can talk with God." He looked at the farmhouse ahead. "Will you be around when the men are ready to build again?"

Elias shrugged. "I make no promise about tomorrow. I go where my God sends me." He motioned straight ahead. "The man is waiting for your arrival."

Chapter Thirty

K atie wrapped the last plate using a section of the *Budget* newspaper and placed the dish in the box. Outside of a few miscellaneous kitchen items she planned to donate, most of her belongings were packed.

She wished she could store away the lingering feelings about Seth too. With Leah home, he wouldn't have to wait for Amos's sister to arrive from Ohio for him to leave. He seemed anxious to return home and probably had arranged his bus ticket already.

She lifted the box and tested the weight. Not too heavy. She closed the flaps and marked a general description of the contents on the container. Now she could focus on the stuff designated for donation.

The *tap-tap-tap* of a hammer drew her attention to the window. On raised toes, she leaned over the sink to peer outside. High on a ladder, a man's pant legs and boots were all that was visible. Apparently Isaac was in a hurry to get the house ready to rent.

Katie lifted the window casing. "The *kaffi* pot is on whenever you're finished, Isaac," she said. It wouldn't take her brother long to patch the porch roof. She'd planned on doing it herself but hadn't found time with going over to Amos's house every day. It was just as well that Isaac did the repairs, though, since she wasn't completely sure how to tie into the existing shingles.

Katie filled the kettle with water and placed it on the stove to heat. Now she needed to locate the box that she'd packed the coffee cups in. She read the label listing the contents on several boxes before finding the one with the cups.

This all seemed surreal—the cabinets empty, her mother's dishes packed for storage, so many childhood memories tucked away in boxes. She recalled the special times, like when she and *Mamm* cooked together, when a snowstorm buried them inside for three days, and the year when they had to walk buckets of water out to the field because they hadn't had rain in days.

But she wasn't fooling herself. Her heart ached for more reasons than losing the house. She missed Seth. Even losing the teacher position hadn't bothered her like she'd thought. Sure, she was disappointed after reading the letter. But it didn't take long to realize she was disappointed she wouldn't have teaching to preoccupy her mind and escape the constant reminder of Seth. When did she stop wanting to be a teacher?

Katie sighed.

She did need a job, and something more than selling fruit and vegetables with Abigail. It would be hard enough living as an old maid with her brother and his family. Even living in Isaac's *grossdaadi haus* wasn't the same as living independently. Alone.

She had to set some goals. Last night she focused her prayers on finding her purpose. The thought even came to her in the early morning hours to raise bees. She wasn't allergic. Lord knew she'd been stung plenty of times as a youth. She could learn to collect honey.

She wrapped more dishes and placed them in the box for donation. Then she pushed the chair against the counter and climbed up to reach the higher shelves. The hammering stopped. A few minutes later the back door opened and footsteps sounded behind her.

"*Kaffi* pot is hot, Isaac," she said, pulling out an armload of glassware from the cabinet. She climbed off the chair and came face-to-face with Seth.

"I'm *nett* your *bruder*, but I hope the offer still stands."

"Um . . ." The dishes wobbled in her arms. "*Jah*, of course." She set the dishes on the counter and ran her trembling hands against her dress apron. "Have a seat and I'll fix you a cup." She motioned to the table, but realized with all of the boxes piled on it, there wasn't a clear space for them to sit. "I'll move—"

Seth reached for her arm, stopping her from grabbing a box. He picked up the box. "Where do you want this?"

"Um . . ." His touch sent prickling needle sensations scooting the length of her spine, rendering her speechless. She turned a circle looking for a bare spot.

"We can sit on the porch," he said and set the box on the table.

"Okay." She spun toward the hissing kettle, then realized she hadn't unpacked any coffee cups. *Ach*, what was wrong with her? She opened the nearest box and searched inside. "So how is Annie? Is her breathing all right?"

"Like it never happened. Did you hear about Amos? His sight returned."

She jerked upright, her mouth agape. "That's *wundebaar!*"

"God's changed him." He went to the stove and removed the kettle. "Amos even met with the ministers this morning to tell them about it," he said, placing the kettle on the cooling rack.

"I'm so glad. That was Leah's prayer that her family would return to church." She pawed through another box, found the cups, then unwrapped the newspaper from around them. "I suppose that sets your mind at ease. *Nau* you'll be able to go back to Saint Joseph County without worrying about them, ain't so?" Her smile weakened. Afraid the depth of her disappointment would show on her face, she redirected her attention and filled the cups with coffee.

"It will be a relief to know they're doing better," he said.

She glanced sideways, caught a glimpse of his steady gaze on her, and willed her knees not to go weak. Her throat dry, she swallowed. "Should we take our *kaffi* out to the porch?" She picked up the cups, but her hands trembled and coffee spilled over the rim.

"I'll carry those." Seth took the cups.

"I'll get the door." Katie rushed past him, held the door open for him, then stepped outside behind him. The patchwork repair on the porch roof caught her eye. "*Denki* for doing the repairs."

"I used the lumber from one of the beehive boxes." He handed her a cup, then moved over to the railing.

"Really?"

"Lumber is scarce around here."

"*Jah*, I know." She knew that too well. If it hadn't been for the lumber shortage, Isaac wouldn't have considered renting the farm. She gazed again at the work, but this time to avoid his probing eyes. "You actually took apart a beehive?"

"Amos had me dismantle all of them." He smiled. "That's what you wanted all along, *jah*?"

"I'm glad for Annie's sake. I wouldn't want her stung again." She sipped her coffee and found she didn't want any more. She moved to the banister and set her cup on the porch railing. "So how long before you go back to Saint Joseph County?"

"I had planned to leave tomorrow." He covered the steps between them, then lowered his cup next to hers. "But I couldn't leave without talking with you."

"Seems you said everything you needed to in the barn. Has Amos's sister arrived from Ohio? I suppose with Leah home and with Amos's sight returned—"

"Katie," he said. His gaze so intent, he didn't blink.

She shifted her focus to the barn.

"I couldn't have taken care of Amos and the children without you. Especially the day Annie was stung."

Did he merely come to thank her for helping? She wanted to ask him to explain what he'd meant in the barn. Why he thought it wouldn't work between them. But she couldn't find the courage. Determined not to veer onto the subject of their failed relationship, she talked about Annie. "I wasn't sure why you wanted me to gather sheets."

"Her airway was closing. I thought the kettle steam would help."

"What were you planning to do with the ink pen?"

His slight shrug wasn't as startling as his sobered expression. "I watched a barn wall collapse on a man. His airway closed." Seth dropped eye contact with her and stared at the barn. He gripped the banister hard enough for his knuckles to whiten. "He made the same high-pitched wheezing as Annie. The emergency worker cut the man's throat and inserted something that looked like a PVC pipe. I thought of trying the same for Annie. The only thing that came to mind was the plastic casing of an ink pen."

"I'm glad you didn't have to use it."

"Me too." He nodded. "Those sounds have tormented me since that day." He fell silent.

After a moment, she touched his arm. "I'm sorry about your friend."

"It was my fault." He cringed as he choked out the words. "I oversaw the barn raising."

His hands trembled, scratching his jaw.

"I stopped building. I couldn't risk making another error and putting anyone else's life in danger." He blew out a breath and then faced her. "That's why I didn't speak up at the first meeting when they announced they wanted to establish multiple crews. I no longer considered myself a master builder."

She lowered her head, ashamed she'd told Andrew Lapp about Seth's experience.

"I shouldn't have snapped at you the day I was working on Amos's barn. It's just that I hadn't led a raising—"

"You were right. I should've minded *mei* own business." Oh, how she wished now she had.

"You didn't know." He smiled, but his mouth quivered and it faded. "My pride kept me from telling you. I know building beehives isn't like building barns . . . I couldn't bear to see the disappointment in your eyes."

"You were worried about what I thought? Why?"

"I couldn't bear the idea of you thinking less of me."

"Less of you? I don't understand."

"You saw through me. That *nacht* at Isaac's *haus*. You figured out I wasn't a beehive maker by choice. But I didn't know how to tell you why I gave up building. I watched you talking with Andrew. I didn't know you were telling him about *mei* experience, but you smiled, pleased with yourself."

"Amos told me you were a master builder. I thought maybe you were reserved because this wasn't your district. I put you in an awful position. I'm really sorry I said anything to Andrew."

"And you think less of me—"

"*Nay*, I don't," she snapped. "There's nothing wrong with being a beehive maker."

He stared at her a moment, then a slow smile crept across his face.

"I said all that at *mei* brother's *haus* because I was upset about the hives' placement near the *schul*." She shrugged. "At that time I still believed the *schul* would be rebuilt."

"Teaching is really important to you, isn't it?"

"It's the only thing I know to do." She sighed. "Do you think I could learn how to collect honey?"

He crossed his arms over his chest and laughed. "You want to be a beekeeper?"

"What? You don't think I'm capable?" She thumbed her chest. "I'm *nett* afraid of bees. Besides, I've been stung plenty of times. I'm *nett* allergic." She looked at the house. "But I guess that won't be possible. Isaac is renting the farm. That's why I'm packing everything into boxes."

He inched closer. "I'll teach you how to collect honey. That is, if you're willing to take instruction from one of your students."

"*Mei* students?" She lifted a brow.

"I figure I won't be off the hook and I'll still have to read with you, ain't so?"

Her mind hadn't unraveled the question before he pulled her

into his arms and kissed her. He pressed his hand against her back, bringing her even closer as the kiss continued. The same prickling sensations sputtered along her nerves as he deepened the kiss.

He lifted his lips. "You mean so much to me," he said in a hoarse whisper.

Her throat tightened as tears of joy budded in her eyes.

He leaned back to catch her eyes. "I love you," he said, tipping her chin up. "I want to marry you." He drew her closer and kissed her again. But the loud sound of an engine rattling and tires crushing the driveway gravel interrupted their kiss. Seth released her as the driver climbed out of his truck.

The driver said something, but with her mind still reeling from Seth's proposal, she hadn't listened to a word.

"I have a delivery for you," he repeated.

She followed Seth off the porch. "I think you have the wrong house," she said.

The driver looked at his clipboard. "Are you Seth Stutzman and Katie Bender?"

"*Jah*, but I didn't order anything," Katie tried to explain.

The man opened a side compartment of his truck and pulled out a large container of ice cream. "I was asked by Elias to give you this."

"Elias? Where is he?" Seth scanned the area.

"I was broken down on the road and he appeared out of nowhere and fixed the engine. I tried to pay him and this was all he asked for." The man motioned to the container. "He wanted me to tell you to enjoy your frolic."

Katie brushed the tears from her eyes as she stared at the carton of strawberry ice cream.

"*Denki*. Thank you," Seth said.

The driver climbed into his truck, gave a quick wave, and backed the vehicle out of the drive.

Seth looked down at the container and shook his head. "He wasn't in the cellar with us. How would he have known?" He lifted his gaze to her. "Unless . . ."

"An angel." Katie smiled. "And he's been among us all along."

He sighed. "I guess Amos wasn't the only one blinded all this time."

He grabbed her hand and led her into the house. Then he set the ice cream container on the counter and pulled Katie into another embrace. He kissed her forehead. "You haven't answered *mei* marriage proposal," he said, giving her a gentle nudge.

She played coy, enjoying the sudden concern growing in his expression. "And you can live with a meddlesome woman?"

He nodded.

Warmth filled Katie's heart. As though it were a dream she didn't want to wake from, she wanted to savor the moment.

Seth stepped closer to her, his eyes growing with anticipation. "You're going to keep me waiting?"

Maybe a little while longer. She glanced at the counter. "The ice cream is going to melt."

"You're worried about ice cream *nau*?"

"*Nay*, about finding spoons and bowls." She looked at the cluttered table. "I don't know which box—"

Seth cleared his throat and raised his hand. "*Teetshah*? Can I help you unpack all of the boxes?"

She smiled. "Trying to earn merit points?"

He spun her into his arms. "I'm trying to convince you to marry me."

"Convince me some more," she said, laughter bubbling over her words.

He lowered his mouth over hers. This time his kiss was slow and long lasting. By the time he lifted his mouth from hers, she was breathless.

"Convinced?" Without waiting for her answer, he captured her mouth again. Then again. He kissed her cheek, then moved his mouth in front of her ear. "Have you *kumm* to a decision? Or are you going to let that ice cream melt?"

"*Jah,*" she said.

"*Jah*, you'll marry me? Or *jah*, you don't mind the ice cream melting?"

"Both." She rose to her toes and draped her arms over his shoulders. "I love you, Seth Stutzman. *Jah*, I very much want to marry you."

"I love you too." He rested his chin on the top of her head, nestling her against his chest.

She sighed. It took losing everything for her to see that God's plan was to give her even more. Her eyes blurred with tears.

Seth pulled away. "I could use a bowl of ice cream *nau*. What about you?"

She nodded. "I'll find the box with the bowls." She pulled the tape off the box marked DISHES and opened the lid. Searching the contents, she found the stack of bowls and removed two of them.

"I was serious about unpacking all of the boxes," he said, peeling the lid off the ice cream container. "I talked with your *bruder*. He isn't going to rent the *haus*."

"What?" She stopped removing the newspaper from the dish. "Peter Wyse plans to rent the farm until he can rebuild."

"I know. I talked with an *Englischer* who needs his old barn hauled away so he can build a new one. Apparently his insurance will pay for a new structure, but it doesn't cover the cost to remove the old building. He's giving us the lumber. The men and I will start removing the wood tomorrow. The Wyse *haus* will be first, but the *Englischer* said he knew of others in the same situation. He thinks we'll be able to remove the lumber from their buildings too."

"That's *wundebaar* news."

Seth scooped a spoonful of ice cream from the container, held it to her lips, then pulled it back teasingly.

She protruded her bottom lip in an exaggerated pout.

Seth leaned forward and kissed the tip of her nose, then fed her the spoonful of ice cream. "By the way, Isaac gave me his blessing to marry you. Abigail reminded me I could move *mei* beehive business to Hope Falls."

Her throat numbed, swallowing the ice cream.

"You're *nett* saying anything. You do want to stay in Hope Falls after we're married, *jah*?"

She nodded.

"*Gut.*" He fed her another spoonful of ice cream. "Amos thinks you'll make a *gut* sister-in-law."

"Meddlesome me?" She almost choked.

Seth laughed. "And don't you ever change. I love you just the way you are."

Reading Group Guide

1. It wasn't until Katie and Seth had been trapped in the cellar awhile before she thought about the gravity of the situation and examined the condition of her heart. How do you think you would respond in the same calamity?

2. Although Seth had prayed that the wall wouldn't collapse, why do you suppose he didn't expect an answer to his prayer? Do you ever continue to worry over things after you've prayed and released them to God?

3. After the tornado destroyed the school, how did Katie react to the possibility of the school not being rebuilt?

4. The members of the Amish settlement pooled their resources to use for rebuilding the community. Can you think of ways you can contribute to your church family?

5. Several times Katie felt prompted to pray without knowing who to pray for. Has there been a time when you were prompted to pray for someone without knowing why?

6. Why do you think Jesus instructs us to pray for those who persecute us? When Katie prayed for Amos, what happened?

7. In what way did the members of the church show God's love toward Amos? How did Amos respond to their kindness?

8. How did Seth's not forgiving himself potentially hinder his future?

9. Why did Katie push Seth to read scriptures to Amos and the children? What are your thoughts about reading the Bible every day? Do you believe it can change someone's outlook on life?

10. Katie told Amos he was spiritually blind. How does spiritual blindness compare to physical blindness?

11. What does Psalm 119:105 say about God's Word?

12. When Katie worked with Thomas, how did Seth's pride affect him? Why was Seth trying to hide his dyslexia from Katie?

Acknowledgments

Above all, I thank my Lord and Savior, Jesus Christ, from whom all blessings flow. He has certainly blessed me with a multitude of support from family and friends.

I would like to thank my husband/general contractor turned pharmacist/DIY home remodeler, Dan, for his help with the construction portion of this book. Your patience with my constant questions is commendable.

To my wonderful friends, prayer warriors, and critique partners. You each know the important role that you played in bringing *An Angel by Her Side* to print. Susanne Dietze, Paul and Kathy Droste, Joy Elwell, Sarah Hamaker, Virginia Hamlin, Bob Kaku, Donna Mumma, Betty Reid, Ella and Bill Roberts, Gail Sattler, Mary Ann Stockwell, Linda Truesdell, Jennifer Uhlarik, and Quanda Watson.

My on-going appreciation goes to Mary and Simon Thon, who introduced me to the Amish while living with them during my college years, and to my Amish friends of Mecosta County, Michigan, who invited me into their homes.

I would like to thank my agent, Mary Sue Seymour of The Seymour Agency, and my publishing family at Thomas Nelson. I have learned so much by working with such talented people. Allen Arnold, former Senior Vice President and Publisher, through your vision and leadership you have built an awesome team! Natalie Hanemann, I'm honored to have you as my editor. Meredith Efken, it was a pleasure working on line editing with you. Special thanks Becky Monds, Ruthie Dean, and the sales/marketing team: Katie Bond, Eric Mullett, and Ashley Schneider. I am truly grateful for everything you all have contributed to bring *An Angel by Her Side* to print.

An Excerpt from
The Promise of an Angel

Mecosta County, Michigan

The maple tree's crimson canopy offered shade for the children in Judith Fischer's charge, and a perfect place to stitch her quilt while viewing Levi Plank as he worked with the men building the barn. With the structure nearly complete, soon the supper bell would ring. Judith glanced toward the house. Her friend Deborah was busy preparing the outdoor tables for the meal. Judith enjoyed helping with the food preparations, but she loved sitting with the children and entertaining them with stories more.

Six-year-old Rebecca pulled on her sister's sleeve. "Tell us another story."

Judith turned back and eyed the tight circle of smiling children. "What color dress will the *maydel* wear?"

"Yellow," said Rebecca.

Little Emily looked down at her own dark dress. "Not black or blue?"

A leaf fluttered from the branch above them and landed on Judith's lap. She picked it up and twirled it by the stem. "In stories, people wear bright colors." She tucked the red leaf into her tightly wound hair, leaving it to dangle from under the head covering. "Storybook characters can also wear wildflowers and colorful ribbons in their hair."

Rebecca raised her hand to shield the late afternoon sun from her eyes as she looked up into the branches. "What's her name?"

Judith repositioned the younger girl's bonnet, then removed the leaf from her own hair and tucked the stem under Rebecca's head covering. Feeling a tug on her other arm, she looked down at her five-year-old brother's gap-toothed smile. "*Jah*, Samuel?"

"Name her Judith."

The girls chimed in their agreement.

Emily's eyes widened. "I'll name the boy in the story."

Judith glanced toward the barn and spotted Levi on the roof. She watched as he removed a nail he'd been holding between his teeth and hammered it into the wood. Judith couldn't help but smile. Levi would make a perfect storybook hero.

"Let's call him Andrew," Emily blurted.

"Andrew?" Judith echoed louder than she intended. She followed the child's gaze to Levi's cousin, Andrew Lapp, and watched as he measured a piece of lumber. He paused, holding the pencil in place against the wood, and smiling, turned toward the children. As his eyes met Judith's, he lifted his hand from the board and touched the brim of his straw hat.

Rebecca scrunched her freckled nose as she looked at Judith. "Why is your face red?"

Judith touched her warm cheeks. Before she could think of how to answer, she heard her sister Martha giggling behind her.

"Supper's ready," she said. "That is, if the daydreamer is ready to eat?"

Judith set the quilt section beside her and stood. Since Martha turned seventeen last month, her entire demeanor had changed. Judith hoped her father would notice the way Martha sashayed to the barn. He'd have something to say about that.

Judith lined up the children to brush the grass off their dresses, meanwhile watching Levi climb down the ladder out of the corner of her eye.

"Am I done?" Emily asked.

She looked at the girl's dress. "*Jah*, run to your *mamm*."

Martha had managed to be at the foot of the ladder as Levi reached the ground.

Sarah, Emily's older sister, fanned her dress by pulling on both sides, then twirled in place. "What about me?"

After a few swipes, Judith sent her on her way. Her jaw tightened as she heard Martha and Levi laugh. She should be the one exchanging pleasantries with him, not Martha. She was the one turning nineteen tomorrow. She shooed the other children toward the house without inspecting their clothing, but held back Rebecca and Samuel.

"Samuel, you stay with Rebecca and me. *Mamm* doesn't need to chase after you today."

He pointed to the supper tables. "I'm hungry."

Judith could see Martha, Levi, and some other girls their age moving in her direction. She pretended to brush grass off Samuel's clothing. "*Mamm* wouldn't want you to *kumm* to the table covered with grass. *Nau* hold still."

"Hello, Judith." Levi paused near the tree, Martha and the

others clustered around him. "You sounded happy being surrounded by children all day."

Judith blushed. He had noticed her under the tree. She thought she'd seen him gaze in their direction a few times.

Martha sighed. "She was filling their heads with nonsense again."

Judith gritted her teeth and didn't comment.

"She's going to lead the children astray. They'll all want to wear lacy gowns and ribbons in their hair." Martha pointed to Rebecca. "See, she has our sister wearing colorful adornments."

Rebecca's lips puckered, and Judith quickly patted the girl's slumped shoulders. "It's okay. Martha used to listen to stories too."

"Before I turned seventeen."

Judith crossed her arms. "And you think seventeen makes you grown?"

Martha planted her hand on her hiked hip and shot her nose into the air. "At least I don't dream of fairy tales. I—"

Judith hadn't noticed Andrew joining their group until he cleared his throat and stepped forward. He reached into his pants pocket and knelt in front of Samuel. "I have something for you."

"For me?" The little boy beamed.

Andrew handed him a galvanized nail. "After supper, I'll help you pound that into a piece of wood."

"Really?" Samuel rolled the nail over his palm, eyeing it as if he held a fistful of candy.

Andrew stood and dusted the dirt from his patched knees. "Sure. You want to build barns someday, don't you?"

Samuel nodded. "And furniture too."

Rebecca peeked around Judith's dress. "Andrew was the name of the boy in Judith's story."

Judith's breath caught as she glimpsed Andrew's raised eyebrows. She sent a furtive glance in Levi's direction, but he and the others were heading toward the house.

Andrew squatted and picked up the quilt Judith had been sewing. "Ouch!" He shook his hand. "I guess I stabbed myself with your needle." He handed her the fabric, taking care to point out where the needle was stuck. "I hope I didn't dirty your work."

Judith looked down at the squares. "It'll come out in the wash." She hoped. When she married, she wouldn't want her wedding quilt marred.

She reached for Samuel's hand and caught Rebecca before she darted away. "You two need to wash for supper." Avoiding eye contact with Andrew, she hustled the children toward the house.

As was the custom, the men stood on one side of the table, the women and children on the opposite side. While Bishop Lapp thanked God for the meal, the completed barn, and the day's fair weather, Judith glanced across the table at Levi.

His thick, broad shoulders gave him a towering build. Hat in hand and head bowed, his sandy-brown hair, damp with sweat, curled into ringlets and fell forward, covering his eyes.

She stifled the sigh that threatened to escape. If her father caught her staring at a boy instead of giving thanks to God for their new barn, she would hear about it. She tried to keep her eyes closed, but as the bishop's prayer droned on and on, she couldn't keep from peering at Levi again.

His eyes opened. He tipped his head enough to look between his coiled locks.

Her heart quickened. Tomorrow she'd be nineteen. In her dreams, she had already accepted his courtship invitation.

His glance passed over her toward the opposite end of the table.

She leaned forward on her tiptoes and craned her neck to see what he was looking at. His gaze had stopped on Martha. Her long, batting lashes and perfect, rose-glowing cheeks stole his undivided attention.

Judith looked again at Levi. He shook his head as a broad grin spread across his face. She wondered what her sister had asked him, and snapped her head in Martha's direction to see her sister's lips form an exaggerated pout. Disgusted at her inappropriate behavior, Judith turned her attention back to Levi to see him shrug at Martha.

Judith squeezed her eyes shut and bit her bottom lip.

This wasn't how she dreamed things would be when she turned nineteen. While a few of her friends dared to speak of what it would be like to live outside the Amish community, Judith valued household duties, knowing they prepared her for marriage. She performed each task with vigor, even unpleasant chores like scrubbing barn-soiled clothes against the washboard, while pretending to be Levi Plank's *fraa*.

Now his playful gestures toward her sister were unbearable. He'd talked about courting *her* once she turned nineteen. She had expected he would ask to take her home after the next singing.

Judith felt a tug on her dress and looked down at Rebecca.

"Where's Samuel?" the little girl whispered.

Judith brought her finger to her lips. Even at age six, children knew not to interrupt the blessing.

She glanced to her other side, where her brother was supposed to be. Samuel was gone. She scanned the immediate area. He wasn't with her parents or with the other children. He wasn't— anywhere. She drew a deep breath. Once the prayer ended, she would search for him. He wouldn't go far. She looked again at Levi, but a blur of blue in the distance caught her attention.

Samuel was squatting on the barn roof with hammer in hand, tapping a board.

Judith moved away from the table and ran toward the barn, prayer or no prayer.

"Samuel!" Her voice boomed in the near silence.

Samuel jerked upright, arms flailing. In the time it took to blink, he disappeared from view.

Judith sprinted to the other side of the barn. *Please, God, let him be okay. He's just a child.* She pushed herself to run faster.

She rounded the corner of the barn and skidded to a halt. A man, an *Englisch* man, was kneeling next to her brother.

The man lifted his head away from Samuel's face. "The boy's alive."

Judith collapsed to her knees as she stretched her hand to Samuel's pale face. "Samuel."

Her brother didn't respond or open his eyes.

The *Englisch* man rose to his feet. "Have faith. Samuel's steps are ordered by God."

When she looked up at the man, his eyes flickered with a bright, wavering light. Her throat tightened, and she was unable to speak.

Then the sound of the others approaching pulled her attention away. Her older brother, David, reached them first.

"Samuel, wake up. Please." Judith wrapped her arms around Samuel and clung to his limp, unresponsive body. "God, please," she murmured.

David's strong hands lifted Judith and set her aside as others swarmed around Samuel.

"No, please don't—" Judith felt herself being pushed aside.

"Don't cause problems," David warned.

She drew in a hitched breath and wiped the tears from her eyes to clear her vision. From somewhere nearby, a voice resonated in a language she'd never heard. While everyone's focus remained fixed on Samuel, she turned a complete circle in search of the source. The voice sounded like that of the stranger she'd found next to Samuel. How had he known her brother's name? And where had he gone?

Filled with an urgent need to find him, she followed the sound of the harmonious chant and spotted the man crossing the pasture, heading into the apple orchard without looking back.

She moved cautiously at first, then with a surge of determination she lifted her skirt and broke into a full run. She lost sight of him, cloaked as he was in the undergrowth of the dense branches and an emerging thick haze that seemed to seep up from the ground. The fog turned solid at her feet, preventing her from following his tracks. He had disappeared.

She shivered at the memory of his penetrating stare. As though she'd looked at the sky through an icicle, his frosty-blue eyes etched her senses. Oddly, her core warmed with an inner peace.

A whoosh of wind, followed by a sound like sheets flapping on a clothesline, startled her. The murky vapor had cleared, and now shadows from the low-hanging branches filled the empty void. Somehow she knew it was pointless to follow, and she turned back.

Once clear of the grove, she sprinted across the pasture, hoping that no one had noticed her absence. Her heart still pounding hard, she steadied her breathing before she edged back into the crowd.

Her father was raising the rear wooden panel off the market

wagon as the men lifted a board that held Samuel. They carried his limp body like pallbearers carrying a pine box.

Judith raced to catch her mother before she climbed into the buggy. "Where are they taking him?"

Mamm lowered a handkerchief from her face. "He needs a doctor. You'll stay with your sisters."

Judith saw Rebecca clinging to Martha. Both stared blankly as they looked on in silence.

Then she glanced at Samuel's white complexion. Eyes closed, unresponsive. The vivid impression embedded itself into her mind.

"Judith."

She looked up at her father.

"Keep your eye on the girls."

His stony expression drove a nail through her heart. It was her failure to supervise Samuel that had caused the accident. Her eyes welled up at the thought of her brother dying on her watch. As the buggy pulled away, her vision blurred again with tears.

The story continues in *The Promise of an Angel*.

About the Author

Author photo by Lexie Reid

Ruth Reid is a full-time pharmacist who lives in Florida with her husband and three children. When attending Ferris State University School of Pharmacy in Big Rapids, Michigan, she lived on the outskirts of an Amish community and had several occasions to visit the Amish farms. Her interest grew into love as she saw the beauty in living a simple life.